With an easy stride, he carried her to the bank of the stream, then set her down. Still holding her with one hand, he bent down to remove her boots. "Come, my Moon Flower," he said softly. "We will bathe together."

Iva stood as though frozen. She was afraid to try to flee, for she knew his strength was far greater than her own. She met his gaze as he looked up at her. Peering into the sable depths of his eyes, she was powerless to move away. He rose to his full height, and she yearned to feel his touch on her face . . . on every inch of her body. Slowly, Shadow Dancer's head lowered. His lips settled over hers, tempting her beyond endurance.

Time stood still as Iva was truly kissed for the first time. Her lips trembled beneath the warmth of his caress. As the kiss grew deeper, she felt her insides melting, her limbs becoming heavier. She had to clutch and hold his strong shoulders to keep from crumpling to the ground.

Shadow Dancer's arms entwined around her as he tenderly supported her against his chest. Lifting his lips from hers, he smiled and held her more tightly. "Moon Flower," he whispered. "You are truly fated to be mine."

KATHLEEN DRYMON

WARRIOR OF THE SUN

ZEBRA BOOKS
KENSINGTON PUBLISHING CORP.

To my sister Barbara

*You are the one who understands
where I've been, where I am,
where I'm going.
Thanks for always being there!*

ZEBRA BOOKS

are published by

Kensington Publishing Corp.
475 Park Avenue South
New York, NY 10016

First printing: October, 1992

Printed in the United States of America

Legend of the Lost Tribe

According to legend, Quetzalcoatl, the ancient Aztec god of light, wind, life, and civilization, was the discoverer of corn and the calendar. He was a pale-skinned, light-bearded man, who one day sailed east from Tenochtitlán—now Mexico City—promising the Aztec people that he would return. He did not return and his image became that of a plumed serpent-bird.

In 1519 when Cortés and his six hundred conquistadors invaded Tenochtitlán, the gates of the city were thrown wide due to the Aztec belief that these light-skinned men riding atop the strange, four-legged beasts were gods.

In those days the Aztec emperor, Montezuma, had a beautiful daughter by his favorite concubine, and when this Aztec princess's dark eyes fell upon one of Cortés's fair-haired, blue-eyed officers, she instantly fell in love. A golden-haired, blue-eyed, female child was born a year later.

The girl child's name was Sharaza, and the Aztec people believed her to be a link to their god, Quetzalcoatl. The young girl grew into a beautiful Aztec princess who was beloved by all.

One morning, while out riding, Sharaza met an Apache warrior, known as Wind Cryer to his people. After this, the couple met each morning, and soon they fell in love.

Desiring to be together forever, the pair fled to the mountains. The Aztec princess took the women and men of her household, and Wind Cryer took those of his tribe who wished to follow him.

Apache lore holds that there is a hidden valley deep within the Rocky Mountains, and it was to this refuge that Wind Cryer and Sharaza took their people to begin a new civilization. These people of the hidden mountain valley have had little contact with the outside world. Until today!

Prologue

The young woman stood in thigh-deep water and held tightly to the reins of a wild, unbroken stallion. The afternoon sun broke through the trees that grew in abundance along this portion of the Platte River. Her golden tresses dipped into the swirling water, rushing about her body and glistening like fiery strands of shimmering gold. Droplets produced an iridescent sheen over her pearl-satin skin. She wore only a sheer, lacy camisole and a thin cotton petticoat; her slim bountiful figure was delicately outlined. She held in her free hand her dark gown of heavy, serviceable material. With gentle strokes she rubbed the gown along the animal's neck and over his face; filling the stallion's senses with the scent of his new mistress. Softly she crooned to the large black beast.

The stallion pranced nervously beneath her hand, the water around his finely shaped legs preventing him from showing his full spirit.

The girl's soft lilting voice had the power to ease the tension in the great creature as she tirelessly rubbed

7

him with the dampened gown and told him of his beauty and strength.

A lone Indian warrior, held in an almost trancelike state by what he saw, watched the scene from the concealing shrubbery and tall pines at the river's edge. Never had he viewed such a wondrous sight!

Chapter One

Dust rose from the prancing hooves as Iva Cassidy sat straight and proud upon the back of the black beast and circled him around the paddock once again.

Delbert Benell sat on the stone wall that enclosed the corral and watched the girl and animal, a wide grin on his face. "I still can't believe you were able to break him, Iva." The young man pushed back the unruly locks of chestnut hair that had fallen over his hazel eyes. The stallion had been on the Cassidy horse farm for a little over two months. Delbert had never seen a fiercer animal than the great black horse the day Bain Cassidy brought him home from a buying trip in Amarillo. He had won the animal in a poker game from a miner, who had sworn that he had won him from a Spanish Don.

"I told you I could break him!" Iva bent forward and stroked the stallion's long, sleek neck. Only her father had believed her capable of taming such a wild beast as Cimmerian. Iva's mother, along with Delbert, had voiced doubts of her capabilities. Bain Cassidy's neighbors as well had shaken their heads when they'd seen the fiercely high-strung Arabian two months earlier. But father and daughter had never had any doubt.

"Iva has a special gift," her father proclaimed. "The

girl can tame the wild beast in any animal."

Delbert's green eyes reflected his inner feelings as he watched Iva turn the stallion about once again. He loved this girl with all of his heart. He could hardly remember a time when he had not loved this golden-haired young woman. From the moment of their meeting six years ago, when her father had brought him, an orphan, off the streets and into the Cassidy house, Delbert had loved Iva from afar. Now, watching her violet-blue eyes sparkle with well-earned pride and seeing her long, golden hair flow down her back, Delbert ached from unrequited adoration.

"See how sharp he looks!" Iva called to him as she led the stallion in a high-stepping trot.

To Delbert's eyes the magnificence of the animal was enhanced only by Iva's incredible beauty. The stallion's well-shaped, muscled legs rose high in the air with each prancing step, his long, silky black tail proudly raised and his head held arrogantly high. Delbert's breath caught in his chest at the sight.

He released the air trapped in his lungs only when Bain Cassidy called out. From atop a wagon seat, Bain was directing a pair of matching, fine-spirited sorrel mares out of the barn and around to the side of the paddock. "I have to drive Iva's mother over to the Cannfield farm. Beth is about to deliver, and she has asked for her help." Bain Cassidy's words were directed at the young man of eighteen sitting atop the paddock wall, but his pride-filled eyes were on his daughter as he watched her take Cimmerian through his paces. To him, the sun rose and set upon Iva Cassidy. She combined all the best of him and his wife Katherine.

Iva heard her father's words, and pulling Cimmerian up close to the paddock wall where Delbert sat, she called out as she watched the youth jump away from the animal and onto his feet on the other side of the stone fence, "I am almost finished working Cimmerian for the day, Father. I hope all goes well at the

10

Cannfields'.'" They had expected this call to come for her mother at any time. Those living on farms and ranches that were this far away from any town could only depend upon their neighbors. The nearest doctor was in Sterling, over thirty miles away, so it was not unusual that her mother would be called on to act as midwife.

"I will take care of the horses, sir," Delbert assured the man who had been like a father to him.

Bain Cassidy nodded his head, confident that Delbert would indeed tend the animals on the Cassidy farm should he not return before nightfall. "Make sure Bold Sweeper does not get in with those mares again. We were lucky we caught him yesterday before any harm could be done. The next time we may not be as fortunate!"

Delbert knew that the mares Bain spoke of were his special picks and were to be covered only by the best stallion on the farm, Rebel Boy. When Bold Sweeper had broken out of his own pasture and into the one that held the mares, Bain's plans for a string of yearlings from Rebel Boy the following year had almost been ruined. "Yes, sir. I'll keep special watch over Bold Sweeper."

Bain smiled fondly at the young man, and for a moment was tempted to reach out and rumple his brown, curly hair, the way he had when Delbert was a boy, but he restrained the impulse. He knew such a gesture would only embarrass the lad in front of Iva. Bain was aware of Delbert's feelings for his daughter, and he did not wish to cause the young man any undue distress. He knew it was hard enough for Delbert to be in love and have to refrain from proclaiming it in order not to show disrespect to his foster family. The boy just needed time to work out his problems. Bain and his wife were very much aware of the situation.

Joining her husband near the paddock, Katherine Cassidy watched her daughter atop Cimmerian. "Iva dear, dinner is on the table. As soon as you finish here, you and Delbert eat and then see to your chores." Tucking escaping wisps of pale blond hair into her bonnet and tying its ribbons beneath her chin, Katherine once again told herself that she would prefer it if her daughter had taken more after her. This preference she had for working with Bain's horses instead of doing household chores was something Katherine was concerned about, yet she had come to realize, over the past few years, that Iva's very nature kept her ill at ease within the confines of the house. The girl was carefree and happy only while working on the farm at her father's side, or breaking one of the fine horses the Cassidys were known to breed and raise for sale.

Iva was well aware of her mother's feelings, and noticing Katherine's frown of concern, she wished to alleviate her fears, knowing that her mother was only thinking of her safety. There had been several discussions about the stallion, and Katherine had insisted that her daughter should not be the one to break the wild beast. Now that the horse was broken and Iva could sit him well, her mother's fears stemmed from the fact that the stallion still acted wild whenever anyone other than Iva tried to handle him. Katherine constantly declared that the horse was bedeviled! "I'm just going to cool Cimmerian down, Mother."

Relief replaced the concern on Katherine's features. "I'm not sure how long we'll be away from the farm, Iva. This is Beth's first child, so it might take some time."

"Don't worry, Mother. Delbert and I will be fine." Iva dismounted and began to walk the stallion around the paddock before taking him to the barn and putting him in his stall.

Leaving the young pair alone for the day—and perhaps the night—was another worry that Katherine had to contend with. Well aware of Delbert's feelings

12

for Iva, she did not trust the boy. Though she was very fond of him and thought of him as a son, Katherine Cassidy was a firm believer in being cautious about such matters. She and Bain had talked the situation over at great length when they had first noticed Delbert's reactions whenever he was around Iva. Neither of them truly would have been against such a match. Delbert was a hardworking young man and could well handle the horse farm once Bain decided to retire. It was just that they both hated the thought of losing their only child, even if she would still be close by. So they held to the belief that Iva was still too young to wed, thinking they still had a few years to enjoy their daughter's company.

Helping his wife onto the wagon seat, Bain climbed back up himself and spoke one last word of farewell. Then the wagon slowly pulled away from the paddock and down the long drive of the Cassidy farm.

For a few lingering moments Delbert stood near the paddock wall and watched Iva as she walked the stallion. To him, Iva Cassidy was the most beautiful young woman he had ever seen. Though she was tall for a woman, she had such grace and elegance that every man or boy who saw her was enthralled. Her slim and willowy, perfectly curved figure, attired in a full-skirted, riding habit which hugged it, seemed to glide across the inner boundaries of the paddock. Her golden, coppery hair, hanging down to the shapely curve of her buttocks, gleamed in shimmering waves beneath the bright afternoon sun. Pulling himself away from the dangerous thoughts her beauty aroused, Delbert murmured in a tone that barely carried to Iva, "I guess I had best go and check on Bold Sweeper." And with this he hurried away from the paddock.

Iva sighed softly as she opened the corral gate and led Cimmerian toward the open doors of the barn. Iva had not missed the long looks of yearning the young man often cast in her direction or the confusion that came upon him when they were alone. Often of late she would catch him blushing, and then he would quickly turn and hurry off on the pretext of seeing to some chore he had neglected. She was thankful that Delbert had not broached the subject of his feelings. She loved him, but not with the fire and passion a young woman reserved for the man of her heart. Her feelings were more those of a sister toward a brother.

Taking the saddle and bridle off Cimmerian, Iva filled his feed bag with fresh oats and then started toward the house. She hoped Delbert would not be too hurt when he discovered her true feelings. She had always believed the right man would one day come into her life, but she was in no hurry for that to take place. Her father needed her here on the farm, and she would hate to have to give up breaking horses.

Opening the back door, she brightened at the thought that perhaps the man of her choice would be much like her father and would not want his wife to do only household chores.

The Cassidy dwelling was a large, single-story, wood-framed ranch house. Most of the furnishings had been brought by her parents from Virginia. She had been only seven years old when her father had taken his inheritance and had bought property outside Sterling, Colorado. Two years later he had started a horse farm and had brought his family to live on this piece of earth he so proudly called his own.

A few years later her father had brought Delbert Benell home when he'd returned from a trip to San Antonio. Being a little girl of twelve who had no one to play with, Iva quickly became the young orphan boy's best friend.

After washing the dust and sweat from her hands and arms, Iva uncovered one of the plates her mother had left on the kitchen work table. As she waited for Delbert to come to the house to eat, she hoped once again that their friendship would not be damaged by the feelings he held for her—feelings she could not reciprocate.

Delbert's mood was quiet when he did arrive. He sat down, uncovered his plate, and kept his eyes on it as he took up his fork and began to eat.

Filling their glasses with fresh milk from the pitcher her mother had left on the table, Iva tried to lighten the tension between them. "Was everything all right with Bold Sweeper, Delbert? I think Father might be going to put him with the two mares in the south pasture this week. Maybe that will settle him down." She smiled between bites of beef stew and fresh-baked biscuit.

Delbert did not comment. A commotion outside, at the front of the house, caught his attention, and with a frown, he got up and went to the sink to look out the window.

What Delbert saw in the front yard of the Cassidy home held him immobile.

"What is it?" Iva thought maybe her parents had forgotten something and had returned to the house, but the noise outside increased. She stepped away from the table and started toward Delbert, intending to see for herself what was taking place.

Her voice pulled him from his stupor, and spinning around, Delbert grabbed Iva by the arms and, in a dead-serious voice, ordered, "Iva, run to the barn. Stay there until I call for you!"

Seeing that his face had turned pale and glimpsing the concern in his eyes, she pulled away. "What on earth is it, Delbert?" she asked. "Why should I go out to the barn?" Moving around him, she looked out the window. "Indians!" she gasped in total disbelief.

Swinging back around, she caught a glimpse of Delbert in the hallway leading into the front room, taking down her father's old, muzzle-loading, long-barreled gun from the mantel and snatching up gunpowder and shot. "Do you think that thing will even work?" she questioned as he began to load the weapon. She couldn't remember when her father had last fired the gun.

Ignoring the question, Delbert shouted at her as the noise outside increased and was becoming more distinguishable as Indian war whoops, "Iva, do as I say! Now!" He ran into the kitchen while shoving the packing rod down the barrel of the gun. Grabbing hold of her again, he all but dragged her out the back door. "Run, Iva!"

Once she was outside the house, some of Iva's paralyzing fear left her. Running toward the barn with Delbert right behind her, she gasped as she heard the sound of breaking glass. "What do you think they want? Do you think they will search the barn?"

They had reached the safety of the barn, but Delbert knew it would only be a matter of moments before the Indians, having found the house empty, would be following in their tracks. And Iva was far too beautiful a prize for any brave to resist. "Bridle Cimmerian and mount him," he said to her. "When I push the back door open, you ride as fast as you can to the Cannfields'!"

"But I can't leave you here alone!" Even as she made this statement, fear was directing her steps toward Cimmerian's stall.

"You won't be leaving me! I have a gun, remember? Go and get help!" Though Delbert had always stayed clear of the black stallion, his terror over what the next few minutes might bring if he did not get Iva away from the farm pushed every other fear aside. Grabbing up Cimmerian's bridle, he clutched the black beast's mane and, ignoring the brandished teeth that tried to bite him, forced the bit between them before strapping the leather bindings around the horse's neck. "Hurry, Iva, take my hand-up!"

Iva was too terrified not to obey. Leaping upon Cimmerian's back, she heard the terrifying war cries filling the back yard and coming closer to the barn.

Running to the back of the barn, Delbert pulled the wood bar free and threw the double doors wide. He automatically reached out and slapped Cimmerian upon the rump; then he shouted, "Ride hard, Iva!"

Cimmerian lunged out of the barn. Unused to being struck, and sensing the excitement of his mistress, he stretched out his long legs. Iva clung to the reins with one hand and the stallion's thick black mane with the other. Her heart beat fiercely in her chest, her one thought being to bring help in time to save Delbert.

Most of the band of Indians had stayed mounted while two braves had broken through a front window of the house. Upon being notified that the place was unoccupied, the group made their way toward the barn.

The leader of the warriors was the first to see the fleeing black stallion and the golden-haired girl upon its back. As he was about to direct his warriors to give chase, a shot was fired from inside the large barn.

Using sign language, the leader directed a few of his braves to subdue, but not harm, the young man he had earlier seen sitting on the paddock wall while the girl worked with the horse. The other warriors followed him as he raced after the black stallion.

Chapter Two

The sound of Cimmerian's thundering hooves as they churned up the meadow grass in the pasture behind the barn was all Iva heard as she urged the stallion toward the forest that ran along the outer fringe of the Cassidy property. If she could just make it to the trees she could use the shelter to conceal herself, and if she kept to the outer boundaries of the thick pines she could go directly to the Cannfield property.

She dared not look behind her to see if she was being pursued by the attacking band of Indians. She could only hold on as her heart beat wildly in her breast and she raced for her very life!

Cimmerian took the low, stone wall that divided the forest from the Cassidy property without hesitation. The dense forest looming ahead did not distract the great beast. Clinging to his back, the girl drove him toward a little-used trail, one that she had occasionally ventured down when she had desired solitude.

"Go, Cimmerian, go!" Iva breathed aloud as she pressed herself to his back, low-hanging branches and shrubbery clawing at the horse's flanks and reaching out to unseat her.

The Indian warriors rode on the backs of spirited, endurance-bred ponies, sure footed and swift. Only moments after Iva entered the forest, they were coming down the trail after her.

Fear laced through Iva's body when she heard the pursuing horses breaking through the underbrush. The shouting Indians were only a short distance behind. Perhaps she should direct Cimmerian off the trail. That thought swiftly took root as she frantically sought some maneuver to escape her pursuers.

Racing across the leaf- and pine-needle floor of the forest, her thoughts only of eluding the Indians, she suddenly jerked the reins to the right and directed Cimmerian off the path the Indians had discovered.

Trying to dodge the trees, Cimmerian ran beneath a low-hanging branch, and even though Iva was bent over his sweat-slick neck, she could not keep her seat upon the animal's back. The thick limb raked her off, and she hit the ground with a thud!

For a few seconds Iva sat where she was, in a daze, her breath trapped in her lungs as she fought to steady the mounting hysteria that threatened to overcome her, hoofbeats and Indian war cries frighteningly close.

Slowing his frenzied pace with the realization that he was now riderless, the large ebony beast turned back to search for his mistress.

Too terrified even to think about the punishment her posterior had taken from her fall, Iva forced herself to her feet, her blue eyes wide with fright. She could not stay there. The Indians could easily find her, for she was only a few feet away from the trail. Hearing a noise off to the side, she expelled her breath as she saw Cimmerian crashing toward her through the underbrush and trees.

Running toward the stallion, she heard loud war whoops, and before she could grab hold of the reins, she was encircled by over a dozen Indian braves, all on horseback.

Terror gripped Iva as she turned slowly around, seeking any opening in the enveloping circle of riders.

To Shadow Dancer, the leader of the band, the

young woman looked much like a wild animal caught in an escape-proof snare. Dried leaves and pieces of pine needles were entangled in the golden hair which flowed in disarray down her back. Her wide, sapphire eyes stared at each brave as she slowly turned within the circle. Her buff-colored riding habit, which had been fresh and attractive when Shadow Dancer had watched her earlier this day, was now snagged and dirty, and in several places there were large rents in the material. As he stared down at her from his mounted position, he realized that his remembrance of her that day at the river did little justice to the beauty he was now viewing. The golden-haired, blue-eyed woman of his dreams was no match for the dazzling creature who now stood before him. Her fear was great, but she held her head high and her features showed her outrage over the attack upon her. Kicking the flanks of his horse, Shadow Dancer left the circle of riders that held her prisoner.

Still searching for a weak spot through which she might make her escape, Iva glared at the menacing horseman as he advanced toward her. Within her, anger intermingled with fear. "What do you want with me?" She demanded as she faced the formidable bronzed warrior who wore only a breechcloth around his loins. He sat his horse silently and appeared to study her in a manner that did not in the least ease Iva's anger or her terror.

The Indian did not answer, but signaling to two of his warriors, he pointed toward Cimmerian.

As the two braves started toward her horse, Iva truly became upset. If these bloodthirsty savages thought they were going to steal her stallion, they had best think again. Cimmerian belonged to her. "Wait a minute!" she shouted and took a step in Cimmerian's direction.

Her warning was ignored. As the pair of Indians advanced upon Cimmerian, his front legs rose high in the air, his hooves striking out at anything that would

20

dare come close enough to test his strength, his teeth bared to bite the closest Indian pony.

"Leave him alone! He will let no one close to him except me!" Iva would have rushed to Cimmerian's side if she had dared to go around the Indian who sat upon his horse in the middle of the circle. "Can't you understand? He will not let you near him!" Tears of anger and frustration filled her eyes as the two Indians kept circling Cimmerian. She feared they would hurt him if he did not submit, and knowing the stallion as well as she did, she was sure he would fight off the Indians until he could no longer stand.

A single Indian word came from the warrior within the circle, and the pair of braves who had been circling Cimmerian stilled their horses.

It was in that moment, as Iva looked to her horse and the menacing warriors surrounding him, that she was taken unaware. The brave within the circle kicked his pony's sides, and when his mount lunged at Iva, the warrior reached down and caught her around the waist. Pulling her off her feet and atop his mount, Shadow Dancer held her tightly against his chest.

At feeling his hands upon her body, Iva fought with every ounce of strength she possessed. She kicked out and flayed the air with her arms as she felt his body against her own. She tried to wriggle away from him, to throw herself to the ground, as she screamed out her rage at being so handled!

But nothing she did seemed to sway the Indian. Even when her fist made contact with his chin, he did not flinch; he appeared undaunted by her efforts.

With an easy movement, he seized both her hands in his larger one, and holding her close to his chest, he left her with no defense except her mouth. Without a second thought, Iva bent forward and bit the hand that clutched her own, hoping he'd release her. This, at least, gained a measure of response other than the tolerance he had thus far displayed. He grabbed her chin with his free hand, and pulling her face up closely to his own, he allowed her a clear view of his darkly piercing eyes and his stern visage.

Iva swallowed hard as she correctly read the look upon his features. Anger. Stilling her struggling for the time being, she watched as the Indian looked down at his hand and viewed the bloody teeth marks.

Releasing her chin, Shadow Dancer ignored her gasp of surprise and anger as he reached down and pulled up the hem of her riding habit. Tearing away a piece of the fabric, he wiped away the blood on his hand.

No man had ever dared to be so bold as to reach down and pull up Iva's clothing! "You brute! You vicious savage!" Beyond control now, Iva felt the Indian's hands tightening upon her, and hearing Cimmerian snorting and kicking up the floor of the forest, she gave free vent to her raging feelings. What could this savage do to her? Kill her? Would that not be preferable to whatever these brutal men planned? She had heard stories about raiding bands of Indians taking white women captive, tales of the terrible things they were said to have done to them. "Let me go!" she screamed, and tried to jump off his horse as she pushed against his broad chest rippling with muscles.

Appearing to tire of this exchange with his captive beauty, Shadow Dancer signed to his men and, kicking his horse's flanks, started back to the forest trail.

"You can't leave those horrible savages with Cimmerian!" Iva shouted and tried to look over his shoulder to see what was happening to her horse. When the Indian paid no heed to her, Iva began to curse him, dredging up every foul word she had ever heard.

Seeming to quickly tire of her verbal abuse, the Indian halted his horse. Again pulling strips of material from her garment, he swiftly tied one strip of cloth about her mouth and the other around her wrists.

Clutched to his iron-hewed, partially naked body as

22

she was, and with her hands and mouth now useless, Iva at last felt total defeat. She was powerless to do anything but glare her hatred, which was tempered only by her fear of her abductor.

Leaving the forest trail, the Indian's horse jumped the low stone fence Cimmerian had earlier taken so easily. Was the savage taking her back toward the farmhouse? Was all of this just some crazy game to these horrible warriors? For the first time since her capture, she thought about Delbert. Had he been able to escape the attack after she had ridden away from the barn? Anxiously she watched for the tall, lean frame of Delbert Benell as the Indian directed his horse around to the front of the barn.

Iva first glimpsed three Indian braves standing before the barn, near them a mounted warrior holding the lead for a string of at least twenty fine-looking horses. She then made out a prone form in the dust at the feet of the warriors. Delbert Benell. Her father's musket was lying several feet away, and as she looked closer, she saw that Delbert had been tied up.

As the Indian leader drew abreast of the three, Iva tried to pull herself out of his arms in order to go to the young man's side. Had they killed him? He was so deathly pale and still.

Her captor must have read her thoughts, for at a nod of his dark head, one of the braves gently kicked Delbert's side and an unconscious groan softly escaped Delbert's lips.

Iva sagged somewhat with relief at knowing that for the time being Delbert still lived. But her anger once again began to surface as the rest of the war party approached with Cimmerian tied between two Indian ponies. A pair of braves had lassoed the large stallion, and each time he'd tried to fight them off or gain his freedom, one of the two had tightened his rope, causing Cimmerian to feel the constricting pain of the lariat, which quickly tempered his spirit.

23

Though Iva was outraged at the treatment given her stallion and at her own inability to do more than sit and view Delbert trussed up and unconscious, she could not interfere. She was held tightly in the grip of a threatening warrior and could only wait to see what he would do next.

Perhaps they only wanted to steal the horses and would then be on their way. She tried to calm her fiercely beating heart, almost overcome with fear. Noticing the large string of horses once again, she resigned herself to the fact that the band's intent was to steal the horses on the farm, including Cimmerian. Steeling herself to the loss of her stallion, she knew that Delbert's life and her own would be in jeopardy if they resisted. The fact that Delbert had not already been slain seemed further proof of the reason for the Indians' presence on the Cassidy farm. The warriors had to be aware that if they harmed either of their captives they would be hunted down and made to pay for their crime. If they only stole the Cassidy horses, there would be little action taken against them. Perhaps the Indians intended to scare them and then depart with their bounty.

At a nod of his leader's dark head, the Indian still on horseback and holding the lead rope which kept the string of horses together, turned and started into the paddock where, earlier, Iva had been training Cimmerian. Freeing the horses within and then tightly securing the gate, the brave then guided his mount back toward the barn and Delbert. Pulling two small leather pouches from the parfleche tied on his horsehair saddle, the brave next made a drawing in the sand with a yellow substance the color of gold. It depicted the sun, and as a finishing touch he outlined it with silver. Upon completing this task, the warrior looked toward Shadow Dancer for affirmation.

Shadow Dancer nodded his head, and the three Indians standing near Delbert mounted their ponies.

Then, without a word being spoken, the band began to turn away from the barn.

Iva had been confused as she had watched the Indian leave the string of ponies in the paddock and then draw the strange design in the sand only a few feet away from where Delbert was lying. As the riders started to pull away from the barn, though, her confusion turned to fear and she would have screamed at her captor that he was supposed to leave her with Delbert, but with her mouth covered, she could only struggle. And she did! Though her hands were tied, she pushed against her captor, taking him unaware, as she tried to lunge off the back of his pony. She threw him off balance for a second, but he quickly braced himself against her efforts and tightened his grip around her waist. The only satisfaction Iva gained was from seeing his leather headband, with a design matching the one the Indian had drawn in the dust, fall beneath his pony's feet.

Tightening his grip on her, Shadow Dancer appeared to be unaware of the loss. With a deep, husky war cry, he kicked his pony's sides sharply and then galloped away from the Cassidy farm, his band of braves following.

Chapter Three

The sun was beginning to lower in the western sky when consciousness returned to Delbert. His head ached unmercifully as he stirred and found himself lying in the dirt. For a moment he closed his eyes and tried to clear the haze that seemed to have settled over him. As he was about to pull himself to his feet, he found that he was unable to rise. He slowly began to remember the Indian attack.

He was tied, he realized as he tried to roll over, and a groan escaped his lips when he raised his face from the ground. The Indians that had run into the barn and overpowered him after he'd fired the musket must have knocked him out and then tied him up.

With the constraints of the rope tied around his wrists, behind his back, and tightly drawn down to encircle his ankles, Delbert could only lie where he was, though he glimpsed Bain Cassidy's gun lying in the dirt not far from his side.

Iva! Her image swiftly filled his mind. Had she escaped the savages? As he became aware of the quiet, he struggled against his bonds, a hopeless gesture.

Iva must have made it to the Cannfields', he told himself. The Indians would never have caught up with Cimmerian! He tried to reassure himself with this thought, but another soon followed. If Iva had made it to the Cannfields', where was the help that should have been forthcoming? Why was he still tied up and lying here in the dust? Surely Bain Cassidy and Baxter Cannfield would have gathered as many men as possible and ridden back to the Cassidy farm to fight off the attacking Indians!

He watched the sun lower over the clear, Colorado sky. It was growing late, and with every moment that passed his fears for Iva's safety intensified. About to close his green eyes tightly to restrain the tears that threatened to flow, he caught a glimpse of something sparkling in the dimming sunlight. One of the Indians must have dropped something, he thought, and throughout the rest of the night, his hazel eyes held on the indistinguishable object several feet away.

As dawn was breaking over a pinkish-pearl morning Bain Cassidy and his wife returned to the farm. Beth Cannfield had delivered a healthy, baby girl in the early hours of the morning, and shortly after seeing that mother and child were resting comfortably, the Cassidys had started for home.

Bain's attention was drawn to something lying on the ground before the barn, and as he drew closer, he stared in total disbelief at Delbert's prone form.

Pulling the wagon up before the symbol drawn in the dust, the older man, who still had much of the strength and quickness of youth, jumped from the wagon seat and ran to Delbert's side.

Stirred awake by the sounds of wagon and team, Delbert cried with relief as he saw Bain rush to his side. "Iva!" he cried. "Did she make it to the Cannfields'?" His only thought was for the girl he loved.

Bain quickly began to cut away the rope with his pocket knife. "What do you mean, Delbert? Why would Iva be going to the Cannfields', and why are you tied up out here?" Bain was totally baffled, but his heart was already filling with dread, the boy's question about his daughter running through his mind.

"It was Indians, sir. They attacked the house, and Iva and I ran to the barn. I made her take Cimmerian and ride to the Cannfields'." At last free, Delbert slowly pulled himself up into a sitting position and began to rub his raw, aching wrists.

"How long ago, Delbert?" Bain's worried gaze went to his wife's pale, stricken face. Katherine now stood on the other side of Delbert.

"Yesterday, shortly after you rode away from the farm. They attacked while we were eating lunch." Delbert now knew that Iva had never made it to the Cannfields'. "They must have caught her!" The statement escaped him and conjuring all the horror it implied.

"Noooo," Katherine moaned, and Bain went quickly to her side and put his arm around her. "Not my baby, Bain! Dear God, not my little girl!" Tears were falling from her eyes as she looked to her husband for some assurance that what they all feared could not be true.

"Come into the house, Katherine. I promise you I will find her." Bain tried to offer his wife comfort, though he knew there would be no peace for any of them until he found Iva and brought her back to her family. "Perhaps she rode to one of our other neighbors," he offered, and for a few lingering seconds he studied the gold sun sign that had been drawn in the sand. Shaking his head without understanding, he began to lead Katherine into the house.

Eager to hold on to anything that would deny the horror of Indians having seized her daughter, Katherine said, "She might have gone to the Barlows'. They are closer than the Cannfields', if she went south instead of north."

Bain nodded his russet head as he began to gather supplies and shove them into a bag he could tie over his saddle horn. He would need extra bullets for the rifle that was in the wagon and food to last at least a few days. If the Indians had carried off Iva, it might take him a while to locate their tribe and then rescue her.

Knowing that her husband was in as much pain as she, Katherine forced herself to begin her daily chores. She was determined to keep herself busy until Bain returned with their daughter. "Take care of yourself." She forced her trembling lips into a smile as she lightly patted the front of her husband's cotton work shirt.

She'd barely got the words out before Bain placed a fleeting kiss upon her lips and started out the back door.

"Sir, I found this near the barn. It matches the design drawn in the dust." Delbert held up a leather headband on which a gold sun was outlined with silver.

Bain Cassidy looked closely at the headband, turning it over in his hand several times. As his finger traced the silver and gold workmanship, his gaze rose to meet Delbert's, and he murmured beneath his breath, "You're right, son. It is like the drawing in the dust. I've never seen anything like it before."

"The Indians must have left those horses in the corral, sir. There are about twenty of them, and they are all in fine shape."

Bain nodded his head as he went to one of the horses Delbert had saddled. It was all a mystery to him, but he did not have the time now to try to sort out why Indians would leave his corral full of horses and draw such a sign in his yard. He tucked the headband into the bag he tied across his saddle horn, after putting his rifle in its scabbard. "You stay here, Delbert, and take care of things until I get back."

"But, sir, I thought I would go with you to search for Iva." Delbert wanted with all his heart to help find the Indians that had attacked the farm.

"You are needed here, lad. We can't be leaving Katherine on the farm without a man to look out for her."

Of course, Bain was right. If the Indians returned for their horses Katherine Cassidy would surely be their next victim. "All right, sir," Delbert said softly, and within seconds he stood alone before the barn as Bain Cassidy galloped off toward the Barlows' ranch, in search of his daughter.

Hours ago Iva's tears had dried upon her cheeks. Her body numb from the hard riding of the Indian band, she was dazed, still not able to fully comprehend that she had been taken away from her home. They had ridden over rich farm land and rough terrain, the Indian ponies seeming used to this form of hard travel. Cimmerian, like his mistress, appeared subdued now, and he followed his captors without complaint.

Shortly after leaving the farm, Iva's abductor had untied her hands and removed the cloth covering her mouth. Strong arms held her, however, as he grasped the reins, preventing her from trying to escape.

For a time Iva held herself stiffly before the Indian, not daring to allow any portion of her body to be drawn close to his nearly naked torso. It was not long, though, before she began to slump wearily against his powerful chest. The day had been an exhausting one. Not only was her mind weary from speculating on what was to happen to her at the hands of these savages, but she was worn out from what she had endured throughout the day—the ride from the barn and into the forest, her fall from Cimmerian's back, and the endless riding—and was fighting to keep her eyes open and her body erect.

Finally, after dark and deep within a forest, near a shallow-rushing stream, the Indian leader at last called to the group of braves to make camp for the night.

As the Indians dismounted and quickly began to set up a small camp, Shadow Dancer slid off his horse's back, then reached up and took hold of Iva by the waist, pulling her from the horse and to her feet at his side.

Her glare, full of heated fury, seared him as she tried to pull away from his touch. "Take your hands off of me!" she got out from between clenched teeth, daring him to react to her outburst.

Shadow Dancer looked down into her weary features. The moonlight that shimmered through the tops of the trees clearly showed her rage. Disregarding her demands for release, he summoned a young brave, who quickly took hold of his mount's reins after Shadow Dancer took his parfleche from the pony's back. Taking hold of Iva's slim wrist, Shadow Dancer began to pull her toward the stream.

Digging her heels into the firm earth, Iva tried to pull back. What did he have planned for her? Now that they had stopped for the night was he going to force himself upon her and then kill her and leave her body in this dense forest where no one would ever find it?

Shadow Dancer, who was also tired from the long day, was beginning to grow a bit impatient with her stubbornness. Again he tugged at her wrist. Again he felt resistance. With an easy motion, he bent down and hefted her up over his shoulder.

Hearing the laughter of the other braves and feeling all eyes upon them, Iva felt real mortification. Instantly she began to beat upon his back with her fists and to kick her legs wildly as she fought for release. If he planned to take her away from the group and then molest and kill her, she certainly would not make it easy for him. She would try to escape from him in the cover of the forest. If she struggled hard enough, and forced him to release her, perhaps she would have a chance to run.

Iva had little choice about where her captor took her. With an easy stride, he made his way down the stream bank and away from the camp. When he reached the desired spot, he set his captive on her feet, one hand still holding her arm.

Iva glared into his obsidian eyes, and as his large, strong hands reached out and began to undo the long row of buttons that ran down the front of her blouse, she gasped aloud as she tried to push his hands away. "No . . . Please . . . Don't!" Her earlier fear gave way to overwhelming terror as she felt the moment of her greatest downfall was at hand.

Shadow Dancer pushed her hands aside as he determinedly finished with the unbuttoning and pulled her blouse from her upper body. Next he began to remove her skirt, amidst the protesting cries and insults she hurled at him.

When Iva stood on the stream bank in no more than her underclothing and boots, Shadow Dancer bent down and, still holding her with one hand, pulled the boots off her feet.

Looking into her face at that moment, Shadow Dancer was momentarily held in the spell cast by her incredible beauty. Shimmering tear drops glistened in her indigo eyes and sparkled against her cheeks. Her curling, copper tresses wrapped around her body, shining as though fire-gold in the moonlight. Shadow Dancer released one of her wrists—he had been holding both of them against her sides—and gently reached up and brushed away a tear. Coyolxauhqui, the moon goddess, surely must have touched this woman. She was more beautiful than a golden moon flower.

Iva stood as though frozen. She was afraid to try to flee, for she knew his strength was far greater than her own, and with her lack of clothing, she dared not tempt him into taking hold of her body once again. His touch upon her cheek unnerved her! It had a tenderness that she would never have expected from an Indian. As he traced the dampness of her cheek down to her jawline, her wide blue eyes rose up to meet his.

The contact jolted Iva and she could not break away.

She looked into those sable depths, felt his touch upon her face, and heard her own heartbeat.

Slowly as though fearing she was but an illusion from his dreams, Shadow Dancer lowered his head. His mouth, very gently, settled over the bow-shaped lips that tempted him beyond all endurance.

Time stood still as Iva was truly kissed for the first time. Her lips trembled beneath the warmth of his light caress, and as the kiss deepened she felt her insides melt, her limbs become heavy; she had to clutch his strong shoulders to keep from crumpling to the ground.

Shadow Dancer's arms entwined around her as he tenderly supported her against his chest. He felt each delicate curve as his senses filled with her scent and his blood rushed hotly through his veins. She was all he had imagined, all he desired!

The kiss consumed her, took her breath and left her mindful of only this powerful man that held her so gently. No longer thinking of the happenings of the day, no longer hearing the night sounds of the forest, Iva twined her fingers in strands of midnight black hair that lay against the broad shoulders. She was lost to all but her daring captor!

Shadow Dancer was the one who broke the spell. His lips drew up in a smile as he looked down into her beautiful face and whispered, "Moon Flower, you are truly fated to be mine."

The intensity of the kiss lingered for a few seconds, leaving Iva unable to respond. But soon his words intruded into her mind. "You speak English!" She gasped, as she stepped back to get a better look at him.

Shadow Dancer gazed down at her without making a response.

"You must take me back to my family!" Aware now that he could understand her, she began to hope that she could make him realize he had to return her to her father's farm. Surely he would know that he could not keep her a prisoner!

Had the kiss meant nothing to her? Shadow Dancer asked himself, and he quickly knew the answer. She was an innocent. She did not know as yet what was to be between them. What Quetzalcoatl had deemed from the very beginning of time. She was his destiny. She was his contact with the god of light, wind, and life—his very reason for being!

Iva indeed had not forgotten the kiss they had shared. Her lips still burned from his touch, but in spite of how wonderful it had felt, she suppressed her feelings for him. She had to regain her freedom! Had to return to her mother and father and Delbert! This man standing before her was an Indian! "Please, you have made a terrible mistake!" She tried to reason with him. "You must return me to the farm. You cannot keep me with you!"

"I brought you to the stream to bathe!" Shadow Dancer spoke English haltingly. He had learned it from a Catholic missionary, a priest his father had captured in a raid and had then brought back to their tribe's mountain valley.

"But I don't want to bathe. I want to go home!" Iva pleaded, her wide, blue eyes revealing all of her fear and frustration.

Shadow Dancer again reached out a long, tan finger and traced her jawline. "I can never release you, Moon Flower. Our spirits have touched. You are my vision of golden light." He spoke softly, wishing to impart his feelings to her without frightening her further.

Iva could not believe what she was hearing! *I am his vision of golden light?* She wanted no part of this craziness! She only wanted to go home! "No!" she gasped, but taking a step backward, she glimpsed the seriousness of his expression. He had no intention of releasing her; she knew it in that moment. He was still her captor, she his prisoner. Despite the kiss that they had shared, the fact that he could speak English. He had kidnapped her, taken her from her home, and if she

34

were ever to be free of him, it would only be by her own doing. Turning upon her bare feet, she began to run.

Shadow Dancer's instincts were sharp, and he was swift. As she started to run, he lunged after her and easily took hold of a handful of golden curls.

Iva cried out in disappointment and fury as he caught hold of her. "Let me go, you beast! I hate you! You . . . you . . . savage!"

"Come and wash, Moon Flower. You are tired and the hour grows late." Shadow Dancer seemed immune to her insults as he pulled her back to the stream.

"I will not bathe!" she declared righteously, determined not to bathe in front of this heathen!

"If you do not you will feel weary in the morning, and we have another long day ahead of us," Shadow Dancer tried to explain.

But, stubborn as a child, Iva crossed her arms over her chest and shook her head. She would not submit to his demands willingly. She suspected he had some underhanded reason for wanting her to bathe, and she was not about to be caught unaware! It was bad enough he had forced her to comply with his kiss! At this thought, she remembered the heated feel of those sensual lips upon her own, and she felt herself flush. She was thankful for the cover of night, which hid her embarrassment.

Bending down, Shadow Dancer unlaced the leather ties that ran from his sandals up his calves, still keeping a sharp eye upon her. Without further argument, he lifted Iva with one arm after straightening, and with an easy movement of one hand, he untied the leather binding of his breechcloth, allowing it to fall to the earth as he started toward the stream and waded into the water.

"What are you doing? Put me down, this minute!" Iva screamed, afraid of what he might do next as she felt the heat of his body through the sheerness of her underclothing. Her heart was racing frantically in her breast.

Shadow Dancer complied. In the deepest portion of the stream, he dropped her into the cool, swirling depths.

Plunging back up to the surface, Iva sputtered and gasped out loud, not believing that he had dared to drop her.

Standing above her in waist-deep water, Shadow Dancer smiled upon her in an easy manner. "We shall bathe, and then we will eat and rest." This said, he went back to the bank. Keeping the lower portion of his body beneath the water, he reached into his parfleche, which was lying at the stream's edge, and drew out a mixture of the sweet-smelling soap his cousin Nokie had given him.

In the light of the full moon shimmering down upon the stream, Iva watched the Indian's every move. Glimpsing the white substance in his hand as he turned back toward her, she began to back away from him, shaking her head. "Don't come near me with that!" She had no idea what new torment he had in mind, but she was not about to submit to it.

Shadow Dancer laughed aloud as he drew nearer and saw her fear of what he held in his hand. Holding the mixture beneath her nose, he pronounced the word in his own language for soap.

Iva eyed the stuff cautiously even though it smelled of the sweetness of summer flowers. It was soap, she realized; still, she warily eyed the Indian.

Shadow Dancer gave her not a moment to keep him at bay; within seconds, he was standing at her side in the rushing water, and without hesitation, he separated a small amount of the soap and rubbed it into her hair.

Iva knew it would do little good to protest. She was wet through to the skin, and this savage would have his way. Enduring his attentions, she stood still as he soaped the length of her golden hair, and then with a quick movement he caught her against his chest.

36

Slipping one arm beneath her knees as she clutched at his neck for fear that he would drop her, he dipped her head back into the cool water and gently ran his free hand through her hair to free it of any remaining suds.

This whole scene is insane, Iva told herself as the Indian set her on her feet and gently drew his soapy fingers along her throat and down the lengths of her bare arms. His movements were seductively ensnaring, and gasping aloud as a heated flush traveled the length of her body, Iva jumped away from him. What on earth is wrong with me? she asked herself. Can this heathen so easily make me forget who I am and why I am here— in this stream—so far from my home and family.

Shadow Dancer kept his distance, watching her with searching, dark eyes as she finished washing. She was exactly as he remembered her from that day when she had been breaking the mighty black stallion. So beautiful with the moonlight showering down upon her. Even through her dampened underclothes, he could see that she had a perfect figure, full breasts whose dark tips strained against the fabric of her sheer top, curves that her lacy pantalets hugged tightly. Forcing his thoughts away from this track, Shadow Dancer strode out of the water. He had no wish to frighten her with his great desire. He would first have to teach her to trust him. He decided to wait a bit longer to tell her that he had left the horses in her father's corral as a bride price, his sun sign in the yard to indicate his honorable intentions toward her. "Come." He spoke the single word as though he held no doubt that she would obey.

As Iva watched from the center of the stream, for the first time she noticed that he was entirely naked. She looked for only a few seconds upon the first naked male she had ever seen, but that short look was sufficient. He stood upon the stream bank, moonlight playing off of his huge, bronzed body, unaffected by his own nakedness. His glistening, black hair lay against his broad shoulders; his muscle-corded arms hung easily at his sides. His torso rippled and glistened with strength, his manhood stood proud and large, his powerful thighs and calves were braced slightly apart, and his feet were firmly placed upon the dampened earth.

"Come, Moon Flower, I am hungry." Shadow Dancer called out to the woman in the water.

Iva could not look back toward the bank. I do not want to look at him again, she told herself, then felt her entire body flush and begin to tremble. She had to have time to gather her wits, time in which to remind herself that this man was her abductor, her captor, her kidnapper! I am beset with these strange feelings for this man only because I am tired and hungry and want desperately to go home! she said to herself.

Shadow Dancer had learned patience at an early age, and understanding much of what she must be feeling, he silently pulled on his breechcloth and awaited her. Though he was tired from the long day, he wanted to lighten the burden of her misery as much as possible. He wanted this woman to be willingly his!

After some minutes had passed, Iva stole another glance at the bank and saw Shadow Dancer, now wearing his breechcloth, leaning against a tree and silently watching her. Slowly she began to make her way out of the water, thankful that he had covered that portion of his body that had brought such embarrassment to her.

"Come here, Moon Flower, and I will dry you." Shadow Dancer spoke softly, his words the only sound coming to Iva's ears.

She would have refused, but as she glimpsed the piece of fur he had pulled from his parfleche, of a sudden she felt bone weary and only wanted to have this nightmare over with, wanted to be able to put on her clothes and find somewhere to sleep. With halting steps she made her way to stand before him.

Shadow Dancer expelled his breath. He had feared

that she would refuse him. Gently he rubbed the fur over her shapely body, drying the droplets of water that glistened on her pearl-satin skin. "You should take these off and allow them to dry," he softly stated, as he touched the strap of her camisole.

Some reason instantly returned to Iva with these words, and she jumped away from him. "I think not!" she declared, and started toward her riding habit and boots!

Chapter Four

Indians! The word conjured up wild imaginings and frenzied terror in the most stouthearted settler in the Colorado area, though for several years now there had been relative peace between Indian and white. Now and then a renegade band of Apaches would descend upon unsuspecting settlers and wreak havoc.

There were numerous stories of murder and mayhem at the hands of the Apaches. The most horrible of these told of the torture and abuse their white captives suffered. The prisoners taken were mostly women and young children, and usually their fate was servitude. They were treated as the lowest creatures in an Apache village, unless fate took a hand and somehow a captive won some small favor in their masters' eyes.

Over the next several days every story Iva had heard over the years came to her mind over and over again. As mile after mile broadened the distance between herself and the Cassidy farm, she sat before her captor, his large, bronze arms wrapped around her, and as each day wore on, her stiffened form slowly began to press against his naked chest. Her exhaustion was so great she could do little but imagine what lay ahead of her as an Indian's captive.

Over the years Iva had glimpsed small bands of Apaches as they moved from one area of Colorado to another at certain times of the year. Her abductor and his party of braves did not resemble any of the Apaches she had seen on the outskirts of Sterling, nor did they favor the Indians she had spotted when her father had taken her and her mother to Denver for a holiday, but she believed this band had to be Apache. No other Indians would dare to attack her father's farm and steal a woman. Only the Apache were known to be so cunning and dangerous!

Her only hope was that her father would rescue her, but as each day of hard travel passed, Iva's eyes turned less and less toward the horizon in search of some sign of her father and a search party.

If her misery was unbearable during the daylight hours, the evenings she spent as Shadow Dancer's captive were sheer torture.

Her warrior captor forced her to remain at his side even while he slept. Each evening he spread out his sleeping mat a short distance away from the rest of his braves, then signing to her, he directed her to lie down at his side.

There was little Iva could do about this. With his massive body next to hers on the sleeping mat, she could scarcely breathe; let alone sleep. She was overcome with the masculine scent of him. In such cramped conditions, the accidental brush of his hand along her ribs or against the outline of her breasts sent her pulses to pounding, and her anger at her body's reaction to this warrior to escalating.

After that first night of her capture, when Shadow Dancer had kissed her, he had not again attempted such an advance, nor had he spoken to her very often in her own language.

Daily he instructed her in his own tongue. Allowing her no food or water, or even a moment's peace, until she repeated the foreign words to his satisfaction.

At first Iva tried to refuse him, but he was relentless; and after her first morning's travel on an empty

41

stomach, she grudgingly spoke the words he demanded.

Stretching out her shapely legs, she wearily sat upon a log that had been pulled up near the shallow pit fire in the center of the Indians' make-shift camp. Iva glared across the cleared space of the camp toward Shadow Dancer. Biting off a piece of the honey-sweetened corn cake she had been given as her evening meal, she inwardly fumed at her mistreatment. She was exhausted, her clothes were ruined, and she was sick of being forced to repeat the uncomfortable-sounding words that he demanded from her lips. Even to receive this simple meal of corn cake and a skein of water, she had been made to endure many long moments of repeating and then repeating again each word that related to her meal.

In Iva's mind the reason for this was obvious: he was forcing her to learn his language. She was to be a slave! He believed that her value would be increased if she could communicate with the person in his village she would belong to. She had no idea that Shadow Dancer had stolen her for himself. She believed these warriors to be a raiding band of braves who would return to their village and trade off their loot to the highest bidder. Somewhere in the back of her mind she remembered being told about a young white woman who had been sold to several different Indian tribes; each time the seller received a higher price for his captive.

Day and night she was plagued with thoughts of escape.

She would not become a slave! She could not allow herself to be taken to their village; for once there, it would be even harder for her to gain her freedom. She held to the belief that her father was searching for her. She knew he would never give up looking, but she also knew that too much time had already passed since her abduction. Each day it grew harder for any kind of search party to find a sign of this small band of warriors.

For over a day now they had been traveling through the mountains, the terrain so rough there would be little sign to lead her father in her direction. She knew that her only chance might well lie in her own abilities!

As she stared at the tall figure of Shadow Dancer, once again noticing his masculine grace and striking handsomeness, she sternly rebuked that traitorous part of her inner consciousness. *He is a dangerous Indian!* No more *than a savage! Savage perhaps! But surely more man than you have ever seen before. . . .* That side of her that enjoyed flirting with danger responded to the rebuke.

She followed Shadow Dancer with her eyes as he walked away from the brave he had been conversing with and, without a look in her direction, started off toward the area where the horses were tied. This was the first time he had left her alone since her abduction. Quickly Iva's glance took in the rest of the camp to see if any of the other warriors were looking in her direction. Most had already spread out their sleeping mats and had settled down for the night, their faces turned away from the fire. The Indian that had been talking to Shadow Dancer soon left the circle of light in the campsite, and praying that he was going to take up his nightly watch, Iva decided there was a slim chance this would be her opportunity to escape.

Forgetting the corn cake in her hand, Iva let it slip to the ground next to the log. Her chest tight, she slowly rose to her feet. She took one more look around before she silently slipped away from the pit fire.

If she could only get out of the Indian encampment she would find someplace to hide! It was a moonless night with a vast array of stars overhead to illuminate her way. The semidarkness hindered her steps, but at the same time it helped keep her from being detected. Starting off in the opposite direction from the one the Indian who had just left camp had taken, Iva forced herself to move slowly, not allowing herself the pleasure of running away from her captor as she desired, fearing that her movement would somehow give her presence away.

The dark shadows of the surrounding trees gave her pause, for she felt that at any moment one of them would suddenly assume the form of her abductor.

Several yards away from camp, she exhaled and started, at a quicker pace, in the direction she believed to be southwest. If she could keep to this course she hoped somehow to find her father. Perhaps as soon as tomorrow morning she would meet up with Bain Cassidy and his search party. This thought pushed her on all the harder.

Every second that passed held a joyful taste of freedom. *Just a bit farther . . . Over the embankment up ahead . . . Keep going . . . Keep going. . . .*

Drawing in a deep, ragged breath, Iva began to run. Believing herself far enough from the Indian camp, she prayed that Shadow Dancer had not yet returned to find her missing. She needed only a bit more time to find somewhere to hide.

Panic and fear dogged her every step as she ran toward freedom. As she raced past a dark clump of shrubbery, from out of nowhere a long portion of shadow reached out and, with a viselike grip, grabbed her arm.

Before she realized what was happening, memories passed through her mind in swift sequence as often happens when one faces a catastrophe. Both of her upper arms were clamped tightly, and she was jerked against a hard, male body.

Iva let out a piercing cry that filled the night air and seemed to tremble upon her lips before a large hand covered her mouth.

A harsh, rasping voice commanded her to silence. Not understanding the words of the one who held her made Iva's fear escalate: the language he spoke was not that of Shadow Dancer's group.

Drawing a ragged breath beneath the hand held tightly over her mouth, Iva took in the dark material of an open shirt and then the fur vest the large Indian was wearing. She had no doubt now that this man was not a part of Shadow Dancer's party, and her terror intensified with her awareness that she received no tenderness from this warrior. His grip was savage, and the sharp point of the large, bladed knife held beneath her chin signified he meant every unintelligible word he harshly uttered.

Still holding his hand over her mouth as he threatened her with his cruel weapon, the Indian began to pull her along

Iva dared not draw breath. She silently prayed she would not stumble and cause her own death as she was drawn through the brush toward a horse. She knew she had to try to fight her captor, but she was powerless to wage any kind of defensive assault with cold steel pressed against her throat. Angry that she had escaped Shadow Dancer only to be caught by another Indian, she threw caution to the wind! With all the strength she possessed, she grabbed hold of the hand holding the knife. If she could somehow dispose of the threat of this deadly weapon, perhaps she could once again gain her freedom. She knew instantly that her strength was no match for his, still she held on to his hand. In those moments she almost believed death would be preferable to the fate that awaited her at this vicious man's hands.

With a movement and a deep-throated growl of warning, the Indian shook off her hands, and as he did, he withdrew the knife from her throat and replaced it in the sheath at his side. His other hand left her forearm, and with lightning speed his long, dark fingers tightly grasped strands of her long hair. With a jerk, he pulled her against his chest, and she was now powerless to fight him. Small, whimpering moans of pain escaped her lips as he gathered up his pony's reins and with a swift movement leaped upon its back.

Still holding tightly to Iva's hair the savage bent and would have pulled his captive up before him on the pony, but at that moment a dark form hurtled through the air, a terrifying war cry pierced the still night, and the Indian was knocked from his horse. His abrupt release of Iva's hair sent her rolling across the hard ground.

The episode was so sudden; Iva could not believe she was witnessing Shadow Dancer's savage assault. From where she lay sprawled upon the ground she caught the glint of a knife blade as Shadow Dancer landed astraddle his quarry. Without hesitation he drove the large hunting knife into the other warrior's chest.

Only seconds had passed before Shadow Dancer lifted Iva from the ground and held her in his powerful embrace.

Is one savage any less evil than the other? The question assaulted Iva's inner conscience as her terror slowly diminished while Shadow Dancer gently soothed her. His large hands caressed her cheek as he looked deeply into her pale features as though trying to assure himself that she was unhurt. Tenderly his fingers laced a trail through her hair and then ran over her trim back, the masculine tenderness of his words making her tremble.

"You are unhurt, Moon Flower. Coyolxauhqui spoke your name upon the night wind and told me of your danger." Shadow Dancer had been brushing down his horse and also trying to win Cimmerian's trust so the mighty animal would allow himself to be brushed down. At first Cimmerian had refused, but eventually Shadow Dancer's crooning tone and light hand had eased him somewhat and he had nervously submitted to the ministrations. As Shadow Dancer had brushed sweet-smelling sage grass over the sleek flanks of the large animal, his movements had stilled, some inner sense of impending danger catching hold of him. Silently he had listened to the sounds of the night.

From deep within his soul he had captured the presence of the moon goddess, Coyolxauhqui, upon the gentle breeze of the night wind. She had called to him the name of Moon Flower, and without hesitation, Shadow Dancer had run back to camp, there to find only quiet.

At first anger gripped him when he did not find Iva sitting before the fire where he had seen her last, but just as quickly he was beset with fear for her safety. Wariness filled him as he was consumed by a sense of impending danger. With all of his inner senses attuned to the threats that could be lurking in the night, he silently drew forth his knife and left the campsite.

As the shock Iva had received slowly began to diminish, she began to gently quake with silent sobs.

Shadow Dancer allowed her time to quiet her distress as her tears rolled down the solid muscular wall of his chest. He offered her the only comfort he knew. His hands gently soothed, and his words tried to imply his concern. "Hush, my heart. I would never have allowed him to take you," he softly crooned as he brushed back the golden strands of hair lying against her cheeks.

"You killed him!" Iva gasped aloud. She admitted to herself that she was glad the strange Indian had been prevented from stealing her, but she was horrified at the swiftness of the justice Shadow Dancer had meted out.

"He is Apache. He would have done the same to me if I had not been the swifter." Shadow Dancer tried to maintain a softness to his speech, understanding that this woman was unused to the harshness of the Indian way of life.

The fact that the dead Indian was an Apache seemed all the more terrible to Iva. In her eyes Shadow Dancer had killed one of his own tribe. "But I was trying to run away from you when he captured me. I want to find my father! I want only to go back home!" She cried out

47

these last words, her slim form sagging against him as though in total defeat.

Shadow Dancer lightly gathered her into his arms and then turned back in the direction of the camp, the dead Indian forgotten now in his concern for the woman in his arms. "You are very brave, Moon Flower." This was his only comment on her confession of trying to flee him.

Iva tried to glance into his features to see for herself if he was making light of the anger he was, in truth, feeling over her attempt to escape. His handsome profile was concealed in the darkness of the night shadows, so she could not make out his feelings. "You are not angry that I tried to escape you?" she dared to ask as she stifled a sob.

"I should not have left you alone. I should have expected such attempts for freedom for the time being. You still have much to learn. If I were in a like position, and I was being held against my will, I also would have taken the opportunity to flee." Inwardly he believed that she would one day learn that they were fated to be together, and with this understanding, she would never again wish to be apart from him.

Iva was amazed by his understanding and by the truthfulness of his answer. This man was certainly like no other she had ever met. She had tried to run away from him and in the process had put herself—and him—in danger, and she had also been the cause of his killing one of his own kind, but he spoke softly of understanding her actions.

Once they were back at camp, Shadow Dancer sent out two braves to scout the area and make sure no other Apaches were lurking about.

Taking Iva to his sleeping mat, he set her down upon the soft, warm furs. "Your hair, Moon Flower, is a great temptation for any brave. No doubt the Apache thought himself looked upon with great favor by Coyolxauhqui." As he stated this he drew forth a tortoise-shell comb and a strip of leather from his parfleche. Once again Shadow Dancer relived the moment when he had come upon the Apache and Iva. He had seen the other warrior's hand cruelly wrapped within the golden strands of her hair, and at that instant an overpowering fury had assaulted him. This woman belonged only to him! No other would ever dare lay hands upon her! He would have to be much more wary in the future, he told himself. She was a precious gift to him, from the gods, and he was responsible for her protection. Gently he began to comb out her long golden wealth of curls, and with an agile swiftness, began to weave her tresses into a thick braid.

Iva silently endured his attentions, unaware of his solemn thoughts. Every now and then his ministrations evoked a sigh from her due to the tenderness of her scalp from the Apache's imprisoning grip on her hair.

When finished braiding, Shadow Dancer surveyed his handiwork as he sat back upon his haunches on the bed of fur. And he looked with great admiration upon Iva's rare beauty. "This night has proven even more fully to me that our paths have been linked by the gods," he murmured softly as her liquid, blue eyes looked upon him questioningly.

Her regard of him touched off a quickening within Shadow Dancer's soul, and he would have drawn her to him in that moment and sated his wild cravings for her had not his rein upon his impulses prevailed. He sensed an opening of trust. He would not shatter this new feeling with his own need for assuagement, though his manhood swelled and pulsed with the desire to claim this woman as his own. He had expected that the binding of her moon-gold hair would lessen the incredible appeal she had over him, but in fact that had had the opposite effect. With her long, wild strands of hair controlled, her natural beauty was plainly revealed. The pearl-like luster of her creamy skin enhanced the

49

outline of her delicately high cheekbones, and her sparkling azure eyes held mysterious depths that could tempt any man's soul as she stared back at him without lowering her thick, golden lashes or blushing under the boldness of his intent regard. Even her petal-soft lips, luscious as summer-sweet strawberries, aroused to fever pitch his raging desire.

For a moment Shadow Dancer closed his eyes against her radiance, and drawing a deep breath he reminded himself that he was a war chief. He held a high position in the inner council of his tribe. He was a man who had imposed control on his emotions all of his life, one who had withstood all manner of temptations of the flesh.

But Iva was an enticement that he had never experienced before, he admitted as he opened his eyes and saw her still watching him. Her beauty was incomparable. The women of his past were as the stars before the early morning dawn, so quickly did they pass from his mind.

Iva sat mesmerized as she looked into the warm, sable depths of his gaze. A flaming spark was set off deep within her breast as he admired her hair and examined her every facial feature. She was held spellbound, the sexual tension of the moment as electrifying as heat lightning before a summer storm. Being a novice in the face of these new feelings, Iva was very curious. She perhaps would have reached out to discover for herself the meaning of this thing flaming between them. The kiss they had shared that first night had replayed itself in her mind often enough over the past few days, and the wilder side of her nature would have chanced discovering what more lay ahead.

Forcing his thoughts in a direction that would help him to regain his self-control, Shadow Dancer pulled a soft hide shirt from his parfleche, and in a voice that sounded rough even to his own ears, he stated as he nodded his head toward the object of his statement,

"Your gown is torn, Moon Flower."

It took a full moment before the spell was broken and Iva realized what his speech implied. Glancing down at her riding habit, she gasped and then clasped her blouse where a large rent had left the lace of her camisole plainly visible. Her skirt also was torn and snagged from all she had been through, she noted. A soft sigh of self-pity escaped her as she remembered the morning she had put the riding habit on. It had certainly been her best, and she had worn it to show Cimmerian off to his fullest. Now as she sat in her rags upon a bed of furs owned by an Indian, she knew little of the feelings of pride she had known that day. She was reduced to the state of an undignified ragamuffin! In misery, she would have wept except that Shadow Dancer's voice caught her attention.

"This will cover you for now, Moon Flower."

Iva melted in her inner being as her hand tentatively brushed the softness of the shirt. Slowly she nodded her pale head. "Thank you, Shadow Dancer," she whispered.

The smile he bestowed upon her for some unknown reason filled her with a light sense of happiness. Softly he spoke the words in his own language that meant thank you, and for the first time Iva repeated his words without complaint.

Chapter Five

As she rested lightly within the shelter of strong arms, the first gray light of dawn revealed Iva Cassidy's features as a trusting blend of innocent girl and lovely young woman. Shadow Dancer, looking down at her, hated to wake her. In her sleep she appeared unaware of the closeness of their bodies. Each shapely curve was pressed tightly against his harder contours. Her gentle breath caressing his hard, flat nipples sent shocking torrents of heated desire coursing throughout his body. He would be more than glad when they finally reached his village and he could devote all of his time and attention to the cause of winning this woman's trust and heart.

Last night they had shared a few moments' reprieve from the distrust and anger that existed between them. Dreading the thought of once again being witness to the fear and resentment on her face when she awoke, but knowing he could put off rousing her no longer, he said quietly, "Moon Flower, it is time to awake to this new day."

His face was only inches from her own, and with his warming breath fanning her cheek, Iva, not fully conscious of what she was doing, stretched alluringly within the coverings on the fur bed, her full lips pouting temptingly at being so disturbed.

Shadow Dancer was more than willing to be the recipient of such welcome gestures. Through the cover of the hide shirt he had given her, he could feel the fullness of her bountiful, ripe breasts pressing against his chest, and her slender legs moved seductively against his own limbs, stirring his simmering passions to a dangerous level.

Still partially caught up in the nether world of blissful sleep, Iva softly questioned, "Why do I have to wake up? I am so terribly tired."

Shadow Dancer's sensual lips pulled back into a smile of pity for her and for himself. She had no idea of what she was doing to him, and though he was well aware of how exhausted she was from their hard days of travel, he told himself that there was little help for it. "Moon Flower, the other braves are stirring about camp. It is time for us to leave my sleeping mat."

At last his words gained a coherent response. Blinking her eyes, Iva gasped aloud as she realized how closely she was lying against the Indian warrior's powerful chest. A bright flush of scarlet touched her cheeks as she quickly scrambled to her feet and out of the warmth of his soft bed.

Regret clearly showed upon Shadow Dancer's features as he rolled off his sleeping mat and secured it. He would have given much this morning to be allowed total privacy with this woman.

Iva tried to put as much distance between herself and Shadow Dancer as possible as she endeavored to calm the trembling of her body. Standing before the shallow pit fire that had been stoked back into existence, she tried to bring some order to her hair and to calm her rapidly pounding heart. In sleep much of her hair had been freed from the long braid Shadow Dancer had made the night before, and untying the leather binding with trembling hands she now tried to bring some order to her wayward curls. She was finding it harder and harder to resist this man, and realizing this, her concern over her tangled emotions grew. Rightfully she could not forget that she was his prisoner, but had ever a captive known such gentle care? How could she hold a tight rein over her wilder nature when at every hand she was easily tempted by his masculine strength and by that husky, sensuously vibrating tone of his, which left her feeling like melted butter every time he spoke to her. How could any woman resist him?

Glimpsing her agitated movements as he readied his horse, Shadow Dancer drew his tortoise-shell comb from his parfleche. Stepping to her side, he brushed her hands aside. "I will do this deed for you, Moon Flower." He spoke the language of his own people as he drew his comb through the golden length of her hair.

Standing so closely at his side, Iva had to accept his offer, but she fought off the weakness she felt in her knees. Something had happened between them last night. An awareness of each other now had come into being, and with the light of morning, it frightened Iva more than she liked to admit. She wanted to ignore these strange feelings this Indian evoked in her. She wanted only to return to her family the same person she had been before he had stolen her!

"We will camp early this afternoon. Tomorrow we will reach my village, and then you will be able to rest." His words were spoken softly in her own language in order that she would fully understand him. With swift fingers, he deftly rebraided the length of her hair. He wanted to offer her an end in sight to their hard travel, and he hoped word of reaching his village would please her.

As she swung around to face him, her fear was plainly visible upon Iva's delicate features. "Please let me go." It was more than a plea for her release; her words were an anguished cry for release from the hold he had over her inmost emotions. Her wide indigo eyes looked up into his, and in their depths he could easily discern her plea for freedom.

Shadow Dancer would have given this woman anything in his power, but he could not grant her this one wish. His very heart beat out her name with every pulsing breath that he took. In her, he had found that rare being that would make him complete. He could no more allow her to leave him than he could separate his spirit from his earthly form. "You will find happiness in my village, Moon Flower." This he could promise her, for he swore to himself that he would do all in his power to see to her happiness as his wife.

"Happiness!" Iva repeated in a scathing tone, though tears threatened. "What captive has ever been happy in an Apache Village?" The tears she had fought to conquer now trickled down over her cheeks as all her imagined horrors resurfaced, all the tales about the women captured by Indians. Did he truly believe for one minute that once he sold her as a slave she would find happiness?

Glancing around, Shadow Dancer noticed that most of his braves were already mounted and ready to leave. He did not have the time this morning to soothe away her fears as he would have liked, he could only offer her some small consolation. Reaching down, he wiped the moisture from her cheeks and looked tenderly into wide, dampened blue eyes. "I am not as cruel as you would believe. My people are not as you fear."

Iva still would have begged this warrior for her release. How could she believe an Indian? How could she put any credence in the words he spoke? But even as she opened her mouth to further implore him to reconsider, he brushed out the campfire and, taking hold of her forearm, silently led her to his horse.

Deep within the mountains the small band approached a shallow stream that veered northward and ran farther into the mountains. Following the rocky bed deep into the hills that were well known to the band, Shadow Dancer held his pace as one by one his braves silently disappeared.

Early in the afternoon Iva's head nodded against Shadow Dancer's broad chest as she fell into a troubled light sleep. It was some time later that she awoke to a loud rushing noise. Opening her eyes, she saw that they were traveling in a narrow ravine bounded on both sides by a thick pine forest. "Where are we?" The loudness of the strange noise still assaulted her ears.

"Some of my people believe this place to be the home of the rain god, Tláloc. Few come here for fear of retribution from the gods. Their fear of that which they have little understanding deprives them of this most wondrous sight, which I would have you witness at my side." Shadow Dancer's husky voice, next to her ear, carried over the thunderous force of the noise up ahead and sent warm shivers running the length of her spine.

Iva sat straighter upon the back of his pony, her eyes wide with expectation of what was lying in wait for her as she tried to ignore his closeness. The forest around them held back the brightness of the late afternoon sun, so it was with a gasp of surprise that Iva was met with the most spectacular view she had ever seen. Shadow Dancer's pony, with Cimmerian following behind on a lead rope, stepped through the path of the ravine and into bold sunlight. "I can well understand why your people would believe this place created by the gods," she breathed out as the incredible panaroma before her held her enthralled. Like glittering sparkles of iridescent shimmering silk a waterfall cascaded to earth, down the side of an imposing mountain, a majestic kaleidoscope of swirling diamond droplets. The rushing spirals were finally captured by the crystalline pond that was the source of the stream they had been following throughout the afternoon. Along the banks of this pond lush meadow grass was interwoven with bursts of wild forest flowers. The late afternoon sunshine fully enhanced the magnificent scene laid out before them.

Shadow Dancer interrupted the quiet that had settled over them. "I come here often and fill my soul with beauty. Perhaps in days long past the gods of my people did linger here about the falls, forgetting the trials of their immortal lives."

Iva turned in his arms and gazed into the warm dark depths of his eyes when she caught the wistfulness in his tone. It is strange, she thought, that such a man as he, an Indian warrior of great power and strength, could share such tender emotions with another.

"We will camp here for the night." The words were still softly spoken.

"But what of the others?" For the first time Iva wondered about the dispersal of Shadow Dancer's group, his words bringing home the realization that they were now totally alone.

"They have gone on to the village. We will continue on tomorrow." Shadow Dancer planned to have the rest of what was left of this day and the coming night alone with her in the hope that he could bring her to regard him with some small favor. Sliding off the back of his pony, he reached up and in an easy movement set Iva on her feet. Without further comment, he took the reins off his mount and turned the pony loose to feed on the tall grass along the pond's edge. Keeping the lead rope on Cimmerian, he staked the large animal out so that he also could partake of the bounty of sweet, tender shoots along the floor of the valley.

Iva could not offer resistance in words to Shadow Dancer's plan to stay the night here near the falls. Though she tried to quell her nervousness at being alone with this man, her uppermost thought was that the longer arrival at his village could be postponed, the more time she would have before being sold into slavery. Silently she drew closer to the edge of the pond and watched the cascading water from the falls hit the surface of the pool in showerings of glistening droplets.

As Shadow Dancer started a small pit fire and pulled a few supplies from his parfleche, he studied her solitary form from the corner of his eye. There was an aura of sadness about her, and being true to himself, Shadow Dancer had to admit that he was not lost to the reason for her distress. He would have gladly gone to her in that moment and wrapped his arms around her, offered her comfort and tried to lessen all her fears; but believing he would only find rejection of such an offer, he drew from his parfleche the sweet-smelling soap he had shared with her on the night of her capture. He would make a gesture that he hoped she would not be able to refuse. "If you wish for privacy in which to bathe, I will be gone for a time." As she turned toward him, suspicion in the depths of her blue eyes, he hurriedly added, "It will take me some time to find meat, a rabbit perhaps for our meal."

It took only seconds for Iva to jump at the opportunity he was presenting. It would be sheer heaven to be able to strip away all of her clothing and take a long, leisurely bath without this large, imposing Indian at her side, watching her every move. How could she refuse this offer when she did not know when she would be afforded a like one? Tentatively she reached out and took the soap he held out. The thought of escape fleetingly crossed her mind, but the memory of her last attempt at freedom followed so she pushed the thought aside.

A smile of pleasure came over Shadow Dancer's features as he glimpsed the sparkle of excitement in Iva's sapphire eyes. Without another word he left her, taking up his bow and quiver of arrows and then turning toward the forest.

For a few lingering minutes Iva watched the spot at which Shadow Dancer had disappeared into the trees. Then, kicking off her boots in the tall grass, she nervously began to pull off her clothing. With anxious glances thrown in the direction the Indian had taken,

58

she quickly washed out her underclothing with a small portion of the soap. The sweet floral aroma of the creamy mixture mingled with the scents of the wild flowers at the pond's edge, and Iva smiled softly to herself, thinking of clean clothes and a welcome bath.

The initial chill of the water as she dove into the clear blue depths left her sputtering, her naked body shivering as she broke the surface. But she swiftly adapted to the coolness of the pond as she washed long dampened strands of pale hair and then every portion of her body with the creamy soap.

With the cleansing of her body completed, Iva was loath to leave the pond. Believing herself to have plenty of time before Shadow Dancer returned, she floated on the surface, allowing the rays from the afternoon sun to warm her naked flesh. As she did so, the coolness of silken soft liquid surrounding her, she lost all sense of time and place. She held her eyes tightly shut as she drifted into a realm of forgetfulness. She did not feel the restrictions of being a captive. The fact that she was so far from home and all those she loved seemed to matter little as she allowed herself to be engulfed in a sphere of nothingness for these lingering minutes. This total pleasure which caused her grip upon reality to momentarily vanish was, of course, little more than a shield of the mind that gave her strength for what she would have to endure next, a small reprieve in which to recoup, to rally her inner strength.

Stepping out of the thick pines that made up the forest surrounding the falls, Shadow Dancer instantly scanned the area around the pond and sighted Iva's underclothing drying upon a clump of bushes. On silent feet he made his way to the fire and skewered the plump rabbit he had killed and cleaned. Efficiently he set the meat to roast over the glowing coals.

With his task completed, Shadow Dancer took a deep breath, for the first time allowing his gaze to seek out Iva in the pond. Immobile, he took in each delicate curve that was bountifully displayed for his viewing.

As Iva floated atop the water, the creamy texture of her skin had a sparkling sheen. The thick, golden threads of her hair radiated across the surface with a gentle motion due to the flow of the water. The darkened budding peaks of her full breasts undulated temptingly in and out of the crystal blue surface, as did her flat belly, her rounded hips and slender legs.

Without a will now, Shadow Dancer was drawn. Easy motions of his hands untied the leather bindings of his sandals and then allowed his breechcloth to fall at his feet along the bank of the pond. Thus far undetected by the drifting woman, Shadow Dancer dove into the depths of the large pond.

Surprise and instant recognition of her surroundings swept over Iva as she heard the loud splash not far from where she floated. Without hesitation she lowered her body under the surface; her wide, blue eyes scanning the water. A strangled gasp escaped her as she witnessed Shadow Dancer's dark head breaking through nearby. "What are you doing?" she cried aloud, and automatically her hands covered her breasts.

Although now less than ten feet from her, Shadow Dancer was deprived of the incredible view of her shapely form he had been privy to earlier. Disappointment filled him, but a wide smile curved his sensual lips. "I also thought to enjoy a swim." He threw back his head, and droplets flew from his hair.

"But you can't!"

Shadow Dancer's smile never wavered but appeared to Iva to grow even larger. "And who is to say that I cannot?" His tone was teasing, and he delighted in the bright flush that graced her cheeks and flowed down her slim throat.

"Why . . . why . . . you are intruding upon my privacy!" Iva could only respond in a highly indignant manner; her foot even began to attempt a tapping motion as her temper mounted. How dare this brute join her in the pond! Surely he had seen her clothing thrown over the bushes along the bank! He must know that she was entirely naked!

"I do not mean to intrude." The smile vanished somewhat, but slowly returned as he added, "I stood for a time and watched you from the bank, but you appeared to have fallen asleep. I feared that if I did not take the opportunity to swim while the sun was still warming mother earth, I would have to suffer the chill of the pond at night."

With his words Iva knew true mortification. He had been watching her as she was floating! At that moment she wished with all her heart she could turn and flee, but she was caught in a trap of his making. She had no clothes on and could not possibly leave the security of the water with him so closely watching. There was no way in which she could retrieve her clothes without further exposing herself. "If you would please turn around, I will leave you to your swim then." Iva thought to try to force him into being a gentleman and turning away as she retreated from the water.

For a few seconds Shadow Dancer seemed to contemplate her request, but all too quickly his grin reappeared and he made his own counteroffer. "I will do as you request, but first I would ask of you a small favor."

What on earth could he want of me? Iva asked herself as she eyed him warily. "What favor would you have of me in order for me to be allowed to leave this pond and your presence?"

"A race! A race to the falls, and the winner will have his wish granted."

With the boyish grin upon his handsome features, Shadow Dancer was hard to resist. Iva weighed the offer of a race in her mind, and the wilder side of her, which she often had to subdue, surfaced at such a challenge. She was a strong swimmer, and had he not said that the winner's wish would be granted? Why not take the wager and change my wish from his turning his back while I leave the pond—to his granting me freedom! Such a chance may not come again. Still the more cautious part of her held back. "If I agree, can I change my wish to anything I desire?"

Shadow Dancer's dark eyes twinkled with good nature. "Whatever your wish is, it shall be granted." Without being told, he was sure that he knew what she would desire of him, but having no doubt about his own abilities and desiring no argument to his own wish when he proclaimed himself the winner of the race, he willingly nodded his head.

Iva knew that she was powerless to give any answer but yes, and at the same moment that she nodded her head, she realized that she had not asked him what his wish would be. Without saying a word she dove into the water and began the race to the falls.

The tantalizing shape of her buttocks greeted Shadow Dancer's eyes, and for a second breath left his lungs as though he had been physically assaulted. Quickly he regained his senses and dove after her.

Indeed, Iva was a strong swimmer. Most of her entertainment while growing up on her father's ranch had consisted of swimming in the river and breaking horses. Both pastimes aided her now. Her strength of limb, due to her many hours in the saddle, to her handling of wild horses, and to her ability as a swimmer, bore her swiftly toward her goal. Her arms swiftly stroked out before her and her legs kicked with a surging power for a woman of her size.

Shadow Dancer was more than a little surprised at his opponent's ability as a swimmer. He had expected to overtake and outdistance her with ease. This was not the case, however, he soon realized as he was forced to push himself harder to gain the victory he desired.

Freedom . . . freedom . . . freedom . . . The word vibrated in Iva's head with each stroke she took as she came closer to the falls. She had not dared to look back to see where Shadow Dancer was, but she had not seen him pass her. She had to win! This was her only chance to be returned to her family. Her only chance!

Shadow Dancer's thoughts ran parallel to hers. He had to win this race or he would lose her. He had given his word, and there was no reneging on the bet. He had to win! And with this thought a mighty influx of power surged through him and his powerful strokes brought him abreast of her.

The falls were but a short distance away, the noise from their cascading descent down the mountain roaring in the swimmers' ears. Each aware of the other's proximity, they stroked and kicked, their lungs bursting with the need for a deep breath of air. All depended upon these last seconds of the race!

With a triumphant burst of energy and a jubilant cry of conquest bursting from his lips, Shadow Dancer pulled away from Iva and, reaching the falls, drew himself up onto the flat platform of limestone rock at the foot of the rushing overflow.

Iva's heart fell as she heard his cry of victory. She did not even notice that he was naked as he pulled himself into a sitting position beneath the falls and awaited her.

Shadow Dancer's first thought was to thank the gods for the strength they had loaned him to win this race. The thought of how close he had come to losing the woman of his heart by being too sure of his own ability and strength scared him more than he would ever admit to any but the gods who had taken pity upon him and had aided him in his time of need. He should have known better than to risk such a treasure, he told himself as Iva reached the base of the falls and, gasping for breath, clung to a protruding rock. He had learned a well-deserved lesson. He would never again challenge this woman. She was a gift of the gods and would stand up to the challenge of any!

Her arms wrapped around the boulder, Iva did not

dare to look at Shadow Dancer. She could not bear to see his look of triumph, and what was more she dreaded the payment he would demand as victor.

Calming the raggedness of her breathing, Iva envisioned all manner of horrible demands this Indian warrior could make, now that she had lost the race. Dreading to look, but knowing that she must face him sooner or later, Iva raised her eyes to meet his.

Her golden curls veiled the smooth planes of her shapely back, and the rest of her form was covered by the water except for her arms which encircled the large rock. As her heart-shaped face turned up and her fear-filled blue eyes held Shadow Dancer's questioningly, he felt his heartbeat stagger. He knew in that moment that she waited to hear his wish, and he also knew that this woman would hold her honor dear: she would ful-fill the wager; whatever the price would prove.

There was not the gloating triumph of one who savors the moment of victory on Shadow Dancer's face as Iva would have expected. Instead she was held by the sable depths of his warm regard. "What wish would you have fulfilled, Shadow Dancer?" she queried, wanting an end to her inner trepidations but believing his words would prove her worst fears justified.

Chapter Six

"Friendship," Shadow Dancer replied. "For this time when we are here at the falls, we will forget that I took you from your home. We will be friends!"

Iva was amazed at receiving this answer. With all the replies she had braced herself for, she had never expected this one. Had she won the wager, she would have demanded the ultimate payment! She would have cried out for freedom, would have demanded that she be given her horse to make the journey back to her father's farm. And she had expected a demand from him which she would be loath to fulfill. She was taken totally off guard by his words.

"Is friendship for this short time too much to request?"

Iva did not know how to answer as she read the seriousness in his expression. Finally she replied, "Why no, of course not." If this was all that he wanted from her, how could she refuse him? As strange as the request was, surprisingly she began to feel her spirits lighten.

Shadow Dancer did not give her time to reconsider. His heart beating wildly, he jumped into the water, near enough to drench her with the splash, and within seconds he was beneath the surface, taking hold of her ankle and pulling her away from the rock she clutched.

"What are you doing?" Iva cried before her head went underwater. She resurfaced and then was pulled down once again.

He was standing but a few feet from her, his dark hair lying in dampened strands on his shoulders, and Iva could not resist a small smile even as she gasped and spit out water. He was devilishly handsome, his dark eyes glowing with mirth, his smile one she could not resist. "Cannot two friends such as we enjoy an afternoon of swimming and playing?"

Iva was about to state the obvious, that she was without clothes and did not feel playful, but the more daring side of her quickly took over. A roar of laughter erupted from her as she took Shadow Dancer off guard, pushing against his broad chest and setting him on his backside at the bottom of the pond. Then she swam away. "Friendship indeed!" she shouted with glee as she looked back over her shoulder and watched the Indian warrior spit out water as she had done only moments before.

As Shadow Dancer had come out of the water, gasping and choking, his view of the tempting beauty had been limited to one shapely hip and the back of her blond head. The wide grin instantly returned to his face, his pulses quickened, and his spirits soared.

Iva's thoughts were on trying to keep her distance from this handsome man. Swimming with rapid strokes, she made for the other bank, her heartbeat accelerating with the knowledge that he would surely be behind her. Perhaps the best thing she could do, she told herself, was count her losses, swim to where her clothes were drying, and quickly leave the pond and dress. Though he would certainly catch a glimpse of her naked body, would this not be wiser than staying in the pond with only the water to conceal her nudity? So far he has acted as though my nakedness is unimportant, her more venturesome self reminded her as she approached the bank and saw her clothes hanging over the bushes.

Why am I acting like such a ninny? After all he only desires my friendship! Perhaps his people swim naked together all the time and this is nothing unusual to him!

Shadow Dancer easily discerned her intentions as he swam after her toward the opposite bank. He had hoped that she would let down her guard for a short time and try to enjoy his company, but as he gained on her, he knew that would not be the way the rest of the afternoon would be spent. She was determined to keep her distance from him, he decided, resolute in her plan to cover that beautiful body of hers.

So it was with some surprise that Shadow Dancer saw Iva veer away from the bank and disappear underwater for a few minutes. When she resurfaced she was on the other side of him, her laughter tinkling upon the afternoon breeze as she read the confusion on his face.

All thoughts of clothing and modesty fled, as Shadow Dancer dove after the comely beauty. Iva squealed with delight as the warrior pulled her underwater, then splashed her mercilessly when she came up. His husky laughter mixed with her own and filled the area, enhancing the mood of carefree abandon.

Iva gave no thought to her own actions; she allowed that bolder side of her nature to take over. After all, she was this warrior's captive. Surely he could overpower her at any time he wished, and he could do to her whatever he pleased. Why not enjoy the moments that were left to her?

Only a short time later, when Shadow Dancer caught her and their bodies were drawn tightly together, did Iva realize that he also wore no clothing. At first she was horrified and again would have left the pond, but Shadow Dancer gave her not a moment to dwell upon their nudity. He acted as though it were the most natural thing, the two of them swimming and playing together. For a time she almost forgot that nothing prevented their flesh from coming into contact. As his hands reached out to her and carelessly touched a full breast or lightly ran over a rounded buttock, he made light of the gesture, keeping their frolic playful and innocent.

It was some time later, as the afternoon sun began to lower, that Shadow Dancer called a halt to their play. "I fear you have worn me out, Moon Flower." He grinned in an appealing manner. "I grow hungry. What of you?"

Iva was also tired, but exhilarated. The water had been refreshing, and for this short time she admitted, if only to herself, that she had enjoyed Shadow Dancer's company. The afternoon had reminded her of the fun she and Delbert had often shared while growing up. "I am a little hungry," she admitted nervously as the problem of clothing once again surfaced in her mind.

"Then come." Shadow Dancer held out a hand. "When we finish with our meal, I will tell you a story of my people."

Iva could not think about a story at the moment. Refusing his extended hand, she kept her body under water. "You go first," she said, then turned her back to him in the hope that he would do the same when she climbed out onto the bank to retrieve her clothes.

Shadow Dancer smiled as he lightly spoke to the back of her head. "We are friends, Moon Flower. This afternoon has bonded us. There is no need to turn from the sight of a friend. Can we not share all things in common?"

Iva choked back her reply and firmly shook her head in a negative response, praying that he would not, after such a glorious afternoon, destroy the moment by forcing her to leave the pond at his side.

"Perhaps our friendship is too new." His words were spoken softly as though in reflection, and as Iva stood her ground she sensed that he was leaving the pond.

A large sigh fled her lips as sheer relief overcame her. Perhaps this tall, handsome Indian was not the beastly savage she had at first imagined him to be. He appeared willing enough not to force her to abide by his will, at least for now, and if this was all done under the guise of friendship, then she was more than willing to accept the olive branch he offered, imaginary or not.

For a brief moment after donning his leather breechcloth and sandals, Shadow Dancer looked aross the few feet of water that separated him from the woman of his heart. He knew a moment's regret that the pleasant afternoon had drawn to a close, but quickly the thought of the coming night clouded his mind. He and Moon Flower would be all alone here at the falls; surely this would lend him the opportunity to bend her just a bit more in his favor! His thoughts took off in joyous flight as he softly began to hum a song of thankfulness. Leaving the edge of the pond, he made his way to the fire he had made earlier.

Hearing the Indian's pleasant humming, Iva chanced a quick glance at the bank and saw him walking away and bending down toward the fire he had earlier built, she realized this would be the only moment she would be allowed to claim her clothes and to dress in private.

Very cautiously she climbed out onto the bank, and as quickly as possible she clutched Shadow Dancer's hide shirt beneath her chin. While she pulled on her tattered camisole and pantalets, her blue eyes constantly watching the back of the warrior as he set about laying out their meal. It was with great relief that Iva finished dressing. Straightening the wrinkled, damp skirt over her hips and swallowing nervously, she silently approached Shadow Dancer, the smell of the cooked rabbit not allowing her to linger for long.

He slowly glanced up, and a soft smile brightened his generous features. "I fear that our dinner is somewhat charred around the edges, Moon Flower."

The carefree mood that the couple had shared earlier

returned with this greeting. Iva sat down upon the piece of fur he had laid out near the shallow pit fire, and stretching forth a slim hand, she gladly accepted the overdone piece of meat he offered her. As she bit through the darkened outer skin, savory juices ran down her chin, and she realized this was the most succulent serving of rabbit she had ever tasted. "Either I am truly starving or this is the most delicious meat I have ever eaten!" She laughed before taking another bite and wiping at her chin.

Shadow Dancer delighted in watching her every movement, but forced himself to restrain the impulse to bend toward her and kiss away the small bit of liquid on her chin. It would be unwise to move too quickly, he reminded himself over and over. Nodding his dark head with gusto over their simple fare, he also attacked the rabbit with enthusiasm.

As the couple finished their meal, Shadow Dancer bent toward his parfleche. "Come, friend, and I will comb out your hair. The tangles will be easier to manage while they are still damp."

Iva could see no reason to refuse him. After all, it was her best interest he seemed to be thinking about, and he was still implying that they would only be friends.

Taking hold of her hand, he led her to a large, smooth rock protruding from the midst of the tall, sweet-smelling grasses growing in the meadow around the pond. From this place they had a spectacular view of the setting sun, a bright orange ball slowly disappearing behind the mountain down which the falls descended. Cimmerian was close by, and his proximity allowed Iva to experience a tranquil contentment as the Indian warrior stood behind her and with strong hands gently stroked the length of her long, curling tresses.

In these moments Shadow Dancer knew genuine bliss. His soul was calm while Iva sat easily beneath the light stroking of his hand; the picturesque setting of the falls and the lowering sun furthered his heightened feeling of peace and well-being.

Iva covered a yawn with the back of her hand. The long ride that morning, the afternoon spent swimming, a full stomach, and now the tender ministrations of this man standing behind her and combing out her hair— all these left her barely able to hold her eyes open. "I thought you said that you were going to tell me a story?" Her words came out hesitantly, as she fought for something to take her mind off of her sleepiness.

Shadow Dancer chuckled lightly against her golden curls, his warming breath sending a chill through Iva. "Why do we not wait until it is time to lie upon my sleeping mat and we can be more comfortable when I entertain you with my tale?" he huskily questioned.

Iva's senses became more alert at the mention of his sleeping mat, even as she fought off the irresistible allure of his voice and touch. She was instantly reminded that they were entirely alone. Perhaps it would be wisest for her to insist that they sleep separately. Perhaps now that she had had time to think about it, she should even reject his offer of a story! Thus far he had not acted in an unacceptable manner, but what assurance did she have that he would continue to do so? She could not let her guard down for a moment, nor could she let herself forget that he was an Indian and not to be trusted, even if he momentarily seemed to hold some strange power over her!

With her quiet, Shadow Dancer sensed something of her thoughts. Not giving her another moment to dwell upon any plan to put him off, he tucked the comb in the waist of his breechcloth and, in the next second, gathered her into his powerful arms. Laughing loudly, he swung her about amid the tall grasses and wild forest flowers.

Her pale hair flowed thickly over his broad arm and hung low against the green grass and the colorful profusion of flowers. Iva's surprise at being so handled

71

shortly turned into peals of breathless laughter, for her head rushed with dizziness and her entire body felt as light as a feather at being held in such massive arms.

Giddy and breathless, her tiredness now totally forgotten, she clutched Shadow Dancer's shoulders to keep from falling as he set her on her feet. He looked down upon her with open admiration. Bright touches of rose touched her cheeks, and her blue eyes, sparkled more colorful than the brightest flower in the meadow. The feel of her hands upon him forced Shadow Dancer to exert an inordinate amount of will to keep from taking her on the bed of wild flowers and sweet-smelling grass and putting an end to his self-imposed abstinence. His entire body raged with a burning want and desire! Taking a deep breath of air into his lungs, he shut his dark eyes, trying to stem the fire that had leaped into flame and now burned deeply in his gut and throughout his veins. At last, with his body under some kind of control, he was able to speak. Keeping his hands lowered to his sides and not allowing himself to reach out and draw her against his chest and rain kisses over her lovely face and the slim, sweet column of her throat, he took a step backward. "Why do we not brush down the horses before we call it a day?"

He was latching onto anything that would take his mind off thoughts of ravishing her.

Iva nodded her head vigorously. Though somewhat surprised by the sudden change in him, she excitedly accepted his offer to let her help tend her large stallion. For the first time in many days she would be able to approach Cimmerian! Her heartbeat quickened as Shadow Dancer, without comment, led her toward the large, black beast.

Leaving her with her animal, and glad for the chance to be able to put a few feet between them, Shadow Dancer watched closely over his pony's back as Iva reaquainted herself with Cimmerian. Her slim arms wrapped around the stallion's neck as she buried her face in the thick muscles of Cimmerian's chest. The horse stood still before her attentions, seeming to welcome her closeness as he whinnied ever so softly. It was a touching picture of two old friends coming together again, and for some strange reason Shadow Dancer felt like an intruder.

"Why do you not make yourself more comfortable for the night by ridding yourself of this shirt and skirt?" Shadow Dancer rose on an elbow as the pair stretched out upon his sleeping pallet before the fire. His dark, warm gaze in that moment easily glimpsed her distrust as she turned toward him.

"I am quite all right, thank you!" Iva held herself stiffly on the bed, her chin rising a notch with the words. Though she had lost the last verbal bout with this Indian, over sleeping upon separate mats, she did not intend to give in on this subject of her clothing. Though it was tattered and wrinkled, she was not about to shed one piece that was covering her body!

"I only offer you this advice as a friend. I would see that you are comfortable and well rested." Shadow Dancer spoke only half the truth.

He sounded innocent enough, but Iva did not trust his intentions. "Will we still be friends when we reach your village?" She wanted to shift the subject away from her clothing and get him to answer some questions about what she could expect in his village.

"I am not a man that lightly gives his friendship and then takes it away, Moon Flower. My friends are friends for my lifetime, and I grant them liberties I do not extend to others." Without thought, Shadow Dancer toyed with one of Iva's curls, his sable eyes tracing her delicate features.

"And what liberties can a slave be offered?" Iva questioned sulkily, jerking her hair away from his touch. Though she still had a strong measure of fear

73

where this man was concerned, her thoughts of what would lay ahead when they arrived at his village overshadowed all other unease.

"Why do I not tell you that story now?" Shadow Dancer ignored her actions and tried to ignore the anger that had appeared on her face. He knew that she would shortly find out everything about his village, so he tried to put his own mind at ease. If she believed her fate was to be a slave, perhaps the idea of becoming his wife would not seem so terrible when the time came to tell her all.

Iva decided she would get nowhere with this exasperating man. He constantly put off her questions about what she could expect as a slave in his village. The afternoon through he had avoided her pointed queries about her future. With a soft sigh of aggravation and worry, she finally gave in, "The story then, if you like."

"This story is one I heard when I was a very young boy. A traveler, who was also a storyteller and a trader of many goods from various Indian tribes, found his way to my village, and my father allowed him to stay with our family for a moon before he continued on his journey." Shadow Dancer took a full breath, glad to begin his story and to try in the telling to take her mind off her fate.

Iva lay beside him and silently listened, his deep voice against her will giving her an enveloping feeling of security.

"I remember the story well—and the night the traveler told this particular tale. I remember that he had built up a large fire in the center of our village. A dark moonless night had already crept over the mountains when he placed himself before the blaze, where he could achieve the greatest effect.

"I no longer can remember the name of the storyteller; but I do remember that his voice was as gentle as a whispering wind, and those that gathered around him that night dared not breathe a word lest they miss a portion of the story.

"He had been to many places telling his stories and trading his goods, and he knew the very ancient stories of my own people." Shadow Dancer's gaze fixed on the beautiful face turned up to him for just a few seconds before he continued. "This night the storyteller told about the spirit horse and the boy who rode upon his back—Spirit Boy. He began by telling the legend of first man and first woman's creation through the sprinkling of blood upon the earth by Quetzalcoatl. Then he explained the existence of the People in the land that the gods had created for their own pleasure and amusement."

"Ket-sal-kwattle?" Iva sounded out the foreign name aloud. And with pride sparkling in his dark eyes, Shadow Dancer nodded his head in approval of her efforts to pronounce the name of this benevolent deity.

Continuing with the story Shadow Dancer felt the blue eyes holding upon him with some interest. "It was at the time when first man had grown old and lay upon his pallet, seeking the peace of death, that the spirit horse with his great white wings stretched wide in flight from the heavens, soared toward earth with Spirit Boy upon his back. Their express purpose was that of bearing the spirit of first man to the star path.

"This plan of life and death was chosen by Quetzalcoatl; and was good! First man would be the first of the people to join the gods in the heavens. But even with immortal beings there are conflicts. Tezcatlipoca, the god of war and sacrifice, was angered by Quetzalcoatl's plan. The two gods—one of war and the other of peace—had been fighting for supremacy over the powers and this was just another reason for the rift to widen between them.

"Tezcatlipoca sent out a large force to capture the spirit horse and Spirit Boy. As they soared over the desert, a whirling noose rose up from the dust and captured spirit horse's leg. Within seconds the Spirit Boy and his horse were pulled to the desert floor, ensnared by tethers that bound the great beast and the boy to the earth.

"First man lay drawing his last breath, the battle over his spirit going on in the desert while Quetzalcoatl, unaware, was indulging himself in the beauties of his gardens. It was a lesser god who brought him word of Spirit Boy's plight." At this point in the story Shadow Dancer took a deep breath in order to dramatize the moment.

"What happened to Spirit Boy and his horse? This horrible god—Tez-cat-li-po-ca—did not harm them?" Iva breathlessly questioned, goading Shadow Dancer to continue with the story.

Shadow Dancer smiled fondly, warmed by her enthusiasm. She was much as a child, this woman of his heart. All of her thoughts were so plainly revealed. Her emotions so quickly would turn from fear and sadness to joy and happiness, and these changes were not lost to Shadow Dancer's ever watchful eyes. He felt some pride in her excitement over his story. Tenderly he reached out a long, bronzed finger and caressed her soft cheek.

"There was a mighty clash of spirit power and strength there upon the floor of the desert. The earth itself trembled like a virgin being dragged toward the nuptial bed, and great rents slashed through the desert floor around the bound spirit horse.

"The god of war—Tezcatlipoca—held great power and caused the forces of darkness to strike out at his enemy. The god of life and peace—Quetzalcoatl—also brought all of his forces together."

"Who won this fight?" Iva all but shouted the words at him, so impatient was she to hear whether Spirit Boy and his horse were saved.

"It was Quetzalcoatl who won this battle between the gods. Spirit horse was freed from his bonds and ascended to the sky. As first man drew his last breath of this life, his spirit was swept up into the arms of Spirit Boy, who took him to the heavens to climb the star path and to be greeted by Quetzalcoatl himself."

For a lingering moment Iva closed her eyes tightly as though savoring the outcome of the story. As a child she had been told her nighttime stories by her father, but none as exciting as this one. She had actually envisioned Spirit Boy and his horse as Shadow Dancer had spoken. "It was a wonderful story," she said at last.

Shadow Dancer silently wondered at this woman who appeared to derive so much pleasure from a simple tale. "There are many more stories that I will tell you." Leaning on an elbow above her, he awaited the opening of her eyes and as these crystal-blue jewels glowed with pleasure but then the light in them dimmed, Shadow Dancer knew instinctively that she had once again remembered that she was his captive. At that moment he would have given all of his wealth and all of his power always to behold the pleasure he had glimpsed in her eyes for those few seconds.

"Will you not free me?"

Her words were so softly spoken, Shadow Dancer at first thought he had misunderstood. Liquid tears caught at the tilted corners of her eyes as her regard held on him and she awaited his reply. Her joy in his story or the enjoyment she had received while swimming with him that very afternoon no longer mattered, Iva could not forget the fact that she had been stolen from her home. It was not right that she was here in the mountains with this man, lying upon his sleeping pallet. She should be home, in the comfort of her own bedchamber and with her family. In her heart Iva knew that she had to make this one last appeal for release.

There was a small catch in Shadow Dancer's throat as he held her beautiful face. How can I tell her no? he asked himself. How can I possibly refuse her her heart's request? But how can I release her?

As a young boy he had been schooled to hide his emotions well, so Iva did not see any trace of his conflicting thoughts. She glimpsed only the closed countenance of one whose mind is already made up.

What could I offer her that would ease her worry? Shadow Dancer asked himself as he reached out and gently wiped away a lone tear that ran down her cheek. "If I tell you that you will not be a slave in my village, will this bring comfort to you, Moon Flower? If I say to you that you will be treated well, that you have nothing to fear, will you believe me?" For his own part Shadow Dancer doubted that anything he could say would lessen her fear and worry over the future. This was the reason he had told her little about himself or his village. He had truly hoped that once she had experienced for herself being treated well, she would resign herself to the fate that he believed the gods had ordained for them both; and at that time he would win over her heart. But now as he looked upon the distress evident in her features, he was not sure that his decision was the right one.

Iva knew that her very life depended upon this man's every whim. He alone held the power to set her into slavery or to free her. She had no choice at the moment except to trust in whatever he told her. Slowly she nodded her head, and dashing away the remainder of her tears with the back of her hand, she presented a tremulous smile. "This day you have proclaimed that we are friends. As you are my friend, I will believe what you say, Shadow Dancer." And for some strange reason at that moment Iva did, indeed, believe what he was telling her.

So touched was Shadow Dancer at realizing that she was going to place her trust in him, he let his thoughts take flight. *First friends and then lovers.* The thought fleetingly crossed his mind as he smiled upon her, and unwilling or unable to stop himself, he bent toward her, his lips catching hers in a tender, all-consuming merging that generated a scorching seduction of the senses. All outer considerations disappeared before the onslaught of such a powerful blending; right and wrong, and even reason, vanished.

Caught up in her tremendous need of his warmth and strength, Iva pressed herself against him, his kiss driving her to mindless oblivion. She felt herself meeting his every advance, his tongue pressing through the fullness of her soft lips, brushing against even, white teeth and circling her own tongue in a compelling dance of fiery tantalization. Her arms wrapped about his powerful neck as he drew her closer against him. Flame seared through the very fabric of her clothing as she pressed against the hard power of his body. He was tempered steel to her womanly softness!

Holding her fully against the length of him, Shadow Dancer boldly pressed the hardness of his pulsing manhood against her. His lips and tongue sent thrilling ripples of delight coursing through her as a low moan escaped her, and his hand, traveling over the loose neck of her blouse and pressing between the fabric of her sheer camisole, sought out the feel of the tender flesh that appeared to be straining for his fondling.

With indrawn breath, Iva admitted to herself that rationality was fleeing her. The feelings this man was evoking deep within her edged her along a steamy path of no return, yet her inner, daring self told her he was all that mattered! She pressed against his hand as it lowered to the throbbing center of her being, her own tongue circling and dancing against his as she felt she would surely swoon, so wonderful were the feelings consuming her.

Seeking and exploring, Shadow Dancer lovingly caressed his way to the warmth of her womanhood, his fingers gently probing while he now seared her face, neck, and the tops of her breasts with his heated tongue and kisses. As he pushed aside the obstruction of her pantalets and inserted a finger into her warm nest, the tight membrane of her maidenhead halted his fired passion. With gentle movements he drew his finger out and straightened her clothes, his dark, warm eyes beholding the passion her face revealed as he heard her gasp for breath.

Never in her life had Iva experienced anything like these feelings! His flaming kisses and searing tongue had brought her unto the very brink of heated desire, and his touch had stirred awake a deep primeval wanting she had never known herself capable of. She had wanted him to keep touching her there between her legs, had wanted to continue to enjoy the feelings he was arousing within her. And, yes, she had wanted to experience all that he could teach her. She wanted! She wanted! She wanted! Actually she was unsure of exactly what it was she did want. She was an innocent to these newfound awakenings, but she did know that she had not wanted him to stop!

Shadow Dancer was no novice in the art of love, and as he looked down upon her and heard her ragged breaths, he knew the emotions she was experiencing. Raging passion suddenly dampened left one feeling empty and neglected. But as he valiantly fought to steady his own breathing and wild heartbeat, he knew that he had done the right thing. This woman was to be his wife; he would not join his body with hers until their union had been blessed. Forcing control of his desires proved to himself as well as to the gods how much he held this woman in high honor. He prayed the gods would look upon them both with favor and would bless their joining after they were wed. It had been at the moment when he had touched the thin barrier that proclaimed Iva still chaste that some small portion of his passion-sodden brain had whispered a warning. It was well that he had heeded it, he told himself as the force of his desire slowly began to abate. Turning on his side, one arm beneath her shoulders, he tenderly kissed

Iva's pink, swollen lips, his warm, inky black eyes lovingly seeking out her delicate features. "You can trust in my friendship, Moon Flower." The words came out on a husky tremor from deep within his chest.

The fact that this man was an Indian warrior who had stolen her from her home did not enter Iva's thoughts. She believed what he told her. Slowly she nodded her head, secure in his arms, lying upon his fur-covered bed and warmed by his seeking regard. The feelings they had shared only moments ago belied his words of friendship, however. There was much more between them, she silently admitted to herself, but just then she did not care to analyze what had taken place between them. It was enough for now that he was holding her. Tomorrow she would once again allow herself to worry about her future. At the moment she was content!

Shadow Dancer watched as her crystal blue eyes closed and, a soft sigh escaping her lips, Iva snuggled closer against his chest. A feeling of ultimate contentment filled Shadow Dancer's heart. For a time he lay still, watching her every movement while she slept. Her beauty was unequaled, her passionate nature all that any man could ever ask for. He could not wait to introduce her to his home, his family. He wanted to share all things with her. The very secrets of his heart he knew he would one day be able to reveal to her. She was his soul mate, the reason for his being, his very breath and heart.

Chapter Seven

His flesh, beneath her hands, warmed her fingertips as they roamed at will over the corded contours of his muscular back. Holding her eyes tightly shut, Iva drew a deep breath as her hands splayed over the wide expanse and with a featherlike touch roamed slowly over his broad shoulders, then to his chest. Feeling the rapid thudding of his heartbeat beneath her palm, with a tantalizing slowness Iva let her fingers caress hard, flat nipples before lacing their way downward . . . over the sculpted outline of each rib and then across his flat-firm belly. With a light downward movement she brushed against his hip, her fingers straying over the dark, crisp hair that grew lightly inches below his navel and then thickened into a wealth of coarse, thickness between the junction of his powerful legs. With bated breath, Iva reached out and her fingers wrapped around . . .

A sound coming from behind Iva pulled her out of the daydream that had held her so totally enthralled. With scarlet face, her hands now rubbing her arms in an attempt to drive away her erotic thoughts, she swung around and faced the man of her dreams.

Under normal circumstances Iva would have prayed that the earth would open wide and swallow her, but as she gazed at Shadow Dancer standing before her, holding the reins to both horses, the erotic daydream was pushed to the farthest reaches of her mind.

The Indian stood silently, his stance that of a proud warrior. His long, black hair was pulled back into a thick braid which fell down the center of his back. One portion of his face was painted entirely black, the opposite side was adorned with a pattern of yellow-gold bars. Around his neck and hanging down his broad, bronze chest was a silver disk about the size of her palm. The amulet was impressed with the design of the sun, which she had seen upon the headband that had fallen in the dust at the Cassidy farm. Upon each muscular forearm he wore a silver bracelet crafted in the shape of a strange serpent-bird, and from his breastbone downward to the indent of his navel ran a long, thin line of the same yellow-gold ocher paint.

Iva's gaze went back up to the painted face, to full, sensual lips pulled back into an alluring smile which instantly reminded her of the daydream she had been indulging in only moments before. She quickly lowered her gaze, as though fearing he would somehow be able to read her mind.

"I have prepared myself for our arrival in my village." Shadow Dancer spoke softly, for he had noticed her unease and believed it due to his appearance. As he had watched her sitting alone near the pond's edge he had remembered what had taken place upon his sleeping mat the night before. He could even now shut his eyes and feel the softness of her flesh, the sweetness of her honey taste. Forcing himself away from such dangerous thoughts, he spoke aloud, "I brought my paints with me." He stepped to his pony's side and, rummaging through his parfleche, drew forth an assortment of small clay jars which contained the ocher paint. "I thought perhaps you might wish to use some, Moon Flower."

The humor in his tone was not lost on Iva, nor did she miss laughter in his dark eyes as he watched her

83

reaction to his invitation. But even as she believed him to be only joking, she could not help sounding rather scandalized by his offer. "No! I mean, I would never . . . I would not dare . . ."

Shadow Dancer laughed aloud at her nervous reply. He had only made the suggestion in the hope of lightening her mood. "Perhaps this is all too new." He relented with a deep-throated chuckle. "But in the future if you decide to try them, you may always use my paints."

"I think not!" Iva's reply was hasty, but as she made it a smile was settling over her lips. This new relationship between them, this friendship, was something that she would have to get used to. Never had she had a friend such as he. His manner was so light and easy, at times humorous, but always there was something more beneath the surface. Perhaps it was the challenge that sparkled within the warm sable depths of his watchful eyes, the dare that he patiently waited for her to reach out and accept. As she stared into his warm eyes for one single second, she was tempted!

Shadow Dancer gave her no more time to search her soul and discover for herself whether she was up to such a challenge. Taking her hand in his own, he drew her toward Cimmerian. Removing the leather cloth covering the clay jar that held silver-colored paint, without comment he dabbed some of its contents on her hand.

Surprise registered, as Iva watched Shadow Dancer place her hand, fingers spread wide, upon Cimmerian's rump. Next to her imprint, he placed his own hand covered with the silver paint, leaving a larger brand upon the animal's flank. His reason for doing such a thing was lost on Iva, and as she looked up into his face, her question was plain.

"When we reach my village, there will be no mistaking the stallion's ownership," Shadow Dancer explained, and stepping to the water, he turned his

84

back to her and washed his hands.

Watching the flexing muscles of his back with each movement that he made, Iva thought fleetingly, Does he wish to imply to those of his village that not only is the stallion his property, but I am also! This thought did not provoke the anger Iva would have experienced only a few short days ago; instead it evoked a warm feeling in the depths of her being that whispered of security.

"After you wash the paint from your hands, Moon Flower, I will braid your hair and we can then be on our way." Shadow Dancer turned toward her, and for a moment he wondered at her silent reflections. Caught unaware, her inner thoughts plainly reflected, Iva did not conceal the desirable warmth that stole over her features. It intrigued Shadow Dancer, but as she quickly turned away and bent to wash, the moment passed.

While they were alone at the falls Iva had let her hair flow freely down her back, but now, with the prospect of being around those of his tribe, Shadow Dancer insisted upon braiding her flaxen curls into a long, thick braid down her back. "Today, Moon Flower, you will ride the stallion." Shadow Dancer desired that his people would first see this woman as beautiful, pride-filled. A woman all would agree would be a fit mate for one of their own.

Iva was truly surprised at his offer. After these many days of having to ride in front of him on his pony, she wondered at this change. She dared not voice her inner thoughts, for fear that he would change his mind and once again make her ride before him. Inwardly she was terrified of what would await her in his village, but at least now she would be able to greet her fate with head held high and atop her own horse. Thoughts of slavery were still ever present, but determined, she forced herself to hold to the promise of friendship that Shadow Dancer had offered.

His words from the night before about her having nothing to fear, his promise that she would be treated well in his village, sounded over and over in her mind as he gave her a leg up and she sat upon Cimmerian's back.

The ride from the falls to Shadow Dancer's village was a rough trek which took them ever higher into the mountains. At times they traveled single file over ledges on the mountainside. Iva feared that at any moment the trail would be too narrow to negotiate. On more than one occasion as the early afternoon swept past, Iva clutched hold of Cimmerian's thick mane as well as the reins for security. Several times they came close to the large, fleecy white snow goats that inhabited the higher ranges of the Rockies. Daringly the goats appeared to traverse the sides of the steep mountains, their kids frolicking with dangerous abandon at their parent's side.

It was in midafternoon, just when Iva had begun to fear they would never halt their taxing pace, that Shadow Dancer led her through a narrow ravine on the side of a mountain. The chasm ran through the mountain top, and after they passed through the narrow gorge that was over a mile long with sloping cliffs on either side, they at last began moving down a winding trail that suddenly opened into a vast, fertile valley.

Pleased to have such rough travel behind her, Iva did not at first notice the village that was hidden within the shelter of the spruce, fir, and pine trees that enclosed the outer boundaries of the valley floor, concealing the village from anyone daring enough to follow the dangerous trail that she and Shadow Dancer had traversed.

Iva watched in stunned amazement as they drew closer to the village. The peaceful scene that stretched out before her was not what she had expected. Even from a distance she could see that this Indian village was not typical of those she had read about or had heard about. The entire settlement was laid out in a vast area of the valley floor. There were none of the hide- or wattle-type shelters she had imagined, instead the structures appeared to be of an adobe construction with turf roofs, their shapes running in relaxed circular patterns. In the center of the village was a large building which was evidently communal.

As the pair on horseback slowly descended the trail leading from the mountain, Shadow Dancer pulled abreast of Iva and said softly, "Speak only the tongue I have taught you, Moon Flower." As she nervously nodded her head, there was a warm, pink glow on her cheeks from their ride, and her blue eyes sparkled with curiosity, though they also held fear. Even in her tattered clothes, sitting atop the large, black beast, she was by far the most beautiful woman Shadow Dancer had ever seen. "Do not be frightened. I will keep you safe from all harm," he added. He wanted to offer her some reassurance and would have reached out and squeezed her hand, but a call went out over the valley floor, one of the posted sentries announcing their arrival and drawing most of the villagers out of their houses and into the streets to await their approach.

Iva swallowed hard. Taking a tighter grip on the reins, she forced herself to look straight ahead as Shadow Dancer led her into the center of the village.

As they drew closer to the houses she noticed that each was covered with colorful frescoes. This art work depicted strange gods, colorful birds, and graceful butterflies.

As the group of people gathered around Shadow Dancer and Iva, she found them as surprising as she found their homes.

Most of the men wore loincloths with flaps at front and back decorated with fringe or tassels as well as being colorfully embroidered. A blanket about one yard wide and two yards long hung under the left arm of each man and was knotted on the right shoulder. Many of these blankets were made of a coarse cotton material, but others were more elaborate mantles adorned with ancient symbolic designs. The women wore lengths of cloth as wraparound skirts. These were made of the same cotton material bleached white and were held up with a narrow belt drawn around loose, short-sleeved tunics. Every garment was decorated with vivid embroidery of every imagined color. As for their hair, it was braided and interlaced with colorful ribbons. The men wore leather sandals much like Shadow Dancer's; most of the women were barefoot. Everyone wore paint and jewelry as adornments, and Iva noticed that several men displayed ornaments that had been passed through the septum of the nose or suspended from a slit in the lip. Iva was overwhelmed by the colors and general appearance of those standing around her. What manner of Indians are these? she asked herself as she tried to make out the words that were being hurled at Shadow Dancer.

Shadow Dancer appeared to welcome the reception, an easy smile spreading over his handsome face as he answered each question put to him. His gaze often went to Iva, however, in an attempt to put her at ease. As Shadow Dancer dismounted from his pony, a disturbance on the outer fringe of the group standing around them stirred the populace of the village to step aside and allow an overweight man who was extravagantly cloaked and bejeweled, to make his way through the crowd and stand before Shadow Dancer and Iva.

"What have you brought back to our village, Shadow Dancer?" The man's voice was rather high pitched and piercing for one so large, and as Iva tried to make out some of what he was saying, she noticed a long, jagged scar on one side of his face. Though his makeup had attempted to cover most of the disfigurement, and the gleaming obsidian stone suspended by a golden link from a slit in his lower lip vied for the attention that might go to the scar, Iva felt a prickling at the nape of her neck as the man's small, piercing, black eyes went over her from head to toe.

Shadow Dancer was well aware that the man before him—the chief of his village and also his cousin—had already been informed about Iva by the braves who had returned the day before. Still, politeness demanded that he answer Gray Otter's question. "I have brought back this woman I call Moon Flower. She is the reason the gods sent me from this valley." Shadow Dancer had never been on friendly terms with Gray Otter, and the hardness in his tone was lost on no one in the crowd, including Iva.

"Have you forgotten, Shadow Dancer, that one of the laws of our tribe is that intruders are not allowed in our village?" The small, black eyes peered at Iva, a bold look of hatred in them that Gray Otter did not bother to conceal. Most of those who were standing around, and who had great fear of Gray Otter, quietly drew back a few steps.

In a protective gesture Shadow Dancer took a step in front of Iva and Cimmerian, as though he would stave off the dark looks of his kin. "It is true, Gray Otter, in the past we have not allowed strangers to enter our village for fear of defilement, but this woman is no stranger to our gods. As I have already told you, I was sent to claim her. She will become my wife!" Turning his back toward Gray Otter, Shadow Dancer reached up and lifted Iva from the back of her horse.

Gray Otter's anger ignited at his cousin's insolence. As Shadow Dancer presented his broad back to him for a few foolish seconds he entertained thoughts of attacking the young man. But that would have been foolhardy indeed, he thought as he drew in a great breath and tried to control his rage. It was not often that Gray Otter was talked to in such a manner, but this cousin of his had always been difficult. He should have had a couple of his braves take care of him long ago. Now Shadow Dancer was held in great esteem in the village. The braves admired his strength, and the elders, as well as his own daughter, praised Shadow Dancer's wisdom and intelligence. To attack him openly would be very dangerous, for his position among the villagers as well as for his own well-being. Gray Otter was no longer a young man, and he was not unaware that his muscles long ago had turned to fat. Caution at last took hold. He again took a long look at the woman now standing next to Shadow Dancer. He had to admit that her pale features were not unpleasant to look upon. Though she appeared rather unkempt, she had an air of sensual beauty he had never seen in the women of his village. And for the first time Gray Otter noticed the fine stallion the woman had ridden into the village. "This fine animal then is the gift that you would present to your chief?" His high-pitched tone lowered somewhat as greed took over and his eyes met Shadow Dancer's gaze.

Shadow Dancer was well aware that his cousin's greatest love was fast horses. Often there were races held in the valley, and vast amounts of wealth was wagered. More often than not Gray Otter's horses were the winners. "I will come to you after I have settled Moon Flower, Gray Otter. I have brought gifts for you and your family." Shadow Dancer tried to put the older man off for the time being.

"But I would have this fine stallion!" Gray Otter would not relent, for he was filled with a deep envy and was driven to claim ownership of the horse and also the woman. For now, he told himself, he would demand the stallion; the woman would come later.

"The animal is Moon Flower's. No other can mount him." Saying this Shadow Dancer grasped the reins of both horses in one hand and, taking Iva's arm, began to lead her through the crowd.

They had taken only a few steps when Gray Otter despite his great weight hurried to their side and, taking hold of Cimmerian's reins, declared loudly so that all could hear. "I shall ride the black beast, and then I shall claim him as is my right as your chief!"

Iva gasped aloud in surprise, and her anger was such that she would have rushed to Cimmerian's side but for Shadow Dancer's restraining hand on her arm.

Gray Otter, though ponderously obese, still occasionally rode his own horses with a strong hand. Certain that he could handle the large, black stallion, he grasped a handful of mane to hoist himself up on the horse's back. He was seated for a fraction of a second upon Cimmerian's back before he was thrown onto his backside in the dust.

It was all over so quickly that those observing doubted what they had just witnessed. No one had ever seen Gray Otter thrown from a horse before. Several hands rose to cover grins inspired by the sight of their fat chief sitting in the dirt, his face a crimson red and outrage choking off his breath.

Shadow Dancer retrieved the reins of the nervous animal as the stallion pawed the earth and eyed the man who had dared to place his huge bulk upon Cimmerian's back. "I will come to your home later, Gray Otter, with the gifts I have for your family." Shadow Dancer spoke to the chief, who still sat in the dust. Receiving no answer, he turned to Iva and the couple walked through the crowd toward the outer portion of the village.

Iva worried about the reaction her arrival had evoked. Now she wished she had paid closer attention to the language lessons Shadow Dancer had given her. It had been clear that the chief had insisted he be given Cimmerian, but why had he and Shadow Dancer shown such animosity toward one another? As Shadow Dancer led her through the crowd, she stole a glance over her shoulder, for one last look at the fat man. He was not attempting to rise, and as their glances met, Iva was witness to the cold fury his features revealed. And the burning hatred on his ugly face—the menace—was not directed solely upon her. It was also meant for Shadow Dancer! "Who is he?" Iva whispered as fear constricted her throat and she held tighter to Shadow Dancer's hand.

"He is the chief of my people and also my cousin," Shadow Dancer replied as he led Iva toward their destination.

Those villagers who had not met Shadow Dancer and Iva when they had first entered the village watched from their doorways as the couple passed their houses. Though Iva did not say any more to Shadow Dancer about what had just taken place, she felt that surely the hostility that had been so evident had not originated with the chief's inability to ride Cimmerian. No, what she had been witness to was a deep-seated hatred, the kind that did not appear overnight and with little reason.

The house that Shadow Dancer led Iva toward had been built apart from the rest of the village. Set off at a small distance, it was easily the largest and most beautiful of the dwellings. The exterior was of glistening white masonry decorated with graceful representations of hummingbirds and butterflies that had been painted by a talented hand. On the entry door the sun sign she now associated with Shadow Dancer had been painstakingly drawn. Iva gazed in wide-eyed wonder as a young boy ran from the back of the building and took hold of the horses' reins. The youth had a wide grin upon his pleasant features as he offered words of welcome to Shadow Dancer, and after a quick peek at Iva, he hurriedly turned his eyes away.

Shadow Dancer ruffled the boy's dark hair and in a friendly tone called him by name. "Have you been minding your mother, while I have been gone, Arez?"

The boy vigorously nodded his head, and stealing

another glance at the beautiful woman Shadow Dancer had brought home with him, he gave Iva a shy smile.

She was aware of the seeming ease with which man and boy conversed. She had made out most of what Shadow Dancer had asked the boy, and of a sudden it hit her that perhaps this boy was Shadow Dancer's son. It was true that there was little resemblance between the two, but Shadow Dancer had asked after the boy's mother. For some strange reason when the youth smiled shyly at her, Iva trembled inwardly, then sternly reminded herself that she was only this Indian's prisoner. What did it matter to her if this was his child and a wife awaited him in this beautiful house? The dampness behind her eyes threatened to spill over into tears, but she forbade herself to make such a display. *I will not remain in this village long anyway,* she told herself to bolster her spirits. *At the first opportunity I will escape! Escape him and this horrible village!*

Iva was feeling confused and disheartened as Shadow Dancer led her through the entrance of his home and the small boy called Arez took the horses away.

Thoughts of Shadow Dancer being a husband and a father were temporarily pushed to the back of her mind as Iva looked at everything about her. The interior of the house was windowless. Its tall ceilings accounted for the coolness that swept over them upon entering. The flooring was a dark, gleaming brown tile with sparkles of gold dust imprinted in its surface, and the interior walls were fashioned around a large central courtyard that led into a colorful profusion of gardens. As the house was of circular construction Iva could only wonder what lay beyond the wide doors opening off the courtyard. "I don't understand any of this!" she got out on a gasp as Shadow Dancer stood near, apparently awaiting her reaction to his home. *What kind of Indian was he, to be the possessor of such wealth?* Everywhere Iva looked she witnessed gold and silver! There were numerous statues of ancient gods, large, circular disks with impressions of early ancestors etched in silver and gold suspended along the interior walls of the building. Intricately crafted wood chests were placed along the hallways, and above each was a colorful, hand-embroidered tapestry depicting the Indian culture that Iva was now finding so confusing.

As her wide eyes returned to Shadow Dancer's face she would have questioned him, but before she could speak an attractive, barefooted young woman approached them from one of the side doors running along the hallway. The tunic over her white wraparound skirt was made of a shimmering bronze material that accented her rich, dark skin and her loose, flowing, straight black hair. Her silent tread over the tile floor lent her an exotic air which instantly filled Iva with a burning jealousy.

"Moon Flower, this is Aquilla." Shadow Dancer appeared not to notice Iva's stiffening as she imagined the worst upon viewing the woman who now stood before her.

This must be Shadow Dancer's wife! The thought filled Iva's mind with imaginings—this woman's long, slender fingers playing over the wide expanse of Shadow Dancer's muscular chest, her lips kissing those same lips that she had tasted only the night before!

As though twisting the blade deeper into her breast, Shadow Dancer added, "This is Arez's mother."

Iva's worst fear became reality with Shadow Dancer's words. Not only was she the captive of this man at her side, she now knew that she had unintentionally committed a horrible sin against his wife. All those private moments she had shared with Shadow Dancer over the past few days raced through her mind. *Each night I lay upon his sleeping mat—next to him! At the falls I swam naked with him! We kissed, touched! I craved him in my daydream this morning at the pond!*

Chapter Eight

The woman called Aquilla, whom Iva believed to be Shadow Dancer's wife, reached out and took Iva's hand and, without speaking, led her down the long hallway that circled the courtyard.

Moments before, Shadow Dancer had made his exit, saying that he would be delivering gifts to Gray Otter and his family. Iva would have begged him not to leave her alone with this woman, but the appraisal by the dark, searching eyes of the woman standing before her prevented her from speaking. Nervously, she swallowed hard, knowing that she had little choice but to follow wherever this woman led. Perhaps all along it had been Shadow Dancer's intention to make her a servant in his home, and now she was left to follow the instructions of his wife. Salty tears burned the backs of her eyes as the searing pain of betrayal lanced through her.

The chamber Aquilla led her into, like the central part of the house, was elegantly decorated, and handcrafted statues had been placed about the room. The marble shelves resting against one wall contained fine earthenware with gilt-edged designs, and beautiful fans composed of multicolored bird feathers were arranged upon the opposite wall along with finely worked tapestries. Rugs, of intricate design and finely woven, were stretched out on the tile floors. Iva had never been in such an impressive room, and as Aquilla stepped to a large hand-grooved chest, a soft gasp escaped Iva when the other woman opened the lid to reveal a wealth of finely made tunics and skirts.

"They are all very beautiful," she said, and the young woman called Aquilla smiled in agreement.

"Shadow Dancer had them placed here for your use." The exotic-looking woman spoke very slowly, also using hand signing so that Iva was able to understand her. Stepping away from the chest, she indicated that Iva should choose an outfit.

Iva stood for a moment, dumbfounded by the generosity of the woman. She had understood most of what Aquilla had said, and she was sure that Shadow Dancer had instructed her through one of the braves who had returned the previous day, as to what to do upon Iva's arrival. "I don't know," Iva murmured, reluctant to allow herself to so easily enjoy the riches of her captor.

"I will go and get you water for your bath." Aquilla again took great care in how she spoke so that the other woman would understand her. It was evident that the woman Shadow Dancer called Moon Flower was very nervous. I will give her a few minutes alone to collect herself, Aquilla thought as she quietly left the chamber to retrieve the water.

With Aquilla's departure, Iva was able to breathe easier. Instinctively her hand strayed to the clothing in the chest. The tunics were made of finer material than the coarse cotton the women of the village wore, and Iva could only imagine how they would feel against her body. She took out a shimmering aqua tunic embroidered with gold thread stitched in the designs of mountain poppies. Next to the tunics in the chest were wraparound skirts and a variety of colorful belts and sashes. Iva could not resist the temptation to hold the aqua tunic up beneath her chin and press it against the

96

outline of her breasts. She took a step backward, and looking down, she tried to imagine how it would look on her. How delightful the cloth felt against her hand, so different from the rough texture of the hide shirt that Shadow Dancer had given her and the tattered, dirty skirt she wore. With a soft sigh she started to replace the clothes. Feeling guilty over her part in what had taken place between herself and Shadow Dancer, she knew she could not accept his wife's kind gesture of sharing her clothing.

When Aquilla returned to the chamber, she glimpsed the other woman starting to return the tunic to the chest. Quickly she set the large clay jar of water down and went to her side. "This tunic will match the color of the sky in your eyes perfectly. Shadow Dancer will be very pleased when he returns and finds you wearing this."

Iva flushed, but refusing to be put off, Aquilla took the tunic, a skirt, and matching sash, then drew Iva toward a corner of the chamber, where, after setting the clothing across yet another chest, she poured the water into a clay bowl and indicated that Iva was to bathe.

There was very little Iva could do to keep herself from cooperating because of the other woman's high-handed manner.

Within moments Aquilla had Iva standing naked and washing the sweat and grime from her body while Aquilla unbraided her hair. Having never seen such golden hair before, Aquilla delighted in combing out the long curling mass until it shimmered with a glorious sheen.

Keeping her eyes lowered to the tiled floor Iva felt her embarrassment keenly as Aquilla helped her to dress in the tunic and wraparound skirt. At first Iva tried to retrieve her underclothing, but with a little squeak of protest, Aquilla pushed these items into a heap on the floor, and shaking her dark head, she explained, "You cannot wear these, they must be

97

cleaned first."

With the completion of her toilet, Iva stood before the other woman and nervously ran her hands down both sides of the tunic. Feeling the softness of the material, she unexpectedly knew a wicked delight in the contact of the cloth against her naked flesh.

Aquilla's gaze held genuine warmth as she let her dark eyes roam over the other woman from head to toe. Slowly nodding her head in a thoughtful manner, she at last spoke. "I now see fully the reason why Shadow Dancer brought you to his home. It is true. You must indeed be a gift of the gods." Pride in her accomplishments swelled within Aquilla as she envisioned what Shadow Dancer's reaction would be when he set eyes on this woman. She had been beautiful earlier, there was no denying this, but now, with her brilliant hair hanging below her waist and the gown matching so nearly the color of her eyes, she was incredibly lovely!

Iva understood some of what Aquilla was saying, and she wondered silently if all this woman's servants were welcomed in such a fashion. Did Aquilla not mind that she had been alone last night with her husband? Surely at least one of the other braves who had returned the day before had indicated that the two were alone. Was it commonplace for the men of this village to treat their wives in such a fashion? Though Iva was now more than a bit confused, her own woman's honor and pride rose to the surface. How dare any man treat his wife in such a manner! Let alone a woman as beautiful and kind as Aquilla. The first chance I have, I will set Shadow Dancer straight, she swore to herself.

With a smile that at last appeared to win over Iva's trust, Aquilla took the other woman's hand and led her toward a small drape-covered alcove. Pulling back the sheer curtains she showed Iva a small sleeping couch littered with embroidered pillows. "You should rest until it is time to eat, Moon Flower."

Rest? How was she to rest when she was so confused?

Aquilla left her standing near the alcove and as the chamber door softly shut, Iva sat tentatively upon the edge of the sleeping couch. I have to get away from these people, she declared to herself. She could not become a part of this strange household! Again she felt the sharp sting of tears, and scorning her feelings for Shadow Dancer, she dashed away the dampness on her cheeks with the backs of her hands. *He said he was my friend! What kind of friend would be so careless of my feelings as to bring me home to his wife after what we shared together?* Unable to control the flow of tears such thoughts of betrayal prompted, she curled herself upon the soft, plush couch, and as exhaustion from the day's long ride and her turbulent thoughts caught up with her, she fell into a troubled sleep. Shadow Dancer's deception and her own stupid weakness for a man that was already married were the last wakeful thoughts to occupy her mind.

It was well after dark when Iva finally awoke. An oil brazier burned in a corner of the chamber, and glancing around the room, she realized that the happenings of the afternoon had not been part of some exotic dream. She was still here in Shadow Dancer's house, and she was just as confused as she had been before she had fallen asleep. There were so many questions she needed answers to. What kind of Indians were these in this hidden mountain valley? Why were their dress and manner so different from those of the Indians she had seen and heard of in the past? But the main question that plagued her was, What is to become of me? Now that she was well rested, she forced herself to deal with the fact that Shadow Dancer had a wife and a son. All he had ever offered her was his friendship, she had to admit. The touch of his lips and the warm pressure of his body were remembrances that she pushed to the back of her mind. He had made no promises other than that she would come to no harm in his village and that he would be her friend. If I imagined anything else it was entirely my own fault, she berated herself. But the pain in her heart was a bit sharper.

Forcing herself to rise from the sleeping couch, she wondered if all in the household were asleep. Perhaps now would be the time to search for Cimmerian and flee from this village under cover of darkness.

Determined to leave her exotic prison, Iva began to search the chamber for her clothes. The tattered skirt and hide shirt were not to be found. Aquilla must have taken them while she slept, she must have also lit the brazier. As Iva glanced down at the soft, aqua tunic, unconsciously her hand caressed the sleek material. She would keep these clothes she was wearing, she decided. Shadow Dancer owed her at least this much!

Making her way cautiously to the chamber door, she looked down at her bare feet, realizing that she had to find shoes of some sort. As she reached out a hand to quietly push the door open, she found herself face to face with Aquilla in the wide central hallway.

The woman smiled with pleasure at finding Iva already awake, and in her language, she instructed, "Shadow Dancer awaits you in the courtyard."

Iva would have resisted; she did not want to see Shadow Dancer, ever again. She wanted only to find Cimmerian and flee. But as Aquilla reached out a slender hand and took her own, she knew that she must follow the woman who silently led her out into the tiled central courtyard.

At first Iva did not see Shadow Dancer, the shadows within the courtyard obscured him as he stood next to a small fountain in the center of the enclosure. When he stepped into the light, Iva's breath caught. How tall and handsome he was. He had washed away the paint from his body and was clothed now in the manner of the other men of his tribe. The blanket knotted upon his shoulder and hanging beneath the opposite arm appeared to be made of a thinner, softer material, but other than that only the difference in his features set him apart from those of his tribe. And as his dark eyes touched her from head to foot in a heated, lengthy caress, Iva fully believed him to be the best-looking man she had ever seen. She flushed as his eyes rose and locked with her own.

"You surely must be hungry after this long day." His husky voice filled her ears as he reached out and drew her toward the back portion of the courtyard where a flower-covered arbor sheltered a small stone bench. Before this retreat a tantalizing meal was set up, its fragrant aromas carrying on the night breeze.

Glancing about as though now afraid to be alone with this man, Iva noticed that Aquilla had silently disappeared. You would think the woman would guard her husband more closely, Iva thought. Surely she must be aware of Shadow Dancer's attractiveness and of the danger of his entertaining another woman in the gardens beneath a star-studded night sky. "Perhaps I should take my meal elsewhere." She tried to pull back.

"Why would you not desire to share this food with me?" Shadow Dancer asked before she could turn and flee, his warm, sable eyes holding hers.

How could she possibly explain to him that the way he affected her was far too hard to combat? Would reminding him that he had a wife and a child bring some reason to this situation? Perhaps this was a usual custom of these people, that a man should share a meal alone with a guest without the presence of his wife, even if the guest was another female. She was more confused than ever as he proceeded to lead her to the bench and then stood, waiting for her to take a seat.

"I have dismissed Aquilla for the evening and will serve us myself." He gave her a warm smile as he bent over the arrangement of bowls set up on a large serving tray made of clay. "There is much that I need to explain," he added as he handed her a bowl.

Dismissed his wife indeed! Iva thought heatedly. No matter what the traditions and beliefs of these Indians were, they had no right to treat their women so outrageously! He certainly did have much to explain, but she was not the one he should be doing the explaining to. It was his wife he should address. Iva wanted only her freedom from him.

Filling a delicately crafted golden chalice with wildberry wine, Shadow Dancer handed it to Iva.

She accepted the goblet, and tasting the sweet brew and finding it to her liking, she took a healthy draught.

"The wine is made by the priests who live on the side of the mountain. For hundreds of years they have furnished this household with the fruits of their labor." Shadow Dancer smiled with pleasure, for she seemed to be enjoying the wine. He began to eat the savory, seasoned meat and vegetables in his bowl, his eyes watching her every movement.

"Do these priests also make wine for the other households in your village?" Although Iva's first thought was of escaping, she had to admit that she was curious about these people living so deep within the Rockies.

"They share it with no other. Though Gray Otter would have it differently. It has been their way since Wind Cryer and Sharaza brought their people to this valley." As Shadow Dancer partook of his meal, he told Iva some things about his people. "The priests are very solitary. They keep mostly to themselves in their temple on the side of the mountain. They tend the wild berries, and they make their wine, which they supply only to this house. The remainder is for their own needs."

Iva had sampled very little of the food in the bowl on her lap, being too intrigued by what Shadow Dancer was telling her to eat. "Who were this Wind Cryer and Sharaza you spoke of?"

"I am descended directly from their line. This house that I live in—and all within it—at one time belonged to them. It has been handed down to their children and to their children's children."

"What kind of Indians were Wind Cryer and Sharaza? Why did they come to this valley, and how on earth did they amass such riches?" Iva, now finding him open to her questions, plied him with several queries at once.

Shadow Dancer once again smiled generously as he set his bowl aside and drank deeply of his wine. He had hoped this evening would be passed in this fashion. He had told her little of his life or himself while on the trail, but here in his home he felt a need to share everything with her. "Wind Cryer was a great Apache warrior."

At this pronouncement, Iva drew in a deep breath and her eyes enlarged. She had been right all along! He was an Apache!

Before she could speak, Shadow Dancer continued. "Sharaza was an Aztec princess. She was the grand-daughter to Montezuma, and her mother was the Aztec emperor's favorite girl child."

"Aztec!" Iva gasped. The history lessons taught by the tutor her father had hired to come out to the farm during the winter months suddenly came back to her. Mr. Samply had taught her and Delbert a little about the Aztecs. They had been a cruel, barbarous people who had been conquered by Cortés and the conquistadors, and then had been brought to hand by the Christian church. Mr. Samply had told stories of the Aztec practice of sacrifice and slaughter.

Shadow Dancer could plainly read her horror and surprise in her expression. "My ancestors were an intelligent, advanced civilization. Their way of life began to change with the invasion of the Spaniards. Sharaza's father was one of the conquistadors, and like him, she was blessed with a wealth of golden hair and eyes the color of a clear sky." His regard of Iva was

103

tender as he tried to explain without frightening her the details of his ancestry. "As an Aztec princess, Sharaza was beloved by all, and whatever she desired she was granted. Except marriage to the man she fell in love with. Wind Cryer was an Apache, not one of her own, so she was forbidden to see him once the couple were discovered together.

Iva anxiously listened to what Shadow Dancer was telling her, but the word "Aztec" was even more menacing to her than the word "Apache," and clutching the goblet tightly within both hands, she was now even more determined to get away from this valley and these people!

"That is why Sharaza and all those in her household fled Tenochtitlán, which is now called Mexico City, under the cover of night. There were others from this city who joined her large party, seeking to escape the Spaniards and their strange ways."

Though Shadow Dancer paused for a moment, his eyes never left her face. "Wind Cryer, the Apache warrior, also took those of his tribe who wished to follow him, but it was the Aztec god Huitzilopóchtli who guided their steps. Often speaking to Sharaza in his strange, twittering voice, much like that of a hummingbird, he led those who followed Wind Cryer and Sharaza through the deserts and into the mountains and finally into this secret valley. The Aztec beliefs have changed much because of the great shaman who came to this land with Wind Cryer. This shaman was known as Spirit Dreamer, and he taught the people of the valley—Aztec and Apache alike—about the love of the great spirit, the love that he held for all of his children. So the ways of sacrifice and war were set aside by the law of Wind Cryer, and the best aspects of both cultures were free to grow here in this valley." Shadow Dancer hoped that he had eased Iva's fears somewhat. He wished her to open herself to his home and people— and to the ways that he knew would be strange to her for a time.

Wee-tzee-lo-potch-tly, Iva silently sounded out the name of the god Shadow Dancer had claimed had spoken in a strange, twittering voice to Sharaza, and had thus led these people to this valley. As she did so, she wondered how many gods these people had. "Your people then no longer hunt down little children to kill?" She glanced nervously at him, remembering one particularly grisly story that Mr. Samply had told to her and Delbert. In this tale a group of Aztec warriors attacked an enemy village, and after killing all of the adults, they took the children back to their own village to be sacrificed. Mr. Samply had said something about the Aztec belief that sacrifice must take place daily for the sun to rise each morning!

Shadow Dancer sighed deeply. "My people are content here in their valley. We do not wage war, nor do we kill little children. The Aztecs of long ago were misled by Tezcatlipoca, their tribal sky god, who demanded human sacrifice from them. The priests of our valley teach the peaceful ways of Quetzalcoatl. Of course, there are those of my village who follow the ways of the Apache and the great spirit. All here are free to follow the ways of the god or gods they desire to believe in."

Iva felt somewhat better upon hearing this. She had been wondering if she had been captured for the express purpose of being used as a sacrifice! A sigh of relief escaped her. "And what are your beliefs, Shadow Dancer?" she softly asked. Then, her mouth growing dry as Shadow Dancer's gaze held hers, she bent her lips to the brim of the chalice.

"When I was a young child my father sent me to the priests to be taught the history of my ancestors—the Aztecs. Upon my return to my father's house, I spent much time with the shaman of our village. This is how my own father and his before him learned the ways and the truths of our two cultures. I was taught at an early

105

age to weigh all the good and the bad in a person, in much the same way I judge the merits of my heritage and of the many gods of my people."

Iva was still confused. This man appeared not to be able to give her a simple answer. How different his beliefs were from those of her own religion. She had been taught that there was but one God. A loving, kind God who was the creator of all things. Her mother and father had nightly listened to her pray to this God as a child. Iva was about to tell him of her belief in but one God, but his next words stilled hers.

"More than a summer past, when a band of my warriors and I were out raiding, I was sought out by my inner spirit so I felt the need to find a place of solitude and pray in the fashion of Wind Cryer's people. Often I find my heart heavy with the need to seek out this god. I left the others of my band and made my way along the river bank on which we had been camping, seeking a quiet place to be to myself."

Iva listened attentively, captured by the vibrating tremor of his husky voice as he told her of his adventure, and for some strange reason she found herself falling even more under his influence.

"I had just begun my prayers, holding my arms wide toward the encompassing oneness of the great spirit, when my attention was pulled back toward the river and to the sounds of a horse and a woman. Parting the brush beside the river bank, I beheld a sight that was imprinted upon my mind forever. I silently watched for a time until the woman vanished, much like a wisp of smoke or some strange dream. I returned to my band, and after our raiding was finished we returned to our valley." Shadow Dancer paused here as he drank of his wine and looked across the small space to Iva. Gazing into her relaxed face, he glimpsed no recognition on her part of the point to his story. As yet she does not understand, he told himself patiently. I must explain further.

106

"Day and night I could not put the woman and horse from my thoughts. I forced myself to go raiding with my band of braves; I hunted high into the mountains, trying to forget. I sought out the priests and the shaman, trying to find answers. Then one night as I lay beneath the stars, the god of love and peace spoke to me of the woman. He told me that it was meant that I would see her at the river and that her vision would fill my heart. She was that portion of my heart each man searches for. She was my soul mate, the keeper of my dreams, and the blending of my inner being. Quetzalcoatl spoke the name of Sharaza and Moon Flower in the same breath. He declared that I seek you out and bring you here to my village to share my life with me."

"No!" Iva declared aloud as she jumped to her feet, the bowl of food falling from her lap and the goblet of wine splattering over the cool tile floor. With each sentence he spoke, she had begun to fear that she was the woman he was speaking of, and now she was certain of it. "How dare you say such things to me!" she cried aloud, having stood all that she could. This man had a wife and child, he had no right to say these things to her. Did he not realize how he affected her? Did he not know that his words cut deeply into her heart? She had to get away! She had to escape him and this madness. She could stay in his home no longer, but must get back to her father's house, where she was safe and did not have to fear that her heart would be shattered into a thousand pieces by a man who did not have one.

Shadow Dancer rose to his feet, and before she could turn and run from him, he grabbed hold of her hands. "Do not tell me no, Moon Flower. I ask you to become my wife. To share my life, my home, my heart."

"No . . . no . . . no . . ." Tears fell from her eyes as she tried in vain to break his grip on her hands and on her breaking heart.

How can this be? Shadow Dancer asked himself.

How could she refuse him if their being together had been ordained by the gods? He was bewildered by her refusal, and then a thought he had not even allowed himself to consider came to mind. "Is there another one in your heart, Moon Flower? Is this why you will not join yourself to me?" His question was softly spoken, though a touch of hardness crept beneath the surface and belied the ease he tried to keep in his tone.

Iva nodded her head, as a sob escaped her. Indeed another stood between them. His wife!

It must be the boy she was with the day I took her from her father's farm, Shadow Dancer told himself. Determined to force the memory of her lover from her, he pulled her into his arms. Anger drove him as he thought of his love in the arms of another, and he forcefully pressed his mouth over hers.

Iva made whimpering noises of resistance, but he held her in a powerful embrace. The ravishment of her mouth by his sent her pulses to thudding wildly. Drowning under the flood of his hungry demand, she fought for sanity. She had to resist him! She had to fight him off! But the pressure upon her lips intensified and the feel of his warm, hard body was more than she could endure. Suddenly her mouth slanted and opened to accommodate his searching tongue, her arms involuntarily went around his broad shoulders, and her searching fingers entwined in long, glistening strands of midnight black hair. She was lost! Totally oblivious to anything but the branding fire of the mouth covering hers. Trapped within the mindless pleasure of being within his massive arms, she was the recipient of his uncompromising passion as his fingers caressed the flesh of her slim throat, then slipped within the top of her tunic and pressed against the fullness of her breasts.

As Shadow Dancer continued to kiss her with a hunger that left no room for breath, his free hand roamed over the slimness of her back, and then, capturing the fullness of her buttocks, he pressed her against him, allowing her to feel his hard, demanding need.

Iva was dimly aware that her own body pressed more fully against his, rubbing against the firmness of his manhood. Her breasts achingly swelled and strained against his searching fingers, and for one wild, passionate moment she wished them freed. Open to his gaze and available to his heated touch. And at that moment she imagined the fire of his lips upon them. A moan of sheer unadulterated passion burned within the center of her being and escaped her throat. She was ablaze beneath his touch! If she did not break away now there would be no escape! "No . . . Please . . . I . . . I can't!" she cried out, her pain so great she might have been in the grips of torture.

"Do not say no to me. I will make you forget him. You will only know my touch, my love." Shadow Dancer fought the demons in his mind. He could not lose her to another! He would not release her!

Somehow his words took form within her befogged brain. "What other man?" she demanded as she fought off another attempt to make her mindless with his kisses.

"The one at your father's farm. The one I saw you with that day." Shadow Dancer did not want to talk, he wanted to teach her that he held the power to make her forget any other man.

"What about Delbert?" Iva's thoughts, by degrees, were clearing, and she wondered what he was talking about. What did Delbert have to do with anything? It was his wife and child that stood between them. She would not become his second wife, if this was what he had on his mind. It did not matter to her whether these people thought that this sort of conduct was permissible or not. She had been raised with the belief that a man took only one wife!

Slowly Shadow Dancer's passion began to cool as he tried in vain to bring her back into that state of thoughtless ecstasy they had shared only moments before. "This boy is your reason for rejecting me, but I will soon teach you what only a man can give you."

"Why you mindless oaf!" The words exploded from Iva and she pushed against his chest to set herself free. "You think I refuse you because of Delbert?" Her fiery anger instantly surfaced. "Why you are the most overbearing, heathen, whoreson I have ever had the misfortune to come into contact with! How dare you set the blame on me! How dare you accuse me and Delbert of being . . . of being . . ." Her face flamed, but she could not get out the words that burned within her mind so she launched herself against his chest and began to strike at him with all of her might. If he thought he could blame her for his adulterous behavior, he would soon learn the truth of the matter. Perhaps he did have some strange power over her, but by God she would fight it to the very end!

Some of her insults Shadow Dancer did not understand. The missionary priest who had taught him English had left out the more earthy expletives and had offered only a gentler understanding of Iva's tongue. But the heat of her tone did not escape Shadow Dancer. Ignoring the text of her anger, he concentrated on the fact that she had denied any involvement with the young man called Delbert. For a full moment, he allowed her to pound upon his chest, the inconsequential pain of the attack helping to clear his mind of the lust that tended to cloud his thoughts. As the full realization of what she had said came, a warm, generous smile settled upon his lips. If in truth she had not loved the other man, then he had no doubt that he could eventually win her over. And he was determined that before this night was over, he would have her consent to become his wife. Firmly yet tenderly taking her hands in his own, he tried to reason with her. "If not this Delbert, then why will you not become my wife? When I touch you I know that you feel the need of my

110

body. And your lips speak of the consent you will not voice."

Iva would have covered her ears if her hands had been free. She did not wish to hear how she acted with another woman's husband. She admitted that she had been shameless, a wanton where this man was concerned, but she desired with all her heart to fight off the power he had over her. Why would he not leave her alone? She tried to break free of his hold. "How can I marry you when you already have a wife?" She cried out at last, all of the shame and pain she felt in those words.

Chapter Nine

For a breathless moment Shadow Dancer stared at Iva's tear-stained features, not understanding what she had meant. "You think I already have a wife?" he softly questioned, and as her golden head nodded and she lowered her eyes because of guilt over the feelings she harbored for him, he gently raised her chin. "There is no other, Moon Flower. I have no wife."

Gazing into the sable warmth of his regard, Iva rebelled. "But what of Aquilla? What of your son? Her son? How can you deny them?"

Shadow Dancer's lips drew back into a large smile, and he clasped Iva in his embrace. Laughing huskily, he swung her around until she was gasping for her breath.

"I can easily deny them, my heart, because they belong not to me but to my friend, Dark Water. Aquilla's family have always served this household, so she does now. And her son Arez, though I am fond of the boy, I cannot lay claim to his parentage. Though I might find it amusing to do so, I am afraid that Dark Water, who is proud of his family, would not take kindly to my claim." Shadow Dancer's heart felt pounds lighter.

"Then you do not have a wife already? You do not wish for me to become your second wife?" Iva still could not believe him and had to question him further.

"Second wife, I should say not! You could never be second in anything!" Shadow Dancer stated righteously. "I have waited these many years for only you, my heart."

Iva began to melt inside at these words. Though she knew she should not have such deep feelings for this man who had stolen her from her home, she could not escape them. He had woven some strange magical web about her heart, and she was powerless to deny the force of her feelings for him. Though she should deny him, should cry out for her freedom, she could not. At that moment knowing that he was not married, not the father of Arez, she was forced to accept the powerful attraction she had tried to deny from the first day of her capture, when he had taken her up on his horse and she had felt the tender strength of his large body. "Is it true that you watched me that day at the river while I was breaking Cimmerian?" she asked softly, daring to believe that for over a year he had desired her as his wife.

"Yes, my love, it is true. I watched you that day, and I could not forget you." He held her against his chest, his ebony eyes encompassing her in a loving regard.

"Then you never planned to sell me into slavery?" Iva thought now of the torture she had endured at not knowing what her fate was to be at this warrior's hands.

"I told you that our people do not have slaves in this valley."

"But what of Aquilla? Is she not a slave? Were those in her family not slaves?" She remembered what he had said about the woman's family having served this household and believed Aquilla and her family to be in the bonds of servitude.

"Aquilla is free to leave my home at any time. She runs it as her mother did before her and her grandmother before that. Her husband, Dark Water, is my friend as I told you, and his craft is working with

113

silver as is his father's."

Iva was quickly learning about Shadow Dancer's village and the people within it. It would appear that the specialty or craft of the parents was handed down to the children through the generations. "But why did you not tell me all of this before now? Before you brought me to your village?"

Shadow Dancer smiled fondly, "Would you have believed me if I told you about my people? Did you believe me when I said that you would not be a slave?"

Iva had to admit that she had not believed him. And now, as she thought about it, she realized that she probably would not have believed a word he told her about his home. This village hidden in the valley and his ancestry were a bit more than anyone could be expected to comprehend without firsthand viewing. Her pale curls bobbed as she nodded in agreement. "I guess I wouldn't have believed you, but you should have explained more to me than you did." Iva could not so readily forget all the fear and confusion she had been forced to endure over the last few days.

"I did talk you into becoming my friend." Shadow Dancer grinned, his hand reaching up and his long, tan fingers caressing her fragile jawline. "Never have I had a more beautiful friend," he added as though remembering the time they had shared alone at the falls.

"Indeed." Iva sighed. "I was so fearful of becoming a slave in an Apache village, I would have agreed to becoming the devil's own friend."

Shadow Dancer's gaze became more serious as he stated with some feeling, "Truly I did not mean for you to be frightened. I was fearful that I would lose you, and this is the only reason I can give for my actions." His head bent, and his sensual, full lips slanted tenderly over hers to drink of the sweet giving of her mouth.

"But what of my parents?" Iva protested as she broke free from the kiss. Now that she was assured that Shadow Dancer's intentions were honorable, though his means had been questionable, she was beset by worry over her mother's, her father's, and even Delbert's anxiety over her fate.

"I left a bride price at your father's farm." Shadow Dancer would have drawn her back against him and partaken more fully of the bounty of her charms, but Iva would have none of that.

Shaking her head, she asked, "What bride price? What are you talking about, I saw no such bride price!" In truth Iva did not even know what a bride price was.

"The twenty horses I left in your father's corral. They were the finest animals from my herd. It took me a full year to choose the best as your bride price."

Though touched by his words, Iva still wondered at his actions. "How do you suppose my father would know that the horses were this bride price that you speak of, and besides, I thought it was the woman who brought a dowry into the marriage." That a man would present a bride price of twenty horses to a woman's father seemed very odd to Iva.

"What is this word that you speak, this dowry?" Shadow Dancer was quickly learning that his mastery of the English language was rather limited.

"A dowry is the gifts or wealth that a woman brings to her husband when they are wed," Iva explained.

"Ah, yes, this dowry that you speak of is much like the bride price a warrior bestows upon the father of the woman he chooses to join him along life's path. Why is it that a woman must bring gifts to her man in your land? Does this man not have the strength and means to care for the woman he would take to his home as his bride?"

This was getting harder to explain by the minute. "No, no, it is just the custom of my people for the woman to bring gifts into the marriage."

"Our way is better." Shadow Dancer's chest swelled with pride in his people. "A warrior is not worthy of a woman if he cannot settle a bride price upon her

115

father." Though his own bride price of twenty horses was very high, to him it proved how much he honored the father of Moon Flower.

"But how is my father to know your ways?" Iva finally relented, though still exasperated. "I am sure he still thinks that I was stolen by a band of Indians! He will have no idea that you desired me as your wife!"

"I also left my sun sign before his barn. Would a thief leave his mark for all to view?" Shadow Dancer did not understand why she was so worried. He believed that her father would have been angry at first, but in time would know that his daughter was safe. After all, he had not hidden his intention to make Iva his own.

"How will my family understand all of this? I still don't understand it!" Iva hadn't quite gotten used to the changes in her situation. How was her father to figure all this out? A bride price, a sun sign drawn in the dust?—would anyone at the Cassidy farm understand the situation any better than she had?

"Would you have me go back to your father's farm and tell him of my wish to join with you?" Shadow Dancer easily recognized her concern for her family, and he was eager to do anything that would make her happy. If that meant traveling the long distance back to the Cassidy farm and facing the wrath of her family, he would. There was nothing that she could request of him that he would not attempt to do.

Iva could well imagine the reception that he would receive at her father's farm. More than likely he would be shot before he could explain anything. Vehemently she shook her head. No, the thought of his being killed or harmed in any way made her legs begin to tremble beneath her, and she had to clutch his shoulders tightly as though to assure herself that this would never happen. She could not allow him to go to her father. "I would prefer to go and explain alone," she volunteered softly.

Shadow Dancer was just as adamant that he would

not risk losing her. He had sworn that he would protect her the night the Apache had captured her, and his oath bound him to do so. Besides, he feared that her father would refuse to allow her to return to him. He could not bear, now he had found her, to lose her. "I will not allow you to go without me." He was unrelenting. "If you insist on going back to your family, I will be at your side!"

Iva immediately conjured up visions of Shadow Dancer being set upon by her father and Delbert the instant they approached the farm. It would be better to wait for more time to pass, she thought to herself. Perhaps her family's anger over her abduction would lessen, and she would be able to send word to them of her safety so Shadow Dancer's life would not be risked. "You cannot go. If you will not allow me to go alone, then we will have to wait for a time when my family's hostility will be lessened. I could not bear your being harmed," she softly confessed.

Shadow Dancer's heart pounded heavily within his chest as he heard her last statement, and searching her heart-shaped face for the full meaning of those words, he swept her up into his arms and eased his large frame down upon the stone bench. "You will join your life path with my own?" He held his breath as he awaited her answer, his ebony eyes filled with hope.

Iva felt herself drowning within the tenderness of his presence. "You are quite sure that your gods approve?" She was only jesting, but Shadow Dancer took her seriously.

"I will not tell you that I have not been tempted by other women, Moon Flower, but I will say that I have never desired another for my bride. I know not the reason other than you fill my heart with light, but I do know that the gods approve and one day they will make their plans for us clear."

How understanding and generous this man truly is, Iva thought as she listened to him. There was such

117

knowledge and understanding in all he said, her heart filled with happiness because he desired her as his wife. And though she knew that her family would not approve, and that her life would not be as she had planned, she slowly nodded her head. "I will marry you, Shadow Dancer. I will become your wife."

The kiss that sealed their pledge was so devastatingly potent it stole away Iva's breath as well as her senses. While Shadow Dancer held her in a gentle embrace that bespoke strength and protectiveness as well as tender love, his tongue, urgent in her mouth, awoke a powerful hunger within her and fanned dormant embers of desire into flame. Her hands stole around his muscular neck, drawing him closer as she pressed her aching breasts to his chest, her own heated tongue gliding against his and then pressing on into his mouth as if compelled to fill a void.

With the taste of her sweetness so startlingly acute, Shadow Dancer moaned aloud and clasped her more tightly. Without a word being spoken, he rose to his feet and carried Iva across the tile flooring of the courtyard and down the long hallway to the room she had rested in earlier. The only sounds were the gentle padding of Shadow Dancer's leather sandals upon tile as he made his way to the small alcove which held the sleeping couch.

As he gently placed her on the bed, Shadow Dancer dredged up the strength to break away, withdrawing his lips as he unwound her sleek arms from around his neck. A fierce aching in the pit of his being resulted from the control he was imposing on himself.

Iva's eyes, now a deep violet blue from built-up passion, widened as she looked into his face, wanting to draw him down upon the sleeping couch with her. As she drew in ragged breaths her only desire was to press her body against his and to quench her intense need of him. She was without shame in that moment, and would have cried aloud her wants except for the soft words that filled her ears.

"My body trembles with my great want of you, Moon Flower. I cannot bear to bring you close to me again, nor can I bear to be apart from you; but soon, my flower, soon we will be joined together, and then these raging fires of desire will be quenched." His ebony gaze held her deep blue one for a few lingering moments, and in his eyes Iva glimpsed the verification of his words. Her heartbeat fluttered all the faster at the realization that he wanted her as much as she wanted him, and it was this knowledge alone that stilled the plea about to come from her lips as he turned from her and quickly left the chamber.

For several minutes she could not move. Then, slowly, one hand rose and lightly pressed her kiss-swollen lips. Her entire body ached for some strange fulfillment that she could only guess at. He had brought her to such towering peaks of desire and then had left her.

"You silly goose!" she told herself. "He left only because he wished to honor you. Could you not see his own desire blazing from those fathomless, sable eyes?" Iva hugged herself tightly as though to bring back those minutes when he had held her. Yes, she had been witness to Shadow Dancer's great need for her. The aching tremor in his voice had told her of his feelings. It was just that his leaving had left her feeling so empty inside.

Some time passed before Iva found the strength to rise from the couch. Having no clothing to sleep in, she took off the tunic and skirt, carefully folded them, and placed them across the chest. Naked, she climbed back onto the sleeping couch and pulled the embroidered blanket of softest cotton up under her chin. She had never before dared to be so wicked as to sleep in the nude, but she was swiftly recognizing the part of herself that craved the temptations of the flesh. She felt seductively free beneath the covers, her creamy-soft skin caressed by the tantalizing feel of the blanket and of the sheer covering of the sleeping couch. Stretching full length she forced her eyes tightly shut, and envisioned Shadow Dancer as he had been just before he had left her. Fleetingly she thought that this was the same man who had stolen her away from her family, but as she remembered the fierce possession of his embrace, all recollections of her abduction and of her family faded before the remembrance of Shadow Dancer.

Chapter Ten

Drawn from a deep sleep by the noises Aquilla made as she went about the chamber setting out a fresh tunic and skirt, Iva propped herself on an elbow and gazed about as though not fully aware of her surroundings. She had been dreaming that she and Shadow Dancer were still at the falls, but seeing Aquilla brought all back in a rush. She was in Shadow Dancer's house. Falling back against the softness of the sleeping couch, she remembered the happenings of the past night. She was not to be a slave in this village; she was to be a wife.

Aquilla looked across the room to the sleeping alcove and catching sight of movement, she spoke softly. "If you would care to dress, the morning meal is set up in the courtyard."

Pushing herself up into a sitting position, the blanket pulled up over her breasts, Iva smiled fondly at the other woman. Now that she knew Aquilla was not Shadow Dancer's wife, she hoped the two of them would become friends. "Please be patient while I learn your language," Iva implored in a combination of English and a few of the Indian words she could pronounce. She had already decided to pay closer attention to the language that Shadow Dancer had been trying to teach her.

Aquilla seemed to comprehend, and with feline

121

grace, she crossed the chamber, carrying a deep purple tunic embroidered with silver thread and a white skirt. She set these garments out upon the foot of the sleeping couch.

"Thank you," Iva spoke in the tongue the other woman understood.

As though she were more than willing to do her part in Iva's education, Aquilla pointed toward the clay pitcher of water, and sounding out each word distinctly, she made it clear that the water had been warmed and that Iva was to help herself to it when she was ready to bathe. Before she left the chamber, Aquilla used the word "food" and pointed out toward the courtyard, supplying the word in her language for that central portion of the house.

Iva smiled gratefully, and as Aquilla left her she rose from the sleeping couch. After washing, she dressed in the clothes the other woman had laid out for her. It will certainly take some getting used to, this being waited upon, she told herself as she ran her hands over the soft texture of the tunic. At home she had been used to hard work, not housework, but work on the farm. Shadow Dancer had mentioned last night that he had a herd of horses, perhaps he would agree to let her work with them. She would have to do something to occupy herself.

Iva considered the present arrangement a temporary affair that would last only until she and Shadow Dancer could return to her father's farm and explain her abduction and their wish to wed. She hoped that Shadow Dancer would have no objection to her keeping herself busy by helping with the care of his horses. After all, she could not sew a straight seam, nor could she cook very well; and surely Shadow Dancer would not wish her to be bored to death by being confined to his beautiful house.

Of course, he will grant my wish, she thought with a smile as she started through the chamber door. She would work at his side during the day, and in the evenings . . . She flushed at thinking of the nights she would spend with Shadow Dancer, and quickly forced herself to concentrate on her plans for their future together. Perhaps they would stay with her parents for a time until they found a property to purchase so they could start their own horse farm. This was the track of her thoughts as she made her way down the hallway and circled around to the central courtyard.

Shadow Dancer greeted her warmly as she approached him. His warm, obsidian eyes glowed as he took in her entire form with a single glance. "You are far more beautiful than I ever dreamed," he murmured as he drew her gently into his arms.

Iva felt her entire being was turning to liquid under his gaze, and as his arms enfolded her all thoughts of future and family and obligations flew from her mind. Her head tilted back for the tender kiss he would bestow upon her lips, and with this touching, her heart soared.

By now somewhat lightheaded, Iva allowed herself to be led farther into the courtyard and over to the stone bench that she and Shadow Dancer had shared the night before.

The courtyard and its gardens were cool at this time of the day, for the thick, flourishing vines of vibrant green interwoven throughout the grilled lattice work overhead allowed only sporadic bursts of sunshine to penetrate this exotic and peaceful refuge. At the center of the courtyard was a fountain, a statue from which water gushed, sparkling and crystalline. Birds with colorful plumages preened themselves near the tranquil pools in the gardens or perched in the trees. Sweet-scented flowers bloomed on the arbors, and many fragrant shrubs were strategically positioned.

Iva remembered the mess she had made when she had spilled her food and her goblet of wine on the tiles the night before, but this morning there was no sign that such an accident had taken place. She knew that Aquilla must have cleaned up the disorder before serving their breakfast. She would have to apologize to her for she certainly did not wish to cause the other woman additional work.

Sitting next to Iva, Shadow Dancer drew her hand into his own and regarded her with a tenderness that instantly went straight to her heart. He raised her hand to his lips and kissed the palm. "Did you sleep well, Moon Flower?"

To Iva the question held an undertone that his words did not imply, and instantly a light blush touched her cheeks. Surely he could not know that it had been some time after he left her chamber before she had been able to find slumber. Slowly she nodded her head, forcing herself to respond. "My room is quite comfortable, thank you."

Shadow Dancer's smile was one of understanding, for after leaving her he had gone to the pastures at the back of the house and had taken a long and very cool swim in the pond to gain a measure of control over his cravings. It had been a good while before he had sought his own sleeping couch. "I will be gone most of the day," he said as once again he took the liberty of filling their bowls with the food that Aquilla had prepared.

Iva looked toward him, concerned over her own part to play here in his village. She had hoped to spend the day with him and had planned to approach him about helping with his horses.

Glimpsing her worried look as he handed her a bowl filled with pieces of seasoned meat, fruit, and a bread made from ground cornmeal, Shadow Dancer ventured to ease her concern over his leaving her alone. "My cousin will pay you a visit this morning. I think you will find her pleasant company."

"Your cousin?" In surprise, Iva looked up from her food.

"Her name is Nokie, and we have always been very close. I am sure that you two will become good friends." Shadow Dancer hoped this would be the way of things. It had been his cousin he had first told about the woman he had seen breaking in the large black stallion, and it had been Nokie who had told him about her dream that he would go back to the land of the pale eyes and would bring the woman and horse back to his village. He admitted now, but only to himself, that he had at first not believed his cousin. Though he had been plagued with visions of Moon Flower, it had not been until Quetzalcoatl himself had spoken to him that he had truly accepted Nokie's words about the golden-haired woman. Though he and everyone else in his village knew his cousin was a spirit woman and possessed unusual powers, it had taken him some time to understand the full scope of her dream concerning Iva.

For some strange reason the name Nokie sounded familiar to Iva, and searching her mind, she at last remembered that first night of her capture when Shadow Dancer had forced her to bathe in the stream; he had made mention then that his cousin—Nokie—had given him the soap he had in his parfleche.

"But what if she doesn't like me? She will not be able to understand me." Iva nervously picked at her food as she thought of the morning ahead of her. She dreaded meeting the people of his village, because she was sure they would consider her an intruder.

Responding with a disarming grin, Shadow Dancer bent over and lightly kissed her sweet, tempting lips. "How can anyone help but love you, Moon Flower?" Looking upon her loveliness he knew full well the truth of his words. "Nokie and I have been close since we were very young." He went back to his meal, and after plopping a wild berry into his mouth, he added, "She has volunteered to help you with your language lessons and to teach you something about our village and our ways."

Iva had hoped that it would be Shadow Dancer who

125

would teach her what she needed to know about this strange tribe of Indians. "And what will you be doing while your cousin is teaching me these things?" She imagined that he would be running off with some warriors to hunt or fish or take part in some other exercise that excluded her.

Shadow Dancer did not miss the slight pouting of her lips, and though he was drawn to those tender morsels and desired nothing more than to feel them beneath his own mouth, he fought the urge. "I will go this day to Atlacol, the high priest. He lives in the temple on the mountain's side. I must speak to him of your presence in the valley and tell him of our wish to join our life paths as one."

Iva felt petty because of her earlier thoughts when Shadow Dancer had said he was leaving her in the hands of his cousin. All the while he had been planning to speak with a priest about their marriage. With an attempt at atonement, she stated, "I will try to get along with your cousin."

"You will find it very easy, Moon Flower. Though Nokie is the daughter of Gray Otter, there is a distance as vast as grandmother earth and grandfather sky between the two. My cousin's heart is always kind. She often helps Cloud Walker, our shaman, with healings and rituals which are important to my people. You will find in her a true friend." Shadow Dancer set his bowl aside. "Now, before I leave why do you not show me how much you will miss me this day?"

Her closeness with this man was something entirely new to Iva, and she blushed profusely. But Shadow Dancer took her bowl from her lap and drew her closer to his side on the stone bench.

"The day will be long until I return to you, Moon Flower." His lips lightly brushed against hers, his warming breath fanning her cheek.

Iva shut her eyes and allowed herself to be entirely ensnared by his seductive voice and featherlike kisses.

As the pressure on her mouth persisted and her lips parted for his roving tongue, she knew nothing but the presence of his large, yet tender, body and the power he had over her senses and her heart.

Drawing away, Shadow Dancer allowed his gaze to roam freely over her beauty, imprinting upon his memory every perfect detail of it. As Iva's eyes opened, they took in his generous smile while his thumb lightly caressed her cheek. "I will be hard pressed to keep my thoughts together this day, Moon Flower. Your beauty will fill my every hour." With this, he rose and, before she could pull her thoughts together, quietly left her sitting on the stone bench in the courtyard.

Iva fought for some control over her breathing. He is more powerful than a potent drug, she thought as her mind slowly began to clear.

Looking around the courtyard and finding herself completely alone, she rose from the bench and, still feeling somewhat lightheaded, decided to explore the gardens while she tried to calm her racing heart. For a time she roamed about the lush, vibrantly colorful plants and bushes; a serene feeling settling over her, and then she followed the sculptured walkway and came upon a pair of statues. For a few minutes she looked in admiration at the stone man and woman standing upon a pedestal. Iva wondered if this pair were some fabled god and goddess of Aztec lore. The creator of the statues had made it plain that the couple had been madly in love. It could be seen in the way their heads tilted toward each other and in the small, endearing smiles cast upon their lips.

"They are Sharaza and Wind Cryer." The woman's voice startled Iva into swinging around and facing the two young women who had silently approached her. "Oh." It was all she could manage upon being taken unaware.

The smaller of the two took the step which brought her directly before Iva. As she spoke her voice was as lilting and soft as music to the ears. "I am Nokie, cousin to Shadow Dancer, and this is my friend Tanza. We did not mean to disturb your solitude here in the gardens."

So this is Nokie, Iva thought to herself as she took in the petite woman whose large, warm brown eyes held hers. Finding the young woman much paler in appearance than others she had seen from this village, and liking her genial smile, Iva could not help but smile in return and greet her new friend in the language of this hidden valley. "Shadow Dancer has told me much about you, Nokie." Iva spoke softly and hoped she would not blunder.

Both young women nodded their heads, as though impressed by her ability to grasp their language so quickly. "We thought you might like our company today, with Shadow Dancer away from the village." It was once again Nokie's gentle voice which touched Iva's ears, and since the girl also used her hands to sign out her meaning, it was evident that Shadow Dancer had warned her of Iva's lack of verbal understanding.

Still it was delightful to have the company of two young women. Iva's fear of being out of place around Shadow Dancer's tribeswomen completely vanished that morning as the three relaxed in the gardens.

The young women were all well aware of the communication problem, so they all used hand signing and Nokie and Tanza endeavored to pronounce the Indian words slowly and in an instructional manner.

Iva was delighted by her two guests, and in short order the three women had become fast friends. It was evident to Iva that Nokie and Tanza were quite different. Nokie was very frail, her manner of speech and action soft and reflective, whereas Tanza was talkative and seemed to overshadow Nokie in almost every respect. Still, the love and affection between the two was obvious to Iva. Though Tanza appeared to greatly admire the smaller woman, she interrupted the conversation quite often in little, excited outbursts.

She appeared to have a great lust for life, yet often throughout the morning Iva found the girl smiling upon Nokie with great admiration. Nokie, on the other hand, seemed to delight in her friend's zest. The pair indeed were total opposites, but as they welcomed Iva into their lives without reservation, she could not help but be quickly won over.

By the time Shadow Dancer returned late in the afternoon, Iva's company had taken their leave and she had changed into a fresh outfit and was taking her leisure in the courtyard, awaiting his reappearance.

Iva had determined in her own mind that she would approach Shadow Dancer about working with his horses that very evening. Though she had spent a pleasant day with Nokie and Tanza, she did not look forward to such a life of leisure on a daily basis.

Shadow Dancer's eyes lit up when he stepped into his house and glimpsed Iva in the courtyard. The deep blue tunic she wore was a brilliant backdrop for her glorious mane of copper curls, and as he quickly stepped to her side, her deep blue eyes sparkled with joy at seeing him. Without words spoken between them, he bent to her and, taking her into his arms, tenderly drew her against his chest. Inhaling the sweet scent of her, he sighed softly as his lips slanted over hers. This is truly the meaning of the word *happiness,* he thought to himself as a timeless minute passed while he lovingly partook of her sweet, honeyed taste.

As ever, once she was within his arms, Iva was lost to reason. Swept along on the rushing tide of his tender embrace, she sensed the taste and feel of him, his strength.

"Ah, my flower, I have longed the day through for this minute when I could hold you in my arms." He placed another small kiss upon her soft lips as he released her and allowed her to sit back upon the bench. Taking a seat beside her, Shadow Dancer took her hand within his own, and for a moment, he studied the graceful tint of scarlet that stole across her cheeks and down her throat.

Feeling the full perusal of his warm regard, Iva flushed all the more until his husky laughter brought a smile to her lips and she lifted her head to gaze in return at his handsome face. "You overwhelm me, Shadow Dancer," she confessed, and felt the flame rise to her cheeks once again.

"You do the same to me, Moon Flower." He laughed lightly and squeezed her hand even more tightly. "Would you care to tell me of your day, or should I tell you first of mine?" He turned the subject, hoping to make her more comfortable.

"There is little to tell on my part. Nokie and her friend, Tanza, paid me a visit, and we had a pleasant time." Wanting to approach him about helping with the horses at the right time, so he would not object, Iva allowed him to pick up the conversation.

"I spent most of the day at the temple with the priests. Atlacol is pleased that I have found the woman I would choose as my life mate. He also believes that the gods have ordained our joining and would seek out their guidance and will for our lives."

There was little Iva could add on the subject of gods and their will. It all seemed very strange to her, but she would keep her thoughts to herself. If Shadow Dancer wished to believe that he had been placed in destiny's hands and had been guided to her by his gods on the day he had first seen her, and under his gods' direction he had taken her from her father's farm, she would not argue with him.

"I also went to Cloud Walker's lodge this day. I have told the shaman of our wish to join, and he and Atlacol have both agreed that the time of the ceremony should be with the new moon." Shadow Dancer was pleased with this news that he had to relay, and as he watched her closely, he hoped he would find the same pleasure revealed on her features. He would be more than glad when the ceremonies were over and he could claim this woman as his own. It was becoming more than he could endure to be in her presence without crushing her against him and sating the ravenous desires that came over him without warning.

Both his words and his closeness made Iva's head begin to swim. It was only a couple of weeks until the new moon. Two short weeks before she would become this man's wife! She had thought there would be more time. Time to tell her parents of their plans, for her to make arrangements for her wedding day. "It will be only two weeks then until we wed." Her statement was more to herself than to him.

Glimpsing the paleness of her features, Shadow Dancer held much concern for her reaction. "What is it, Moon Flower? Do you still hold misgivings about my intentions? Do you doubt what I feel for you here, in my chest?" His fist rested upon his heart as he appealed to her, and he wondered if she still believed that he was joined with another. Did her pale face and wistful tone of her voice mean that she had reconsidered and did not wish to become his bride? His worries were reflected in the somberness of his dark eyes.

Held by the power of that dark regard, Iva knew that this man—Indian or savage the world might call him— was the only one who would ever bring forth such overpowering feelings in her. She had once believed that she would never marry. Wishing only to work on her father's horse farm, she had not desired to be tied to a husband who would make unwanted demands upon her. But now, looking into Shadow Dancer's face, she knew that she would put everything aside to be his wife. Of course, the ceremony would take place here in his village, but after they were proclaimed man and wife before his tribe, then surely they would return to her father's farm, and she would be able to have the life she had always expected. "Will I be able to help you with your horses?" Her chin tilted at a stubborn angle as though she would fight for this right. I had best find out now, she told herself, whether this man, like so many others, thinks a woman's place is in the home.

Surprise filled his dark eyes, but a slow, lazy smile settled over Shadow Dancer's lips as he realized the seriousness with which she questioned him. "If it is your desire to work with horses, I will not tell you no. Do not forget, I have seen you taming the great black stallion, so I am well aware of your abilities with animals. If I feared for your safety, then I would try to sway you from what you desire, but my belief is that the gods have blessed you with the gift to tame horses, and I would not wish to interfere but will be pleased with the help that you give."

Iva could have cried aloud with the happiness she felt at hearing these words. Here was the man she had waited for, the man who would become her husband, the one who understood her need to be herself. "Can we start tomorrow? You don't have to leave the village again, do you? I am usually an early riser, so don't worry about having to wait for me to get up." As excitement overtook her, everything came out in a rush.

With her eyes sparkling with joy and her happiness revealed upon her face, Shadow Dancer thought her much like a child. But her exuberance was contagious, and within seconds a large grin split the warrior's face and he was nodding his dark head. "Tomorrow morning I will, indeed, take you to the herd of horses in the pastures behind my house."

For the first time Iva eased up and placed a kiss upon his lips. Though it was but a fleeting gesture of thanks, the contact went straight to Shadow Dancer's heart, and he quickly wrapped his arms around her.

If this was all it took to see happiness upon her face and to be greeted with the touch of her lips, Shadow Dancer swore that he would never refuse her!

Chapter Eleven

One day slowly passed into another as Iva began to adjust to the strangeness of her new life. Her grasp of the Indian language continually improved, with the help of Shadow Dancer and Nokie, Tanza and Aquilla, who all seemed to enjoy teaching her. And she kept busy, for she was now allowed to spend most of her mornings and afternoons exercising and working with Shadow Dancer's horses. She now appreciated Aquilla's efficiency, finding that her clothing was laid out each morning and that Shadow Dancer's house was run with seeming ease.

Upon occasion Iva reflected that she would miss many things about this beautiful valley; Shadow Dancer's magnificent house, for one thing, and all the attention given her by Aquilla, for another. But being anxious to return to her family, and worried still that her mother and father must assume the worst after her abduction, she awaited the day when she and Shadow Dancer would leave this valley and enter the outside world.

"The entire village is very excited about you and Shadow Dancer joining your life paths, Moon Flower. There is little that the elders speak about these days but the preparations being made by the women, and of course the men of the village cannot wait to have a reason to gamble and try to best each other in their games." Lying on her back and gazing up at the scuttling clouds overhead, Tanza turned her dark head in Iva's direction and then bit into a piece of bread that had been made from ground corn. Aquilla had sent the nourishing snack along with Nokie and Tanza, who had sought out Iva at Shadow Dancer's house and had been told they would find her in the back pastures working with Shadow Dancer's horses.

Moments before joining the two young women, Iva had finished brushing Cimmerian down, and she now sat upon the piece of soft material Aquilla had sent along for that use. Looking at Tanza with some surprise, she said, "I had not expected that our wedding would be such a big event." In truth she had hoped they would just go through a simple ceremony; she was not looking forward to gaining the attention of the entire village.

"There will be games for all and much feasting. Shadow Dancer is much loved and commands regard as high war chief of our village." It was Nokie who proudly spoke about her cousin.

The joining ceremony was scheduled to take place in only two days, but Iva tried not to dwell upon the coming affair. Every time her mind filled with thoughts about the day when she would truly become Shadow Dancer's wife, curiosity about what they had shared thus far quickly occupied her mind. It was true that she knew what took place between a man and a woman, so she had an idea of what to expect, but each time Shadow Dancer took her in his arms she experienced a craving deep within herself that cried out for some kind of release, and Iva was unsure whether this was normal or whether there was something wrong with her! When her mother had taken her aside and told her what every young girl should know, she had not addressed the subject of inner feelings. There had been no explanation given for the way Iva's heartbeat accelerated or her knees began to tremble whenever Shadow Dancer was near, for the way her cheeks flushed after each hungry kiss they shared.

Nokie noticed the tension that overcame Iva with this talk about the joining with her cousin, and being intuitive of another's feelings, she softly questioned the young woman, "Is there something amiss, Moon Flower?" This young woman with the golden curls did not seem as excited about the prospect of wedding Shadow Dancer as Nokie would have thought. Perhaps it was their different backgrounds and cultures that plagued the girl. If so, Nokie hoped she could say something that would ease Iva's mind.

Aware that Nokie's interest in her had sharpened, Iva turned crimson. Taking a sip of water from her goblet, she hoped that her companions did not notice her discomfort. How on earth could she tell these two young women who had befriended her the disturbing thoughts she had about the man she would marry? Perhaps she was the only one to have ever experienced such overwhelming feelings in a man's arms—a quick flame sparked within her at just the remembrance of a tender word her virile warrior had spoken—perhaps there was something terribly wrong with her! Deep within was there some wanton, perverse nature that a virtuous young woman would not possess, and if she spoke of it aloud, would her companions condemn her?

It was Tanza, not Nokie, who seemed of a sudden to understand Iva's mood, and after a few more minutes of silence, she spoke to her in a serious tone. "You know, Moon Flower, once you are joined with Shadow Dancer there will be some things in this village that you will no longer be able to do."

"Such as what?" Iva questioned as she took a piece of cornbread and dipped it in honey before putting it into her mouth.

Nokie regarded her friend warily, as though unsure of what she would say. Her pale, slender hands, their small veins barely visible, nervously plucked at her food as though she feared the inevitability of what was to come.

"Well, there is the house of pleasure for one!" Tanza grinned widely and pulled herself up into a sitting position as she warmed to her subject, glancing from one young woman to the other.

"Really, Tanza, I cannot believe you would say such a thing!" Nokie exclaimed as though for once she was truly shocked by what her friend was saying.

Tanza's grin never wavered and her gaze held Iva's. "Well, it is true! You are not even permitted through the back door and into the corridor, if you are joined with a warrior!"

"What on earth is this place you call the house of pleasure?" Puzzled, Iva looked from the grinning Tanza to the scandalized Nokie.

"It is not the type of place you should know of, Moon Flower." Nokie attempted to put the subject aside, for she felt very uncomfortable speaking about the house of pleasure!

But Tanza laughed heartily and lightly shoved Nokie's shoulder as though she believed her to be kidding. "Why, every young woman should know about the house of pleasure!" Her dark eyes twinkled with mischief as they settled on Iva, and she thought to herself that Nokie could be a stick in the mud at times. What harm could there be in telling Moon Flower about the house of pleasure? "If you wish, Moon Flower, I will take you to the house of pleasure this very evening! You can see for yourself what takes place there!" The young woman was still smiling.

Nokie gasped aloud, her mind quickly filled with all manner of images of decadent behavior. She had heard much of the house of pleasure, spoken by the women of the hidden valley in hushed tones, but she herself had never dared to venture anywhere near the large building that stood on the outskirts of the village. She tried to intervene. "My cousin would not wish for Moon Flower to go to this place, Tanza!"

It was one of those rare times in all the years the two young women had been friends that Tanza was aware of Nokie's displeasure with her. But, as always, the young woman pressed on. "There is going to be a meeting of the high council tonight, Moon Flower, and Shadow Dancer will surely go. He will not even know that you have left the house to go with us. And besides, Nokie, we will only watch what takes place from the back corridor. What harm can there be in that?"

Listening to Tanza, Iva was beginning to feel some of the other girl's excitement over the prospect of visiting this house of pleasure that Nokie seemed to believe was off limits. "Tell me what takes place in this house of pleasure." She looked from one young woman to the other, and of course it was Tanza who responded.

"It is a house in the village that is operated entirely by the warriors of a large family!" The young woman laughed, and Nokie's face turned crimson as she softly moaned aloud.

Iva still did not quite understand what the girl was getting at, and she wondered why Nokie was acting so strangely. Perhaps she had missed something in Tanza's exchange. "What on earth is it that these warriors do?"

"Why, Moon Flower, the task of these men is to devote themselves to entertaining and pleasuring women!" Tanza straightforwardly stated, provoking another moan from Nokie.

For a full moment longer Iva sat as though not comprehending, looking from one young woman to the other, but slowly the full magnitude of what Tanza implied penetrated. "You mean . . ." Her eyes enlarged as she stared at the still-grinning Tanza.

Tanza eagerly nodded her dark head as she at last recognized understanding upon Iva's face, while Nokie knew there was little sense in trying to interfere now because it was already too late. Tanza would have her say upon the matter of the pleasure house, and there was nothing that could be said to sway her. "The house has been here in the village seemingly forever. It is said that the family in charge of it are descended in direct line from Sharaza's household. It is also said that they practiced their trade long before this valley was found. The priests condone the house as a means to keep a single woman or widow from stealing another woman's husband, and it is run entirely by the braves of this one family. Oh, what warriors they all are!" Tanza dreamily wavered as she ended her explanation.

"But why on earth would we wish to go to this house?" To Iva, the place sounded much like the house of ill repute run by women in the town of Sterling. That was called Sal's place. It was a whorehouse!

Nokie relaxed somewhat upon hearing Iva's question. She decided that Shadow Dancer's choice as life companion was much more sensible than her own choice as friend.

"Tell me truthfully, Moon Flower. Would you not like to see for yourself what takes place between a man and a woman?" Tanza had not missed Iva's earlier reactions when questioned about marriage to Shadow Dancer. Though she herself was still unwed, she did have a young man that she cared about, and she was not entirely lost to the strange feelings that stole over her while she was in the presence of Soaring Hawk, the handsome warrior who was courting her.

Iva was more than a little surprised by the girl's words, and for a few seconds she silently wondered if Tanza had somehow guessed at her earlier feelings. "You mean to tell me that you can go to this house of pleasure and watch what goes on between the men and women?" she at last got out. Then, for some strange reason, her breath held as she awaited Tanza's reply.

"This is not a good idea! We should not be talking about this house of pleasure! What would Shadow

138

Dancer say?" Nokie could well imagine the anger of her cousin if he ever found out his intended had visited such a place as the house of pleasure!

"He will never have to know!" Tanza seemed rather intent on taking Iva to this house of pleasure. Turning her gaze back to her, she stated, "There is a long corridor which runs the length of the entire house. It's purpose is to allow viewers to watch unnoticed through viewing holes made in the walls."

Iva was not sure that she wanted any part in what seemed to be a sordid affair. She thought it rather reprehensible to participate in such voyeurism!

Watching her very closely, Tanza easily read her feelings. "I know it sounds rather unsavory, watching others through a viewing hole. I, too, felt this same way, until I went with some friends one night. It is really rather enlightening for young women such as we to know fully, without having to experience the actual act, what to expect when we take a warrior as our mate."

Iva slowly turned the other girl's words over in her mind. It was certainly true that she knew very little except what her mother had told her, and remembering those feelings she experienced every time she was in Shadow Dancer's arms, she knew that her mother had left much out of the telling. What could it hurt? she asked herself. "Will we not be recognized if we go to this house?" She was thinking of Shadow Dancer's reaction if he were to find out that she had gone to this place known as the house of pleasure. Since his cousin was worried about his reaction, she certainly should be.

Tanza eagerly announced that she would bring three masks to hide their faces. "No one will be able to recognize us, don't worry! We will meet shortly after dark outside of Shadow Dancer's house." The adventuresome young woman quickly began to make plans for their secret outing.

At first Nokie thought to refuse to go along, but

looking at Iva, she quickly realized how easily Tanza could talk the girl into trouble. I had best go, she reasoned, to ensure that all goes well. Slowly she nodded her dark head, though her features were grim. She would have to pray throughout the rest of the day to the moon goddess, Coyolxauhqui, to seek her protection for this evening's event!

"What kind of women participate at this house of pleasure, Tanza?" Iva whispered softly as the three young women made their way through the dark streets of the village. The afternoon through she had worried about what she would see taking place at this house of pleasure when they arrived. Several times she had told herself that when the hour came for her to meet Tanza and Nokie, she would tell them that she had changed her mind, but when Shadow Dancer had left shortly after dinner to go to the meeting of the high council, Iva had quickly changed her tunic and had awaited the moment when she would meet her two friends. The temptation of having many of her questions answered, those concerning the feelings that stole over her when she was in Shadow Dancer's presence, was just too great!

"There is a law in our valley which forbids adultery, with a penalty of death. It is those whose husbands have been killed while out hunting or raiding, or whose life mates have been carried to the star path by some other means, who usually use the services of the house of pleasure. And there are also those maidens who do not wish to join themselves with a warrior—for their own reasons—who find themselves seeking out the warriors at the house of pleasure." Tanza appeared to be a wealth of information about this subject.

"Are you sure no one will recognize us?" Iva could not help worrying, and her hand automatically went up to make sure that her golden hair was covered by the dark hood attached to the cloak Tanza had brought for her use. Being out at this time of the evening with Tanza and Nokie would certainly be hard to explain to Shadow Dancer, she thought as Tanza led them down one more dark street and then, nearing the very outskirts of the village, turned onto a side path which wound around the back portion of a large house.

"This is it! Just keep your hair covered and do not take off your mask for any reason and no one will ever be the wiser about your identity." Tanza grinned as they reached a back door, and before opening it, she covered her own smiling face with a brightly colored mask that portrayed a feathered parrot. The other two girls quickly followed suit, Iva's mask that of an ocelot—sparkling, bejeweled, and cotton-quilted— and Nokie's that of a brightly feathered peacock. As the girls made themselves ready, it was Tanza who pulled the door wide and took the first step into the back foyer.

Standing nervously with the other women, Iva swallowed the knot in her throat as an Indian boy in his late teens approached them. It was Tanza who once more took charge. Whispering something to the boy, she placed some trinkets in his palm.

Silently the youth, who himself had two more years before he could participate in the sexual activities of the house of pleasure, turned and began to lead the three young women through a low, framed doorway that opened into a long, narrow corridor. This passage appeared to run the length of the entire building. Small, dish-shaped braziers set in alcoves against the walls provided dim, yellowish lighting, and as Tanza took both of her companions by the hand and began to lead them down the passageway, the boy silently disappeared.

The coolness in the narrow hallway caused a shiver to run through Iva, and she drew the mantle more closely about her. The light given off from each brazier reflected against the opposite wall and Iva soon found

141

that at each small area provided with light there was a small viewing hole that enabled those in the outer hallway to be privy to the activity going on in the small chambers alongside the passageway.

"The first time I came here with my friends, there were several other women in the corridor. We are lucky that we are alone tonight." Tanza said softly as she drew the pair to the end of the passageway. She then put her eye up to the peephole that had been bored in the wall long ago.

As she watched Tanza looking through the viewing hole, the full magnitude of what they were doing settled upon Iva. *I should not be here doing this! This whole affair is insane!* She should take Nokie by the arm and get as far away from this house as she could, she decided. Then that rebellious side of her took over. *Silly girl, what can it hurt to take a look since you are already here? You can't deny that you truly want to!*

Nokie hung back against the outer wall of the hallway, not possessed with the curiosity that overwhelms most young women. As though lacking a will of her own, Iva slowly took the steps that brought her up against the opposite wall of the corridor, and stood facing one of the viewing holes. Drawing a deep, tentative breath, she placed her face at an angle so, with one eye, she could easily glimpse what was taking place beyond the passageway wall.

Iva softly exhaled as she stood rooted, taking in the sleek, muscular, naked form of a young man of medium height as he erotically began to undress a middle-aged woman who wore, over the upper portion of her face, a feathered half-mask. Her long hair hung in black silken rivulets down her back, and it was all that now covered her abundantly proportioned curves when the man set her tunic and skirt aside.

A catlike smile came over the woman's lips, and drew Iva's attention, just before the woman reached out for the bronzed dark-haired adonis. Though the man was

142

not tall, he was of a powerful size, and Iva's face flamed beneath her mask as her eyes traveled over his full length. His hands traveled over the woman's entire body, his knowledgeable touch eliciting carnal moans from her. As she threw her head back, the man's mouth sought out her full, ripened breasts and suckled them hungrily.

At that moment Iva knew that what she was doing was wrong, but she could not pull herself away from the viewing hole. She stood, mesmerized by the lust-filled sight before her, watching the man's mouth and hands slowly travel over the woman's ribs and belly and then settle between her legs. It was not so much the actions of the man that held Iva's full attention as it was the raw, sensual delight of his partner, who entwined slim hands in the long strands of her lover's dark hair and forced him ever closer to her woman's jewel, her limbs visibly trembling with passion as the man appeared to overwhelm her with the skill of his sexual assault.

No sounds could be heard in the outside corridor from the chambers within, but Iva knew that the woman must have cried out for her mouth had opened as her body had begun to undulate in spasms of heated passion. With the slow relaxing of her body, the man lifted her in his arms and carried her to the large sleeping couch arranged in the middle of the chamber.

Taken by surprise, Iva watched the woman push against the Indian man's chest, and after he complied by lying down upon the soft bed, the woman lowered her lush form atop him, then boldly reached out and wrapped her slender hand around the fullness of his throbbing man-root. Guiding it toward the desired haven, the woman lowered herself full upon him. Impaled as though a wild thing, she rode her lover as though he were an unbroken stallion.

Iva heard the soft moan of pent-up, unfulfilled desire that escaped her own lips as she forced herself away from the viewing hole. Her body sagged against the wall of the corridor, and her breathing came in short, ragged breaths. So this was what the act of lovemaking entailed! All those rampant feelings that had been so elusive and at the same time seductive while she had been in Shadow Dancer's arms were but the prelude to these wanton, lustful actions she had just witnessed. At last she regained some control over her ragged breathing, and slowly strength began to return to wobbly knees. Opening her eyes, Iva saw Nokie standing where she had been earlier and watching her intently.

"Remember where you are, Moon Flower. These are not the ways of those in love." The dark eyes that stared out of the peacock mask appeared centuries old and full of unquestionable knowledge as they held upon Iva. "Perhaps we should go now."

At that moment the only thing Iva was able to do was nod her head in agreement.

"It is getting late, Tanza." Nokie spoke to the other girl softly but firmly as she stepped to her side. "We should get Moon Flower back before Shadow Dancer returns and finds her missing from his home. My cousin would not take kindly to our having brought her to this house." Nokie's voice held censure of their evening's visit, and when Tanza kept her eye against the viewing hole, she shook her head at her friend. Nokie had only agreed to accompany them in order to watch out for her cousin's woman, and now that Moon Flower had seen what they had come for, it was time for the three of them to leave.

Tanza tried to shake off her friend's hand as Nokie took her by the forearm. She was loath to abandon her view of the handsome warrior and the Indian woman in an entanglement of arms and legs upon a sleeping couch.

From the moment she had pressed her eye to the viewing hole, Tanza had been unable to look away

144

from the sensual scene being enacted within the chamber. As the woman had lain upon the sleeping couch, the warrior had bent over her, massaging her body and limbs with a heated oil which he had poured into a clay bowl set at the side of the sleeping couch. His strong fingers had roamed enticingly over her body, leaving a dampened path of glistening ointment over darkened skin.

The heated oil held aphrodisiac powers and had left the woman writhing upon the sleeping couch as the brave set the clay bowl aside. The slightest brush of the man's fingers across her body now had her pressing herself against him in an undulating manner that made clear exactly what her need was.

Titillation was this warrior's greatest pursuit. Ignoring the maneuvers of the shapely woman, who tried to capture his hand and force it to her breast while her lower body pressed hungrily against his muscular thigh, the brave took up from the side table a delicate feather which had been taken from a young eagle. With much skill the man seductively let the feather wander over the woman's body, its soft caressing of the tips of her breasts and the tender insides of her thighs bringing to life a steaming desire in her.

The woman was blinded by her wanton passion! Head thrown back against the soft furs, she reached out demandingly, seeking something to quench the fierce, flooding desires that raged throughout her body. Finally, her own hands cupped her breasts and rubbed the aching, rosy tips, her body bucking, twisting, and turning as she searched for fulfillment.

At last the warrior appeared to take pity on her. As if in a single motion he allowed the feather to fall next to the sleeping couch, discarded his breechcloth, and mounted the woman.

From where Tanza stood she could glimpse the full length of the brave's manhood, as, with a single thrust, he entered the woman, her legs immediately wrapping about his hips and drawing him more fully into her aching depths.

It was at this moment that Nokie tried to pull her friend away from the viewing hole and, with determined tugs on Tanza's arm, finally got the young woman's attention. "Tanza, Moon Flower and I are leaving!"

The high-spirited girl was not all that happy to be pulled away at that moment, but after taking a few deep breaths of air to clear her senses, she followed along as Nokie led her and Iva down the long, cool corridor, and out of the house of pleasure.

The night air instantly revived all of them, and without a second thought Tanza began to relate in vivid detail all that she had witnessed. When she told them of the heated oil, her eyes sought out Nokie's face in the moonlight, and without any guilty thoughts, she asked, "Do you think you could make up some of that oil? I would love to try something like that out on Soaring Hawk. That is, of course, after we are joined," she hurriedly amended.

Absently Nokie nodded her head. She had been taught long ago at the temple of the high priest to make potions and healing medicines. The oil Tanza spoke of was one that, when heated made the skin ultra-sensitive, and if placed on the body in areas of great sexual awareness, it increased stimulation of sexual desire.

As the young woman talked on without pause, Iva reviewed in her own mind what she had seen as she had pressed her eye to the viewing hole. The image of the woman's naked body climbing atop the Indian man's, of her being impaled upon his manhood, left her clutching her hands tightly beneath her dark cloak. The woman certainly appeared to find great pleasure in this action, Iva thought, and immediately a raw ache began to grow deep within the lower portion of her own body.

*   *   *

Not wishing to be faced by Shadow Dancer and to be forced to hide her nervousness over her actions of the evening, as soon as Nokie and Tanza saw her off at Shadow Dancer's house, Iva hurriedly went straight to her bedchamber. Without lingering, she quickly shed her clothes, and after a few quick strokes through her hair with a comb, she climbed beneath the soft coverings of her sleeping couch.

Lying naked beneath the coverings, Iva felt her body was aflame when her skin came into contact with the sheer, wispy material. She felt the prickling sensation of each nerve ending as her breasts strained, the tender, pink buds heady with feelings which rippled heatedly over her entire length. Moaning aloud, she rolled over and pulled the coverings over her head, trying to force erotic images of the warrior and the woman with the half-mask out of her mind, at the same time trying to quell the sensual needs raging through her.

"I knew good and well that I should never have gone to that damned house!" she cried out softly. Now, instead of feeling satisfied with the knowledge of what would happen between her and Shadow Dancer, her body ached from some secret wanting! Only it was no longer a secret!

Chapter Twelve

The interior of Iva's bedchamber seemed filled to capacity with women of every size and shape, so many they threatened to spill out the doorway and into the hall and courtyard beyond. Everyone seemed to be talking at once, turning Iva this way and that. One woman rubbed her body with a scented oil while another brushed out her long, golden curls. Still another helped to entwine separate strands into plump, full braids, which were pinned atop her head before the entire mass was captured within a finely spun, silver-threaded snood.

Standing in the center of the chamber, her hair already arranged and a thin, cool wrap knotted above her breasts, covering her body, Iva was the center of attention, as she had been for most of the after-noon.

She was to become the bride of one of their most highly regarded warriors, and it appeared that not a woman of the village would miss out on contributing to her toilet for this special occasion. Earlier Iva had been ushered by the younger women of the tribe to the stream that ran through the back of Shadow Dancer's pastures. Despite her protests they had laughingly washed every inch of her body with a creamy, exotically scented soap. Nokie and Tanza had both helped to wash her hair, and smiling, they had brushed her hands away as she had tried to halt their ministrations and to let them know that she could wash herself.

"This is the way of our people." Nokie smiled. "Years past our princesses were bathed by their women in this manner daily."

"But I am not a princess!" Iva tried to object, feeling ill at ease with the attention she was receiving.

"You will be a princess as soon as you are joined with Shadow Dancer!" Nokie answered, and amidst giggles, the young women drew her from the stream and, wrapping her in the piece of cloth they had brought for the occasion, hurriedly led her back to her chamber, where the elder women of the tribe awaited.

As though in a daze, Iva no longer attempted to push away the hands that came at her. Those women who were too old to join in with the ones encircling her sat on pallets on the tile floor and directed the younger women in how best to make Shadow Dancer's future bride more beautiful.

A few of the women brought out small gourds of paint and, as one, began to paint Iva's toenails and fingernails. One woman bent down and, at the small indenture above Iva's right ankle, deftly painted a colorful plumed serpent-bird. Her face was not painted with the yellow ocher paint or the designs with which these women adorned themselves on a daily basis, but the woman who applied the facial makeup traced a line of deep purple above each of Iva's eyelids and with an indigo stick accented the bottom lids, these touches enhancing her deep blue eyes. A fragile, jade and blue, winged hummingbird was artistically painted on the creamy flesh of Iva's right breast. Then the knot holding her covering was undone, and the material fell to the floor.

Iva's hands were brushed aside as she made a futile attempt to retrieve the covering. Amidst the giggles of the old women and the grins of the younger attendants, Iva was then turned this way and that as her naked body was adorned for her wedding night.

Aquilla laid out a tray of jewelry that included a finely linked gold chain to which a diamond-shaped polished stone the color of fired amber was appended. This chain was placed around Iva's waist, the stone settling provocatively over the indent of her navel. A delicately fashioned collar of gold was placed around her throat, and with fragile grace it lay against her collarbone. Silver bracelets fashioned in the design of golden, plumed serpents with jade eyes were placed upon both of Iva's forearms.

Following the jewelry, a glistening white tunic, cut low at the top so it descended toward the valley of her breasts, was carefully settled over her torso. Hanging down over her thighs, it covered much of the matching skirt the women next put on her. Gold thread had been used in the embroidery of both tunic and skirt, and as a finely spun golden mantle was placed over Iva's shoulders, all of the women stood silent, each studying the woman standing before them.

"It is true that she is favored much like Sharaza!" The old woman looked intently upon Iva and spoke aloud to a companion sitting next to her.

The other ancient eagerly nodded her head. "Shadow Dancer spoke before the council and told all who would listen that Moon Flower was his destiny. Predestined from that day that Sharaza and Wind Cryer set eyes on one another. He spoke loudly that night before the council fire of her golden beauty and of how he had been led to her father's horse farm by the gods." The old woman's words were spoken as if in awe of the powerful evidence of Shadow Dancer's words. All in this village had grown up hearing stories of Sharaza and Wind Cryer, and with the help of the many statues in the village, each woman present knew exactly what their ancient princess had looked like.

Now, as all eyes beheld Iva, none could say that Shadow Dancer had been misled. The woman dressed in white and gold, standing in the center of the chamber, seemed exactly as they imagined Sharaza had been when she had stood before her attendants on her wedding day.

"There must be a powerful reason for the gods to bring her back amongst us," another whispered softly.

Iva heard some of what the women were saying, and believing it to be no more than nonsense, she opened her mouth to set them straight. Her being here had nothing to do with their ancient princess. She was going to marry Shadow Dancer for reasons of her own. But with this thought, another swiftly followed and her lips slowly drew together, for at this moment her reasons for marrying Shadow Dancer had somehow fled her. Exactly why was she going to marry this man she knew so little about? Was the mindless ecstasy she knew while in his arms enough to see them through a lifetime together?

A frown marring her features, Nokie stepped to Iva's side before she could dwell further upon her inner thoughts, and softly said, "You are very beautiful, Moon Flower. My cousin is a very lucky man indeed. I have brought you this." She held out her hand, and in it, wrapped in a soft piece of hide, was a necklace. Upon the small round disk centered on its silver chain was the hand-painted scene of a golden-haired woman and a dark-haired warrior standing hand in hand, at their knees a small child.

"This is beautiful, Nokie, I will treasure it always." Iva's words barely carried over the other women's talk. She was still feeling somewhat confused, and could not tell if the man and woman on the necklace were supposed to be her and Shadow Dancer or if they depicted Sharaza and Wind Cryer.

"The necklace is not exactly for you, Moon Flower." Nokie appeared embarrassed by the mistake. "It is the

151

custom of my people that a couple exchange bridal gifts during the hours of their first night together. I did not expect that you would know of our ways, so I decided to bring this gift for you to give your husband. I painted the scene myself with much love for you and my cousin."

Even as Iva was touched once again by Nokie's kind nature, her use of the word husband brought home the seriousness of the event that was to take place. Kissing the other woman's cheek, Iva murmured, "Then this gift shall be doubly treasured."

As though anxious to have their handiwork beheld by the rest of the village, the women in the chamber encircled Iva. Holding up the back portion of her mantle as though it were a wedding train, they ushered her out of the chamber and through the front door and into the street.

At an almost breathless pace she was led toward the center of the village, and amidst the laughter and shouts of villagers who were standing around, she was brought into the central communal building. This large, circular structure was as lavishly designed as Shadow Dancer's own house. The walls of bleached masonry were extravagantly painted in frescoes, depicting a multitude of scenes relating the history of these people, starting from their arrival in this valley. The flooring was tile, and in the center of the building a large, shallow circle had been set into the floor. In this pit a fire had been built, and it was to this the women now led Iva.

She had been told that this communal building was used for those special occasions when all the villagers came together. It was also the place where the council of elders met and where the council of chiefs planned for the protection and survival of the village. This evening the building would house all those of the village who would turn out to attend their high war chief's marriage.

Now Iva was left alone as the women joined their families and friends. Nervously she watched as the villagers, in a colorful procession, began to fill the building. To the people of this hidden tribe, Shadow Dancer was nobility, and great feather headdresses and the finest, most colorfully embroidered blankets and tunics were worn in his honor. Over the pandemonium Iva heard the noises made by bone whistles, rattles, bells, and drums. The high notes of a flute mixed with the other sounds and added to the confusion.

She stood alone before the burning fire like a virgin sacrifice of some primeval day. The deep beat of a drum seemed to pulsate in her head and to throb with her heartbeat, tinging her growing anxiousness with full-fledged fear. How ever had she come to this state? Dressed in queenly array of silver and gold, she awaited a man she knew little about, but he would soon become her husband. She turned and looked at the strange people around her. True, there were the faces of those that had befriended her over the past weeks, but even they appeared unfamiliar at this moment. I have been swept along on a tide of unreality, she told herself as she wondered how she had ever agreed to this whole affair.

As her eyes touched and held upon the intimidating visage of Gray Otter, who was standing next to Nokie, Iva noticed an insulting gleam in his beady, black eyes as they roamed at will over her body. I have to get out of here, she told herself. I have to escape! She could not go through with this marriage. She could not allow herself to become like these people. She could not stay in this same village with this man who was chief, yet who glared his hatred at her without troubling to conceal it.

Turning away from Gray Otter's glare, Iva glimpsed Tanza standing close to another woman and smiling and conversing as though everything were quite normal. The beating of the drum was vibrating now, and

Iva felt as though she were suffocating. Faces, painted brightly and grinning with expectation, swam before her, and in that moment she felt herself swaying! She had to find her way out of this building! She had to get some air. Had to clear her head!

Swinging toward the direction from which she had been led into the building, Iva would have run toward the doorway with but one thought on her mind—escape—but as she took a step, her attempt was halted. The drumbeat intensified as the music from the rattles, the bone whistles, and the flute sharpened, and then a large, masked man came through the doorway, followed closely by a procession of masked attendants. The leader stood out above his escorts, not only his height and breadth of shoulder drawing every eye within the communal lodge, but his richly appointed costume as well.

Iva's blue eyes sought out his identity as she looked upon the mask designed in the form of a serpent inlaid with turquoise, a band of quetzal feathers and golden earrings hanging down each side. A golden vest decorated with quetzal feathers adorned this man's broad chest, and a collar of precious stones, a gold disk suspended from its center, hung around his neck. His cloak, with bright red borders around the shoulders, fell over his thick, powerful thighs. It was adorned with jade and obsidian stones, and trailed little golden bells. In his right hand he clutched a shield ornamented with gold and mother of pearl, its outer border fringed with silver and a pendant of quetzal feathers residing in its center.

Iva was riveted to the spot, so forcefully was she held in place by the jet eyes staring out from behind the mask. She felt encased, surrounded by that gaze, as though only she and this masked giant who was silently approaching existed.

Her heart slamming violently against the wall of her chest, Iva watched the villagers part before this newcomer and his colorful procession. She could not break free of those deep ebony eyes, their caress almost a viable thing.

As he stood directly before her, Iva's knees buckled and she had to will herself to stand upright. When his hands rose, she flinched, so caught up in the savage pageantry of the moment, she almost believed him to be some dark, ancient Aztec god who had come out of nowhere to claim her life as a sacrificial offering. A gasp escaped Iva as he lowered the serpent mask and handed it to one of his attendants.

As was the ancient custom of the villagers during the marriage ceremony of royalty, with the mask lowered, a high-pitched chattering filled the building and the noise of the whistles and flutes increased.

Iva was not aware of this, for the flaming glow within Shadow Dancer's eyes held her ensnared. In those few moments as he stood before her, neither saying a word, she was totally lost to love. The power he now exerted was not equaled by anything she had ever felt before. He consumed her with his regard, held captive the very beating of her heart. All thoughts of escaping this man fled before the potent storm of his presence. He was the reason why she was here before these villagers. The overpowering feelings raging within her were reason enough to join herself with this man.

As the chattering and the music slowly abated, Shadow Dancer placed himself at Iva's side. The long line of male attendants silently disappeared into the crowd, except for two. These, Iva noticed, wore identical masks, each made to represent an eagle, wisps of white feathers arranged on the outer edges. One after the other these two lowered their masks and threw them into the burning flames in the central fire before taking their places in front of the couple.

Iva had been told some of what would take place. Though she had not been informed about the manner in which the groom would gain her side, she had been instructed that the high priest, Atlacol, and the tribe's

155

shaman, Cloud Walker, would perform the ceremony which would join her to Shadow Dancer. She assumed these were the two men standing before her. The high priest Atlacol was dressed in a long black tunic that touched his ankles. His hair, mostly gray, hung matted and unwashed around his shoulders and down his back. As his piercing, black, fanatical eyes touched hers, Iva had to suppress the shudder that threatened to course through her. The light from the fire allowed her to glimpse a reddish tint to Atlacol's hair as he turned away from her, and noticing that his earlobes had been lacerated, she realized that the redness was blood. She would learn later that Aztec high priests often shred their earlobes in a form of penitence. In contrast, Cloud Walker's kindly dark eyes looked to Iva out of a weathered and wrinkled countenance, helping to quell her fear, as the old shaman reached out and lightly touched first her forearm and then Shadow Dancer's.

Sensing some of her distress, Shadow Dancer placed one arm around her back, his reassuring strength helping Iva to stand silent and watchful before the high priest and the shaman.

It was Cloud Walker who began the rites by dipping his gnarled hand into the small leather bag tied at his waist and withdrawing a powdery substance, then throwing this into the fire, evoking rising amber flames which spiraled wafts of incense throughout. This done, the old Indian drew forth a gourd which had been fashioned into a rattle, and turning slowly toward the four directions of mother earth, he called aloud for the blessings of the great spirit over this union as he shook the gourd over his head. When at last he faced Shadow Dancer and Iva again, his gaze encompassed them both in a timeless vision of past and future.

Then Atlacol, the high priest, drew a portion of Shadow Dancer's colorful blanket around Iva's shoulders and in the ancient Aztec custom proclaimed the pair joined together from this day forth.

Again the chattering of the villagers rose, and rattles, whistles, bells, and flutes filled the chamber with sound.

Iva looked around at the many faces staring at her, in a daze, her glance going back to Shadow Dancer and his warm smile that told her the ceremony was finished. "Is it over?" She had always imagined that when she married the event would be a monumental experience. Where were the words of love and faithfulness, the "I do's" repeated to one another? She should feel giddy over the fact that this was her wedding day and the man standing at her side was now her husband, but she felt only a vast emptiness.

Drawing Iva to his side, Shadow Dancer whispered against her smooth cheek, "You are mine throughout this life and all eternity."

She felt something at hearing these words. She could not deny it! Her heart began to beat at a swifter pace, even as a trembling overcame her limbs. The ceremony, performed so strangely by priest and shaman, had joined her in marriage to this man, and the night before her was her wedding night!

Wrapping his arm around her waist, the colorful blanket still held around both of them, Shadow Dancer swept Iva along toward the door of the lodge as the villagers followed. Shouts and songs and music filled the newlywed's ears until the moment Shadow Dancer shut the door of his house on all intrusions.

Silently Iva stood at his side, overwhelmed by the events that had taken place in the past few hours. She was now a married woman according to the tradition of these mountain Indians, and she was standing in her husband's house—without a clue as to what she should do next.

With a soft sigh, Shadow Dancer turned away from the closed door and toward his bride. She appears to be overcome by the happenings of the evening, he thought as her crystal gaze rose to meet his. There was a sense of fear and disorientation about her which was not lost to his thoughtful appraisal. "When I entered the communal lodge, Moon Flower, and my eyes beheld you standing all alone before the center fire, I felt the very breath leave my body at your beauty. I am an honored man that you have pledged yourself to travel down my life path with me." His words came out on a soft breath as the braziers burning brightly against the wall allowed him to feast his gaze upon her loveliness.

Iva blushed and nervously took a step away from him. Now that the deed of their wedding was accomplished, she knew there was no need to hold back the feelings that Shadow Dancer had denied them full exploration of in the past. And unbidden images of the man and the woman in the house of pleasure stole into her mind.

"Come, Moon Flower." He held out his hand in her direction, and when she did not take it a slight frown marred his brow as he pondered this. Did she so quickly regret that she had joined herself to him? Was this some joke of the gods? To bring him so close to his heart's desire and then force him to watch from afar without allowing him to sample fully the depths of his longing? "Aquilla has left us a meal in the gardens," he murmured absently, ensnared within his dark thoughts.

Iva felt she had been given a reprieve when he spoke of the meal. She tried to forget her visit to the pleasure house and all the images that night still evoked. Of course Shadow Dancer would give her time to adjust to the fact that they were now wed. A tentative smile nervously replaced the fear Shadow Dancer had noted, and she reached out and took the hand he offered.

This gesture eased Shadow Dancer's mind somewhat. Though he would have wished for a warmer reception from the woman who had just become his bride, he reminded himself that she was an innocent. This was no trick of the gods. He would have to take each step very carefully in order not to frighten her. A generous smile settled on his lips and he realized that he had all the time in the world in which to gain her full trust. His heart was light and full of love as he led her through the courtyard and out into the gardens. Settling her on the stone bench, Shadow Dancer excused himself in order to get the wedding dinner Aquilla had prepared for them.

In a nervous manner Iva rubbed the soft material of her tunic, her fingers outlining the gold thread that decorated her wedding dress. Her parents would certainly be surprised if they could see her now! With this thought, tears filled her eyes. She had always imagined herself marrying within a church, her father standing next to her and giving her over to the man of her choice, her mother watching tearily as her only daughter was placed into the care of another. Surprised? More than likely they would have been shocked if they had seen her standing before a fire in the center of a communal lodge as an Aztec high priest and an Apache shaman performed the marriage rites for her and a high war chief.

The Cassidy farmhouse was silent at this time of the evening. The animals, as well as those within, had already settled down for the night. The only telltale sign of life was the oil lamp burning dimly on the kitchen table. The sound of a horse coming down the drive brought both Katherine Cassidy and Delbert Benell out of their beds.

"Is it Bain?" Katherine breathlessly questioned as she clutched her robe about her breasts and looked anxiously toward Delbert who stood at the kitchen door, holding the old rifle and peering out into the dark night.

For the past month Delbert had been queried in this same anxious tone each time the farm received a visitor. He prayed that whoever was riding slowly up to the house was indeed Bain and his daughter and not attacking Indians. The strain of Iva's abduction had about run full course, and he feared that he would not be able to take much more of not knowing before he would have to set out in search for her himself. He had not already done so because of his loyalty to Bain and because he did not want to leave Katherine on the farm by herself.

As the rider dismounted and started up the steps of the back porch, Delbert's face became more animated than it had been since Iva's abduction. "It's him!" the young man shouted over his shoulder. "He's at last come home!" He did not allow himself to look beyond the tall form of Bain Cassidy as the older man stepped through the doorway.

Bain looked gaunt and haggard as he dropped his saddlebags onto the kitchen floor and, running a hand through his hair, sat down upon one of the wooden kitchen chairs. His blue eyes held a hollowness as they rose to take in his wife, who was standing near the sink.

"You didn't find her?" Katherine had to ask. The question was uppermost in all of their minds, and Bain had dreaded answering it since he had started the long trek back to the farm.

"It's as though she has vanished from the face of the earth. We picked up sign of the Indian's ponies the first day out and followed it without rest for two days. After that the sign became harder and harder to pick out until at last it was impossible to spot." The horror Bain saw on his wife's face was what he had been feeling himself for the past month. "I'll not give up, Katherine. I only came home to get fresh horses and some food. The men who went with me had to return to their homes. I can't be expecting them to give any more of their time."

Katherine Cassidy's tears had long since dried up. She could not cry, she could only keep herself busy and

160

try to keep her mind off the torments she imagined her only child was enduring, if indeed Iva was still alive.

"I'll leave in the morning and try to pick up the trail we were following. Those damn Injuns couldn't have just disappeared! We had to have missed something!" Bain tossed the headband with the sun sign on the table, miserable. "I can't call it quits!"

Katherine knew her husband well enough to be certain that he would never give up the search for their daughter. How could he, when Iva was all that they had? "I'll fix you something to eat," she offered in a subdued tone.

"It can wait till morning. All I want now is our bed." Bain rose to his feet and, with Katherine at his side, left the kitchen.

Delbert remained, standing by the door. He had heard everything Bain had said. There had been no sign of the Indians or Iva! His heart hammered in his chest as he dashed a tear from his cheek with the back of his fist. He had not allowed himself to give in to the awful defeat he had felt over the past month because he knew that he had to be strong for Katherine, but the bad news Bain had brought home was too much for the young man.

Going to the table, through a blur of tears, he glimpsed the leather headband. Picking it up, he ran his fingers over the gold and silver. Then he shoved the headband inside his shirt. Filling a flour sack with a few provisions and taking up Bain's old rifle, he silently left the Cassidy house. He would find Iva himself, or die trying.

Chapter Thirteen

Iva was deep in thought when Shadow Dancer returned to her with their wedding dinner. For a few lingering moments, he stood off to the side of the courtyard, several feet away from the bench, and feasted his gaze upon her rare beauty. The oil torches in the garden permitted him to view his bride, and their light reflected off the gold and silver of her wedding outfit. The silver snood capturing her golden curls sparkled like twinkling stars, enhancing the creamy smoothness of her soft skin, and the golden mantle around her shoulders held her within its shimmering sphere. Shadow Dancer's heart ached with adoration and he felt himself to be the most honored of men! At this moment even the gods must be looking down upon him with envy!

He must have made some small noise, perhaps an indrawn breath, for Iva's heart-shaped face turned in his direction and her fathomless blue eyes held and locked with his sable depths. There was a timeless quality to this glance. All of the unspoken words of the heart were carried upon the burning current that ran between them, and fear of the unknown vanished before this onslaught of emotions. A deep yearning of the senses replaced the distance the events of the evening had put between the couple. Shadow Dancer silently stepped before her, set the food he carried aside, and took her hands in his.

"My entire life has led me to this moment, Moon Flower. You are the beginning and the ending of my life circle; the completion of my soul. I give unto you my most treasured possession, my gift to you on our becoming as one on the path that this life will lead us down." He held out a soft blue piece of cloth.

The tears that sparkled within the depths of her topaz eyes were not prompted by fear of what tomorrow would bring as this man's wife or by a longing for family and friends. They arose from the fullness welling in her heart. There could never be another for her but Shadow Dancer. If she returned to her family, she knew that she would never again know a day's happiness. She had changed since that afternoon when she had been captured in the forest near her father's farm. Shadow Dancer had changed her, and she could never return to yesterdays. Carefully she drew back the cloth to glimpse the gift he held. Lying upon the soft blue material was an exquisite crystal tube containing a blue hummingbird feather linked to a gold chain which fashioned it into a necklace of incredible beauty.

Reaching across her, Shadow Dancer brushed away a tear as it caressed her cheek. "This necklace was one that Montezuma himself wore. He bestowed it upon his granddaughter Sharaza at her birth. It has been handed down throughout the generations, but has rarely been worn. I give it to you now as my gift of love, for I treasure you above all things."

She could not stop the tears that came as she looked upon the priceless necklace and knew that it had been given to her out of love.

"Are these tears of regret, Moon Flower?" Shadow Dancer's heart stilled within his chest as he waited her answer. His earlier fear that the gods were playing some great trick upon him made its way back into his mind when she did not speak but sat weeping over the gift she held in her hand.

Slowly Iva shook her head in denial. "Never regret, Shadow Dancer," she softly replied. "These tears are for the happiness that fills my heart."

This was all he needed to be told. Within seconds he was sitting upon the stone bench and holding Iva tightly against his chest. "You cannot imagine the fear that filled me when I thought you had found that you had made a mistake by joining yourself with me." His embrace tightened as he whispered the words against the side of her forehead.

"I am sorry you thought this. It is only that everything seemed to be happening so quickly. Are you sure that we are truly married?" She was still uncertain the ceremony that had taken place in the communal lodge was truly a wedding. She had always believed a wedding took place in a church before God.

Shadow Dancer looked deeply into her eyes, hoping once and for all to ease her troubled mind. "Our joining ceremony was as real as the white man's in the house of his God. The Apache believe in the great spirit, the Aztecs have their gods. Our joining together was performed before the God of your people as well as the gods of my own people. You are mine, Moon Flower, have no doubt."

As Iva listened to him her doubt about the validity of their marriage slowly began to dissipate. Surely, she decided, the one true God she had been taught to worship had been witness to their joining. For the first time she really believed that the man holding her was her husband. A smile slowly settled over her lips. "I have a gift for you." Without waiting for his comment, she quickly left the gardens to retrieve the necklace that Nokie had given her.

Shadow Dancer gave her a tender smile when she placed the piece of soft hide in his hand. As her blue eyes sparkled with delight, he opened the fold and revealed the necklace. Holding it to the light, he studied the picture of the woman, the warrior, and the small child standing at their side. "The child is a little girl," he softly stated.

Iva had not noticed this earlier. "I am afraid I did not know your custom of exchanging gifts on the wedding night, but Nokie gave this to me to give to you."

"It has been touched then by the spirit world," he said appreciatively.

"Do you think the couple are Sharaza and Wind Cryer?" Iva did not understand what he'd meant when he'd spoken of the spirit world, but she had been curious about the couple painted on the smooth round disk.

Almost in reverence Shadow Dancer traced a tan finger over the beautiful figures, outlining the little girl; then eyes of deepest jet rose up to Iva's sparkling blue. "They are us, Moon Flower."

Held by the possession in his warm eyes, Iva could say nothing.

"You are my soul mate!" Shadow Dancer whispered as his head bent toward her and his lips caught hers in a spellbinding promise.

Iva's lips parted as she felt the slight pressure of his searching tongue, her mouth welcoming the warm intrusion, and slipping her slender arms around his neck, she pressed herself fully against him.

For a time the pair were lost in the sheer taste of one another. Their kiss grew deeper and their passions heightened. Shadow Dancer enfolded her in his embrace as though she were the rarest of gems. And she was the total culmination of all his desires. He had waited his entire life for this moment. Lightly he caressed the slim column of her soft throat with his index finger. The fact that she now belonged to him seemed to temper the urgency he had felt in the past while holding her in his arms. Now he wished only to take his time and show her the rare delights they had been unable to fully explore in the past.

As his warm, moist tongue sought out each hidden crevice of her mouth and his finger covered the pulsebeat of her throat, Iva gave herself up to the raw ache of desire.

It was Shadow Dancer who broke the embrace. With a loving smile, he brought his finger up and tenderly drew it across her smooth cheek. "We have both waited long for this moment when we can claim the right to share our deep feelings. I admit that my desire for you is great, Moon Flower. I would not wish this night to be passed in haste. Let us go to my chambers." The words were spoken rather breathlessly against her ear.

Though a shiver brought on by nervous anticipation coursed through Iva, and bold images from the house of pleasure flashed in her mind, she could not speak. Shadow Dancer drew her to her feet, grasped their bridal gifts in one hand, entwined the fingers of the other in hers, and led her out of the gardens and courtyard, down the long hallway, and through the door that led into his chambers.

Iva stood silently in the center of the room as Shadow Dancer lit the two braziers resting on stands near the sleeping alcove. Nervously she glanced around the chamber, noticing that it was quite a bit larger than her own and, though much more lavish with darkly appointed accents, that it had a masculine feel.

With a sigh Shadow Dancer drew the blanket from his shoulders and removed the golden vest. As he began to unlatch the golden collar around his neck, his warm, sable eyes held upon Iva who stood in the center of the chamber. Her winsome look stoked his pent-up desire, and slowly he made his way to her, reaching out and unclasping the golden link of her cloak, and allowing the garment to slip to the floor.

Iva did not speak. Indeed, she was barely able to breathe as he stood before her in all of his magnificence. He was darkly handsome, and his hair hung unbraided over his shoulders. His powerful chest and arms bared he slowly drew the silver snood from her hair, and glimpsing the glimmer of appreciation in his dark eyes, Iva felt she would swoon beneath his touch as his long fingers untwined each golden braid and then ran lightly through the tangled strands, allowing her tresses to cascade down her back.

For a moment her unleashed beauty was enough for Shadow Dancer to feast his eyes upon. As he drank his fill of the golden bounty of her hair and the rare comeliness of her features, her amethyst eyes holding upon him, with a light movement, he reached out and unclasped the catch that held the white and gold embroidered tunic over her shoulder.

His breath was expelled when her full, upthrust breasts with their pinkened tips were exposed, the jade and blue hummingbird capturing Shadow Dancer's attention as did the delicate, golden points of the necklace she wore about her neck, both furthering his temptation to reach out and caress her. His fingers went to the small, colorful drawing of the bird and as Iva's soft moan filled the chamber, he bent his head and in delicious patterns of tender seduction, his heated tongue outlined the artful painting.

Iva's fingers entwined his dark hair, her breathing ragged as she stood before him, her flesh accepting his tender lips, her breasts straining for more of his passionate attentions.

Shadow Dancer was greedy in his desires as his heated, moist tongue slowly drew away from the hummingbird and his mouth covered one ripe rose-colored nub. Suckling the sweet-tender morsel, he gathered the fullness of the other breast in his palm, his fingers stroking in a swirling motion around the areola until that rose-crested bud strained against his touch, and without words being spoken, Shadow Dancer knew that this breast also desired the attention of his mouth and the lavish strokes of his tongue.

Only her fingers entwined in Shadow Dancer's hair

kept Iva from melting to the floor, so passionately lost was she to the ecstasy of his touch.

For a timeless period Shadow Dancer seemed satisfied to feast upon the sweet-tender flesh of her breasts, her taste and scent a powerful elixir for his senses.

Iva clung precariously to sanity as Shadow Dancer lovingly lavished one breast and then the other. Deep within her passion's embers were igniting into towering flames. She ached for fulfillment, her body a seething cauldron of steaming desire as she pressed her length against him and, in so doing, felt the hard, pulsating length of his manhood pressing against his breechcloth and her wraparound skirt, its very heat searing her belly.

The vehemence of her ravenous craving was not lost to Shadow Dancer; his own body raged with a burning need that matched her own. With a movement of his hand, he freed the wraparound skirt and his agate eyes roamed freely over her entire length, Iva feeling the heat of his gaze.

With no more thought than to worship every glorious inch of her, Shadow Dancer slowly lowered to his knees before her, his kisses raining on the tender underflesh of her full breasts and over her ribs to the tiny indent of her belly where the diamond-shaped amber stone resided, suspended on a fine golden chain. "My very soul envies even this tiny treasure," he breathed aloud as his kisses roamed over her belly and his tongue playfully dueled with the stone for placement next to her flesh.

His ministrations and his words, spoken in a husky tremor, set Iva's pulses to fluttering.

His hands captured the fullness of her shapely buttocks as she stood before him on trembling legs, and his kisses lowered from the amber jewel to lightly sear her hips and feather across the short curling, pale hair that covered the junction of her womanhood. A large gasp of astonishment mixed with incredible pleasure filled his ears as his mouth and heated tongue found that most treasured spot and, with a penetrating, consuming fever, plundered her very core, delving deeply into her and carrying her toward the highest pinnacle of pleasure. His mouth spiraled her soul into a vortex of impossible feelings. Swept heavenward, Iva collided with rapture's searing reward and could but hold on to his shoulders, her head thrown back and her cries of release filling the chamber.

Unable to withstand such an onslaught, Iva felt her body dissolving as a trembling started within her and raced throughout every portion of her body. At that very moment Shadow Dancer lifted her and carried her to his bed, depositing her on soft pillows and furs.

For a moment Shadow Dancer looked down upon her flushed beauty, his desire for her so strong he had to enforce control on his own body. He wanted only to bring her joy with their joining. As his gaze held hers, he untied the leather binding of his breechcloth and allowed it to fall at his feet.

Iva drew in a deep, ragged breath as her eyes left his and lowered to the pulsating length of his manhood. Though he had been naked in her presence in the past, she had never allowed herself to appraise this part of his body. Momentarily fear shone in the depths of Iva's eyes as they rose to meet his.

Shadow Dancer lowered his large frame to the bed and drew her into his arms. Again the warning sounded in his brain to go slowly, but his body reacted to the touch of her soft flesh, the contact goading his loins. He knew that it would take little to inflame her desires once again, and that was what he set out to do. Tenderly he slanted his mouth over hers, his kiss chasing away her fear as his hands moved seductively down her arms, caressing her soft flesh.

Within moments Iva's soft moans were of delight, of pleasure, as his hands gently roamed over her body and his lips devoured her sweet mouth. His kisses rained over her eyelids, over the gentle slope of her cheekbone and down across her fragile jawline. In his loving ministrations he traced a dampened path over the slim column of her throat and feathered kisses over the swollen fullness of her breasts, his mouth slowly covered each pink-tipped nipple and feasted greedily; Iva threw her head back and gasped.

Hoping to further her reception of him, he lowered his hand to the golden triangle of her womanhood, a finger easing slowly into its warm velvet heat and teasingly backing out.

As his finger retreated, Iva pressed her lower body toward his warmth, wanting to capture the feeling of this fullness within her. Never had she felt so wanton! Her entire body ached for something more, for something only this man could give her! She wanted at that moment only to experience womanhood.

Knowing the moment was right, Shadow Dancer rose above her, and as the velvet tip of his heated lance touched the moist haven of her opening and her body pressed upward to meet him, his heart sang with incredible joy. This woman would hold nothing back. She would share all with him, and their joining would be unrivaled throughout eternity.

As his throbbing, thickened love tool slowly lowered and her velvet sheath opened to receive him, Shadow Dancer's sable eyes caught those of crystal blue. "The rest of my life will be spent loving you, Moon Flower. Our meeting has been written in the stars, and there shall never be a love like ours. You are my bond with the gods, my reason for existing!" With this, he slowly began to penetrate her a bit deeper. Forcing extraordinary control over himself, he strained to avoid causing her more pain than was absolutely necessary.

The instant Iva's maidenhead was pierced, Shadow Dancer drew back somewhat as he felt her pain in his own heart. Glimpsing the hurt on her face, he quickly caught her lips with his own.

The kiss they shared was the most tender Iva had ever known. All of Shadow Dancer's love was in the joining of their lips. His sensual lips caressed, lightly ensnaring her, forcing her to forget the fleeting moment of pain caused by his entry and to dwell only upon the pleasures they had already shared and soon would share again. "I am sorry, my love. Trust me when I say that you will never know such pain again."

Iva felt that she could easily drown in the love flowing from the face looking down at her. She knew what she had endured was worth this glimpse of tender adoration. Her family, her friends—her whole life until she met this man—meant nothing to her at this moment. He was everything. His people would become her people, his desires her own. This man, her husband, would become her life. In her own mind Iva had at last committed herself to Shadow Dancer, and knew she would never turn back. With a soft cry for the tenderness that filled her heart, she wrapped her arms around his neck as she drew him back to her lips and, in turn, kissed him tenderly. "I love you, Shadow Dancer."

No further words were needed. His body slowly began to move atop hers, and she welcomed the movement without pain, her hips slowly beginning to undulate temptingly.

Shadow Dancer's only thoughts were of pleasing this woman who so completely filled his heart. Her soft, yielding body was a seductive temple of love to him, quenching his incredible thirst with its heady draught and setting his very soul afire with its taste.

Iva also was now beyond herself. Nothing in the world mattered except this man atop her, and the exquisite, breathless pleasure he was bringing to her. As her inexperienced body started of its own will to move and respond in the same pulsating motions as Shadow Dancer's, the full extent of his manhood eased within her sleek, hot passage and then drew back out to the very brink of the lips of her moist desire, the effect leaving her desirous of the vein ribbed, throbbing length of him. And, as over and over again he continued to fill her and then ease out of her, a glorious sensation grew in the very depths of Iva's being. For the first time she knew what true pleasure was, her body trembling and erotically quivering as she was caught up in the blinding rapture of fulfillment. Her lips opened and she called out her lover's name, then tightly clutched his back as surging ripples of cascading pleasure coursed through her.

Shadow Dancer, engulfed by the sensations her quivering sheath brought to him and by the sweet pleasure coursing through his veins, lost all coherent will. Succumbing to the overpowering pull upon his senses, he allowed his body to have its way.

As the pair slowly settled back into reality, Shadow Dancer drew Iva up against his chest, her naked limbs entwined with his own, his fingers laced through her golden curls, and his loving agate eyes looked deeply into her face. "Are you all right, my heart?" Now able to take a deep breath he remembered that this had been her first time lying with a man, and never before had he felt such concern for a woman as he did now for this one he claimed as his own. It was as though her pain were his own.

The pain that Iva had experienced at the start of their lovemaking was the farthest thing from her mind at this moment. She was totally saturated with the most delicious feelings of languor. Her body still tingled from his touch, her thoughts dwelling only on the incredible pleasure he had awakened deep within her depths. She had never imagined this act of joining oneself with a man could be so utterly wonderful. Not able to speak yet, Iva could but shake her head in response to her husband's concerned question.

For a time he held her, neither talking as they

marveled over what had taken place. Finally, as the embers of their passion slowly banked, it was Shadow Dancer who rose from the sleeping couch and retrieved the clay bowl of water from across the chamber. As his bride lay before him, he tenderly bent to her and washed the maiden's blood from the inside of her tender thighs.

Accepting his tender ministrations, Iva was saturated within the feel and regard of her husband's love. Each touch given went straight to her heart.

As Shadow Dancer finished the task and set the wash bowl away from the bed, he gently eased the jewelry from her neck and arms, and drew forth the bridal gift he had given her. With an easy movement he clasped the necklace behind her neck.

Iva sat up on the bed and looked down at the crystal tube containing the hummingbird feather, now lying against the fullness of her naked breasts. As her eyes then rose to her husband's, a small smile came over her lips and she softly stated, "I must remember to tell Tanza as soon as possible that her time has been wasted in her trips to the house of pleasure." Iva was remembering the scene she had watched in the back corridor of that house, and how she had been so caught up in the raw sexuality of what she had been viewing. She now knew that what had taken place between that warrior and the masked woman could never be compared to what had taken place this evening with Shadow Dancer, the man she loved. There had been none of the affection that was shared, no tenderness or concern for the other. There had been only sex between the two, and she now knew that there was much more to be had!

Shadow Dancer looked askew at his young bride as he wondered about her words. "What do you know of this place called the house of pleasure?" he questioned, his hand lightly caressing the tender flesh next to the crystal tube.

Iva instantly knew that she had made a mistake in mentioning that place. She remembered Nokie's worry that her cousin would find out that they had paid a visit to the house, and now as she looked into his features she glimpsed a touch of hardness in his black gaze. "I . . . I . . ." Unsure of how to explain what she meant without telling all, Iva sat before him, knowing that she could not lie. Drawing a deep breath, she tried to explain herself without further raising his ire. "There is a back corridor that runs along a portion of the house, and women can go there and view what takes place within the chambers."

"I have heard this in the past," he stated, his gaze upon her, and she glimpsed the surprise on his face at her knowing so much about this house.

Something in his look touched a stubborn note within Iva, and she sat up straighter before him. Why was she acting like some weak-kneed child who was being berated by her father? She had done nothing wrong that night she had gone to the house of pleasure with Tanza and Nokie. She had been curious and she had satisfied that curiosity, or at least she had thought so at the time. She remembered anew the feel of lying beneath Shadow Dancer's magnificent body. It seemed peculiar to her that the men of this village knew some of the same feelings women in the outside world felt when their men paid visits to such houses, those operated by women. "I was curious about this place and Tanza volunteered to take me one night." There she had said it!

"Curious?" Shadow Dancer questioned softly, the muscle below his cheekbone flexing with his agitation at her confession. "Was there no other way to satisfy your curiosity? Could you not have asked someone?" He was thinking about his cousin. That Nokie herself was still a virgin and would have been as unknowledgeable as his bride did not cross his mind.

"We did nothing wrong," Iva stated in a forthright

174

manner, and at the same time she wondered who on earth he would have expected her to go to with her questions about sex.

Shadow Dancer was not lost to the instant firmness of her chin and the quick inner flame in her blue eyes. He had known that she was unlike other women. Once more he was being shown that she had a mind of her own. First she had insisted that she be able to work with his horses, and now he had found that she had visited the house of pleasure. Slowly a smile came over his lips as he once again gazed at her beauty, and it fleetingly crossed his mind that she had remained untouched though she had visited the house of pleasure. "Then it is a good thing that we have been joined. You will not need to make another visit to this house. I will answer any questions you may have from this day forth."

Iva instantly grinned in return as his good humor surfaced. "Oh, I don't know, there may be some things a husband cannot explain to his wife, and perhaps if I wear a mask and cover my hair, no one will recognize me as a married woman if I return to this house of pleasure." Only teasing him, she batted her long lashes, and her eyes now sparkled with a playfulness that was not lost on Shadow Dancer.

In an instant he was pulling her back into his arms upon the sleeping couch. "Then I promise you that I will be doubly diligent in trying to sway you from taking such a path, my love." His lips sought hers and drew out their sweetness, and softly he murmured against her mouth, "I hold all the answers that you will ever want, my heart."

Within seconds the couple were once again discovering the pleasures that could be found within each other's arms, their tender touches and pleasurable kisses heightening their passions until they at last came together in a scalding burst of sensual heat.

Responding to his caresses and his words of love, Iva

175

succumbed to the feelings abounding in her. His fingers elicited a rapturous trail of fire as they trailed over her full, firm breasts. And when his tongue followed suit, scorching her flesh with endless kisses, she knew this man was truly hers, for now and forever. Whether time stood still or was borne on wings, there would be no changing her fate.

The pressure of the rigid shaft slipping into her tightness and slowly stretching that moist, warm haven to accommodate his engorged size held the power to chase away all thoughts. Cupping her buttocks in his hands, he pushed deeper, and the pleasurable assault drew forth a soft moan as Iva clasped his shoulders tightly and wound her shapely legs around his hips. Moving her own hips up and down in an undulating motion that matched his, she surrendered to the incredible pleasure that overcame her as Shadow Dancer glided deep within her and then slowly eased out in a rocking motion, at the same time feathering kisses over her eyelids, her cheekbones, the pulsebeat at her throat while he murmured heated love words behind the fiery kisses.

Their souls were joined, and their bodies blended in sweet, consuming passion as they soared together upon phantom clouds while seeking the release that awaited them.

As the night grew old and the braziers dimmed and then guttered, the couple upon the sleeping couch did not take notice. Totally immersed in their lovemaking, they were aware only of each other.

4 FREE BOOKS

TO GET YOUR 4 FREE BOOKS WORTH $18.00 — MAIL IN THE FREE BOOK CERTIFICATE T O D A Y

Fill in the Free Book Certificate below, and we'll send your FREE BOOKS to you as soon as we receive it.

If the certificate is missing below, write to: Zebra Home Subscription Service, Inc., P.O. Box 5214, 120 Brighton Road, Clifton, New Jersey 07015-5214.

FREE BOOK CERTIFICATE

4 FREE BOOKS

ZEBRA HOME SUBSCRIPTION SERVICE, INC.

YES! Please start my subscription to Zebra Historical Romances and send me my first 4 books absolutely FREE. I understand that each month I may preview four new Zebra Historical Romances free for 10 days. If I'm not satisfied with them, I may return the four books within 10 days and owe nothing. Otherwise, I will pay the low preferred subscriber's price of just $3.75 each; a total of $15.00, *a savings off the publisher's price of $3.00.* I may return any shipment and I may cancel this subscription at any time. There is no obligation to buy any shipment and there are no shipping, handling or other hidden charges. Regardless of what I decide, the four free books are mine to keep.

NAME _____

ADDRESS _____ APT _____

CITY _____ STATE _____ ZIP _____

TELEPHONE (____) _____

SIGNATURE _____ (if under 18, parent or guardian must sign)

Terms, offer and prices subject to change without notice. Subscription subject to acceptance by Zebra Books. Zebra Books reserves the right to reject any order or cancel any subscription.

GET
FOUR
FREE
BOOKS
(AN $18.00 VALUE)

Chapter Fourteen

Awakening as the first shafts of sunlight stole into his chamber, Shadow Dancer's first thought was of the woman wrapped so snugly against his side. Turning his head to gain a better view of her beauty, he drew in a deep breath.

He could not recall how many times over the past year he had awakened and imagined this woman lying at his side. From that first glimpse of her standing in the river beside her horse he had desired her, but through all of his imaginings, he could never have envisioned the full extent of his feelings for Moon Flower. She was simply everything to him!

As he allowed himself these quiet moments to study her rare beauty, even in sleep she seemed to reach out to touch his heart with her innocent loveliness. Her thick, golden curls wrapped around her body and twined about his arm, the sweetly scented tresses filling his nostrils with the scent of exotic flowers. Her heart-shaped face was tilted toward him, and he lovingly traced each gentle feature. The thick, pale sweep of lashes delicately dusting her rose-hued cheeks sent a fierce pang of desire through him, an urge to gather her tightly into his arms and kiss those closed lids until she awakened and he could once again gaze into the depths of blue in which he often felt he would drown. With a will, he forcefully held out against such a notion, continuing his enjoyable viewing of her. Her lips, in sleep, appeared to pout in the most provocative fashion, and her small, firm chin lay trustingly against one of the cloth-covered pillows. Viewing her without disturbance, Shadow Dancer knew that if he were to ease away the cool piece of material draped over her body, he would find more of her incredible perfection. Never had his senses been so overwhelmed. This completeness that she brought to him was a new thing that seemed to capture him totally.

With a small, sleepy sigh Iva snuggled closer against her husband, her body stretching with her inner feeling of well-being. As she slowly came out of her sleepy state a small smile played on her lips.

Shadow Dancer could have spent the rest of the morning lying next to her and admiring her breathtaking beauty, but he was just as pleased by her wakening. "Well, at last, my sweet." He bent over her and kissed her sweetly tempting lips in a morning greeting that promised much for the day ahead.

As Iva opened her sapphire eyes she wondered for a second if she had truly dreamed the wondrous delights that she had shared with this man the night before, but as she felt the heat of his loins touching her thigh, she knew no dream could have compared to this man's touch.

Ever so gently Shadow Dancer's hands glided across her silken flesh, stoking the embers that still glowed warmly from the night before. As his mouth covered hers, he rose above her, spreading her shapely thighs and, with a loving thrust, delving into that most desired shelter of her warmth.

Without thought, Iva rhythmically began to respond to his movements. He swept her upward, higher and higher and then soaring, gliding as though through all time and creation they searched for rapture's pinnacle amongst the fleecy murmurings of their own beginnings.

A breathless eternity passed, their bodies moving together, stroking and satisfying all cravings, waiting only for that indescribable moment's pleasure when they would collide with love's brilliance. And as Iva's soft cry of release filled the chamber, Shadow Dancer could not halt the shudderings that ran through him. Clutching this woman of his heart in a fierce embrace, he also spiraled over the fiery brink to total fulfillment.

As they held one another tightly, Shadow Dancer feathered tiny, breathless kisses over her face and neck. Seeming not able to have enough of her taste and feel, he whispered softly near her earlobe, "My love for you rages without control and burns deep within my very soul!"

Iva sighed softly, feeling totally adored. With each passing moment, her love for this man was growing stronger. "Will it always be like this?" she softly questioned on a breath.

"Each morning I will wake you in the same fashion, if you like." Shadow Dancer lightly chuckled as he rolled over and pulled her atop him, his strong hands smoothing out the golden tresses flowing over her back.

Iva's laughter joined his as she playfully punched his ribs. "I didn't mean that, Shadow Dancer." Her cheeks flushed pink at what his words implied.

His mood turning more serious, he lightly caressed her jawline as his sable eyes drank of the beauty before him. "I know what you mean, my heart: has there ever been a love like ours? Has ever the joining of two people been so complete?" He did not answer his own questions, but looked to Iva to supply a reply.

Slowly her head began to nod as her gaze became a thoughtful regard. "It could not be possible for any other two people to feel this same way, could it?"

Tightening his grip upon her, Shadow Dancer softly spoke. "The gods make no mistakes, my love. Of all the people on this earth, they have brought us together and have joined us. Our hearts are now one. Our souls have touched, and with our blending we have changed for all time. Yes, Moon Flower, our love will always remain the same, only perhaps growing in intensity with the passage of time."

His words touched Iva's core, and silently she wondered at her fortune in finding a man such as he. Without saying another word, she bent her head and slanted her lips over his, as though sealing the promise of his words with the tantalizing joining of their lips.

A short time later the couple shared a hearty breakfast in the gardens, afterward leaving Shadow Dancer's house hand in hand, they joined the other villagers who proclaimed this day a holiday.

The entire village appeared delighted over the fact that the wedding of Shadow Dancer and Iva had granted them a day of inactivity. The time was given over to feasting, gambling, and playing games. The village women laughed and visited as they cooked and tended the younger children, the older men of the tribe, along with those who held a taste for gambling, sat before their homes and played a well-liked game called patolli.

A dice game, it was played upon a mat which had been painted entirely black, the scoring board in the form of a cross. The counters were large black beans in which several holes had been made, and a numerical symbol was painted on each. Before a man threw the dice, he would rub them between his palms and, in the act of throwing, would call out the name of the patron god of the game.

Iva and Shadow Dancer watched for a time as a group of men played patolli. Iva was amazed to see how much the men lost on a simple throw of the dice. There were precious stones, mantles, headdresses, and plumage lost on a single wager. One man lost his horse, and as he left the group shortly after, Iva's heart wavered over his ill fortune.

The villagers were carefree and in the spirit for

merrymaking. Shadow Dancer and Iva, as the newly-weds and the cause for this day of pleasure, were the object of many giggles and light jokes. But everything was done in fun, and the couple were more than able to withstand the humorous remarks cast in their direction.

It was nearing the noon hour when Dark Water, Aquilla's husband, found the pair and invited them to his house for a light meal. With Arez off playing with the other children of the village, it was a pleasant group of four who shared a delicious meal in the small garden behind Aquilla and Dark Water's home.

A ball game was planned after the noon meal, and later in the afternoon there was to be a horse race, so it was not long that the four lingered in the garden over their food.

As the group made their way toward the outer portion of the village, to a smooth, masonry court shaped in the form of the letter *I* and flanked by two tall walls of stone, Iva's thoughts wandered to the horse race that would take place later in the day. From the first moment she had heard about that event, her excitement had grown. She wanted to race too! The only problem was, she was not sure how her husband would react to a request that she and Cimmerian be allowed to participate.

With her thoughts thus occupied, Iva listened as Aquilla tried to explain the ball game to her after Dark Water and Shadow Dancer, both players, left their sides. It was not long before Iva believed herself to have a small grasp of what was to take place, but as she watched the players on each side pulling on leather gloves and covering their knees and hips with leather guards, a small trail of fear laced its way within her heart. Shadow Dancer also was covering his body with the protective gear.

Nokie and Tanza joined Iva and Aquilla as the villagers shouted out wagers and the teams took their sides. The object of the players on each team was to drive a hard rubber ball through a stone ring set vertically in the middle of each wall; the ring was surmounted by an image of the patron god of the game. Winning strokes counted only when made by hitting the ball with the hips, buttocks, or elbows.

When the game started and both sides ran after the ball and fought for possession, Iva grimaced as three men collided and fell heavily to the ground. Her heart hammered swiftly in her chest as she followed Shadow Dancer's every move. He and Dark Water were on the same team, and at the moment it was Dark Water who was in control of the ball, Shadow Dancer who was guarding him, his large body blocking the efforts of the other team to break through his defenses and prevent Dark Water from racing to the other end of the court and scoring a point.

Her breath caught as Shadow Dancer sent one warrior to the ground and then another came up behind him unaware and dodged to the side, his leg kicking out at the ball and almost sending Dark Water to his knees before Shadow Dancer blocked the attack and sent this man to the ground with his fellow player.

Aquilla laughed with glee as her husband steadied himself and rushed onward. Dark Water kicked the ball before him, then maneuvered it into the air and, with his elbow, shot it through the ring on the wall.

Most of the villagers were now standing around the court and watching the teams playing this daring game. As Dark Water made the ring, a volley of shouts and calls were thrown back and forth among the men, and the women laughed and teased those who had men on the opposite team.

It all appeared to be good-natured fun, but Iva could not quell the feeling that this game was a bit too dangerous. As both teams scampered once again to gain possession of the ball, Shadow Dancer once more was in the thick of things, but this time it was he instead of Dark Water who gained the hard ball, Iva's heartbeat quickened as her husband turned about and, with a quick maneuver, carried the ball with him as he raced toward the other end of the court, his team setting up a defense, the other team trying to block his progress. "Oh, my God!" Iva cried aloud, and she would have rushed onto the court to Shadow Dancer's side if Nokie had not clutched her arm, when a large warrior from the opposite team threw himself headlong into Shadow Dancer's path and sent her husband to the ground, then stole the ball and started off in the opposite direction.

Shouts of encouragement were heard as the man bested Shadow Dancer, and when Shadow Dancer limped off the court another warrior hurriedly put on gloves and leather shields to take his place.

"He is fine, Moon Flower." Nokie smiled as she tried to calm the other woman, not wishing her to make a spectacle of herself in front of all the villagers.

"But he's hurt!" Iva at last broke free of Nokie's frail grip upon her just as Shadow Dancer limped off the court.

Shadow Dancer grinned at her in an easy manner. "Where are you hurt? Is it serious?" Iva was so upset that she was mixing English with the Indian language she had been trying so hard to master.

Wrapping his large arm around her shoulder as though needing her support, Shadow Dancer drew her face up so that he could look down into it before placing a kiss upon her worried brow. "I am unhurt, my love. I allowed myself to fall in order to gain your side more quickly."

Iva stared at him in total disbelief. "You mean you let me believe you hurt just so you could leave the game?"

"Exactly, my heart!" Shadow Dancer grinned the wider. "Sometimes the game lasts well into the afternoon, and once I had started playing I kept catching glimpses of you from the corner of my eye, and I wanted only to be at your side once again. I thought perhaps we could watch the game together from the shade of that tree," He pointed to a large pine a short distance away from the court.

Iva could have shouted out her anger at him for the worry he had caused her. "But I thought you had been hurt!" she at last got out in a strained voice as she tried to pull herself out of his arms.

Shadow Dancer would not let her go. Seeing growing anger replacing her earlier concern for him, he quickly set about soothing her. "There truly was no other way out of the game, Moon Flower."

"Then you should never have joined in to begin with!" Remembering vividly how her heart had fallen at the sight of him hitting the ground, the terror that had taken hold of her over his supposed injuries, she was not about to be easily swayed by his honeyed words.

"But I was thinking only of you, Moon Flower, and how hot you must have been standing there in the sun and watching the game. My mind was running rampant with thoughts of sharing the cool shade of the pine tree with you at my side. If I had not faked an injury, surely one would have come upon me with my mind not on the game."

How could Iva resist him any longer? Slowly a smile replaced the pout upon her lips, and she playfully scolded as she hit at his chest with her fist. "For a moment, I thought you truly were injured!"

Shadow Dancer felt his heart lighten with her smile, and avoiding the full impact of her fist, his ears filled with her confession of worry, he quickly began to apologize. "The next time I will tell you beforehand of my intentions. And I promise you that I will make it up to you for all the worry I have caused. Your every wish shall be my command for the rest of this day!" He held his fist to his heart as though making a pledge.

The smile on Iva's lips soon turned to a grin. "There had better not be a next time, Shadow Dancer," she declared as she began to speculate on what his words implied. If indeed she would be granted any wish, perhaps this would be the time to approach him about entering the horse race.

Shadow Dancer laughed aloud as he took her hand and began to lead her toward the tree, and as he sat down in the shade, he pulled her down upon his lap. "Of course there will not be a next time, my love." He boldly kissed her full upon the mouth, not caring that some of the villagers had watched them leave the court area and make their way to the tree, and were still watching as Shadow Dancer pulled Iva onto his lap.

"Did you mean what you said, Shadow Dancer?" Iva questioned in a soft tone as soon as her lips were released, and she placed her arms around his neck. There is no time like the present to ask him if I can race, she told herself. It was not likely she would find him in a more amiable mood than at this very minute.

Shadow Dancer's mind dwelt only upon the sweetness of her pink, tempting lips, the feel of her full breasts pressing lightly against his chest as she raised her arms to grasp his shoulders. Absently he nodded his head, at that moment he would have agreed to anything she asked.

"I do then indeed have a wish that I would like to have granted this day." She jumped right in feetfirst.

"Whatever your wish you shall indeed be given your heart's desire." Shadow Dancer imagined that she had seen some trinket at the gold- or silversmith's house or that she had some other trivial thing upon her mind, and as he was intent upon running his fingers along the pale contours of her throat, he nodded his head in agreement as he spoke.

"The horse race, Shadow Dancer. I would like to ride Cimmerian in the race this afternoon." She knew that he had been paying little attention to what she was saying, but as his head rose up a notch and his eyes looked into hers, she at last realized that she now had his full attention.

Taken by surprise, Shadow Dancer at first appeared speechless, but quickly recovering, he slowly began to shake his dark head. "I am afraid that what you wish is impossible, Moon Flower."

Iva had had the morning to think of the many reasons Shadow Dancer would present against her riding, so now she swiftly replied, "Why is it impossible? I can ride as well as any man, and I know that Cimmerian can run faster than any other horse alive!" Her enthusiasm was evident in her voice and the animation of her gestures as she appealed to her husband to consider her request.

"But women do not ride in the horse races that take place in this village." Shadow Dancer did not wish to refuse her; he merely hoped to make her understand his position.

"Then it is about time for a woman to do so!" Iva replied, not for a moment willing to back down. Just because she was a woman was no reason for her not to be allowed to participate in the fun of a horse race! Often in the past she and Delbert had raced her father's horses, and more often than not, Iva had been proclaimed the winner.

Hating to see the joy leave her beautiful face at a refusal, and in truth not having a good enough excuse for her not to ride, for he remembered the legend of Sharaza herself competing in horse races, all Shadow Dancer could do was slowly nod his dark head in agreement. "I guess you are right, Moon Flower. It is time that the women of this village have the choice of riding in the horse races." Though even as he said this, he doubted that any other woman besides his headstrong, young wife would venture upon such a course.

At first Iva was unsure she had heard him correctly. She had expected him to put up a much stronger argument. But when his words penetrated, she threw her arms around his neck and, in her excitement, rained kisses over his handsome face as she eagerly agreed to use all the caution she possibly could.

Only a moment later Iva jumped to her feet, and looking down at her husband relaxing upon the lush grass beneath the tree, she excitedly coaxed him to rise. "We must hurry, Shadow Dancer, to get Cimmerian readied for the race!"

Shadow Dancer moaned aloud as he forced himself to stand, the plans he had had for a pleasant afternoon at her side beneath the shade of the pine tree forgotten as he took her hand and the couple made their way back to the pastures behind his house in order to fetch Cimmerian.

The horse race was to be held in the center of the village, and as the participants began to make their way to the starting line, Iva felt the curious stares of the tribespeople. Forcing herself to look directly ahead, she used a firm hand to direct Cimmerian toward the starting line.

The number of villagers swelled near the area where the horse race was to begin as word traveled quickly through the valley that Shadow Dancer's new wife, Moon Flower, was going to be racing her black stallion. Bets were lavishly made and challenges accepted, the riders themselves wagering on their mounts and the villagers wagering on their favorite horses and riders.

Surprise was easily read on many faces as the crowd watched the slim young woman with the brightly colored blanket covering her legs sit astride the high-strung stallion and, with a firm hand, control her mount's nervousness as she held him at the ready near the starting line.

No objections were voiced out of respect for Iva's

husband, not until Gray Otter pushed his ponderous bulk through the crowd and, standing only a few feet from Shadow Dancer, pointed a plump finger in Iva's direction. "What is this, Shadow Dancer? Do women now join in on a horse race between men?"

The sharp retort that instantly came to Iva's mind did not leave her mouth, for she glimpsed the twitching of the muscle beneath Shadow Dancer's cheek and the thin smile that belied his anger. "There is no law, Gray Otter, which says a woman cannot participate in the games of our people, in fact, if you recall the legends of our people you will remember that Sharaza herself raced her horses and also spent many hours playing patolli with the men of her village. Moon Flower can ride well and her horse is swift, I do not feel threatened as a man that my wife wishes to race."

Each word that came out of Shadow Dancer's mouth was taken as a personal afront by Gray Otter. "She is but a woman! She holds no power to threaten any man!" His beady black eyes went back to Iva. Again he was confronted by her rare beauty and by the proud black stallion that had unseated him before his entire village, and once again swift-surging fury threatened to overcome him.

The smile upon Shadow Dancer's lips reached his eyes as he allowed his gaze to travel over his wife's form as she sat atop Cimmerian. "I do not deny that Moon Flower is indeed a woman." He said this very softly as though in praise of what filled his regard. "But woman or not," his gaze hardened as it went back to Gray Otter, "I will wager my entire purse that she wins this race!"

At first Gray Otter did not respond. Silently he stepped before a sorrel stallion on which a brave was mounted, and for a full moment his dark eyes appraised man and mount. "I would take your wager, Shadow Dancer," he finally said, "and I would make one of my own with your wife." His eyes now turned to

Iva, and as they traveled over her length and settled upon the swell of her breasts, he drew in a deep breath. She wore the crystal tube necklace which he had coveted since the first time he had set eyes upon it. By all rights, he believed the necklace, as well as everything else that Shadow Dancer owned, should be his. He was the chief of this tribe, as his father had been before him! It should be he who lived in the house that once belonged to Wind Cryer and Sharaza. It should also be he who received the wine from the priests, and his household should receive the first picks from the crops every year. He hated the fact that the elders of the village still considered Shadow Dancer and his line royalty.

"What is your wager then?" Iva demanded as she faced his ill-favored gaze, which seemed lost to what was taking place around him for it was concentrated on the necklace she wore around her neck. With Shadow Dancer so close by, and now holding claim to be his wife, Iva did not fear this overweight chief as she had upon their first meeting.

"Straight Arrow rides my horse in this race." The black eyes rose up and clashed with Iva's deep blue ones. "My wager is my stallion for the black! If Straight Arrow wins, the black beast is mine!"

Iva did not need much time to make a decision. She had already looked over each horse that was to race, and though the sorrel looked stronger than the rest, she truly believed with all her heart that Cimmerian was the best horse entered this day. "I accept, Gray Otter," she replied evenly without even looking in her husband's direction to see his reaction to the wager.

Gray Otter seemed pleased, as he imagined the black stallion belonging solely to him. He would take the wildness out of the beast himself, he swore, and he would enjoy every minute of the taming. As his eyes slowly left her face and touched upon the crystal tube containing the perfect hummingbird feather, he boldly

189

expanded his wager. "I will also wager one—no two—of my best mares against the necklace that you now wear."

Iva's hand automatically went to the necklace around her neck. This was her wedding gift from Shadow Dancer! She could not even think about wagering it! Slowly she began to shake her head, but before she could open her mouth to refuse him, Shadow Dancer took up the bet.

"My wife's stallion and her necklace, this is a good wager, Gray Otter. I hope that your horses are as worthy." His eyes sparkled as he glimpsed Gray Otter's displeasure with his words.

Iva would have protested wagering the necklace since it was her wedding gift, but when she looked at Shadow Dancer and glimpsed the proud stance of his straight back and wide shoulders as he faced his cousin, she knew there was more going on between the two men than a wager over a horse race. Gray Otter's actions were those of a man holding a longstanding grudge, and Shadow Dancer was not one to back down, no matter that the one standing before him was chief of this village. To say a word against wagering the necklace, Iva realized, would only make Gray Otter gloat in the face of her husband and before his tribe. With a determined glint in her blue eyes, she swore to herself, as she reached down and patted Cimmerian's sleek neck, that she would give this race her best efforts and would make her husband proud of her!

As the riders readied their horses, Iva tucked the crystal-tube necklace within her tunic and allowed it to lie against her breasts, as she tried to maintain control over Cimmerian, the stallion anxiously pranced behind the starting line. Unused to the many colorful Indians standing around the horse racers, Cimmerian flared his nostrils and widened his eyes as he several times threw his head back and rose up on his hind legs.

At just such a moment, when Cimmerian's front legs

pawed the air, the shout was given and riders and horses thundered across the starting line. Iva instantly recovered her animal and, pressing herself against Cimmerian's back, she and her mount shot across the starting line and within seconds were pulling past the last rider and horse and then the next.

With her golden hair flying wildly behind her, Iva shouted, "Go, Cimmerian, go! Give it all you've got, boy!" As she kicked out at his flanks, they raced through the center of the village, circling to the right and back toward the starting line, Cimmerian overtook the next horse and then the next.

It was Straight Arrow on the back of Gray Otter's horse that had taken the lead. Iva could feel the crystal tube lying against her breasts and seeming to burn her very flesh, she pushed Cimmerian harder as they drew closer and closer to Straight Arrow.

Cimmerian and Straight Arrow's mount were now neck and neck, the crowd's shouts filling the riders' ears. Iva could feel the laboring of her horse even as her own breath came out in short gasps and her heart beat at a frantic pace. Kicking out a final time, she shouted, "Now, Cimmerian, go!"

As the finish line came into view and the villagers hurried out of the way of the racing horses, the tense muscles in Cimmerian's sleek body strained as he gave his all. With a mighty burst of energy, he pulled away from Straight Arrow's mount and flew across the finish line.

Amidst the uproarious cheers of the bystanders, Iva was helped to her feet by her husband as soon as Cimmerian halted a few feet from the finish line. Grinning his pleasure and his pride, Shadow Dancer welcomed the hearty compliments given him by the other warriors, while many women of the tribe circled around Iva and, with admiration upon their faces, congratulated the golden woman now known to them as Moon Flower on winning the race.

Iva felt a warm glow within at seeing her husband's pride in her. The rest of the villagers were joking and laughing as they settled their bets and relived the outcome of the race, retelling how Cimmerian had lunged out in front of Straight Arrow's horse and had cleared the finish line by a head.

Arez approached, grinning broadly, and took the reins out of Iva's hand, promising to see that Cimmerian was cooled down and later well fed. As the boy left with the stallion, Gray Otter approached the group gathered around the happy couple.

As the chief handed the reins of his stallion over to Shadow Dancer's keeping, his visage was masked in dark anger. "I will have the mares delivered before nightfall." With this, his dark eyes went to Iva for a moment before he turned and left the area where the horse race had taken place. To Gray Otter this was another slight that he had been handed by Shadow Dancer and his family. As he made his way toward his home, he swore to himself that one day he would have revenge and in so doing he would have all that Shadow Dancer now laid claim to!

"And I tell you again, Meci, we should have taken care of this cousin of mine years ago!" Gray Otter paced about the dank, bare chamber, his gaze once again settling upon the dark-robed, Aztec priest sitting before a small table. Frowning, he wondered if he was making a mistake by petitioning for the man's help in this matter. Upon occasion, in the past Meci had helped him handle a few delicate matters that Gray Otter had wanted to be kept secret. Having confided in the priest some years ago about his relationship with Shadow Dancer, he now felt somewhat uneasy as he waited for Meci to come up with some plan that would help to ease his mind. "I told you when Shadow Dancer first brought the pale woman among us that she would become trouble. She is influencing the people more and more in Shadow Dancer's favor."

Meci had heard about the horse race, and knew that Gray Otter's hatred of his kin had deepened with the fact that the woman known as Moon Flower had bested him this very afternoon. "As I have already told you, Gray Otter, there is little cause for your worry." The red-veined dark eyes looked up out of a wrinkled visage, as long, unclean fingers appeared like talons from the folds of the priest's robe to wrap themselves around the stem of a goblet. Bringing the wine to his lips, Meci sipped deeply of the strong brew. "Your secret is safe. Your worry is for nothing. Who would ever guess at the deceit that raged within the hearts of your ancestors?"

"I should have followed my instincts and had Shadow Dancer destroyed long ago! I knew the day would come when he would take a bride. Now there is the chance that his line will become strong once again!"

"Perhaps you are right." The matted gray head nodded as though deep in thought. "It might be wise to lay a trap to snare our foe, and have done with the matter for once and for all." Meci put down the goblet of wine and steepled his fingers before him upon the wood table. "There will be a higher price to be met for this deed than those in the past." Once again those bloodshot eyes with their unearthly gleam fixed upon Gray Otter.

"What is it that you want?" Gray Otter questioned, at the moment willing to give almost anything to have Shadow Dancer removed from his life. He could not even sleep any longer without thoughts of Shadow Dancer and the golden woman plaguing him.

"It is time that I become high priest." Meci puffed out his chest beneath the dark robes, his eyes never leaving Gray Otter's face. "Atlacol is too lax in the ancient beliefs of our ancestors. There are few Aztec rights performed any longer here. The priests follow the dictates of Quetzalcoatl, and spend their days worshipping images of butterflies and flowers. As high priest, I would bring back the old ways and reacquaint our people with the gods of years past who made the Aztecs a people that were invincible!"

"You would have me name you high priest?" Gray Otter questioned with some disbelief. As Meci nodded his head and seemed not in the least surprised by Gray Otter's reaction, the chief responded, "I hold no authority over what takes place here in the temple, you ask that which I am unable to give." In Gray Otter, a small tremor of fear had taken root with Meci's request. Atlacol held much power. Gray Otter had heard it spoken by many of the people that Atlacol was closer to the gods than any human alive. How would he possibly overstep such a one? But looking across the table at Meci, he asked himself how he could not. His own future and that of his family were at stake.

"The dearer the price paid, the more valued the request." Meci seemed to read the chief's mind, and he watched as Gray Otter's head slowly nodded in agreement.

Chapter Fifteen

For several days after their joining Shadow Dancer and Iva stayed secluded at the falls. They spent their days learning each other's likes and dislikes, their nights on Shadow Dancer's sleeping pallet, discovering the incredible joys that were to be found in their union.

Tomorrow they would return to Shadow Dancer's village, and like the last time they were at the falls, Iva dreaded leaving this paradise. She did not fear what awaited her in the hidden valley, as she had in the past, but she knew that with their return everyday life would interfere with the happiness she had found these past days while alone with her husband.

With a soft sigh, which signified not only to herself but also to Shadow Dancer, that reality must be faced, Iva gazed through the canopy of trees overhead as she ran a cool hand over her husband's naked chest. "Why does Gray Otter dislike you so much?"

They were lying in the tall grass side by side, allowing their bodies to dry in the afternoon sun. For a lingering moment Shadow Dancer held his eyes tightly shut as though talk of Gray Otter was the most unwelcome subject his wife could have brought up. Then he opened them, resigning himself; for he knew that sooner or later he would have to tell her the story of how Gray Otter's line became chiefs of the village. Feeling her gaze move from the trees overhead to him, Shadow Dancer rolled upon his belly and, leaning upon his elbows rested his chin in one palm. "As I have already told you, Moon Flower, my family descended from Wind Cryer and Sharaza. The first chief of our tribe was Wind Cryer, then his first son and so on. In the custom of the Apache, this is how our village's chiefs were determined."

"Then how can it be that Gray Otter is now chief?" Iva questioned. It seemed to her that for Gray Otter to be chief today, there would have to be a closer relationship between him and Shadow Dancer than that of mere cousins.

Shadow Dancer wrapped a golden curl around his finger and, for a moment, seemed to study the silken texture. "My grandfather, Golden Eagle, was the last in our direct line to serve as chief of my people." Shadow Dancer hated to admit even to himself how much this story of his ancestor bothered him.

"My grandfather was a peaceful man, and everyone in the valley loved him for his wisdom and kindness. He served his people well, but one day he disappeared from the valley and never returned. There were those who claimed that he met with foul play, but nothing could be proven. It was my grandfather's cousin who claimed the chieftainship by right of greater strength, for Golden Eagle's only son was but an infant when his father disappeared. Sky Hawk, Gray Otter's father became chief, and the line of chieftainship was changed."

"Then is this the reason for Gray Otter's hatred of you?" This was puzzling to Iva, for if anyone had reason to be angry, it should be Shadow Dancer. He would have succeeded his father as chief.

"Gray Otter is eaten away with jealousy. He covets everything that belongs in the line I was born to. My house, the riches that are in it. He believes everything should be his, but the high priest in his father's time

196

would not allow the belongings of my grandfather to be given to Sky Hawk's kin. Everything except the title of chief was given to my father, and this fact consumes Gray Otter with hatred!"

"He certainly does not conceal his emotions very well," Iva added, understanding more now.

"Gray Otter has always been thus. Do not let his actions worry you." Shadow Dancer would not have his wife afraid of his cousin or of anyone else in his village.

"I do not fear him for myself," Iva confessed softly as her eyes looked into his.

"Fear not for me, my heart. Gray Otter would never confront me openly. He is not a brave man, and even with his power, he would be hard pressed to find anyone in my village to lift a hand against me or what is mine." His words expressed more confidence than he truly felt, for Gray Otter was an enemy to be reckoned with. "Let us not waste another moment of this day with talk of Gray Otter. There are more pleasant things on my mind than my cousin." He tried to dispel thoughts of Gray Otter as he rolled onto his back and pulled her into his arms, and when she lay against his broad chest, his mouth plundered hers with a searing intensity that drove away all thought except for the pleasure he was causing within the depths of her.

Iva gasped aloud as waves of white hot heat washed over her entire length. She could not think, she could barely breathe. As the kiss waned and she drew back slightly to catch her breath, Shadow Dancer's lips plied her throat, lowering to her collarbone and to her full breasts, making a path from one taut peak to the other. He suckled gently on one pinkened tip, his teeth lightly grazing the erect nipple, and then feasted upon the other.

Iva moaned aloud, throwing her head back as rioting-wild sensations raced through her. Her breasts strained toward his skillful play. Her fingers, roaming over his muscle-rippled back to his powerful shoulders, soon were wrapped within the midnight strands of his hair. Enveloped by his powerful strength as he lowered his body and she parted her legs to receive him, Iva rose up to meet each sensual thrust, every inch of her being attuned to his masterful skill.

Caught up in a whirlwind of emotions, the couple was hidden by the lush grass that rose from the sweet-smelling earth. As the late afternoon breeze whispered within the canopy of trees overhead, Shadow Dancer's husky voice filled Iva's ears with all the adoration and love he was feeling for her.

Buried deeply within her, his rigid manhood clasped tightly within the satiny depths of her warm sheath, Shadow Dancer was instantly drawn into an eddy of exotic pleasure. As he moved with her in a steady, rhythmic motion, his head bent and his mouth covered hers.

Iva met the hard crush of his kiss with her own, her lips parting to accept the urgent thrust of his tongue. Over and over he kissed her, his probing tongue delving deeper and deeper into her tantalizing sweetness as he plunged his staff more frantically into her velvet heat.

Iva was swept away upon the tide of ecstasy racing through her and leaving her clutching at him as though he were her only anchor, shudders of rapture leaving her trembling.

With overwhelming satisfaction, Shadow Dancer sensed the pulsations that shook her body, and within seconds he also was moaning softly and clutching her tightly, his own release found.

Sighs and soft love words filled the area around the falls as the couple were gradually drawn back to their surroundings.

The three Apache warriors had been paid handsomely in gold. Their instructions had been clear and, but for one exception, would be carried out to the letter. The Indian would die, but the golden-haired woman would go with them.

They arrived at the falls just as dusk was settling over the valley, and watching from the cover of the forest close by, they quietly appraised the tall, powerfully built warrior and the shapely blonde as the pair ate their evening meal and then readied themselves for bed.

The leader of the three was a thick-featured Apache, known as Black Wolf. He was notorious for doing any kind of dirty work that would gain him coins for whiskey and tobacco. It was to him that Meci had sent word, and having met with him one evening deep within the mountains, the priest had laid a bag full of gold in his palm. The promise of more gold had brought Black Wolf and his two cronies to the falls this day.

"Tall Pine, you will take the woman on your horse. Blue Snake and I will take care of the warrior." Black Wolf began to lay out their plan of assault as soon as the three had made their way deeper into the forest so they could talk without being detected. "We will wait for a while after they have bedded down, and then we will attack."

Blue Snake nodded his head in agreement. This was not the first time he had been at Black Wolf's side during such an ambush. Always in the past his friend's plans had proven wise, and he saw no reason why they would not work this time.

"I thought you said that the woman was also to be killed?" Tall Pine questioned, wondering why Black Wolf would wish to complicate matters by taking the woman along with them when they left the falls. "Should we not take care of her right here with the brave?" Unlike Blue Snake, Tall Pine had been on no other ventures with Black Wolf. He had been promised a sizable amount of gold for throwing his lot in with the two warriors, but he was curious to know what Black

Wolf's plans for the woman were. He had hoped they would be able to get this job done quickly so he would be able to return to his new bride's family without much delay.

Black Wolf looked to Blue Snake before answering. Pressing a forefinger against the bridge of his wide nose, he pictured the white woman and a lecherous gleam filled his black eyes. "The woman will not live much longer than the brave, only she will die as I am riding between her pale thighs, and I will hear her cries of passion as my knife enters her heart!"

A half-moon rode high within the starlit sky as the couple, wrapped in each other's arms on their sleeping pallet, fell asleep. Even though they planned to leave the falls early the next morning they had been unable to resist assuaging their bodies' desires one last time before they closed their eyes.

Iva at first thought herself caught up in the confusion of some strange nightmare when she heard the whinnying cry of a horse and the shouts of warriors. Then, she was pushed aside, and her heartbeat all but stilled as she opened her eyes to see strange Indians attacking Shadow Dancer. She opened her mouth to scream, but wasn't sure anything came out for one of the Indians grabbed hold of her arm and pulled her from the pallet.

Trying to get to her knees, she was clawing the earth for something to use as a weapon when she glimpsed a large club being held high over her husband's head. "Shadow Dancer!" Her cry filled the camp just as she was grabbed from behind and hauled onto the back of a horse.

"Noooooo!" she screamed and automatically began to fight off her attacker, her head turning as she tried in vain to see the form of her husband once more.

Tall Pine easily overcame the resistance of the

woman in his arms. In a quick maneuver, he caught up both her wrists in one hand and, kicking the sides of his mount, left the chaos of the camp. He had been told to wait for Black Wolf and Blue Snake where the ravine began to shallow out. It was not far to go, but as the forest began to come between them and the campsite, much of the noise of the attack quieted. Now he had only to deal with the wildcat in his arms.

Iva tried everything she could to get away from the Indian. She kicked at his horse and at him, she tried to bite the hand that held hers captive, she even tried to butt her head against his chest. Desperately, she had but one thought in mind—to get back to Shadow Dancer! It was as her elbow made contact with the Indian's windpipe that he knocked her off his horse, and with a leap he sat astraddle her on the ground.

"You will get all you deserve, white bitch!" he panted close to her face as he held one hand under her chin and gripped both her cheeks with his fingers. Feeling her slender form, a shirt its only covering, wriggling beneath him, Tall Pine was more than a little tempted to carry out the fate Black Wolf had planned for her! He had not thought he could desire another woman since his joining with his sweetheart only two moons past, but something about this white woman fired his blood. Perhaps it was the excitement—the ride into camp, the screaming and fighting, and now her curves lying beneath him—that fired him onward. Reaching out with his free hand as he held tightly to her face with the other, his body pressed upon her, he glided it over her slender leg. Her fighting him furthered his passion as he fought to draw the hand upward, his fingers splaying over her soft flesh and inching toward their goal.

Powerless, but struggling and turning her head to and fro in an attempt to escape his strong grasp and the weight over her, Iva feared the worst as she felt the Indian's hand upon her leg and knew exactly what he intended. A long, shuddering sob escaped her even as she fought with every ounce of her strength.

Just at that moment when Iva held little hope and felt the hand slipping further upward on her flesh, the Indian was knocked from atop her.

In the shadows of the trees it was hard to see who her savior was, but as she heard the scuffling that ensued, she prayed it was Shadow Dancer. Let him be alive, she silently pleaded as tears coursed over her cheeks. *Let it be Shadow Dancer who is my rescuer!*

Only a second or two later she heard the angry voice of her husband. "Why are you here at the falls? Why did you come so far into the mountains?" He spoke the Apache tongue to the Indian who lay mortally wounded by the hunting knife now pressed against his throat.

"It was Black Wolf who was paid to do the deed. I never met the one who wanted you and the golden woman dead." Tall Pine almost choked on the words. Knowing that his death was not long in coming, he was confessing what he knew.

Shadow Dancer had learned more than he had expected. He had gotten nothing from the other two who had attacked him. The assault had been so sudden he had drawn his knife from beneath his sleeping mat and stabbed the Indian who had come at him with a club and then had rolled to his feet to fight off the next warrior who came at him. It had not crossed Shadow Dancer's mind that the attack had been planned, he had only wanted to find out if there was a reason why these three were only a day's ride from his village. Looking down he saw a frothing bubble of blood spurt from Tall Pine's lips and roll down his chin. Rising, Shadow Dancer glanced down without remorse at sightless eyes. He had seen what this Indian was about to do to his wife.

Stepping away from the body, Shadow Dancer took a step toward Iva and instantly found her in his arms. "Are you all right?" she asked over and over, her hands tracing his upper torso as though looking for a wound.

202

"I thought you had been hit with the club." And with this a shudder coursed through her as she saw in her mind the Indian holding the club and swinging it down toward her husband.

"I am unhurt, Moon Flower, but what of you?" Shadow Dancer prayed that he had arrived in time, but he needed to hear her say the words.

Nodding her head, Iva hugged him tightly around the waist. "I am fine, my only concern was for you." Of course, this was not true, but at the moment little else but Shadow Dancer seemed to matter.

A short time later Shadow Dancer sat before the campfire, Iva held tightly in his arms, and as she at last fell asleep, he went over in his mind once again what Tall Pine had said. Who could have wanted him and Moon Flower dead?

The town of Sterling was just coming alive as Delbert Benell rode slowly down the dusty main street. Besides the few supplies he had taken from the Cassidy farm, he had also brought with him fifty-four dollars, his entire savings. He planned to buy from the mercantile store the supplies he would need. He also wanted to make inquiries of several of the townsmen, in the hope that they could start him on a trail that would lead to Iva and the Indians who had stolen her away. He knew word had traveled through Sterling about Iva's abduction shortly after it had occurred, but he was hoping that someone knew something Bain Cassidy had not already been told.

Wainright's mercantile was just opening its doors when Delbert tied his horse to the hitching post and stepped onto the wood plank sidewalk that ran in front of the shops along the main thoroughfare.

Carl Wainright, a well-liked middle-aged man, called out to Delbert in greeting as he secured the door open and, with straw broom in hand, began sweeping the front of the store. "Come on in and look around. I didn't have the time yesterday to sweep, so I figured I had best do it this morning before the missus sets her eyes on this dust and goes off into a tither." The small pot-bellied storeowner motioned Delbert through the front door as he quickly attempted to swipe at the perpetual dust that came from the sidewalk and street beyond.

Looking around at the shelves lined with food, dry goods, and farming supplies, Delbert waited for Mr. Wainright to step behind the long counter so he could order his supplies. He bought a new rifle, as well, and left the old one he had carried from the farm with Mr. Wainright to return to Bain. He then pointed out a sharp-bladed knife with a leather sheath that he studied for a moment before strapping to his side.

Before leaving the store, Delbert pulled out the Indian headband he kept in his shirt next to his skin. "Mr. Wainright, I wonder if you have ever seen anything like this before?"

Carl Wainright pulled his wire-framed spectacles from his shirt pocket and then reached out for the headband that was being held out toward him. "Is this something them Indians left behind when they attacked the Cassidy farm?" he asked, his gray eyes looking over the rim of his glasses at Delbert. Like everyone else he had heard of the Cassidy girl's abduction, and glancing down at the headband he had in hand, he studied it carefully in the hope that he could offer the young man some information.

After studying the sun sign for a few minutes and turning the leather band over and over, the store owner at last pulled off his specs and handed the headband back to Delbert. "Nope, can't say I ever did see anything like it before. That's real gold and silver though."

Delbert had his first taste of disappointment, but as he tucked the band away into his shirt, he asked himself what else he could have expected. He had known from the start that it wouldn't be easy to track down the elusive band of Indians. Bain had been searching for a good month and had come up with nothing. Gathering his supplies, the rifle tucked under his arm, he thanked Mr. Wainright as he started to the door.

"You might like to ask old Willy Handcock if'n he's ever seen an Indian headband like that one you're carrying. If anyone in Sterling might help you, it would probably be Willy. He's been around these parts a lot longer than most, and he claims he used to trap game in the Rockies and used to prospect for gold."

"I'll do that, Mr. Wainright, thanks a lot." Delbert appreciated any help he could get even if it was just the name of a drunken old prospector.

"You might want to be looking behind the Lucky Star for Willy. I heard not long ago that he built some kind of shack back there," Mr. Wainright called out as Delbert started through the door.

The Lucky Star was closed at this time of the day, but there were a few old-timers sitting in chairs on the sidewalk out front, and without a second thought Delbert pulled out the headband and asked each one if they had ever seen anything like it before.

After looking with some interest, all three shook their heads. "Tain't nothing I ever seen afore, son." One of the men stated, and the others agreed.

The rest of the day Delbert met with similar replies. No one had seen an Indian headband like the one he'd displayed nor did anyone know anything about the strange band of Indians he had described. It was not until late in the afternoon that Delbert searched for Willy Handcock behind the Lucky Star saloon.

The old man's shelter, constructed haphazardly against the back of the Lucky Star, would be more aptly described as a lean-to, the doorway consisting of an old dirty blanket that afforded the dweller little privacy. As Delbert approached, a short-legged, wiry-haired terrier sat before the shelter and growled menacingly at the intruder on his domain.

The feisty little animal posed a limited threat, but the ruckus he caused brought a shout from within. "Put a lid on it, Mutt! Dad blast it, if'n yer fretting at one of them whores from Sal's place again, I'll cut out yer dang tongue!" A shaggy, gray head poked out from behind the blanket and from a wrinkled creased face, red-rimmed light brown eyes looked directly at the young man standing near the shelter.

"Mr. Handcock?" Delbert stared a bit nervously at the unkempt, large figure that loomed within the doorway.

"Aye, lad, what ya be wanting with me? Do I know ya or something?" Willy was usually not too friendly with people he did not know, and even those he did know he tried to keep at a distance. His aim in life was to avoid all outsiders unless there was a little profit to be made from associating with them.

"Mr. Wainright from the mercantile told me that maybe you could help me." Delbert had not missed the hard edge to the rough-looking man's voice, and he hurried to explain his reason for being there.

"Well, that sounds like Wainright, sending every orphan off the street to nag at me door!" Willy could be downright unfriendly when it suited him.

Delbert tried to ignore Willy's bad mood, and digging the headband from his shirt, he held it out in the older man's direction.

"Get the hell gone for a while!" Willy shouted at his dog as he took a step out of the hovel and almost tripped over the mongrel. "What ya got there?" He cast a wary eye in the direction of the band that glinted in the afternoon sunlight.

"It's an Indian headband. Mr. Wainright thought you might know something about the Indians that made it." That was all Delbert wanted to offer at the moment.

"Where'd ya find this, boy?" Willy's large head rose up as he pulled his gaze away from the headband and his eyes settled upon Delbert.

"Have you ever seen anything like it before?" Delbert questioned in return, finding a glimmer of hope in the fact that Willy had not handed him back the headband right away and denied knowledge of its origin.

"It 'pears to be a sun sign of some kind. It's made of pure gold and silver, so it probably come out of the mountains. Did ya see the Injun that wore it?" The red-rimmed eyes fixed upon Delbert and awaited his answer, alert with some interest.

"I got a glimpse of him." For obvious reasons Delbert was dealing cautiously with this man.

"So what'd he look like?" If there was one thing Willy Handcock hated, it was trying to pry information out of some two-bit greenhorn! "Don't ya be fergetting, ya come here looking for me, I didn't fetch ya out!"

Delbert conceded the truth of this statement, and though he still mistrusted the rugged-appearing man, he decided then and there that he had little choice but to answer him. This man might be able to help him find the Indians that had stolen Iva. "He was tall, and rather large built for an Indian, I think. He wore only a breechcloth, but it was different than any I had ever seen before. There was some kind of stitchwork covering back and front. Those with him looked about the same, except a few had blankets tied over one shoulder and the blankets hung to their knees." Delbert searched his mind, trying to remember everything he could about the Indians that had raided the farm.

"Why ya trying to find these Injuns?" Willy questioned as Delbert reached out and pulled the headband out of his hands and quickly tucked it back into his shirt.

"I work out at the Cassidy farm. About a month ago a band of Indians attacked it and abducted Iva Cassidy." What do I have to lose? Delbert asked

207

himself as he told this questionable-looking character everything.

"So the little girlie got stolen by savages, did she? Seems as how I heard something 'bout a month or so back about it."

"What do you think, Mr. Handcock? About the headband, I mean. Do you have any idea what tribe of Indians it could belong to?" Delbert still clung to the slim hope that Willy Handcock would be able to help him.

"Call me Willy, everyone does." The large man belched loudly as he stretched to his full six feet and rubbed at his eyes with the palms of his hands. Taking his hands down, he looked directly at Delbert as he offered, "Come on in, boy, and take a load off. I be needing a drink while I think on what ye've told me about them Injuns."

Without waiting for Delbert's response, Willy pushed the blanket aside and silently disappeared into the lean-to.

Delbert had little choice. Drawing a deep breath, he followed. No one else had even offered to talk about the situation with him, and he certainly would not turn away this offer to think about the matter. Stepping around the still-growling mongrel that Willy had called Mutt, he pushed the blanket aside and went into the dark interior of the crudely made shelter.

"Just sit yerself anywhere." Willy offered as he pulled up a jug of whiskey and, holding it with a finger through the handle, took a long, thirsty drink.

Delbert looked around the crowded, unclean single room, but seeing no chairs, he stood near the doorway as though at any moment he might have to make a run for it.

"Knock the junk off that crate. It'll do good enough." Willy jabbed a finger in the direction of a crate that had been used as a table of sorts. It held a tin plate that contained some dried-up beans, plus an odd assortment of dirty clothes.

Feeling ill at ease, Delbert pushed the debris aside and sat down on one corner of the crate. "You said you needed time to think about what I told you?" he asked, not wishing to stay in this hovel any longer than necessary.

"Aye, boy. Let me look at that band one more time." Willy took another long drink from the jug before setting it on the floor next to the mattress on which he was seated.

Not trusting Willy, Delbert cautiously pulled out the headband, knowing that the silver and gold upon it's facing made it an object worth stealing. Slowly he extended his hand in Willy's direction.

For the longest time Willy studied the headband in the dim light of the cabin; then he began to speak. "I heard a story once, a long time back, 'bout a strange tribe of Injuns that live deep in the mountains."

"Do you think it could be the same band that attacked the farm and stole Iva?" Delbert clutched at the first bit of hope he had been given since Iva's abduction.

"It's some kind of legend the Apache speak about. Something about a lost tribe. They say this tribe's valley is full of gold and silver." As Willy glimpsed the ray of hope that came over the young man's face, he added, "Now I ain't saying that this here band comes from this valley. I'm just repeating what I heard a long time back. The Apaches claim one of their own joined up with some Aztec princess and founded the lost tribe."

"Aztec?" Delbert repeated the word in total disbelief.

"Like I already said, it could just be some crazy story the Apaches made up, but then some of these Injun legends do hold some truth to 'em." Willy turned the headband over, and as his brown eyes went back to Delbert there was a greedy gleam in their depths.

"Do you think I could find out something about this

legend for myself?" Delbert doubted that this old rooster had ever heard of such a legend, but if there was the slightest chance he was telling the truth, he could not overlook it.

"Naw, laddy, the Apache would more than likely take yer scalp and feed yer carcass to their camp dogs!" Willy grinned as though that struck him as quite humorous.

"Then how am I going to find out if there is such a valley?" Delbert swallowed the anger that came over him at Willy's words.

"The only way I be seeing it straight, boy, is if'n I go along with ya. I know the Apache pretty well, and they know me."

"You mean that you would be willing to help me find Iva?" Delbert could not believe this man had offered to go along with him.

"If'n this here headband is a sample of the silver and gold to be found in this hidden valley, yes sir, ya can be counting me in." Willy slapped the headband across his knee to emphasize his statement.

Delbert couldn't care less about silver and gold. He just wanted to find Iva, and he would use any means available to do it. If Willy Handcock was willing to lead him to an Apache village to find out about this legend, then he would not argue with the man's motives. Delbert had his own doubts concerning this legend about a valley full of silver and gold, but if it could obtain him a guide, so be it.

Once Delbert agreed that Willy would go along, the man pulled himself from the mattress on the floor and began to stuff some clothing into a cotton sack. "I ain't got but a dog and a few things to pack. I do be having a packhorse though, as well as Saber, me riding horse."

"You mean you want to leave now?" Everything seemed to happen so quickly around this man.

"There ain't no time like the present, laddy. The sooner we find out where this valley is, the sooner ya can find yer little girlie and I can find enough gold to make me a rich man! Now while I be getting me things together, be a good lad and go on down to the livery and tell Sam to fetch ya my horses." Willy dug two more jugs of whiskey out from beneath a pile of debris and set them with his sack of clothes.

Delbert nodded his head, glad to be away from the cramped, ill-smelling quarters that Willy Handcock called home. His spirits were higher than they had been in some time, with the prospect of having some place to start his search, even if that involved the unlikely pursuit of a legendary tribe.

A few minutes later Delbert was once again overtaken by doubts as the livery man presented him with a bill for twenty-one dollars for the care and feeding of Willy Handcock's animals.

"I'll be paying ya back every dollar just as soon as we find that valley of gold, partner." Willy grinned when Delbert handed him the bill with every expectation of being reimbursed immediately, and there was little Delbert could say.

Shortly after, two men, three horses, and a dog named Mutt slowly left the town of Sterling in pursuit of legendary silver and gold—and a lost tribe of Indians. Delbert was locked into an unlikely partnership, for better or worse, for the time being.

Chapter Sixteen

"No, no, Moon Flower. This dark green thread will better suit your material." Nokie smiled warmly as she took the lighter green thread that Iva was about to use.

"I don't know if I will ever get the hang of this," Iva complained as she threaded her bone needle. "I did very little sewing while I was growing up. My mother probably would have enjoyed my company about the house, but I was too busy helping with the horses in the barn." For the past few months Nokie had devoted much of her time to trying to teach Iva how to embroider, and once again Iva was endeavoring to explain her ineptness.

"The time was not right when you lived with your mother for you to indulge yourself with womanly talents." Nokie calmly explained, her words seeming to hold much truth. "I myself did not learn such skills as embroidering and painting until my teen years."

Iva imagined this gentle young woman would have been born knowing such arts. "Why is this, Nokie? I would think Running Spring would have insisted that her daughter learn such things in her younger years." Iva was well aware that Running Spring was well known throughout the valley for her beautiful needle-work, and now after biting off the length of green thread that she needed, she sat back and looked upon the frail young woman with curiosity.

"I know that you may not see it in my father, Moon Flower, but he is truly a good man." Nokie was well aware of the ill will between her father and her cousin's family. Usually both women refrained from speaking much about Gray Otter. "When I was very young, I knew what I wanted of my future, and my father allowed me to pursue my heart's desire."

Iva's only reply was one finely arched brow rising over a blue eye, for she believed Gray Otter's generosity toward his daughter to be somewhat out of character.

Nokie laughed softly as she glimpsed the look Iva gave her. "I know that my father can be very difficult when it comes to Shadow Dancer, and the horse race, of course, certainly did not smooth his rumpled feathers where you are concerned."

Iva began to laugh as she pulled needle and thread through the piece of material on her lap. That is certainly an understatement, she thought as she remembered the last time she had seen Gray Otter in the village; he had glared at her with dark gleaming eyes.

"Well, as I was telling you," Nokie continued with a knowing grin, "my father allowed me to pursue my own talents."

"And what were these talents, Nokie?" Iva could not imagine what this thin, pale young woman would pursue other than womanly duties.

"I spent many hours of my days studying with the priests in the temple."

"You did?" Iva's reaction was one of total surprise. She knew that Shadow Dancer had spent much of his youth with the priests and the shaman of the village, but she would never have expected that a female would be allowed to participate in the learning such men could teach.

Again soft, tinkling laughter filled the peaceful garden. "In the ancient Aztec culture there were priestesses who were much like the priests. They studied and performed many of the rituals the priests carried out, but they were more sought after for their influence with the goddesses than the gods."

"That is what you studied?" Iva still could not believe the young woman, and for the moment her sewing lay forgotten in her lap. "You truly wanted to become one of these priestesses?" Iva could not hide the surprise in her tone. Shadow Dancer had made mention that many in his village believed his cousin to be a spirit woman, but he had neglected to tell her that Nokie was also an Aztec priestess!

"I am sure that my practicing arts as a priestess are not exactly what you are imagining." Nokie smiled at Iva's surprised reaction. "I have the gift of foresight and often help Cloud Walker with healings, and upon occasion women of the village seek me out for a potion that can help their lives."

"Foresight and potions?" Iva's eyes lit up as she questioned her companion. "What kind of potions do these women want you to brew up for them?" She envisioned Nokie working some form of black magic late at night beneath a full moon.

The smile never left Nokie's features as she answered, "Some of the potions are for simple womanly maladies; others are for women who desperately seek to have a child. I have even made up potions to attract a warrior to the woman who desires him as her mate. The gift of sight I have had from early childhood."

"And the potions, do they always work?"

"If the woman receiving one does exactly as I instruct, then it will always work, yes." Nokie seemed very sure of herself.

"And what do you see for my future and Shadow Dancer's?" Iva did not believe all of this, but she was curious about what Nokie would say.

"I know that since your joining with Shadow Dancer there have been a few mornings when you have stayed

214

abed late because you have felt a bit unsettled in your stomach."

"However did you learn about that?" Iva was amazed, but searching her mind, she knew that she had told no one about the light queasiness she had experienced a few mornings before leaving her bed. Could Aquilla have somehow guessed and told Nokie?

"Aquilla has told me nothing, but I do know why you have experienced these feelings." It was as though Nokie could read her mind.

"How can you, when I am not sure myself?" Iva protested. For the past couple of weeks she had had some suspicions, but there was no way anyone else could have guessed that she might be carrying a child; it was far too early!

"If you are not sure then you simply have not given yourself the time to search out your body and learn for yourself, but I suspect you have known for some time that you are carrying Shadow Dancer's child."

For a moment Iva could not speak. At hearing the words spoken aloud, her heart lurched strangely in her breast. "But how can you know this, Nokie? I have not even told Shadow Dancer yet!"

"I have been aware of this for some time, Moon Flower. It is wonderful when my gift of sight sees such welcome news."

"Do you think Shadow Dancer will be pleased?" Iva ventured. Perhaps fear of her husband's reaction had kept her from telling him of her suspicions. After all, they had not spoken about children, and they had only been wed a few months.

"Your child will be well loved by Shadow Dancer and everyone of this village," Nokie stated with surprising assurance, as though once again she had seen into the future.

"I will tell Shadow Dancer tonight." Iva smiled, and setting her sewing aside, she hugged Nokie tightly as she imagined her husband's reaction to her news.

The evenings were growing colder as winter moved upon the valley. Shadow Dancer and his young wife were cloistered within their chamber, eating dinner as a warm fire blazed within the fire pit built into one corner, the smoke rising up through the smoke hole that had been fashioned from baked clay.

"You seem quiet this evening, Moon Flower." Shadow Dancer observed as he once again allowed his gaze to roam over his wife's gentle beauty. "I hope you had a pleasant day with Nokie."

Iva nodded her head, content for the moment to relax in her husband's company and savor the secret she held within her heart. "Tell me of your day, husband."

They were sitting upon a bed of soft furs before the fire, and when he finished his meal, Shadow Dancer set his bowl away from him and stretched out in a comfortable position, his head resting upon one arm so he could fully regard his bride. It appeared as each day passed she grew more lovely. "There is little to tell you of my day, my sweet. Several braves and I went to the mountains to hunt, as you already know, and if I have not already told you, it was your husband who killed the large buck that was brought back to the village." Shadow Dancer winked teasingly. "Dark Water found sign of a large bear, but we did not see this great creature. It is probably traveling through the mountains, looking for a cave to claim as its own before the snows are banked too high."

Putting the bowls that had earlier contained their dinner, aside, Iva allowed her eyes to roam over the muscular contours of her husband's wide chest and flat stomach. If the child beneath her heart was a son, she hoped he would one day look exactly like his sire. A thoughtful smile graced her lips as she thought of that time to come and of how women would be attracted to their son.

Shadow Dancer could not help noticing that Iva was paying little attention to what he was saying. She seemed many miles away as her gaze played over his body with a warmth that not only aroused him but made him curious about her mood.

"What do you think of children, Shadow Dancer?" Iva softly questioned as she drew a lone finger down the bulging strength of his forearm.

"In this life, children are everything. They are created to take our place, to carry on, and perhaps change the mistakes we have made before them. A child is a wondrous gift of the great spirit."

His words did not exactly tell Iva what he thought about becoming a father, so Iva had to search him out a bit further. "And do you think of having children of your own?"

"I think of one day having children with golden hair and eyes the color of the sky." Shadow Dancer grinned as he reached out and caressed her creamy smooth cheek.

Of course he assumes that one day we will have children, Iva told herself, but what will he think if he knows he is shortly to become a father?

Ignoring Shadow Dancer's tender touch, she plunged on, "How long do you wish to wait before you have a child, Shadow Dancer?" As if he truly has any choice in the matter, Iva thought.

Something in the way her eyes held his at last drew Shadow Dancer's complete attention. "I would wait only as long as necessary." He pulled himself up so that he was sitting directly in front of her, his gaze searching out her face. "I will be the proudest of men when we share the joy of having a child made from our love."

"Oh, Shadow Dancer, then I am so happy!" Iva cried as tears rolled down her cheeks and she threw her arms around his neck.

"Does this mean? Are you telling me . . . ? We are

217

going to have a child?" Shadow Dancer held her from him and gently wiped at the salty drops coming from her blue eyes, her smile telling him all he needed to know. A loud war whoop filled the chamber as he jumped to his feet with Iva in his arms, spinning about the room and cradling her close to his chest. "I am to be a father?" He stopped and looked down into her flushed face as though still not believing what he was hearing.

"Yes . . . yes! I am so glad you are happy!"

"Happy? I have never known such happiness, Moon Flower! You have brought incomparable joy into my life and now we shall bear the proof of our incredible love!" Shadow Dancer's lips covered hers in a tender blending of their feelings. He loved her beyond words, and now he was being fully blessed.

Iva was consumed by his mouth, her joy knowing no bounds as they sank to the soft fur before the fire. With the tenderest care Shadow Dancer disrobed her, her body gleaming like pale alabaster as she lay upon the dark cover of the bed. Brushing out her golden hair, his agate eyes admired the glistening highlights that shone like burnished copper. With slow purpose his gaze traveled over her length, lingering upon the fullness of her breasts, touching upon her trim waistline; his adoration of her growing as he thought to the day when she would swell with the growth of their child. His heart leaped within his chest as his eyes rose to meet hers, now deep blue with passion. With that glance they shared the secrets of their hearts, all the unsaid words that lovers never seem fully able to express.

Without a word spoken, he came to her, his lips slanting over her mouth as his body pressed unto hers. They joined as lovers desperate to fully share all, her body opening to him, welcoming his full, throbbing heat as rapturous sensations assaulted them both.

His large body tenderly rocked back and forth as he set a loving pattern and she willingly followed each thrust, each touch and caress. His slow and gentle strokes became stronger and swifter as his arousal began to intensify, and they soared urgently toward the promise of fulfillment, until there was no holding back or halting the ecstasy. For a time they labored lovingly as though there were no beginning or end to the dynamic spinning of their senses. But soon their bodies could contain the striving hunger no longer, and each demanded the passionate climax lying in wait. They strove in unison as they irresistibly sought the ultimate peak of pleasure, and with a last long stroke, they found it together. After a time each spasm and tremble ceased, and they were languidly drained. But still they clung together, their lips lightly touching, while Shadow Dancer whispered words of devotion.

Their love silently spoke of all the promises of tomorrow, each loath to be released as they fully savored the contact of flesh against flesh. They treasured this moment upon their bed of furs. It was theirs forever. With light kisses and caresses, they allowed their bodies to cool and relax, in the aftermath of their fierce union sated and content. And wrapped in her embrace, Shadow Dancer lay awake long after his bride had drifted off into slumber, marveling over the fact that he would soon be a father.

Only a prickling of fear disturbed his thoughts when he remembered the attack upon him and Iva at the falls. He had been unable as yet to find out who had sought their deaths, but he had been watchful; and with the news of the coming child, he knew that he would have to be even more so.

After a while one Indian village began to resemble another as Delbert and Willy Handcock sought information which would lead them to the "lost valley of gold," as Willy so aptly called it.

True to his word, Willy did know the Indians well,

and if it were not for this fact, Delbert would have parted company with the drunken, ill-mannered brute weeks ago. As it was, while on the trail, he tried to keep his distance from the man and his mangy dog. At night Delbert went to bed early, leaving Willy to the company of his jug of whiskey and Mutt. During the days, however, it was harder to avoid the older man's complaining and ill temper, but Delbert kept his thoughts to himself, hoping that soon they would locate someone who could help them find Iva.

In almost all of the Apache villages they had thus far visited, the people had confessed to knowing of the legend of the lost tribe, but no one had known the whereabouts of the valley, and Delbert was beginning to believe that there was no lost tribe secreted in the mountains. As each day passed he was beginning to be more and more certain that he was on a wild-goose chase, with Willy Handcock leading the way.

"We should be arriving at the Apache village by midmorning tomorrow," Willy stated in between mouthfuls of stew made of beans and the rabbit they had shot on the trail that afternoon.

Delbert didn't answer, but sipped his mug of coffee as he sat across the fire from the old man and the now-sleeping Mutt. The weather was getting colder, and Delbert was thankful that he had thought to bring his jacket. Pulling the collar up around his neck, he wished once again that he was back at the Cassidy farm.

"Like I already told ya, this is the last Apache village in the area. If'n they can't help us, we might as well hole up fer the winter and start over again come spring."

"Start over?" Delbert sputtered. He threw the remainder of his coffee into the blazing fire. The prospect of spending the entire winter with this ornery ruffian held little appeal, and starting all of this over once spring came held even less.

"Yeah. We'll probably be able to hole up in old Red Fox's village fer the winter. Come spring there's bound to be someone who can tell us something about that valley of gold. There's got to be something we missed!"

"I don't think we missed anything, because I don't think there is such a valley. The Indians that raided the farm were just that, *Indians*. They weren't from some ancient Aztec-Apache tribe that's been hiding away for centuries in the mountains." Delbert pulled out his bedroll and settled himself some distance from where Willy's saddle and bedroll were spread out. Shutting his eyes tightly, he tried to contain the anger that had been building up in him over the past few days.

"Ain't ya just like all the other worthless greenhorns that set out on their own and find they can't cut the rough going?"

Willy sneered across the fire at the young man's back. Then he threw his tin plate down near the edge of the fire and settled down on his bedroll next to Mutt. He raised the jug of whiskey to his lips as he once again went over the image of the silver and gold headband in his mind. *There is a valley, and it's just like the Injuns claim. Full of gold and a lost tribe of Injuns! The boy will see.* He swallowed another deep draught of the strong brew. *He'll see that old Willy Handcock's not just another washed-up prospector!*

Chapter Seventeen

As the two men on horseback rode into the Apache village, the camp dogs yelped and bit at their horse's hooves. Many of the villagers turned out to take in the arrival of strangers.

"Leave all the talking to me, boy," Willy called over his shoulder as his dark eyes swept over the village. "There 'pears to be something mighty heavy going on here that don't look too friendly fer us. There are too many braves here. It looks like old Red Fox has got himself some company." Willy directed his large horse through the crowds that were forming around him and Delbert. He knew it could be dangerous to venture into an Apache village the size of this one, and if Red Fox had himself company, and that company was a group of young bucks wanting to stir up some trouble, that could mean bad news for any white man within miles.

Holding out a hand in friendship, Willy halted Saber in front of the formidable-looking group of braves standing in front of the chief's buffalo-hide tepee. He looked at each brave in turn before settling on the oldest of the group, Chief Red Fox. "It is good to see you once again, old friend." He greeted the chief in the Apache tongue. "The years have treated you kindly, Red Fox, and you also, Mangus Colorado." Willy was sure now that something mighty important was taking

222

place in Red Fox's village. Mangus Colorado was a Chiricahua Apache, and he and his braves were a long way from home. They had been rebelling against the white man and the proposed peace treaty due to be signed between the U.S. Government and the Apache of Arizona and New Mexico in the summer. Willy had heard a lot of tales lately about raids and looting and killing.

"It has been many moons, Willy Handcock, since we have seen you in our village. Why is it that you have come to us?" Red Fox's hardened features looked from Willy to the young man behind him.

Indeed it has been many moons, Willy thought to himself. It had been well over ten years since Willy had taken one of the women from Red Fox's village as his squaw. He and the woman, Running River, had gone into the mountains to prospect for gold, but a year later the woman had died in childbirth. Willy saw now that the time he had spent in Running River's village had resulted in a relationship with her tribe that had not been forgotten. Seeing that Red Fox held no malice toward him, the older man relaxed in his saddle. "Me and the boy here," he pointed a thumb over his shoulder, "we've been on the trail fer a couple of months now looking fer his sister. She was stolen a while back by a band of braves." Willy knew it would make it much easier to claim that Iva Cassidy and the boy were close kin, so that was how he always presented their mission to the Indians they approached.

"We have no white women in our village. There were two women, but a moon past they were traded by Long Bow to a Comanche. He received three fine horses in the trade." Red Fox smiled with pride over his belief that his warrior had come away with the best trade.

"Oh no, Red Fox, we know that it weren't any of yer braves that stole the boy's sister. Gimme that band, boy." Willy turned in his saddle and held a hand out in

Delbert's direction.

Willy was dealing far differently with this tribe than the others they had come across in the past, Delbert had noticed. He nervously pulled the headband out of his shirt, and his mouth grew dry as he handed it to Willy.

"The braves that attacked the boy's farm left this behind." Willy handed the headband down, and it was Mangus Colorado who took the band and studied it for a few minutes before handing it over to Red Fox.

"You and your friend are welcome to rest for a time in Prairie Bird Woman's lodge. She is the woman of Bear Claw who was killed two winters past by a Pawnee. The old woman will be pleased to have you in her lodge." Red Fox made this invitation while still holding the headband; then he and the braves around him turned and started through the entrance flap of his lodge.

Delbert started to voice a protest as he watched the Indians, with the headband, disappearing into Red Fox's tepee, but Willy gave him a dark look and growled low under his breath, "Keep yer yap shut, boy! They will study the band among themselves and let us know in their own time if'n they know who it belongs to."

"But that's the only lead I have to Iva," Delbert protested as he and Willy were led by a brave to the thatched-roof, bark lodge of Prairie Bird Woman.

The brave that led them to the lodge went within to tell Prairie Bird Woman that Red Fox had sent her guests, and as he disappeared Willy Handcock turned swiftly around and stared hard into Delbert's face. "Do ya have any idea who that large warrior was that took yer band from me?"

Delbert silently shook his head.

"Well, boy, that there Injun could well be one of the meanest critters yer probably ever gonna meet up with. He's the father-in-law to Cochise, and he don't cotton none nowadays to any white man. More'n likely he's right now trying to talk Red Fox into taking our scalps! So if'n I were you, I wouldn't be making no fuss about that headband!"

As the brave came out of the lodge and pulled back the entrance flap for the pair to go inside, Delbert still felt nervous at having the headband out of his sight, and as the older man entered ahead of him, he murmured, "I don't care who the Indian is, I still wish we had kept the headband with us!"

The interior of Prairie Bird Woman's lodge was similar to those of all the other bark structures in the village. It was conically shaped, like a hide tepee, with a dirt floor that had a center pit in which fires served for cooking as well as warmth. Room was sparse, a sleeping couch was in one corner, food, tools, and water in another, and most of the woman's worldly possessions were scattered about.

In the Apache language, Willy greeted the bent, ancient-appearing woman wrapped within a tattered blanket and huddled before a low-burning fire. "We thank you, Prairie Bird Woman, for your generous hospitality."

To Delbert the old woman looked like an aged bird as her bent head rose on a frail neck and her black eyes stared at them with an intense regard. Nervously Delbert smiled and nodded his head. Not able to speak the Apache language, he could only go along with Willy's greeting.

"Sit and warm yourselves." The old woman surprised them both by speaking halting English, but of course this was the reason Red Fox had sent them to her lodge, knowing that they would be able to converse easier.

"Well, we be thanking ye kindly fer the offer." Willy grinned and made his way farther into the lodge, Mutt following closely upon his heels. "Can't say, it won't be a pleasure to sit fer a time by yer fire."

"The dog, out!" She pointed a bony finger toward the entrance flap.

"Mutt ain't used to staying outside," Willy objected, but looking at the stern visage of Prairie Bird Woman, he knew there would be no arguing, and started back outside, Mutt again following.

Delbert certainly did not complain about the mongrel being ousted from the old Indian woman's lodge. Every time he looked in the dog's direction, he felt himself beginning to itch from imagined flea bites. He hid the grin that threatened to come over his lips as Willy stepped past him, then felt the woman's gaze directed upon him as he made his way to her fire.

"Food." The woman pointed to a smoke-blackened pot at the edge of the blaze and then her finger indicated a bowl and a bone spoon.

Hard tack and beans had been the better part of Delbert's main diet for the past few months, and his belly growled as he inhaled the aroma coming from the pot. He bent over and began to ladle out a bowlful of the wild onion and venison stew that was simmering. "Thank you," he responded as he took a seat on the dirt floor close to the fire.

The old woman nodded her head as she watched the young man's every move, seeming pleased when the stew in his bowl quickly disappeared.

Willy had to find a piece of horsehair rope to tie up the dog, for Mutt, used to going everywhere with his master, was intent upon following him back inside the lodge. Now that Mutt was tied, his whining yelps could be heard throughout the village. "Dadblasted mongrel!" Willy complained as he joined Delbert and Prairie Bird Woman inside the lodge. "Beats me why I don't just get rid of the mangy son of a bitch!"

Delbert would have voiced his agreement to this, but he thought better of the idea, knowing how fond Willy Handcock was of his flea-ridden mongrel.

"What ya got there, boy?" Willy questioned. He

stepped to the fire and eyeing the empty bowl in Delbert's hand, he licked his lips as he spied the pot of stew.

The old woman did not hurriedly offer Willy her food, but as the silence stretched on in the lodge and Delbert set his bowl down next to him, she at last relented. Looking at Willy, she nodded, and being a man that does not have to be asked twice, Willy Handcock took her movement as a most generous offer. Taking up Delbert's bowl, he greedily filled it again and sat down, noisily proceeding to wolf down the food and then spoon himself another bowlful.

A large belch sounded as he finished the second helping. "That was sure good, Prairie Bird Woman." He set the bowl down and, with the back of his shirtsleeve, wiped away the portions of his meal that had dribbled down his chin. "Me and the boy here will see if'n we can't be killing a deer come tomorrow, to pay ya back!"

Delbert said nothing. He had learned early on that Willy Handcock would lie whenever the mood struck. More than likely Willy had no intention of hunting to replenish the old woman's larder.

"Well, come on, boy. Let's go and get our bedrolls and spread them down and rest our bones fer a time, at least till Red Fox decides if'n he knows anything about that headband." Willy pulled himself to his feet and waited for Delbert to do likewise.

Delbert felt uncomfortable as he sensed the woman's eyes upon them when they left her lodge. "Why did you tell her that we would hunt for her?" he questioned as soon as they were outside.

"'Cause we just might! Ain't her lodge a sight more comfortable than being outside in the cold? I done told ya we might have to hole up fer the winter, and what better place than a warm lodge?"

"And I have already told you, I am not going to waste the entire winter in an Indian village and then start this whole thing over again come spring!" Delbert stomped away from Willy as he searched about for his horse.

Catching up to him, Willy grunted, "Don't be so dang pigheaded. Maybe old Red Fox or Mangus Colorado will be able to tell us something about that headband so we'll be able to leave this village and freeze our asses off up there in them mountains as ya seemed determined to do!"

It was not until the next morning that Delbert and Willy were called to Red Fox's lodge. Mangus Colorado and his braves had left with the breaking of dawn, along with several warriors from Red Fox's village. The old chief had given those of his braves who wanted to follow Mangus Colorado his blessing, but his own decision had been to stay neutral in this fight with the white man.

"I am afraid that I cannot help you to find those that stole your friend's sister," Red Fox said as he handed Willy the headband. "None of my braves, and none of those in Mangus Colorado's group, have ever seen such markings like those on the band."

Willy had hoped they would have been given some information here in Red Fox's village, but he was not that surprised by what Red Fox was saying. Looking across the fire at Delbert, he knew that the boy would not want to go any further in their search for the lost valley of gold. "Well, I reckon as how we done looked about everywhere we can. We'll start back out come morning, Red Fox. We thank ya fer yer hospitality."

"I am sorry that I could not be of more help," Red Fox added as Delbert and Willy got up to go.

"So am I, old friend," Willy stated with much truth. He had hoped to become rich on this venture with the boy, but it appeared that all he had done was kill time.

Once again Delbert and Willy Handcock spent the

night in Prairie Bird Woman's lodge. Their bedrolls were stretched out near the warmth of her fire, and as Delbert shut his eyes, he was aware that the old woman lying upon her sleeping couch was watching him intently. His last waking thoughts were of what she was thinking.

The following morning as Prairie Bird Woman sat huddled in her usual place near the fire, Delbert rolled up his bedroll. While he was gathering his few belongings together, the headband fell out of his shirt, which had come untucked during the night.

Prairie Bird Woman's quick eyes noticed the headband as it fell to the dirt floor. As Delbert picked up the leather band, he turned it over, and the design was visible from where the old woman sat. A cry tore from her lips as the sunlight coming through the opened doorflap touched upon the sun sign. "Ah-eeeeee." She scrambled to her feet, and as quickly as her bent form would allow, she gained Delbert's side, her gnarled, work-worn hands grasping the headband.

Delbert was more than a little surprised by his hostess' reaction. With widened eyes he regarded her as though she had taken total leave of her senses.

Murmuring Apache and English words that were barely audible, the old woman rubbed her finger over and over the sun sign, as though she expected it to vanish off the smooth leather facing of the headband.

Fearing that she was totally demented, Delbert watched as Prairie Bird Woman at last clutched the headband to the tattered dress that covered her ancient bosom and her eyes latched upon his. His heart lurched. She knew something about the headband! But that is impossible, he told himself in reply to that thought.

"Where did you get this?" Prairie Bird Woman asked, still clutching the headband tightly as though fearing it would be snatched away from her at any minute.

"It belongs to the Indian who raided our farm and stole my sister." Delbert, too, found it easier to explain that Iva was his sibling.

The old woman closed her eyes. "I had almost given up hope," she murmured aloud.

She made little sense to Delbert. Still thinking that she had lost her wits, he spoke softly. "The headband is the reason we are here in Red Fox's village. We had hoped someone here would know the whereabouts of the band of Indians that raided the farm and could help us find Iva."

The old woman quickly shook her head in the negative. "None in Red Fox's village knows of the place where the mountains meet and the valley is guarded by the eagle's nest."

Delbert did not know if the old lady was really insane or if her gibberish held some hidden meaning. "Do you know where this valley is?" He had dared to ask the question, and now, his breath trapped in his chest, he stared into the coal black eyes before him.

Prairie Bird Woman had thought she would die before anyone would ever ask her this question. Slowly she nodded, then her eyes teared over as she mumbled a reply before turning and going back to the warmth of her fire. "I know where the valley of the people is, I know. I could never forget. Over and over he told me the way."

Delbert dared to believe that she was telling him the truth. Nervously he followed her to the fire and bent down across from her, hoping that this was not some insane moment on her part. "Who told you where the valley is located, Prairie Bird Woman?" he softly probed.

As though his question had drawn her back to reality, the old woman's head rose and her dark gaze settled upon the young man before her. "Golden Eagle, my father."

"How did your father know of this valley?"

230

Excitement burned in Delbert's green eyes as he questioned the old woman.

"My father was chief of the lost tribe many years ago."

"The chief?" Delbert gasped aloud. This was unbelievable!

Tears trickled down the leathered cheeks and splashed over the sun sign on the headband Prairie Bird Woman held in her lap.

Delbert was totally unprepared to deal with her grief. He said nothing for a few minutes, allowing her time to pull herself together, but when her tears subsided, he asked, "Are you sure this headband is of the tribe in the hidden valley?"

"This is the same sign which belonged to my father's family. I would never forget it. Though he was blind, my father drew it over and over in the dust. When I was a young girl, he told me that in ancient days the Aztecs called their most valiant braves Warriors of the Sun. Golden Eagle was descended from the house of the sun sign."

Delbert felt as though all the air had been knocked out of his lungs. Feeling weak, he sat down and gazed with disbelief at the old woman. She was not insane as he had at first believed. "Can you tell me how to get to this valley? I must find Iva! I have to make sure that she is safe and bring her back to her family!" Desperation was in Delbert's voice as he made his appeal.

Prairie Bird Woman slowly shook her head. "I can never tell the whereabouts of the valley. I made a promise long ago to my father never to give away the words he told me."

"But you must tell me! You are the only one who knows!" Delbert jumped to his feet in his agitation. "How am I to find this valley on my own? I have been searching now for months! How can I save Iva?" His own eyes filled with tears as he glimpsed the hard tilt to the old woman's chin and knew that she would never

231

tell him or anyone else where the valley was. She was prepared to go to her grave with the secret locked in her heart.

"I will lead you to the valley of my father's people." Prairie Bird Woman's soft voice reached Delbert's ears over the inner turmoil of his soul.

"You would lead the way?" How was this ancient crone going to lead him and Willy Handcock anywhere? She looked as though she could drop at any moment just by walking from one side of her lodge to the other!

"There are things I must set straight in the valley of my father's people. I promised my father that before I died I would take word of him to his family."

"But I could do that for you!"

"No other can do what must be done." A poise came over the haggard woman. "I must be the one. If it is to be believed, I must be the one."

Prairie Bird Woman was resolved to go along. Delbert knew that he would not be able to sway her. If he was to find the valley, his only hope lay in letting her show him the way.

Reading his resignation on his features, Prairie Bird Woman stated, "We shall leave this village when the first snows thaw in the mountains."

"But that won't be until spring!" Delbert wailed aloud. He could not bear the thought of Iva staying with her captors throughout the long winter months.

"It would be foolish to go into the mountains now. There would be no getting through the passes; they will be snowed over," Prairie Bird Woman reasoned.

Delbert knew that she was right. Still it rankled him that he would be detained here in Red Fox's village as Willy Handcock had predicted.

For the first time Delbert saw a smile come to Prairie Bird Woman's wrinkled features. "The young are always impatient. I remember when I was young. I, too, believed that time seemed to pass much too slowly," she said.

Prairie Bird Woman felt younger than she had in years. She had thought that she had little to live for, and had only awaited the day when the great spirit would call her name upon the night breeze and she would join her husband Bear Claw and all her loved ones in the land of paradise, the hunting grounds. Now, suddenly, everything had changed. At last she would be able to fulfill her promise to her father. She would return to his people and tell the tale he had told her so many times while she was growing up!

Chapter Eighteen

Shadow Dancer had left in the early hours of the morning to go on a two-day hunting trip with Dark Water and several Indians from the village. Alone, Iva stretched languorously upon the cool bedding. Shadow Dancer's warmth was absent, but the clean, masculine scent of him still lingered on the covers that surrounded her. A small smile filtered over her lips as she thought of his departing love touches before he climbed from their bed to begin his day.

Closing her eyes, she again envisioned his powerful body covering her own. She could taste the coolness of his flesh as she imagined her lips raining kisses over the straining muscles that ran along his powerfully corded neck. The taste and feel of him had been potent, so potent that it had been Iva who had pressed him down against her, her hand against the firmness of his lower back and buttocks.

His manhood had been hot and burning as it had brushed against her belly for only a second and then, hard and pulsing, had found her hungry womanhood. She had cried aloud at first entry, the largeness of his love tool carrying her beyond caution or control, and had pressed against him, wanting to feel all of him within her, to know the full depths of pleasure that awaited her. He would be gone for two days, and she would miss him terribly. This thought had spurred her to move even more feverishly beneath him.

They had made love twice the past night, and still Shadow Dancer had not had enough of the incredible pleasure this woman alone gave him. Every cell in his body was attuned to but one purpose, that of awakening any dormant embers of desire and carrying her over the boundary of rational thought to sweet-sensual pleasure's domain.

A shudder much like that which had shaken her early this very morning once again coursed over Iva's body as she relived that eruption in her very depths when her husband cried out her name as he also was swept within passion's vortex.

A soft sigh escaped Iva's slightly parted lips, her flesh tingling with remembrance. *Shadow Dancer*. The name swirled within her mind as she indulged herself a few seconds longer in reliving the departing kiss they had shared, one that had nearly consumed her.

Feeling somewhat at a loss as she thought of the two days ahead of her without her husband, Iva slowly forced herself out of bed. After dressing, she headed out to the gardens.

As she ate the breakfast Aquilla had prepared for her, she thought over her options for the day. She could spend it in Nokie and Tanza's company. They were always pleasant, and she did have much sewing still to complete. But then she thought about the horses she had won from Gray Otter, and she decided perhaps she would go to the back pastures and work with Cimmerian and her husband's animals. Perhaps the mares she had won would be worthy to be covered by Cimmerian, she thought as she finished her meal. After all, she told herself, she should be looking to the future for her husband and their child. She could certainly do her part by helping tend her husband's horses and make their lines strong and valuable.

Only a short time later Iva made her way through the

gardens and set out on the path that would take her to the pastures where the horses were kept. Suddenly she was halted by a childish voice. Shading her eyes from the glare of the morning sun, she watched a young boy approach her.

"I have been instructed to bring a message to you, Moon Flower." The boy appeared to stand in awe of the golden woman. His dark eyes were wide with fascination as well as apprehension.

Not recognizing the youth, Iva smiled warmly as she asked, "What is the message?"

"There is someone who wishes to meet you at the temple this evening. You are to be there with the setting of the sun."

For a minute Iva was taken by surprise. She had expected that he had brought some word from Nokie or Tanza. "Why would someone want to meet me at the temple? Who sent you with such a message?"

"I was told to reply only that it is of great concern to the safety of your husband. You are not to forget that you are to come with the lowering of the sun, and he said you are not to tell anyone your destination or there could be danger!"

"Danger for who? For Shadow Dancer?" Iva's hand went to her throat as she thought of her husband in some kind of danger.

The boy shook his head. "I do not know," was the only response he gave before turning and striding away, heading back toward the village.

For a few minutes Iva stood where she was and watched the boy's retreating back. A frown marred her lovely brow as she thought over his words. Whoever could have sent her such a message? What had he meant by saying that her meeting a stranger at the temple could be of great concern to her husband's safety? Why would the boy not tell her who had sent him? Turning her blue eyes in the direction of the temple that housed the priests of the village, Iva took in

236

the imposing structure that sat upon the side of the mountain. If she did as the boy said and left in time to arrive with the setting of the sun, she would surely have to return to her husband's house in the dark.

From where she stood the Indian temple appeared stark and ominous against the backdrop of the mountain. Iva had no desire to go to such a place, and certainly not alone at night. Slowly she began to make her way toward the pastures. She could not forget that the boy had implied there could be some danger to Shadow Dancer, but the child had only repeated what he had been told. Was Shadow Dancer in some kind of trouble? Did this person who instructed her to meet him at the temple know of some danger her husband should be warned about? Her thoughts quickly went to what had happened to them at the falls, and fear began to grow within her. What would happen if she did not go to the temple? Would Shadow Dancer be harmed?

As she came within view of the horses and heard Cimmerian whinnying softly at her approach, she tried to put the message the boy had brought her to the back of her mind. But the strangeness of the communication made her uneasy for the rest of the morning and throughout the afternoon.

Iva spent most of the day with the mares that had once belonged to Gray Otter, trying to win the animals' trust. The stallion that Cimmerian had beaten in the horse race was allowed to run loose with Shadow Dancer's horses for the time being, but Cimmerian did not allow Iva far from his sight as he grazed on the sweet grass and his mistress brushed and soothed the two beautiful mares until they began to whinny softly at the sound of her soft voice. She filled their nostrils with her scent by rubbing them down with her wraparound skirt. The short-sleeved tunic which reached to her knees covered her sufficiently, yet allowed her to work with the animals unhindered.

While she worked with the horses Iva tried to forget her meeting with the young boy. After finishing with the mares, for a time she rode Cimmerian over the pastures. By midafternoon they halted near the pond behind her husband's house, and Iva dismounted to splash some cool water on her arms and throat. She was tempted for a minute to cool off her entire body in the liquid depths, but she decided against it and instead allowed Cimmerian to graze freely near the pond's edge while she rested beneath a tree and ate some of the fruit that Aquilla had given her before she left the house that morning.

Lying in the shade, Iva gazed up at the canopy of leaves and wondered what Shadow Dancer was doing at this minute. Were his thoughts upon her, as hers were on him? A soft sigh escaped her, as once again the message she had been brought filled her thoughts. She wished Shadow Dancer had not left on this trip. If he were here in the village he would go to meet whoever it was that would be waiting at the temple.

Sitting upright once again, Iva realized she had little choice but to go to the temple. She could not ignore the message. What if someone did have information about some danger that lay in wait for Shadow Dancer? She would never be able to forgive herself if something happened to him and she had had it in her power to warn him.

The decision made, Iva did not return to the outer pastures, but instead kept Cimmerian with her as she made her way back to the house. She secured the stallion with a horsehair lead until the appointed time for her to set out for the temple.

Changing into a clean tunic and skirt, her pale curls pulled back and a dark cloak thrown over her shoulders, Iva left her chambers. She would leave in time to ride Cimmerian to the mountain and up the path leading to the temple. She regretted now that she had not sought out Nokie and told the other woman what she was about to do. Perhaps Nokie would have volunteered to go with her. But Iva had not sought out Nokie because the message had directed her to come alone and tell no one. She feared that if she did not obey, whoever it was she was going to meet would not appear!

For some reason though, Iva could not just leave without telling someone her destination. Seeing Aquilla coming from the kitchen area, she approached her. "I'm going to take Cimmerian for a ride, Aquilla. I think that I might go in the direction of the temple." She tried to make her voice appear light so as not to arouse suspicion in the other woman's mind.

One fine brow arched over Aquilla's dark eyes. "The hour grows late, the sun will be gone soon. Would it not be better to take this ride another day?"

Iva was in total agreement with her, but trying not to let her own worry show, she smiled. "I will not be long. Go on home to Arez whenever you wish. Don't worry about me. I will eat when I return." Appearing much more confident than she felt, she turned around and headed out of the house.

Cimmerian was more than ready for a long ride. It had been some days since his mistress had paid him so much attention, and with the sun lowering and cool evening breezes descending over the valley, he was in fine spirits as they left the house.

Iva gave the stallion his lead as he galloped through the pasture toward the mountain on which the priests' temple stood. It was not until they approached the path leading to the temple that Iva slowed their pace.

The temple in which the Indian priests dwelled glittered with a marble brilliance now that she was closer and the setting sun was lowering directly behind its arched roof. Slowly Iva directed Cimmerian along the steep path, the arching straightness of the trail demanding caution though the sun was lowering and Iva would have hurried the stallion's steps in order to have done with this meeting and quickly return to the village.

The temple had been built many years ago as a place for the priests to worship the gods of their ancestors. It was also a place where those of the people who sought out the truths of their past and of their future could come to study and to accept guidance in their lives. As Cimmerian touched flat ground at the end of the trail, Iva stared in wonder at the sight before her, marble-slab steps that led upward.

Tentatively she dismounted and, for a few minutes of indecision, stood holding Cimmerian's reins. Drawing a deep breath in order to steady her nerves, she realized that no one was going to appear and she would have to climb the steps to the temple. She gently patted her stallion's sleek neck before tying the reins to a nearby bush. "I will only be gone a minute, Cimmerian," she whispered softly as she tried to bolster her own spirits before she left her horse's side.

Nervously she approached the steps. There must have been at least fifty of them leading upward. Seeing no one about and knowing that she had no choice but to climb, Iva slowly began the ascent.

At the top of the steps, she found a great pale slab of sandstone and marble laid out before the temple and encircled on the outer edges by hand-hewn and sculpted rock.

I should have thought to bring some kind of weapon with me, she thought. Looking around as she stood on the hard flooring, Iva noticed that torches had been lit and they illuminated the outer walls of the temple and the intricately carved massive front door. As she stood in front of the imposing building with its jewel-like glitter and ancient carvings, she was unsure of why she had been foolish enough to come! Just as she made up her mind that she should turn around and go back down those steps, a dark cloaked figure stepped through a side door that Iva had not noticed.

For a moment she dared not breathe as she stared at the silently approaching priest. When he stood only a few feet from her, a gnarled hand appeared from the folds of the cloak and, with a silent motion, indicated that she was to follow.

Iva was not able to glimpse the man's features behind the cowl drawn forward over his forehead. He turned around as though expecting her to do as instructed, but she stood her ground though her knees were trembling. "Who are you? What do you know of danger that is being directed toward my husband?"

The stranger in black turned around for a fraction of a second, and at that moment Iva thought she glimpsed gleaming, dark eyes. The voice was secretively low as he said, "You must follow. We can talk in here."

Iva still thought to turn away, to flee the temple and this stranger and return to the village, back to the safety of her husband's house, but she thought she detected a touch of urgency in the man's tone, and thoughts of harm coming to Shadow Dancer would not let her leave. One foot and then another followed after the dark figure. Finally, passing through the small side door, Iva looked around her as the man led her down a long, cool hallway.

Torches lit the corridor and glistened off its tile flooring. Colors—Indian red, salmon pink, gold ocher, light emerald green, and indigo blue—reflected off the sculpted walls and shimmered in beautiful frescoes, enhancing depictions of the Indians' numerous gods and their paradises.

The cloaked figure hurried down the corridor, and Iva tried to keep up with him, realizing that he was taking her deep into the interior of the temple.

Fear gnawed at her insides as she was led through a small garden and halted before the door of a tower. A key glistened in the moonlight as it appeared in the gnarled hands of the man, and with an easy motion, he opened the creaking, wood door.

Iva hesitated before entering, but feeling she had gone too far now to turn back, she followed. The minute she stepped inside the tower chamber, she knew that she had made a terrible mistake. The door swung hard behind her and slammed, and at the same time she was grabbed from both sides!

Chapter Nineteen

Bound hand and foot, and with an Indian warrior she did not recognize standing at each side, Iva glared her hatred and fury upon the dark-cloaked figure standing in the shadows of the small, dank, and musty-smelling room. He kept his features obscured, remaining in the shadows with the cowl drawn over his head. Only the low tones of his voice as he gave directions to the two Indian men hinted at his identity. But exhausted from attempting to fight off her attackers, and fearful of what would happen next, Iva did not concentrate on that voice. She did not know if her captor was Atlacol, the high priest of the village, or a lesser priest she had perhaps met over the past weeks.

In a trembling voice, she questioned the cloaked man. "What do you want from me? Why are you doing this?" The reason given to summon her to the temple had been a ruse. It was not Shadow Dancer who was in the danger, she was.

"What do I want from you?" Heinous laughter filled the space of the small chamber, then abruptly halted as the low voice hissed, "You have a purpose, have no fear. You, the golden one whom the gods brought to this valley, will be the very instrument which will cause the destruction of the line of the sun sign! With you gone, Shadow Dancer will be easy prey! His strength and cunning will desert him, and at that time I will be there!" Again the strange, evil laughter filled the chamber.

Chills laced through Iva, not only for herself but for her husband who was unaware of the plot against him. "You hate my husband so much?" The blood had totally drained from her face, but she had to try to find out why this man wanted to destroy Shadow Dancer. If she were to lose her life this night, at least she would attempt to learn something about this man's motives.

"Hate? I have no feelings at all where Shadow Dancer is concerned. He stands in the way of all that I desire, and through you I will see my life's goal completed!" The golden woman's beauty stood out like a polished gem in the dimly lit chamber, even trussed up as she was. For a moment the priest regretted greatly that he would not have the time to fully sample her golden body. He would love to run his hands over her shapely curves. Delight would course through him if he could hear her cry out aloud as his seed pumped into her hot woman's depths. But he knew that he could not dare such a thing! The golden woman had been touched by the gods, and for him to touch her flesh could surely mean his own end. No, it was better he dispose of her and then deal with Shadow Dancer. Turning to the two braves that stood at Iva's sides and held her upright, he said in the same low hiss, "Take her away! Go through the gardens, and keep her silent!"

Iva tried to pull away, her mouth opening to scream for help, but this time a piece of material was slipped over it and tied behind her head. Without preamble she was dragged toward the door, the two braves doing exactly as they were told.

As the warriors took the golden woman from the tower chamber, Meci flung the dark cloak across the small table. A slanted grin, like a leer, revealed his yellowed teeth in the torchlight. He had felt an unusual sexual power while standing in the presence of the golden woman, and perhaps this too was because she had been gifted by the gods! Turning to the dark stairway that led upward, he took up a lit torch and made his way to the second floor of the tower. Unlocking a door, he stepped into the chamber, the torchlight gleaming across bare floors and exposing a small cot placed against the opposite wall.

A young girl of about the age of fourteen stood up, visibly trembling as her dark eyes met those of the priest. The fight had long ago been beaten out of her, and she stood awaiting her fate as the dark-cloaked man placed the torch securely against the cold stone wall and slowly turned toward her.

His black eyes gleamed with an unholy light as his dark priest's robe fell to the tile floor. With one movement his breechcloth was freed, and to the young girl's gaze his thrusting organ appeared swollen and terrifying.

Meci approached, thinking only of the golden woman, his hand reaching down and gathering his scrotum as though he held a formidable weapon.

The young Indian girl would have screamed, but past experiences had taught her this brought no help, only increased abuse. She clamped her jaw shut as she was flung to the cot and mounted without regard.

Totally defenseless, Iva was dragged to the back wall encircling the gardens and pulled through a low stone archway. Her heart hammered wildly within her breasts. At any moment she expected one of the two braves to plunge a knife blade deep into her chest.

Surprise combined with terror as the two braves dragged her along and she saw in the distance silhouetted in the moonlight the shapes of two horses and riders.

"Is this the one?" one of the horsemen questioned. His words seemed to be a mixture of her husband's language and another Indian tongue. In the grip of terror, Iva had a hard time making out what he said, but the braves at her sides appeared to understand him well enough.

"This is the one. She is bad medicine. Our people believe her a witch, so be careful of her trickery! If you do not keep her tied, she might well disappear."

"My wife is a Shoshone woman, she will keep an eye on her. She knows much about witches. She will cast a spell that will conquer the power that woman holds." The Indian sitting atop his horse seemed confident of his wife's abilities to combat witchcraft.

"The Shoshone women are wise in their use of power, but I warn you, the golden woman is possessed of the craft of seducing a man when he is unaware. She should be kept tied for a few days at the least." The Indian at Iva's side did not wish the Paiute to fall victim to Moon Flower as his tribesman, Shadow Dancer, had. The priest had told them both much of this woman's evil, and because of what they had learned, they had agreed to secretly come to the temple this night. They would be glad when she was gone from the valley, and they believed Meci when he said those who had had dealings with the golden woman must be purged and made clean before their gods once again. That was why they would support Meci's plans for Shadow Dancer.

"Have no fear, friend. My wife will watch over the woman. She is to be the sixth wife of her brother. She may well have to use her powers of seduction to claim a place at Bull Feather's side!" The hint of laughter in the horseman's tone brought smiles to the two Indians' lips.

With no more words needed, one of the braves lifted Iva up and placed her before the Paiute. The horseman gave a slight nod of his head then kicked the sides of his pony, and the other rider, a woman, followed behind, leaving the two braves watching after them.

Iva squirmed and wriggled, trying to throw herself from the horse and win her freedom, but tied, she was powerless in the Indian's arms, unable to put up any real opposition to her abduction. The Indian held her against his chest, her struggles not seeming to affect him in the least.

Tears fell from Iva's blue eyes and saturated her gag. Each step the Indian's horse made in the opposite direction from her husband's village left her with a deeper ache in her heart. Shadow Dancer, she silently cried, but knew that her longing for her husband was for naught. He would not even find her missing from his village for another day! Despair, the likes of which she had never known, filled her, and thinking of her unborn child increased the flow of her tears.

The hunting had been good throughout the day, and making camp early in the evening, Shadow Dancer and Dark Water joined the other braves around the fire. Stories of the day's hunt were retold and praised or laughed about. Dark Water had killed a large elk, so the story of his downing of the stag was told more than once.

After eating some of the roasted elk, Shadow Dancer left the group to brush down his horse and then find his sleeping mat. As the others of his group talked on into the night, his thoughts centered upon his wife. This was the first time they had been separated, and though his thoughts had been pleasant enough during the day, when they turned toward Moon Flower, this evening he felt strangely uneasy.

After tending to his horse, he stretched out upon his sleeping mat, and for a time tried to find sleep. But each time he shut his eyes he was plagued by images of his bride. Usually thoughts of Moon Flower filled him with a pleasant warmth deep within, but for some reason tonight was different. A chill swept over him as the moon was covered by dark clouds, and gazing up into the dark velvet night, he felt an emptiness fill his soul.

Trying to put from his mind the feeling that something was amiss back at his village, Shadow Dancer could not find sleep until the late hours when he at last told himself that he would follow his heart and leave for the village in the morning.

The others could carry on with the hunt. He would return to Moon Flower, he decided, and at last was able to sleep.

The Paiute man and Shoshone woman talked long into the night. Some of what they said Iva could make out, their words resembling the speech of her husband's tribe, but for the most part, crazed from all she had experienced in the past few hours, she drifted in and out of awareness. She did not know what they were going to do with her or why they had taken her away from the temple. In the back of her mind was the thought that they were taking her away only to kill her later!

The pair rode on throughout the moonlit night, leaving the valley far behind. They traveled southward, and not until the break of dawn did they halt their mounts near a shallow running stream.

The woman dismounted first and helped Iva down from her husband's mount, holding her around the waist to keep her from falling to her knees. Leading her over to a tree, the Indian woman helped her to sit with her back resting against the trunk.

Leaving Iva's side, she then went back to her horse and retrieved two small leather pouches. Her husband led the horses to the stream and patiently stood near them as they drank their fill.

Returning to Iva, the woman bent down and pulled the gag from her mouth. Opening a pouch, she pulled out a piece of dried meat and indicated that Iva was to eat.

Iva drew in a deep breath through parched lips before shaking her head and trying to speak. "What are you going to do with me?" The words came out raspingly even to her own ears, but the woman appeared to understand her.

Pointing to her own mouth, the woman indicated that Iva was to eat first. "Talk after eat," she stated as she glimpsed Iva's resistance.

Having no choice in the matter, Iva at last nodded her head and bit off a piece of the dried meat. She hoped that she could communicate with the woman after the meal. Iva swallowed hard, and when she tried to speak again, the jerky was once more pressed against her lips. Taking another bite herself, the Indian woman left Iva's side to retrieve water for her to drink.

When the prisoner had eaten and drunk enough to satisfy her, the Shoshone woman leaned back on her heels and grinned widely, showing two missing front teeth.

"Where are you taking me?" Iva did not wait for her to cover her mouth with the gag before she began asking her questions.

Reaching out a tentative hand the Indian woman lightly caressed the golden hair that hung wildly over Iva's shoulders and down her back. "We are going to the village of my brother, Bull Feather. You will be happy there among the Shoshone."

"But why? Why would you take me from my husband's village?" Iva prayed that she would have the time to convince this woman that she should be returned to Shadow Dancer's village. The Indian woman seemed kind enough, not threatening at the moment.

"We were not told that you had a husband." A worried frown appeared upon her dark brow for a second.

Iva sighed softly, believing that if she could convince this woman there had been a mistake she would be returned without delay. "My husband is known as Shadow Dancer. He is a mighty warrior, and will not be pleased with what is happening to me." She thought perhaps a light threat would increase the worry of the woman.

For a moment the Indian woman appeared confused, but then, slowly, her grin reappeared. "Husband not matter. Go to Bull Feather's village. Far away. Husband no more! You have new husband in Shoshone village."

At first Iva thought she had misunderstood. "I have a husband—Shadow Dancer."

The Indian woman's dark head shook back and forth. "New husband, Bull Feather."

Iva shook her head as though trying to clear it. This could not be possible! She had been taken from the temple to be married off to an Indian in a faraway village?

The Indian woman did not immediately cover Iva's mouth with the gag; instead she untied the rope at her feet and indicated that Iva should tend to her needs in the bushes away from the stream where her husband was watering the horses.

While being helped to her feet, Iva tried once more to make the woman understand that she could not go along with her and her husband to this Bull Feather's village. "I must be returned to my husband's village. I am carrying his child!"

The woman's smile never faltered as she looked Iva up and down, then studied her midsection. "Baby good. Bull Feather has five wives, no baby. Baby good!"

Chapter Twenty

The pace set by the Paiute man, Iva had learned he was called Talking Bear, seemed relentless. Except for the night of her abduction and that first morning when Iva had traveled in front of him on his pony, she rode atop the couple's packhorse, her hands tied in front of her, her mount plodding along behind the man's. Throughout much of the day Iva slumped wearily upon the packs on the animal's back, but the woman seemed not at all bothered, as though used to such a hard trek, and followed behind without complaint. The only rest they had came in the middle of each afternoon when Talking Bear signaled that they were to make a small camp. They would eat food from their packs, or what they had acquired during the day, and then sleep for a few hours. Awakening before the setting of the sun, Talking Bear would brush out the small campfire while the woman packed their belongings, and then they would travel throughout the rest of the night.

Iva's feet had been left untied since that first morning and she had not been gagged, but Talking Bear had threatened on more than one occasion to replace the gag when she pleaded with the pair to return her to her husband's village. Unlike his wife, Spotted Fawn, Talking Bear grew impatient with her cries for release and her threats of what would befall them when

Shadow Dancer caught up with them.

After a week's hard travel, one afternoon the couple did not pack up their belongings as they usually did. Instead they lingered around the camp, Talking Bear built up the campfire and, without a word, left the campsite to hunt fresh game. Iva wondered at this sudden change in routine, but she said nothing as she leaned back against a tree and watched Spotted Fawn, beside the campfire, softening a piece of rabbit fur.

"I will be glad to return to the village of my brother." Spotted Fawn smiled as she looked up from her work. "It has been three winters since last I saw Bull Feather. Talking Bear came to our village that cold winter with his trading goods, for then as now he went from village to village trading those things that people need. I enjoy traveling with him, but at times I miss those companions of my youth and my family." Spotted Fawn enjoyed talking to the pale woman. She missed the companionship of a female while on the trail with her husband, and whenever possible she visited with the golden woman.

Iva's hands were untied periodically, but only in the presence of Talking Bear. At the moment she wished they were free so she could rub her wrists. Though the rope was not tight enough to hinder circulation, it had chafed the insides of her wrists. Trying to put this from her thoughts, Iva once more tried to win Spotted Fawn over to her cause. "It is very sad to be away from those you love." She released a soft sigh as though in total agreement with the other woman.

Spotted Fawn nodded, at the moment unaware of the path the pale woman was leading her down. She and Talking Bear had decided that they would not give the golden woman a name until they reached the Shoshone village. Perhaps Bull Feather himself would like to have this honor. "Those in my village will learn to love you; do not fear. They will think you touched by the great spirit, for they have seen few white women."

252

"I do not fear the people of your tribe," Iva lied, for in truth she was terrified of what she would find in the village Spotted Fawn and Talking Bear were taking her to, and doubly afraid of this warrior called Bull Feather! "I fear only for my heart, because I know now that it will never mend from the great hurt I have suffered at being taken from my husband!"

"Such pain will heal in time. You will soon learn to forget this one that was your mate. Bull Feather has many wives, and they will all become your sisters. You will share many things with them, including my brother." Spotted Fawn discarded the pale woman's words. The life of an Indian woman was hard, and at an early age they were taught to adjust to whatever surroundings were forced upon them. Many of her village had had husbands who had died in battle or while out hunting. They had gone on. The pain of such a loss healed, and the women found happiness once again on another warrior's sleeping couch.

Tears, both real and forced, came instantly to Iva's eyes and rolled down her cheeks. "I will never be able to love again. Shadow Dancer holds my heart!" Her words came out softly, almost reverently, as the image of her husband filled her mind.

Spotted Fawn let the fur drop onto her lap as she looked over to the woman she and her husband held captive. By nature she always endeavored to see the bright side of everything. This was one of the things that had attracted Talking Bear to her, she knew, and it was why he considered her to be a good traveling mate. But at the moment, looking at the tears falling from the pale woman's eyes, Spotted Fawn felt a great sadness. "There is nothing I can do to change the way of things now. We will arrive in my brother's village as the sun fills the sky tomorrow."

Iva grasped on to this first ray of hope she had had since her abduction, Spotted Fawn's sympathy for her and her plight. "But you can untie me! You can let me go back to my husband. You can tell Talking Bear that I escaped you. He will never know!" Pleadingly, she looked at the Indian woman, her excitement growing.

For a minute Spotted Fawn seemed to consider allowing her husband's captive to escape, but at last she shook her head. "Talking Bear would not believe these words if I told them to him. I have never been able to speak falsely without his knowledge. He would be angry with me, for he wanted a gift to give my brother after this long time of being away from the Shoshone village."

"But he can give him something else!"

Again the dark head shook in the negative. "There is nothing else worthy of Bull Feather. Women and food mean everything to my brother."

Iva would have protested, but Spotted Fawn interrupted. "You see my brother was very angry with Talking Bear when last we saw him in the Shoshone village. He had wanted Talking Bear to remain in the village and forget his trading. Bull Feather had wanted what my husband had in his packs—for his people— and he was fond of the entertaining stories that Talking Bear told him. But Talking Bear is not a man to stay in one place for long, so early one morning when the village was still asleep, my husband and I left Bull Feather's village and we have not returned since. The gift from my husband to Bull Feather must be great to appease the wrong my brother will still carry in his heart."

"But why does this gift have to be me?" Iva cried aloud in frustration.

"You are beautiful," Spotted Fawn said simply, and as she picked up her fur once more, she added, "Bull Feather's other wives are not as pleasant to look upon as you. He will take great pride in owning a woman such as you. He will consider you his most valuable treasure. My husband realized this when first he was approached by the man with the black robe in your village. The man had desired Talking Bear to take your life, because he claimed your golden features a curse, but my husband quickly thought to take you to my brother. I think Talking Bear also wishes to be able to return to the Shoshone village."

Iva quickly realized that she was getting nowhere with the Indian woman. Granted, she was thankful that she had not been killed, but thinking of the Shoshone village filled her with dread. Slowly she rose, and responding to the worried look Spotted Fawn directed toward her, she said, "I am only going to relieve myself." As the other woman slowly nodded her understanding, Iva quickly made her way to the opposite side of the camp.

This being her first opportunity alone, once behind the cover of bushes, Iva looked around, trying to decide where Talking Bear had tied the horses. Perhaps this would be her only chance to escape before they arrived at the Shoshone village, and she was not going to allow the opportunity to pass without grabbing at the chance. Walking silently around the camp, Iva expelled a deep breath when she spied the horses. Even though her hands were tied, she was confident that she could still ride. Later, after putting some distance between herself and Talking Bear, she would find a sharp rock on which to cut away her bindings.

The days she had endured away from Shadow Dancer had been full of pain, but at this moment she knew that this same pain would see her through whatever she had to suffer in order to regain his side. Without a second thought, she pushed her way through the underbrush and came upon the two ponies and the packhorse. The animals had grown used to her scent, so they continued silently feeding as she approached. Her heart hammered wildly in her chest, freedom only seconds away. Her tied hands reached out to the lead rope that secured all three animals.

At that very moment Talking Bear stepped from

behind a tree and clamped a strong hand over her arm. His visage was darkly fierce as he pulled her against him in anger, before shoving her back in the direction of the camp.

Spotted Fawn looked up from where she sat, surprise upon her features as she saw her husband leading the pale woman back to the camp area.

With a grunt of disapproval, Talking Bear gave Iva a shove that landed her on the ground next to Spotted Fawn.

"Did you think that I would not try to return to my husband?" Iva shouted at him as tears filled her eyes.

Talking Bear did not answer, but instead directed a hard look at his wife, silently telling Spotted Fawn that she must keep a better eye on their captive. Then he put the rabbit he had trapped on a makeshift spit and set it over the campfire.

"My husband is not pleased that you try to run away. The people of your own village believe you are a witch, and Talking Bear does also. It is better that you do not leave my side again until we reach the village." Spotted Fawn was unsure of what Talking Bear might do if pushed too far by the pale woman. True, he wanted her as a gift for Bull Feather, but she had glimpsed in his gaze fear of the golden woman's unknown powers, and she was aware that fear could often make a man such as her husband react without first thinking.

"I am not a witch!" Iva declared loudly, her anger because her attempt to escape had failed overriding any fear she might have of the two Indians.

"I believe you speak truth. I have seen a witch before, and you do not have the look of evil about you. But my husband has never seen a witch, so he is wary of you."

Now Iva knew why Talking Bear quickly turned his head away whenever she caught him looking at her, and she could not remember a single time when he had talked directly to her. Thinking back, she realized that more than likely he had been watching from outside the camp while she had been trying to escape, expecting her to perform some kind of witchcraft with him out of sight. A small smile filtered over her lips. A fearless man such as Talking Bear, who traveled through the wilderness from village to village, was frightened of a woman he had been told was a witch. She wondered if he thought her capable of turning him into a crow or some such creature.

Spotted Fawn glimpsed the smile on the pale woman's lips, and her own smile returned. "Stories claim that my husband has spoken to grandfather bear while on his travels, but he is frightened of a pale woman who carries the sky in her eyes." Her laughter erupted, and Iva could not help smiling more broadly. "Men can be much like children. What they do not understand frightens them!"

Trying to get herself comfortable because both her hands and feet were now tied, Iva softly sighed, resting her hands upon her abdomen. At least no harm had come to her unborn babe as yet. She silently gave thanks for that. Talking Bear's fear that she would try to escape again during the hours of night had led him to bind her ankles. As she silently lay near her captor's sleeping pallet, Iva realized how lucky she had been to be handed over to this pair of Indians by the dark cloaked man from the temple. After Spotted Fawn's earlier confession, she knew that almost anyone else would have done as bid and put an end to her life. The Shoshone woman, in truth, had been very kind to her, and seemed only to want a friend. Talking Bear was a different matter, but now that Iva knew of his fear of witchcraft, much of his behavior was explained. The only immediate problem she had was the fact that they would reach the Shoshone village the next day. Once there, it would be harder for her to escape. She tried not to think of the warrior called Bull Feather. The thought of any man other than Shadow Dancer claiming her as wife filled her with a deep dread.

Lying upon the sleeping mat that Spotted Fawn had provided, Iva gazed up into the star-filled night and centered her thoughts upon her husband. She wondered if he was at this moment searching for her. Had he been able to find any sign of her disappearance near the temple? Surely Cimmerian had returned home the evening of her disappearance, and with Aquilla knowing something of where her ride would have taken her, perhaps a search had started even before Shadow Dancer's expected return. "Shadow Dancer," she sighed softly, and the name was carried upon the breath of the night wind.

Talking Bear moved about restlessly on the sleeping pallet he shared with his wife. Tomorrow afternoon would see them in his wife's village, and he would be glad to be rid of the pale woman. He had been uneasy traveling about with her from the start, but today his worry had increased. A feeling of doom, for himself and those of his wife's village, came over him right before he fell asleep.

Chapter Twenty-One

Shadow Dancer jerked wide awake, feeling that he had been caressed by the silken touch of Moon Flower. The fluttering leaves overhead, stirred by the night wind, seemed to call out her name, and intently listening, he could almost imagine that he heard her soft voice calling out to him. His heart tightened in his chest as he imagined the abuse his wife might be suffering at unknown hands if she had been taken from his village.

Gazing up at the stars sparkling in the dark velvet sky, Shadow Dancer relived the moments when he had found his bride gone from his home. He had left the hunting party upon waking, unable to shake the feeling that something was not right. Throughout the day of traveling he had regretted that he had not left the night before when he had first begun to worry about Moon Flower.

It was not until late in the afternoon when he reached the valley, and going directly to his house, he stepped through the front door to be met by Aquilla, her face drawn with worry but her relief plainly visible when she saw he was at home. "Is Moon Flower well?" These were the first words to come out of his mouth.

"She has been missing since yesterday evening when she left to go out riding, Shadow Dancer. There are braves out now looking for her, but no one knows of her whereabouts. There is no sign of her to be found!"

"Did she not tell anyone where she was going riding?" Shadow Dancer had never expected that he would find his bride missing from their home. His chest constricted with true fear, for in the back of his mind he had expected to find her here awaiting his return.

"She told me only that she was going for a ride late yesterday afternoon. She did say that she would ride toward the temple." Aquilla could not hold back her sobs any longer. When she had come to the house early in the morning and had found Cimmerian out front and Moon Flower missing, she had fought with her inner self to achieve calm; but now, facing Shadow Dancer, she could control herself no longer. "I tried to tell her, Shadow Dancer, that she should wait to take her ride, but she would not listen! Perhaps the great, black stallion threw her off his back and she is suffering somewhere all alone!"

"Cimmerian returned without Moon Flower?" Shadow Dancer knew how close mistress and horse were, and he could not imagine the stallion leaving her side if there had been some kind of accident. Urgent fear for his wife's safety swept over him, and though he tried to appear calm so as not to add to Aquilla's upset, he could not stem the worry in his voice. "Where has the search party looked? Perhaps she was thrown near the temple, and one of the priests took her in to tend her." He grasped on to anything that would bring some reason to the situation.

"Several braves have been out all day, searching the pastures leading to the mountain. The priests have been questioned at the temple, and none have seen Moon Flower."

"Send Arez for the black stallion." Shadow Dancer strode through the main portion of the house as he threw orders over his shoulder. "I will take the time to change, and then I will search for Moon Flower myself!" And he silently swore that he would not return to the valley until he found her, wherever she might be.

Aquilla did not argue but hurriedly left through the back gardens to find her son and send him for Moon Flower's horse. She only wished that her husband, Dark Water, were here so he could go with Shadow Dancer on his search. She had an uneasy feeling that all was not right with Moon Flower, and Shadow Dancer could be in great danger in going after her. She knew, though, that she could say nothing of this. Shadow Dancer would not be swayed from finding his bride!

It was as Shadow Dancer left his chamber that Nokie entered the house. Her features were pale, and the dark circles beneath her eyes attested to her worry and lack of rest. "I knew that you would return soon!" She threw herself against his broad chest, her tone brittle as though at any minute she would fall to weeping. "You must go and find Moon Flower, Shadow Dancer." Even as she said the words she knew they were foolish. Of course, her cousin would find his wife. His soul was incomplete without her!

"I will find her, Nokie." Shadow Dancer made the solemn promise, as he embraced his cousin, offering her comfort even though his own heart was being severed. "Did you speak to her yesterday? Did she say anything to you of riding toward the temple?" Shadow Dancer could not understand Moon Flower's reason for riding toward the temple so late in the day, but knowing how close his wife and cousin had become he hoped that Nokie could offer him some bit of information that Aquilla had not known.

"I did not see her yesterday, Shadow Dancer." Nokie fought to gain control over her emotions, knowing that it would help little if she fell to weeping.

Shadow Dancer could tell there was something Nokie was not telling him. His dark eyes searched her face. Ever since childhood he had been able to see some hidden message in her dark eyes when she had had one of her visions. "Have you seen into the spirit world, cousin? Have you glimpsed anything that can help me in the search for my wife?" His breath held in his chest for a brief moment as he waited for her to speak, knowing that she might well be the only link to learning where Moon Flower was.

Slowly Nokie's head nodded. "I awoke last night and my soul was filled with an overpowering terror. I could not identify its reason or source, so as those in my father's household slept, I brewed a potion in offering to the moon goddess, Coyolxauhqui. I beseeched her to calm this strange fear within me, and as I broke off pieces of sage and burnt them in offering, Moon Flower's name came over me. Then, held within the power of a trance, I glimpsed a man and a woman, not from our tribe. My viewing was through Moon Flower's eyes, and I felt the power of the fear that filled her." Nokie drew in a deep breath before continuing. "I felt the constraint of bindings on my hands and legs. I felt as Moon Flower felt, powerless to fight off those that wished me ill!" Nokie had been unable to tell anyone of the terror that had visited the past night. She had waited for Shadow Dancer to arrive in the village, for she knew that he would consider wisely what she had experienced.

Knowing from the past that Nokie's visions were not to be taken lightly, Shadow Dancer questioned, "While you looked upon this man and woman that were not of our people, did you glimpse anything else? Was there some sign that would take me to the place where Moon Flower came upon them?" He had no doubt that all Nokie said was true, but he needed more information.

"She did not come upon them, Shadow Dancer. I felt her bonds as she was lifted from her feet and placed upon the back of a horse." For a moment Nokie allowed Shadow Dancer to take all of this in; then her eyes brightened and she gasped. "I do remember seeing a garden wall, and there was an arched doorway, but the designs on the enclosure were not those of the people in the village. Perhaps it was the temple garden!"

"The temple gardens?" Aquilla had said that the priests had all been questioned, but not one had seen anything of Moon Flower. Would not someone have seen something if she had been taken away by strangers?

"Of course, Shadow Dancer, it must have been the gardens behind the temple! As a girl, when I went to the temple to study, I spent many hours in the back gardens because they were used so little and offered privacy. You must start there with your search!"

Shadow Dancer also remembered the gardens behind the temple. Nokie was right in stating that they were isolated. Even the priests preferred the well-kept gardens that had been built on both sides of the temple, the old gardens now being overgrown. This was the only real lead Shadow Dancer had. If Nokie believed that Moon Flower had been taken from the gardens at the back of the temple, then he would search that area. Pulling the slender woman against his chest for the briefest moment, as though this situation were only another link that drew them closer together, he promised aloud to his cousin as well as to himself, "I will bring Moon Flower back."

Nokie nodded her head as he drew away, impatient to be gone, and Shadow Dancer started out the door. She knew he would keep his word, or he would die in his attempt to regain his wife. His life and Moon Flower's were linked. One could not exist without the other!

At first Cimmerian put up some resistance as the large warrior climbed onto his back. Bucking several times, he tried to unseat him, then pranced about in agitation at the unfamiliar weight. It took time and patience for Shadow Dancer to calm the horse enough to give the beast his head and allow him to race across the pastures leading in the direction of the temple.

As horse and rider approached the front of the temple, Shadow Dancer's dark gaze scanned the area. He could see no sign that Moon Flower had been here, but as he directed Cimmerian around to the back of the temple, he noted where it appeared that someone had secured a horse to a small bush only a few feet away from the steps leading up to the temple door. The bush was all but stripped of its greenery, and the hoofprints around the bush indicated that the horse had been agitated and had broken loose from its constraints. Could it be possible that his wife had come to the temple to meet someone? Shadow Dancer asked himself as his dark eyes thoughtfully surveyed the area in front of the temple. Had she tied Cimmerian to the bush with the intention of returning for him?

Seeing nothing else that could aid him in reenacting his wife's disappearance, Shadow Dancer went toward the back of the temple, where the old gardens stood. Nokie claimed that she had seen a garden enclosure with designs like those of the temple, and as he directed Cimmerian toward the area, Shadow Dancer's gaze caught upon the tracks of horses. Was this where the man and woman of Nokie's vision had taken Moon Flower upon one of their horses? He was confused. All he could do now was speculate on his wife's disappearance. But as he glimpsed the trail the riders had taken away from the temple, he knew that he could not chance turning away from the only clues he had.

Over the course of the next few days Shadow Dancer found that the pace the riders set was a hard one. Several times he had to backtrack when he had lost their trail, then search for a sign. Whoever it was that he was following knew the art of casting off travel markings. But the tracks he now followed were his only lead, so Shadow Dancer was determined to follow them to their destination. Even if he was wasting time and they did not hold his wife captive, perhaps those he was following had some knowledge of the evening Moon Flower had disappeared. He prayed that there would still be time to rescue her if he had indeed made a mistake and had to turn around and start his search all over again.

Exhaustion finally forced him to seek sleep. Cimmerian also was showing signs of fatigue from the hard pace they had been keeping. Still, Shadow Dancer lay upon his sleeping mat for some time before sleep overtook him. His mind went over the very first time he had seen Moon Flower, working with Cimmerian on her father's farm. Her radiance had been crowned by the sunlight which reflected off her golden hair, and that was how he held her in his heart. From that moment he had been bound to her, not able to find peace until he had made her his own, and now his heart ached with her loss. Inside, he railed at the fates that had stolen her out of his hands! A tear slid from the corner of his eye and ran down his cheek unnoticed, his pain almost unbearable. Slowly he murmured a prayer to the god. Quetzalcoatl, pleading with him to keep his wife and unborn child safe until he could rescue them!

Later in the night Shadow Dancer was awakened, he was certain of her touch, the sound of her calling him filling his heart.

Talking Bear did not hurry the women of his camp the following morning. He brushed down his horses and allowed them to openly graze on the thick, green grass growing near the campsite as he went through his trading packs.

It was midmorning when he gave Spotted Fawn a bundle that she in turn presented to Iva. Later Iva would realize that the morning was to be spent in preparation for their arrival that afternoon in the Shoshone village.

"What is this?" Iva asked from where she sat against the tree. She had remained quiet since yesterday when she had been caught in the attempt at escape. She had not given up her desire for freedom, nor was she resigned to her fate as a captive. But after Talking Bear had caught her just as she had reached for the horse, and after getting little sleep the past night, for the first time since she had been stolen away from her husband's village, Iva felt weary of spirit.

"Talking Bear would give you this as a gift." Spotted Fawn bent to the other woman and set the package, bound in soft leather hide, down upon the grass next to Iva.

Untying the leather straps to release the binding and reveal the contents, Iva looked down at a beautifully beaded, soft doehide dress for only a moment before her gaze went back to Spotted Fawn.

"Your clothes are torn and dirty," Spotted Fawn said by way of explanation.

Iva nodded her head, knowing that the true reason was that they both wanted to impress Spotted Fawn's brother with the gift they had brought him. Iva did not care what their reasons were. She was tired of wearing the same tunic and skirt, and the doehide dress looked wondrously soft. "Thank you," she said as she picked up the dress without argument.

Spotted Fawn seemed happy this had gone so easily. She had feared that the pale woman would make every attempt to keep her own clothes on, and this also had been her husband's thought and the reason he had not given his captive the hide dress before now. "You may wash at the stream. If you wish I will go with you and cut away your bindings."

Iva knew that Spotted Fawn was risking much in trusting her, but upon reflection, she knew that her chance of escaping in broad daylight was very slim.

266

Talking Bear would not be far away, and Iva had no doubt that Spotted Fawn was much stronger than she appeared and would make every attempt to restrain her if the need arose. She had already learned that this pair would do almost anything to hold their prize for Bull Feather.

Still, it felt good to wash and to get out of her dirty clothes. Iva's spirits were much revived as she sat next to the stream's edge while Spotted Fawn gently combed the tangles from her hair.

At first she let the golden strands fall down the pale woman's back. Spotted Fawn later entwined thick braids that hung over both her shoulders. "You are indeed very beautiful," Spotted Fawn stated truthfully, and there was not a tinge of envy in her voice. Bull Feather will be very pleased with his gift, she thought to herself as the pale woman's hair glistened brightly beneath the morning sun.

Chapter Twenty-Two

Riding atop the packhorse, with Talking Bear leading the way and Spotted Fawn following up in the rear, Iva entered the Shoshone village in the late afternoon when the sky was a pinkish blue. Shouts broke out throughout the village, proclaiming their arrival, and looking behind her, Iva glimpsed the wide grin on Spotted Fawn's oval face. The woman was glad to be home once again.

The three rode directly into the midst of the towering, conical structures. Dogs barked, and women left their duties of cooking or tending the drying racks to welcome the visitors. Talking Bear and Spotted Fawn's names were called out, but all eyes soon turned to the woman upon the packhorse, her hair the color of the moon, the pale blueness of a clear sky within her eyes.

Appearing fearless before his wife's entire village, Talking Bear rode directly toward the largest Shoshone lodge. As the three were encircled by what appeared to be the entire tribe, he dismounted. After helping Spotted Fawn from her mount, he reached up and set Iva on her feet.

Spotted Fawn was hugged by the women. And men and women alike converged on her with questions about her travels, but little was said to Talking Bear.

Those who dared to look him in the eye, quickly turned their heads away. I expected no less, Talking Bear told himself as they stood in front of the lodge of his wife's brother. He had left this village on bad terms with Bull Feather, and none would dare to go against their chief and welcome him into their midst prematurely.

The people of this village were far different from those of Iva's husband's tribe. There was a primitive air about them. The women were dressed much like Spotted Fawn and Iva, the hide of animals covering them, while the men wore unadorned leather breechcloths. There was none of the bright-colored jewelry or the painted features Iva had grown used to seeing, nor were the lodges that formed this encampment as appealing as the decoratively painted structures in the hidden valley.

Aware of the curious and the distrustful eyes upon her, Iva stood nervously between Talking Bear and Spotted Fawn. Understanding little of the language that was being spoken, she realized that Talking Bear and Spotted Fawn were much more talented than she had first supposed. She would later learn that Talking Bear was a master of many Indian tongues, which had aided him greatly in his trading in the many villages he had visited over the years, and Spotted Fawn, being a quick learner, was also well versed in the languages of a number of tribes.

As the excitement around them intensified, one older Indian woman braver than the rest questioned Talking Bear and Spotted Fawn, "Why is it that you return after all of this time and bring this white woman amongst us?" Her dark eyes were not very kindly as they fell upon Iva. Her son had been killed by the white man, and as far as Singing Wind was concerned a white woman among them could only bring trouble for the Shoshone village.

Spotted Fawn did not deign to answer, nor did she venture to explain to Iva what the woman had asked. Pushing aside those standing in front of her brother's tepee, she pulled back the entrance flap. Taking hold of Iva's wrist, Spotted Fawn then bent low and stepped into the lodge. Talking Bear followed the women, knowing this was the moment when they would find out what their reception would be. Now he and Spotted Fawn would face Bull Feather!

The interior of the large lodge was dimly lit, the smoke hole in the hide roof allowing the only light other than that given off by the small, center-pit fire. Trying to adjust her vision from the bright sunlight to the dimness, Iva quickly tried to take in her surroundings.

It was a busy lodge. Two women sat near the fire sewing, working with pieces of fur and bright shiny beads, while a heavyset Indian woman bent over the large, blackened cook pot over the fire. The whispers and laughter of more women could be heard in the shadowy corners of the lodge. As Iva's eyes adjusted she glimpsed furs piled against one hide wall, near a variety of food supplies. Clubs and spears and numerous other weapons were set in a corner.

As the three entered the lodge much of the activity within stilled, as though the occupants were allowing those who entered a minute to regain their vision.

Hearing light female laughter come from the opposite corner from where she was looking, Iva swung her head about, and the sight she took in forced the breath from her lungs in a loud gasp.

Sitting upon a large sleeping couch piled high with plush furs and adorned with a brightly colored head rest was the largest man Iva had ever seen. He appeared to be in his middle thirties, yet was gargantuan as he sat with his long legs stretched out upon his sleeping couch. Two female Indians sat next to him, combing out his long, black hair. Iva watched with growing alarm as the huge man's coal black eyes went from Spotted Fawn to Talking Bear and then rested once again upon her. As fear traced a chill path up her spine,

270

Iva thought to herself, This must be Bull Feather! This must be the man I have been brought to this village to wed!

No greeting or gesture of welcome was forthcoming from the man for his sister or her husband, but his gaze held for an uncomfortable amount of time upon the woman with the sun in her hair. Then, ignoring the two women at his side, Bull Feather rose to his full height, which was even more towering than Iva had at first imagined.

Stepping away from his sleeping couch, the giant, with two steps, was standing before Iva. From across the room she had thought him uncomfortably heavy, but the man standing before her, only a breechcloth covering his loins, was by no means obese. Perhaps he was a little bit thick around the middle, but even so, his shoulders were amply wide and muscles rippled across his bronze chest.

As though Bull Feather and Iva were the only two within the lodge, his dark gaze looked down and caught eyes of deepest blue. Her knees trembling, Iva felt faint as she looked up at him. She flinched as his hand left his side and went to her thick strands of blond hair.

Noting the amazement in her brother's eyes as he touched the white woman's hair, Spotted Fawn took advantage of the moment and spoke. "Brother, my husband Talking Bear brought you this woman as a gift. We thought she would please you as your sixth wife."

Iva could not understand what Spotted Fawn was saying, but she prayed that she had made a mistake, that this was not the famed Bull Feather Spotted Fawn had spoken of so much over the past week. It would be hard enough for her to try to escape this Indian village without having this brute of a man watching over her!

His hand still resting in Iva's hair, the massive Indian

271

looked down at his sister. "I have my sixth wife. She shall be my seventh!"

Gasps of surprise came from the women within the lodge. As every eye was directed upon Iva, she nervously clasped her hands, afraid that any moment she would try to break free and run from the confines of the tepee.

But she was not given the chance, for Bull Feather's large hand encircled her upper arm and pulled her along with him to his sleeping couch. When he pushed her down amongst the furs, all Iva could think of was that this huge beast of a man was going to assault her in front of all the people who filled his lodge. She opened her mouth to scream, her hands positioned before her face as if to defend herself.

Hearing the piercing sound she made, Talking Bear stepped forward and tried to calm her as Bull Feather sat down upon the sleeping couch and settled Iva between his legs, his hands once again caressing her golden curls. "He is only curious about your hair. Do not be afraid."

Iva's second scream did not leave her throat for Talking Bear's words quieted her, but they could not stop the trembling that came over her as her legs were positioned between the powerful legs of the giant Indian.

Ignoring her scream and her trembling, Bull Feather gazed in utter amazement at the woman on his lap as he leaned against the backrest of his sleeping couch. Never had he seen such hair, nor had he seen any woman with such pale skin and eyes. His long, bronze fingers ran through her tresses, feeling their silken texture. For a moment he was so consumed by her he forgot everyone else in the lodge.

"My brother's people do not leave these mountains. They have seen few white people besides the trappers who hunt the mountain game. I knew that he would be pleased with you." Spotted Fawn in her own fashion was trying to relieve Iva's fear, for the Indian woman had glimpsed the sheer terror in those blue eyes.

Iva tried to pull away from Bull Feather, his solidly built thighs squeezed around her and held her still. "Please, Spotted Fawn, tell him I wish only to be returned to my husband," Iva begged as huge hands smoothed the tips of her pale curls.

Talking Bear shook his head at his wife, wanting nothing to spoil this moment and draw Bull Feather's anger upon them anew. But Spotted Fawn ignored her husband's gesture. She decided that she could at least speak the white woman's words aloud, and then her brother could decide for himself whether or not he would keep her against her will. "Bull Feather," she called aloud, trying to capture her brother's attention, "the woman with the sun in her hair would tell you that her desire is to be returned to her husband."

For a moment the Indian's hands stilled in Iva's hair, and the women in the lodge stared at their husband with much interest, now that they knew the white woman was not willingly coming into their midst. Bull Feather's hands shortly began their stroking once again. "She no longer has a husband. I will not release her!"

After Spotted Fawn interpreted her brother's words, a sob caught in Iva's throat. Bull Feather's strong fingers turned her chin so that she was forced to look directly into his face. "Tell her not to weep," he commanded his sister. "She will be treated kindly. Perhaps I will even make her my first wife!"

An outraged grunt filled the lodge, and an angry Indian woman jumped to her feet. She glared at both Bull Feather and the pale woman on his lap before storming out of the tepee.

Low-toned laughter filled the lodge at the woman's departure. The other Indian women thought it about time that Bull Feather's number-one wife was deprived

273

of her lofty position and of the power to boss them around.

Spotted Fawn ignored her brother's wives as she repeated Bull Feather's words to Iva, thinking they might please her. "Bull Feather says he will make you his first wife if that will make you happy to stay here in his village."

"But I do not want to become your wife! I already have a husband!" Iva cried into the massive Indian's face, certain that she was experiencing every woman's worst nightmare!

Bull Feather was surprised by this woman's reaction to him. Women had always appreciated him. In fact, upon occasion they appeared to throw themselves at him. That was why he had so many wives. Women seemed unable to get enough of him, and he truly could not get enough of them! Brushing away her tears with his thumb, Bull Feather picked up one of Iva's slender hands, looking at the palm and then the back before his eyes rose to Talking Bear. "She is as beautiful as a pale lily. Thank you for this fine gift, brother. You and my sister are welcome to stay as my guests, here in my lodge. Our Shaman has gone to another village, but I will send a warrior to bring him back to perform the ceremony that will join me to this white woman."

"That is good, Bull Feather, for I have brought much with me in my trading packs, and I have learned many fine stories with which to entertain you." Talking Bear was very pleased that Bull Feather had forgiven him.

Unable to understand their words, Iva knew without being told that the two men had set aside their anger. The gift of Talking Bear and Spotted Fawn had had the desired effect. Though Iva was to become a sacrifice, the pair were once more welcome within the bosom of their family!

That evening, Iva who was now called Pale Lily,

watched from the sidelines as Bull Feather's wives presented dinner to their husband and his guests. The six women of the lodge seemed to have only one interest in their lives, that of pleasing their husband. They appeared to cater to his every whim. A wife sat on either side of him, choosing the choicest pieces of meat from the cooking pot over the fire. Another tempted him with fresh berries that she herself had picked that day, while yet another refilled his bowl of stew. The large Indian chief seemed to take all their attention as his due, and as the evening progressed and his dark eyes more often went to Iva, who sat between Spotted Fawn and Talking Bear, Iva's unease magnified.

She had had only a few minutes alone with Spotted Fawn after they had arrived at Bull Feather's lodge, and that had been when Spotted Fawn had requested that the white woman help her bring in their sleeping mats.

"I told Bull Feather that you are to have a child," Spotted Fawn had stated as soon as they were outside.

"Will he allow me to return to my husband?" Iva stopped in her tracks, grasping at the slim hope.

Spotted Fawn shook her head, her ready grin quickly coming to her lips as she remembered what her brother had replied. "Bull Feather loves children. He says that he will be the child's father. He will treat it as his own."

Iva groaned aloud, but even as the other woman took hold of her arm and began to pull her toward the horses to get their sleeping mats, Iva would not budge until she had said her piece. "I cannot be your brother's wife! He has too many wives as it is!" She tried once more to appeal to the other woman's kind nature. "I would never be happy, don't you understand?"

Relaxing her grip somewhat on the white woman's arm, Spotted Fawn seemed to consider what she said. Slowly her head began to nod as though she were in agreement with her. "Come, we must hurry and return to Bull Feather's lodge. I will think on what you have said." Spotted Fawn in truth wanted this woman to be happy. If she was happy, her brother would be happy!

Clinging to this slim promise that Spotted Fawn would at least consider her plight, Iva slowly began to move her feet. She prayed that Spotted Fawn would help her to escape. She needed only a horse, a few supplies, and to be told the direction she should take in order to return to her husband's village.

Sitting now across the shallow pit fire between Talking Bear and Spotted Fawn, and witnessing the fawning of the other women over Bull Feather, Iva was irritated by their lack of good sense. Where is their pride? she asked herself, since the man's wives appeared to get along rather well and seemed willing enough to share their husband. For a second Iva imagined herself in a like circumstance with Shadow Dancer, and she knew for a certainty that she would not calmly submit to such a way of life. She would be scratching and kicking at any woman that dared to touch her husband.

With the completion of dinner, the two men relaxed near the fire, and Talking Bear enthusiastically began to tell the mighty chief a story, while the women placed the sleeping mats around the floor of the lodge. Iva was more than willing to lie down next to Spotted Fawn and try to find some rest. At least the sleeping mats had been stretched out a distance from the fire, and she could hide from those black searching eyes that had sought her out all evening!

It was some time before the rest of the women retired and a while longer before the voices of the two men quieted and the only sound in the lodge was the occasional snap of a log in the fire. Iva could find no sleep for thoughts of Shadow Dancer, and desire to escape the Shoshone village consumed her. Silently she prayed that her husband would find her before it was too late. She knew that he was looking for her, but the threat of Bull Feather touching her filled her with fear. It had been bad enough being forced to endure his hands on her hair. She did not want to think of what would happen to her if she did not flee this village before the giant claimed her as his mate!

A feminine giggle interrupted Iva's thoughts, and rising up on an elbow, she looked toward Bull Feather's sleeping couch and glimpsed the naked form of an Indian woman atop his large body. The woman's movements were frantic as she pumped her body up and down, not seeming to care who in the lodge saw her or heard the sighs of pleasure that escaped her.

Before Iva could lie back down she was confronted by Bull Feather's dark regard. He appeared to have been watching her lie upon the sleeping mat, on his face an intensely hungry look, while he was being pleasured by one of his wives!

Feeling her cheeks burning furiously, Iva huddled back down upon the sleeping mat and drew the furs up over her head!

A few minutes later after hearing the Indian woman's soft cries of release and then silence, Iva sighed softly to herself. Perhaps now she could get some sleep! But as the late hours of the night passed and at least three other wives climbed upon his bed, one at a time, and rode him as though he were a randy stallion, Iva covered her ears with her hands beneath the fur covering. The man was insatiable!

Chapter Twenty-Three

Dazed, Iva stared openly at Spotted Fawn. "He said he would do what?" Gasping, she shook her head as though she had not heard the other woman correctly.

"Bull Feather said that he would send all of his other wives back to their father's lodges if this will please you. You will be his only wife, Pale Lily!" The Indian woman was excitedly trying to explain to the white woman what a great honor Bull Feather was bestowing upon her.

"But I don't want him to do that! I don't want to become his wife at all!" Iva exclaimed in great agitation. She certainly did not want to be that frightening man's only wife! She had not slept until the early hours of the morning because of the women going to his bed. Not refusing any, he had given each and every one what she wanted! It would be a nightmare to have to contend with such a man on a nightly basis!

Spotted Fawn thought the white woman a strange creature indeed. Her brother was placing her above all his other wives and still she was not satisfied. "The Shaman will arrive in the village today. The joining ceremony will take place this evening," she said. After the ceremony was performed Spotted Fawn hoped that the woman would change her attitude and be happy here in the Shoshone village. Perhaps it was just a white woman's way, that she could not be pleased.

Their conversation was taking place in the morning, near the river where the two women had taken their baths, and clutching a handful of grass in her agitation, Iva fought back tears as she looked at the woman sitting next to her. "Please, Spotted Fawn, you have to help me leave this village! You are the only one I can turn to." Iva had been hoping for more time until the marriage ceremony would be performed, but upon learning that it would take place in the evening, she was desperate to get away from Bull Feather!

"I will be pleased when you become my sister, for I feel that you have a good heart and I hope that we will become friends. I cannot help you, though, as you ask. Bull Feather already believes it is meant that you become his!"

Iva would have continued to appeal to Spotted Fawn, but at that moment two of Bull Feather's wives approached, along with several other Indian women.

The glare of hatred in the eyes of the huge man's wives caught Iva off guard. Inside Bull Feather's lodge these same two had not shown the slightest hint of malice, not even the wife who had stormed out of the lodge shortly after her arrival yesterday had directed any anger at her.

"You are causing us to be driven away from our husband!" the larger of the two Shoshone women cried out as the group drew closer to Spotted Fawn and Iva. "Bull Feather sees no other woman now but the pale one!"

"See how they hate me!" Iva looked at Spotted Fawn and tried to use this confrontation to further her argument for escape. Jumping to her feet, she called out to the group circling around her and Spotted Fawn, "I don't want Bull Feather! You can keep that monstrous man for yourselves as far as I am concerned. I just want to be set free."

"Pay them no heed." Spotted Fawn rose and stood at

Iva's side. Though she had not understood the white woman's words, she had sensed their meaning. Directing her anger at the women standing around them, Spotted Fawn dared any one of them to further abuse the white woman with her tongue. "Come, Pale Lily." She turned back to Iva. "There is much that must be done to ready you for your joining ceremony."

Iva decided that nothing she could say or do would get this woman to change her mind about helping her flee this village. Silently she stepped past the Shoshone women, aware of their heated stares.

It was early afternoon when Bull Feather, Talking Bear, and several other braves returned to the village, a large, bull elk drawn behind them on a travois. Entering his lodge, Bull Feather scanned the interior, his dark eyes skimming over each woman until he beheld Iva. A large grin then curved his mouth, and with a motion of his hand, he signaled her to come to him.

Iva looked from the giant across the lodge to Spotted Fawn sitting at her side, then, her head lowered over the sewing in her lap, she thought for a moment that she could simply ignore Bull Feather's presence in the lodge.

Spotted Fawn was the one who drew the bleached hide dress from Iva's lap, and taking her hand, she drew her toward the entrance flap. "Let us see what Bull Feather wishes to say to you, Pale Lily."

Stepping back outside through the entrance flap, Bull Feather awaited the two women. Not knowing what to expect out of this large man, Iva was shaking by the time she and Spotted Fawn left the lodge.

Thumping his broad chest, Bull Feather pointed to the elk, wanting to show his future bride his powers as a hunter. "Bull Feather can feed and clothe many in his lodge! Pale Lily want Bull Feather all to herself, no other wives, that good! Many babies will fill Bull Feather's lodge instead!"

Iva had not a clue as to what he was saying so loudly that he drew the attention of many in the village. Looking at Spotted Fawn, she glimpsed the easy smile coming over the Indian woman's face once again. "What did he say?" Iva asked nervously, at the moment not even sure that she truly wanted to know what the giant had shouted.

"Bull Feather shows you he is a mighty hunter, by allowing you to see the elk he has brought back for his lodge. He also says that instead of his wives being fed and clothed by the game he brings to his village, you and he will have many children together, and he will provide well for them!" Spotted Fawn giggled aloud and covered her mouth with a hand as she saw the white woman blush profusely.

Every eye in the village now rested upon Iva, and she was mortified. "Nooooo," she at last stammered. "You must tell him, Spotted Fawn, that he must keep his wives. I don't want to join with him and have his children! I already have a husband!"

Of course Spotted Fawn was not about to tell her brother the white woman's words. Instead she told him that the woman he called Pale Lily agreed that he was a great hunter, and she would be happy to have his children.

"You told him what I said?" Iva asked when she saw the wide grin that stretched the large man's lips, for she doubted that Spotted Fawn had done as she had instructed.

"Those words would not please Bull Feather, Pale Lily. The joining ceremony is to be held this night. Would it be good for Bull Feather to be angry?" The Indian woman's reasoning was simple, even if her determination to please her brother exasperated Iva.

*　　*　　*

Bull Feather did not return to his lodge after he left with the other braves to trim out the elk. Talking Bear retrieved from his brother-in-law's tepee the things Bull Feather needed for the ceremony that evening, and Iva was left in the capable hands of Spotted Fawn to prepare for her joining with the giant who frightened her beyond measure!

The other women in the lodge did not offer to help the white woman for the joining ceremony. Each in turn had been told early that morning that she would be returning to her father's lodge the following day, so all resented the intruder with the golden hair keenly. Six pairs of dark eyes watched hostilely as Spotted Fawn helped Iva put on the beautiful bleached-hide dress that had come out of Talking Bear's packs.

Spotted Fawn then presented Iva with a matching pair of calf-high moccasins, and her dressing finished, Iva silently brooded over her fate while the Indian woman combed out her hair and pleated the thick length into twin braids which extended down her slender back.

If only there were some way to prevent this ceremony from taking place, Iva thought with mounting panic as the moments passed. She knew it would soon be time for her to leave the lodge to meet her fate at the hands of the warrior who would claim her as his bride!

It was late morning when Shadow Dancer came across a small band of Shoshone warriors. Keeping his presence well hidden, he followed them at a distance. It was a hunting party, he realized, as the largest man of the group, who appeared to be their leader, downed a large bull elk.

The trail Shadow Dancer had been following over the past week had come to an end in this forest, and he could sense that there was an Indian village not far away. It had been only chance that he had come upon this band of Shoshone braves, but wanting to follow where they led, he silently pursued them.

Following the hunting party back to their village, Shadow Dancer secured Cimmerian in a strand of trees near the river and then silently made his way closer to afford himself a better view.

His heart began to hammer wildly in his chest as he glimpsed a small group standing in front of a large tepee. He could not make out the words at that distance, but he glimpsed the glitter of golden hair as two women stepped out of the lodge. "Moon Flower!" he breathed aloud, and almost stepped out of concealment and rushed to her side. But good sense prevailed as his eyes went over the warrior who stood a foot taller than all those around him.

His breathing coming in short, rapid breaths Shadow Dancer watched the interaction between the large brave and the two women. Peering intently, he tried to discern whether Moon Flower was in any immediate danger, but within moments the two women reentered the tepee and the group of braves walked away. Shadow Dancer let out his pent-up breath.

He had found her at last. His heart sang with joy. She appeared unhurt as she stood outside the lodge, but he could not be sure from such a distance. As it had so often in the past week, his mind once again focused on the babe Moon Flower was carrying, and he prayed that all would be well.

Using all the cunning and caution he had learned as a child, Shadow Dancer reclaimed Cimmerian and led him deeper into the forest. He was already formulating a plan for the rescue for his wife!

Iva was all but dragged through the village by Spotted Fawn when the appointed time for the joining ceremony came. Many small campfires had been lit outside the lodges for the occasion, and in the center of the village a large ceremonial blaze had been set. Dressed in her outfit of bleached doehide, Iva looked ashen as she and Spotted Fawn approached the villagers standing around the fire.

At that moment she remembered, her eyes filling with tears, how frightened she had been when she had been led to the ceremonial lodge in her husband's village on the evening of their joining, how she had wanted to run away from those standing around and watching her. Then Shadow Dancer had entered the lodge, and the warmth in his dark eyes, his very presence, had stilled the terror in her heart. This evening she knew that no one could quell her fear. The giant standing in wait for her before the ceremonial fire frightened her more than anyone she had ever known. That this ceremony would join her to him as his wife in no way would end her terror.

Bull Feather's large arm stretched out, his hand pulling her to his side, his sparkling-bright dark eyes devouring her with a hunger that consumed her. He had waited, from the first moment he had set eyes upon this white woman, to finish the joining ceremony and claim her as his own. His large body ached with the need to fill her. As his dark eyes had looked upon her the past night while his wives had pleasured him, he had had only this white woman upon his mind!

In the moment when Bull Feather drew her to him, Iva believed that she was going to faint. The shaman stood before them, the entire village was looking on, and just as Iva felt her legs begin to buckle, the night air filled with a deep, vibrant war cry that chilled even the stoutest of hearts.

Quickly reviving, Iva felt the giant's hand tighten upon her arm as though he, too, knew that help had come to her. Her heart leaped as a large, menacing rider appeared within the firelight, atop a prancing black stallion. The horse rose up upon its hind legs just as the warrior waved his war club threateningly in the air. His flashing black eyes fastened upon the white woman as the war cry again was torn from his lips!

"Shadow Dancer!" Iva cried aloud, and instinctively she tried to free herself from the grip on her arm and run to her husband.

Everyone in the Shoshone village stared at the warrior atop the mighty, black beast, and there was not a heart that did not skip a beat as the war cry filled the night air.

Bull Feather was the first to react. He knew without being told that this menacing warrior was the white woman's husband and had come to claim that which had been stolen from him. He shoved Iva back toward his sister and her husband, at the same time reaching for the spear and war club always kept nearby.

Shadow Dancer had planned throughout the day to approach the lodge he had seen Moon Flower come out of that afternoon. He had intended to do this under the cover of darkness, and while all in the village slept, wanting to rescue his wife without chancing the harm that could come to her if his rescue caused a disturbance. But as he had watched the village from closer in after dark, he had seen Moon Flower being pulled along by the Shoshone woman toward the center of the encampment, and when he had taken in the large fire burning brightly and the giant warrior waiting beside it, Shadow Dancer had been consumed by anger. He knew, without being told, that this was some kind of joining ceremony, and the large warrior was attempting to claim that which belonged solely to him. At that moment a war cry tore from his lips as Cimmerian galloped headlong into the Shoshone village!

Chapter Twenty-Four

His large, bronze body glistening with raw muscular power, Shadow Dancer seemed an avenging god of ancient lore as he sat atop the prancing black stallion, a club held high above his head. The light of the ceremonial fire caught his piercing black eyes which went first to the woman of his heart and then to the large man at her side. That look of unbridled rage singled the giant out, challenging him to come and meet his fate for daring to lay a hand upon Shadow Dancer's wife.

Bull Feather was determined that no one would take the white woman with the sun-touched hair away from him! His own war cry mingling with Shadow Dancer's upon the night air, he circled the fire and, with cunning ferocity, charged, his spear ready to let fly, his large fist tightly clutching the war club he held overhead. I will put an end to this man and his claim to the white woman! he told himself. Heat rushed boldly to his loins with that thought and it brought him a feeling of power.

A cry broke from Iva's lips as she stood next to Spotted Fawn, her blue eyes wide, and watched her husband kick Cimmerian's sides and charge forward to meet the brave who was approaching him. At that moment Shadow Dancer gave no thought to his opponent's size.

The spear left Bull Feather's hand in those first few seconds when the great black horse was set into motion. With a slight movement of his body, Shadow Dancer avoided its deadly point, and in the next second the two warriors were clashing with their war clubs.

As Cimmerian drew abreast of the large man, Shadow Dancer hit Bull Feather across the shoulders. But Bull Feather's club struck out, catching its target on the forearm. The impact sent Shadow Dancer off the stallion's back, but with a lithe motion, he rolled to his feet. Standing before his enemy with but a war club and coursing anger over his wife's abduction, Shadow Dancer emitted a low menacing growl of warning right before he charged the other warrior, not paying any notice to his foe's greater height and weight.

But where Bull Feather was fleshy, Shadow Dancer was tight, hard muscle. And Bull Feather's great height made him more ungainly than his swift opponent. Shadow Dancer hit him across the chest as Bull Feather struck out with his club and missed. Then Shadow Dancer's quick arm retracted and caught the mighty Bull Feather across the midsection, knocking him to his knees, the huge man's breath whooshing out of him as his club flew off to the side of the ceremonial fire.

When Bull Feather got back to his feet, a wicked-looking, sharp-bladed knife was clutched in his fist.

Iva took a step toward them, intending somehow to intervene, but as she did so Shadow Dancer quickly threw aside his war club, and drew the dangerously sharp hunting knife he'd worn strapped to his side.

The two warriors circled each other cunningly, each awaiting an opening in the other's defenses. It was Bull Feather who made the first move, his huge body lunging into Shadow Dancer and sending him sprawling backward, his knife striking a telling blow evidenced by the thin, red line that appeared across

Shadow Dancer's ribs. A wicked-looking grin came to the giant's features as though that first show of blood was an indication of the outcome of the struggle.

Not by so much as a flinch did Shadow Dancer indicate that he had been harmed. He clutched the larger man's right wrist in a tight grasp, tripped him, and then rolled atop him, his own knife held high and ready to do harm.

Bull Feather knew in that instant that he had terribly underestimated his opponent. The warrior holding his wrist was far more powerful than he had at first suspected. Being flat on his back with Shadow Dancer atop him and holding his wrist, Bull Feather fought to grab the hand that clutched the knife of his foe.

The two men struggled on the ground for some minutes, Shadow Dancer seeming the more worthy fighter since he remained atop his adversary. As the warriors' movements brought them close to the circle of the fire, Bull Feather screamed aloud, for the hand holding his knife had been forced into the leaping flames. Momentarily his grip lessened, and he sought relief from the heat that touched his flesh.

Letting go of the giant's wrist, Shadow Dancer brought his fist down squarely upon the larger man's chin. Bull Feather in turn threw Shadow Dancer off, and as both men regained their feet, their shadowed features were dark with hatred and rage as they fought for breath.

But Shadow Dancer did not give the giant a moment to regain his senses. Still clutching his hunting knife, he leaped into the air, and with both feet struck the larger man full in the chest, knocking him flat once more. This time, though, Shadow Dancer was at the ready. He straddled Bull Feather's big belly and chest, placing the blade of his hunting knife against Bull Feather's throat. His challenging, black gaze looked into the large man's eyes as though questioning whether his opponent wished to live or to die!

Shadow Dancer easily read the defeat in the giant's eyes as they held for a minute on his own. Slowly he rose to his feet, his knife clutched in a defensive manner and extended toward the larger man. Then he looked about to find his wife.

Iva had watched the entire battle, her heart hammering crazily in her chest. As Shadow Dancer's eyes sought her out, his name flew from her lips and she ran to him. "Shadow Dancer!" she cried again as she was caught up against his side, his large arm going protectively around her as his dark gaze circled the villagers around them as though he dared any to attempt to stop him from claiming his wife.

A piercing whistle left his lips and within seconds Cimmerian stood next to them. Still holding his knife defensively, Shadow Dancer helped his bride to mount, and in a lithe movement mounted behind her and, with a kick of both heels, urged the mighty stallion to leave the Shoshone village.

Iva rested her head against Shadow Dancer's chest, her ear filled with the sound of his heartbeat.

Only a few minutes outside of the Shoshone village Shadow Dancer reined in Cimmerian, his hands tenderly drawing Iva's face upward so he might regard it in the moonlight. "You are unhurt, my love?" He appeared to hold his breath while waiting for her answer.

Tears streamed down Iva's face. "I am fine now, Shadow Dancer!" She threw her arms around his neck and pressed her face against the curve of his throat, glorying in the fact that she was once again in the arms of the man who loved her.

"And the babe?" Shadow Dancer knew she had been through a terrible ordeal, but he would not be at peace until certain that his family was once again well and in his keeping.

"The babe is unhurt," she whispered, grateful for his tender concern.

As she raised her face back up toward his, he lowered his lips, and for a wondrous time, they shared a kiss that spoke of the fear they had both known, of the long moments passed in separation, and of the binding love that filled their hearts. His lips played over hers in a consuming brand, seeking and sharing, wanting only to once again know the oneness that united them throughout this life and all eternity.

Iva clutched him tightly to her, glad that her life had been put back in order. She had been almost lost to a terrible fate, but this man, her husband, had saved her. She could not seem to get enough of the taste, the feel of him.

It was Shadow Dancer who first came back to his senses. Drawing his mouth away from hers as though it pained him, he lightly caressed her cheek as he looked deep into her eyes. "When I came back to the village and found you missing, I was mad with worry!" He hugged her tightly as though reliving those moments.

"It was so horrible, Shadow Dancer!" Iva tightened her grip on him. "I should never have gone to the temple to meet the man that sent me the message! I should have known it was a trap, but I was afraid not to go, for the boy who brought the message said that the meeting concerned your safety; and when I remembered what had happened when we were at the falls, I was afraid that something would happen to you!" A long sob shuddered through her.

"So that is why you went to the temple." Shadow Dancer thoughtfully responded. He had wondered so often during the past week just what had drawn her to the temple, but he had never imagined that she had been lured there under the pretense that he was in some kind of danger. "You say the one that brought you the message was a young boy?" His mind quickly tried to piece together the information she had given him.

Iva shook her head, knowing where he was leading. "I did not recognize him, Shadow Dancer." Again tears brimmed in her eyes and dampened her thick lashes.

Noting the stress she was under as she imparted all she had gone through, Shadow Dancer kissed her forehead tenderly and tried to soothe her. "Do not think of this now; we will talk more later. Just let me hold you and know that you are safe." He urged Cimmerian into motion while he held Iva close to his heart.

Throughout most of the long night Shadow Dancer kept Cimmerian moving at a steady pace, wishing to put as much distance as possible between them and the Shoshone village.

Iva made no objections. She was soon asleep in her husband's arms, rocked into slumber by the motion of the great stallion. The past week had been a nightmare, but now she and her unborn child were safe and once again under Shadow Dancer's protection.

It was during the early hours of the morning that Shadow Dancer found a safe place for them all to rest for a few hours. Allowing Cimmerian to freely graze, he spread out his sleeping mat and then tenderly lifted Iva onto it.

Throughout the ride, Shadow Dancer had occupied himself with thoughts of what had drawn his wife to the temple and had set her abduction into motion. Much had been left unsaid, but as he looked down into her beautiful face he felt the power that drew him to her. As his lips descended to the softness of her mouth, he was lost, drawn fully into the web of love's tender illusion. His heated tongue entered the sweetness of her mouth, and he sought out all the honeyed ambrosia he had thirsted for over the past several days.

At that moment Iva fully realized how much she had longed for this man who held her. Her slim arms wound around his neck, pulling him closer to her, as her own tongue dueled with his in a heated reclaiming of their love.

Their time of separation seemed as nothing as their hands sought out the tender pleasure spots of each other's bodies, their breathing ragged and short as they ached to once again rekindle the ecstasy that always accompanied their joining.

Shadow Dancer handled his wife as though she were more precious than gold. Each caress was given in wonder, each kiss holding the capacity to awaken the most lingering desires. He devoured her and she him as they rediscovered the burning rapture that lay in wait.

His heated kisses awakened a trail of steaming need, his mouth roaming from her lips down her slim throat and over the fullness of her breasts to their rose-hued tips, which he drew one by one into the moist cavern of his mouth, his tongue gently teasing each tender bud as he suckled lightly and drew forth sensuous shivers of ecstasy from her.

Iva's body flamed with need as she clutched Shadow Dancer's head to her breasts. "Please, please," she cried aloud as she pushed against him in her craving to sate it.

Shadow Dancer's own body trembled with desire, the sound of her voice pulsing through every vital organ of his being. There was no reason for her to beg. The throbbing length of his manhood sought out the harbor of her warm, moist sheath as he rose up above her, his mouth and tongue playing wantonly over her breasts even as her lower body arched upward to receive his hard, pulsating fullness.

Gathering her curving buttocks in his large hands, Shadow Dancer pressed her body more fully against his own, allowing more of him to enter her velvet depths. With the feel of him completely filling her, Iva cried out, her satin-smooth legs wrapping about his hips. Her body trembled, sheer ecstasy consuming her, and then, with his next deep surging thrust, she knew the fullness of love.

Her body felt liquid, yet the very center of her being seemed to burst with sparkling, jeweled lights. She was spiraling toward the outer reaches, showered by stars. Her whole frame quaked uncontrollably from the assault upon her senses.

Shadow Dancer gloried in the delights of their joining. His dark gaze fixed upon her in fathomless adoration, he also was swept over the precipice to fulfillment. His sensations, seemingly pulled from within him, were of dizzying brilliance. He released an animal-like groan of satisfaction as the life-giving liquid bearing his seed was pumped fiercely upward.

As Shadow Dancer clutched his wife to him, he knew the depth of his love for her. She was all, and without her he would be a dead man. This night she alone had breathed life back into his soul. "I love you beyond anything this life has to offer, Moon Flower," he said, breathing raggedly, and placed loving kisses over her eyelids and across her cheek.

"Oh, Shadow Dancer, I feel the same way! I love you so much! I thought I would die when I was forced to stand before Bull Feather who was about to claim me as his wife!" Iva was certain that she would have fought the giant Shoshone with all her strength. She would never have given in willingly to him, for she was now with the man meant for her. Only Shadow Dancer touched her heart.

Hearing his wife's words, Shadow Dancer silently swore that she would not be stolen away from him again. He held her tightly against his length, his hands tenderly brushing the golden curls from her cheeks, and as he felt her relax against him, he softly questioned, "Did you see the man you went to meet at the temple?" Whoever that was, he told himself, he would seek him out and put a halt to his wretched life!

Gently Iva shook her head. "He was cloaked, the hood pulled over his head. It was too dark for me to make out his features. There were two Indians helping

293

him, but I did not recognize either one." She knew that she could not offer him much aid in finding the culprits that had tried to destroy their lives. "I'm sorry I cannot tell you more."

Shadow Dancer kissed her tenderly upon the forehead. "Do not worry, my heart. Try to sleep now. You are safe." Shadow Dancer did not want her to be concerned. When he returned to the village he would try to gather more information. Now the most important thing was that he had regained his bride. Whoever had dared to abduct her, would one day pay in full!

Chapter Twenty-Five

The ancient, Indian woman known as Prairie Bird Woman rode stretched out on the travois that had been fashioned for her comfort, the device pulled by the packhorses that Willy Handcock had brought along. Every now and then throughout the long, hard days of travel, the old, gray-haired Indian woman would call out directions, her bony finger pointing always toward the vast mountains of the Rockies and keeping them on a steady course.

The day they left the desert and reached the mountains' foothills, Delbert insisted that they halt early and set up camp. Over the past several days the Indian woman had looked pale and exhausted, and seeing her now upon the travois, he feared for her very life if they did not allow time for her to rest. No matter how long it took them to find the hidden valley, Delbert was determined to keep going, but if the old woman took sick or died along the trail, he knew they would never find Iva and that valley.

Willy objected to the delay in his usual unpleasant manner, claiming to Delbert that Prairie Bird Woman was just fine and only wanted to drag out the trip because as their guide she felt important.

Delbert scoffed at the other man's reasoning. Halting his mount and the packhorse in a spot that appeared safe enough to make camp, he ignored Willy's complaints and began to see to the horses.

Leaving Delbert to the camp duties, Willy went out to scout the area and hunt fresh game for the evening meal.

"That one no good! He bad blood!" Prairie Bird Woman spat on the ground in irritation as Delbert began to help her get off the travois. "He good for nothing, and Prairie Bird Woman glad dog stay behind in village! Bad enough man so ornery, little yelping dog drive all mad!"

Delbert laughed aloud in agreement as he went around the campsite gathering wood for a fire. "It was Willy Handcock that offered to help me find Iva. No one else would start out on such a venture." He tried to explain to the Indian woman why he had cast in his lot with the ill-tempered prospector. "The truth is, though, I'm glad his mangy, little dog stayed behind with your nephew, Spotted Pony. I hope by the time we return the aggravating dog will have disappeared!" Delbert started the fire and began to dig out the pots he would need for preparing something to eat.

Prairie Bird Woman grinned widely at the young man's words. Her nephew had told her before she had left that he was going to give the dog to the shaman of the village, Wolf Dreamer. The old woman knew well the fate of the little dog at the shaman's hands, he would be a tasty morsel in Wolf Dreamer's stew pot! "When find girl in valley, then young man happy?" She did not explain her thoughts; but instead from where she sat on the ground as Delbert laid out their supplies, she fixed sharp, dark eyes upon him.

Happy didn't even come near describing what Delbert would feel when at last he found Iva. "Iva and I grew up together. We have always been close," he answered, holding in his true emotions as he looked over his shoulder at the old woman and wondered what she could have on her mind. Usually Prairie Bird

Woman kept to herself. She was not given to asking personal questions, nor did she reveal very much.

"What if, when find girl, she not wish to leave valley?" The old woman's dark eyes held upon Delbert in a searching manner. "What if girl joined with warrior, and he will not release her?"

Until this very moment Delbert had not thought of anything beyond finding the hidden valley and rescuing Iva from her captors. "Why would she not want to return to the farm with me? Her mother and father are there, and she would know how much they have suffered since she was taken from them. Besides, Iva loves the farm. She likes working with horses." The old woman is just trying to goad me for some strange reason, Delbert thought. Why would anyone not wish to return to the Cassidy farm? To Delbert the kind of life he and the Cassidys had shared before Iva's abduction could not be surpassed. Anyway, he reasoned, who would want to stay with someone who had kidnapped them? As for the Indian woman's other question, he would not even consider it. Of course Iva could not be involved with some Indian warrior. Iva belonged to him! He had waited almost his entire life to claim her as his own, and nothing was going to stop him!

Shaking her gray head, Prairie Bird Woman gazed upon him with sad eyes. She had found over the long winter months that she rather liked this young man called Delbert. If given the choice, she would have proclaimed aloud that she liked him much better than his coarse, unclean companion. But she feared at the end of their journey Delbert would find much heartache. She knew without being told that the girl he searched for was not his sister as he proclaimed. She could read his feelings for the missing girl in his eyes every time he spoke her name.

"We will break camp early in the morning and start the trek into the mountains. I hope you will be up to it,

Prairie Bird Woman. I can imagine the ruckus old Willie would cause if we delay more." Delbert deliberately tried to turn the subject away from Iva and what would happen once they found the hidden valley. I will worry about that when the day comes, he told himself.

"I will be fine! Do not worry about Prairie Bird Woman, I will not be the cause of any lagging. I did not sleep well last night because I knew we would reach the mountains today. That is why I am so tired. Tomorrow I will be fine once again!"

The old Indian woman was as determined as ever, Delbert realized as he began to spread out her pallet of furs, which she had brought along to make the travois ride more comfortable and to serve as her bedding.

After watching her settle her frail form upon the thick furs, Delbert went in search of fresh water. Once he was alone, he again went over the questions Prairie Bird Woman had asked him. What would he do if some warrior from the hidden valley had claimed Iva as his wife? Anger coursed through him. Delbert was not the same young man he had been when he had first started his search for Iva. He had changed greatly over this past winter, had become stronger, more self-assured. Prairie Bird Woman's nephew, Spotted Pony, had taken him under his wing and had taught him how to hunt with a bow and arrow, how to silently approach game. Spotted Pony had also taught him how to wrestle and fight in the Apache fashion. Delbert was now sure that he would be able to handle himself in any situation. And without doubt, he would fight any man that dared to stand between him and Iva.

That evening after the rabbit Willy shot had been cooked and the pots and dishes had been washed, the camp settled down for the night. But Delbert's sleep was troubled. A vision of Iva came to him, as he had seen her that day when she was riding Cimmerian around the corral.

The dirt kicked up by the prancing stallion's hooves now appeared to be a cloud of gold dust, and the golden-haired beauty upon the back of the black horse laughed aloud with enjoyment, her sparkling blue eyes like topaz stones.

She called to Delbert, who sat on the corral fence, but he was powerless to move. He could do nothing but sit there, admiring her beauty. At that moment he saw the Indian warrior enter the corral on horseback. Delbert heard Iva call to him again, and he fought the invisible bonds that held him still.

His name pierced the night air just as the Indian reached her side, both of them appearing to vanish in a puff of gold dust! Sitting straight up on his sleeping pallet, Delbert cried aloud, "No!"

Willy Handcock's hand encircled the trigger of his rifle, and at the same time he crouched low upon his bedroll. As his searching gaze fell upon Delbert from across the campfire, his tension eased and with some agitation at being woke up, he mumbled. "Dadblamed greenhorn kid! Yer gonna have the whole Injun nation down on our heads, if'n ya keep up yer bellowing!"

Prairie Bird Woman had also been startled awake by Delbert's outburst, but wisely she kept her thoughts to herself. Her dark eyes filled with sadness as they stared through the darkness of night in Delbert's direction. He must be dreaming about the young woman he seeks, she thought to herself. He must worry that she is already lost to him!

Summer and fall fled, and with the passage of the long winter months, Iva grew even lovelier in her husband's regard. As her body grew larger with the growth of their child, Shadow Dancer was always willing to lend her his assistance. Eagerly he would stretch out a hand to assist his young bride in her attempts to rise from a sitting position, his supportive arm was quickly placed around her waist to help steady an ungainly step, and he offered comfort when her mood was low. He was her mainstay in these days, and they grew even closer.

It was becoming warmer in the hidden valley, though afternoon breezes circulated from the mountains above and turned the evenings pleasantly cool. One morning, upon awakening, Shadow Dancer turned to his beautiful bride and announced that the entire day would be given over to their enjoyment. "I declare this day a holiday!" He grinned and, settling his mouth over her sweet tempting lips, drew her into his embrace, the mound that was their child pressed against his midsection. Suddenly feeling a healthy kick, Shadow Dancer laughed and swore that their child agreed with all he had said.

That afternoon as the couple picnicked near the edge of the small pond behind Shadow Dancer's house, Iva truly believed that her life could not be any more wonderful than it was now. As the couple sat close together upon the blanket Shadow Dancer had spread out, Iva laughed delightedly as she watched a gold mantle squirrel shrilling loudly at a fat, slow-moving woodchuck that had trespassed on its domain.

Shadow Dancer's chest constricted with the pleasure-pain he always felt when touched by his wife's beauty. She was a source of enjoyment, her loveliness seeming to permeate him and at the same time overcome him. Reaching out, Shadow Dancer caressed Iva's soft curls, his finger and thumb rubbing a fine silken strand lovingly. As he smiled, his thoughts were more upon her than the antics of the animals she was watching.

It had been some months now since the attack at the falls and his wife's abduction from the temple, and as each day passed it was becoming easier to put the events from their minds. Shadow Dancer had sought diligently for some clue that would lead him to those who had participated in the abduction of his bride, but his efforts had been to no avail. He had turned up no lead that would bring the culprits to light. At one point he had thought of returning to the Shoshone village and questioning the brave Iva had been handed over to that night at the temple—Talking Bear—but he had decided it was unwise to be gone for the length of time it would take him to go there and then return to the valley. Even leaving Iva's side for a day worried Shadow Dancer.

"Nokie says the baby will surely come before the next full moon." Iva took her husband off guard as she turned away from the entertainment the wildlife provided and interrupted Shadow Dancer's thoughts.

"This does not surprise me." Shadow Dancer remained relaxed, his dark eyes beholding her warmly as his hand moved away from the soft texture of her hair to rest upon the swelling of her abdomen. "Are your thoughts plagued with ill feelings when you think to the hour at which you will be taken with labor to deliver the child, Moon Flower?" Something he had sensed in her tone had brought about his question. He did not wish her to be frightened, and he hoped that he would be able to offer her his strength.

Iva considered his question. They had discussed this subject of her delivery several times during the past few months, yet it always made her uncomfortable. Here in the valley there was no doctor, nor was her mother present to act as midwife. She had only Aquilla and Nokie to rely upon through her ordeal. "Perhaps I am a bit nervous about what will take place, Shadow Dancer, but truly I am trying not to be afraid." She squeezed his hand, not wishing to worry him. "Besides, I plan to ask Nokie to make me up a potion!" She grinned warmly, hoping to ease his mind as well as her own.

"You, my sweet, are surely enough of a potion for me!" Shadow Dancer kissed her full upon the lips, savoring the sweet taste of her as his hands roamed over the soft flesh of her slender arms.

Iva leaned against her husband's chest, more than willing to be the recipient of his loving attentions. Her own mouth opened and welcomed the warm invasion of his tongue, and at the same time her fingers lightly caressed the broad expanse of his chest.

At that moment the idyllic interlude was shattered by a call from Arez. Shadow Dancer withdrew his lips from Iva's, and still holding his wife in an easy embrace, he responded from where he sat. "What brings you out here?" he asked the boy. He thought that perhaps Arez had come for a swim in the pond and had come upon them by surprise.

"My father sent me, Shadow Dancer, to bring you the news." The dark-haired boy took a deep, ragged breath as he tried to recapture his normal breathing. His father had told him to run all the way, and he had not stopped until he had arrived at Shadow Dancer's house, where his mother had told him that Shadow Dancer and Moon Flower were picnicking by the pond.

"What news could be so important to send you rushing about to find me?" Shadow Dancer had to keep a smile from coming to his lips as he glimpsed the lad's serious manner, certain that Arez's father, Dark Water, had sent news that he had at last killed the large bear he had been hunting for the past few days. Dark Water always was one to boast, Shadow Dancer thought to himself, and lately his friend had seemed to be doing more of it because Shadow Dancer was reluctant to leave his wife's side as her time of delivery drew near to go hunting.

"There are some strangers approaching the valley. The warning has been sounded, and the braves are now gathering their weapons to confront those that draw closer to our village!" Arez spoke in a rush of excitement, and his dark eyes kept going back in the direction of the village, where he knew all the other young boys would be gathering up their makeshift weapons and following the braves, anxious to view those that had found the entrance to their valley.

Shadow Dancer looked down at his wife, and blue eyes met his dark ones. "All right, Arez, tell your father I am coming right away." Shadow Dancer only waited for the boy to run off before he rose and drew Iva up to his side. As he took her hand, his dark eyes appeared to seek out her thoughts. "Please, Moon Flower, go back to our home. I will return to you as soon as I am able to leave the village."

She was not going to return alone to their house. "I certainly will not. I am not a child!" The strangers entering the valley might be a party led by my father, Iva thought. Her heart leaped in her breast at the thought of seeing him once again after these many months of separation. There was so much she wanted to tell him. She wanted him to meet her husband and to know how happy she was. Her hand went to her belly, and she knew that she would have to do a lot of explaining!

"You will do as I have told you, Moon Flower!" Shadow Dancer shattered her vision of a happy reunion with her father. He had quickly come to the same conclusion about the strangers, but his vision was not as happy as his wife's. If the intruders were here to seek out his bride, he did not want her anywhere around. He would deal with them alone. But first he needed to find out what was taking place in the village, and he could not do this with her at his side.

"You are my husband, Shadow Dancer, but make no mistake, you are not my lord and master. I will not be ordered about by you or anyone else!" Iva's temper was so fierce that she began to step around him, determined that she would see for herself if it was her father coming into the valley.

Her words dashed against Shadow Dancer like cold

water, but he knew she was right. She was not a woman to be ordered about, and he would have her no different. Taking a deep breath, he tried to make amends. "I am sorry, Moon Flower, I did not mean to give you orders. If it is your will, you may go to the village. I only ask that, as my wife, you do not interfere with what will take place."

"Of course I won't interfere, as long as these visitors are treated fairly!" Since she had lived in the valley with Shadow Dancer she had heard of no outsiders entering it besides herself, and at the moment she had no idea what kind of reception these Indians would give strangers. If Gray Otter's treatment of her was any indication, she had better be present to intervene if it became necessary; she would not allow her father or anyone in his party to be harmed. But with that thought she wondered what she would be able to do to prevent it.

The past several days of mountain travel had been rough going, taxing not only on the old Indian woman but also on Delbert and Willy Handcock. Each morning upon rising and breaking camp, they had pressed the horses to bear them upward, the Apache woman finally having to revert to riding atop the packhorse because of the narrow ledges they had to negotiate on the mountain. They had left the travois behind, but the old woman, determined as ever, guided them onward toward the hidden valley. Always she pointed her bony finger upward in a direction that Willy Handcock swore no man nor animal would venture.

Today as they traveled through a ragged ravine on the side of a huge mountain, slowly approaching a gorge that held towering cliffs on either side, Prairie Bird Woman became so excited she could not keep herself from calling out. "This is the joining together of

304

the mountains; it is just as my father told me long ago! We must be almost there. The valley should be on the other side of the gorge. There will be an eagle's nest on the face of the cliff at the end of the canyon. The sacred eagle's nest has stood for centuries, watching over the people of my father!"

Delbert felt the old woman's excitement as he clung to his saddle horn to keep his seat. She has to be right, he told himself. It was not possible that she made this whole thing up! The stories her father told her have got to be true; there has to be a hidden valley!

Just as Prairie Bird Woman had told them, the chasm opened into a wide, fertile valley. All three riders sat upon their horses, and though each had prayed for different reasons that they would find the valley, they now gazed down into the basin of green grass as though in disbelief.

At first the basin appeared to be only that, a fertile valley, but upon looking farther, past the border of trees, glimpses of civilization could be seen. Smoke curled over the tree tops, and a cow lowed in the distance.

"We have at last found the lost tribe of my father's people!" Tears streamed down the bronze, leathered cheeks of Prairie Bird Woman as she remembered the pain she'd seen long ago upon her father's face, but she shed tears of happiness also.

"Well, I'll be damned! It sure looks like we done found the valley of gold!" Willy Handcock's large hand slapped his thigh. His dark eyes were staring down toward the valley, and his greedy mind was imagining the riches that would soon be his for the taking.

Iva! Delbert held that one thought. The golden-haired young woman filled his mind as he realized that he had at last found the Indians who had abducted her.

"Let's not be dallying up here any longer than needful!" Willy declared to his companions. Then he slapped his horse with the reins. "I can't wait fer a hot

305

meal and to see if'n any of these Injuns got themselves any strong drink!" He had been out of whiskey for weeks and his mouth watered at the thought of a mug of strong brew.

Prairie Bird Woman and Delbert both followed him down into the valley, neither wanting to linger behind but both unable to really believe that their hard journey was at an end!

As the three led their mounts through the brace of trees that bordered the valley, a call in a language neither Willy nor Delbert understood sounded loudly across the valley's floor.

Prairie Bird Woman, taught by her father the language of his people when a child, knew that it was a signal for the warriors of the village to gather up their weapons and prepare a defense against the arrival of the intruders. Remembering also her father's dire warnings that outsiders were not welcome in the valley, Prairie Bird Woman worried over the reception her party would receive. Each man had had his own reason for searching for the hidden valley, but now Prairie Bird Woman asked herself if she would feel guilt if they were not welcomed with open arms.

Before the three strangers on horseback could reach the edge of the village, most of the tribespeople had turned out. In large groups, they searched for a sign that the intruders were near. The warriors carried bows and arrows, spears or lances, and wicked-looking clubs. The women, along with the children, for the most part stayed behind the men, but their loud voices intermingled with the deeper ones of the males as they also protested this violation of their privacy!

By the time Shadow Dancer and Iva reached the village, the people of the valley had already encircled the three riders. Their weapons at the ready, they seemed about to do the intruders harm.

Gray Otter's angry voice carried loudly over the shouts of the villagers. "Take them from their horses!

Be sure that you get all of their weapons! They are evil and cannot be trusted!" He shouted these instructions to his warriors while Meci the priest stood at his side.

Shadow Dancer made his way through the group gathered around the strangers. Iva stayed close behind her husband as he broke through the mass of angry braves. Eagerly her blue eyes sought out the outsiders. When she saw the old Indian woman and the two men standing in the encircling crowd, she blinked back tears and her heart lurched.

"Delbert!" she cried out. And without giving a thought to what her husband's people, or her husband, would think, she ran to the young man and threw her arms around his neck. Tears rolled down her cheeks now, tears of joy at once again seeing her lifelong friend. "I can't believe that it's you, Delbert! How did you find me?" She wept as she remembered seeing Delbert trussed up and lying in the dirt by her father's barn.

As he wrapped his arms tightly around her, Delbert was just as emotional. His long journey was over at last! He had found Iva! Even though he had always hoped to be reunited with her, he had, deep down, feared that she would be forever out of his reach. Now after these many months of not knowing whether she was alive or dead, or whether he would ever see her again, he was holding her. His tears were soon mingling with hers as they clutched one another tightly, the way they had when they were children!

It was Gray Otter who broke the stunned silence that gripped the villagers when they saw Moon Flower run up to one of the strangers and embrace him. "The intruders must be put to death!" he shouted loudly. "They have broken our sacred law by entering our valley and they must not be given the chance to bring more outsiders into our midst!" Deep in his belly Gray Otter was beginning to feel the hunger for revenge. All could see that the golden woman now known as Moon

Flower had at last been found by a loved one. What better way to achieve vengeance against his cousin and his wife than to have this young man she was embracing put to death?

Once again the shouts of the villagers rose, now in agreement with Gray Otter's menacing words. "But the old woman is of the people!" one warrior stated loudly in defense of Prairie Bird Woman, for she was an Apache and wore the clothing of her people, which was not lost upon the speaker. Quickly others sided with him.

"Then she shall live until the pale ones have been taken care of. Once they are out of the way, she will be able to speak. We will hear her words and find out if she led the outsiders into our valley!" Meci spoke out in a strong voice before Gray Otter could say anything else, taking charge in a decisive manner. He realized this was a chance to further his influence, and he was not about to let the opportunity pass. Meci's plan to have Shadow Dancer killed upon his return to the village after the long search for his wife had been foiled. He had not expected the golden woman to return. If she had been murdered in the mountains, upon Shadow Dancer's return to his people, Meci would have ordered a trusted brave to take his life. But Shadow Dancer had brought back his bride, and now he would not roam far from the valley, so there was no opportunity for an attack. In addition, the entire village had found out that the golden woman was going to bear Shadow Dancer a child. This had brought Gray Otter to the temple with threats that Meci would never become high priest if something was not done to prevent the child from being born. Meci had not been able to formulate a plan, until this moment.

The priest's words had stirred the people to anger. They wanted vengeance on the intruders. Assuming a protective stance in front of Delbert, Iva glared at Gray Otter and the priest at his side. "You cannot kill them!

308

They have done nothing wrong," she cried out, and slowly the angry villagers quieted down in order to see what effect her defense of the strangers would have on Gray Otter.

"You forget yourself! I am chief in this valley! My word is law!" Gray Otter puffed out his chest, his own dark stare hard and threatening as he glared back at the woman who had dared to openly defy him and Meci.

Shadow Dancer did not hesitate to come to his wife's defense. "Moon Flower is right! You cannot demand the lives of these men without a meeting of the high council! This one is my wife's kin, I will defend his right to be among us!" Though Shadow Dancer had at first felt keen disappointment because Iva's family had at last found her, he could not allow the young man to come to harm.

Several warriors backed away from the group encircling the outsiders as Dark Water and a number of braves stepped boldly to Shadow Dancer's side to place their weapons at his disposal.

As Gray Otter looked upon the warriors bravely standing at Shadow Dancer's side, a crafty gleam came into his eyes. He knew when to give in. He was not sure that his own warriors were as loyal to him or the priest at his side. "The high council will meet then!" Gray Otter shouted, but the crafty gleam did not leave his dark gaze. It was law that the sentence of death could only be given by the high council, but Gray Otter had a plan. "You, Shadow Dancer, will not be able to attend the meeting. By claiming the outsider as kin, you have given up your right to vote on the council!"

Gray Otter's point struck home. Shadow Dancer now knew there was little he could do in defense of the intruders, for the law did declare that one could not defend a relative before the high council. The two men would have no defense.

Iva looked to her husband, her face pale, her terror evident. "They cannot do this, Shadow Dancer!" she cried, her voice pleading with him to intervene somehow against the decision that Gray Otter and Meci had made.

Delbert could not understand a word of what was going on, but it was easy enough to spot the tension between the fat man with the disfiguring scar, who stood next to the man with the black robe, and the large Indian at Iva's side. "What is happening?" he asked her softly, feeling the friction in the air.

Iva could not bear to tell this dear friend that his very life was at stake. For a moment, unable to look in his direction, she kept her face turned toward Shadow Dancer.

It was Dark Water who offered some small measure of hope. "I will defend these outsiders in your stead, Shadow Dancer. My place on the council may not be high, but my voice will be heard this day by all." There was determination in the Indian's voice as he promised to do his best for his closest friend.

Shadow Dancer thanked his friend warmly, and with a glance he showed his gratefulness to all those braves who had come to his aid against Gray Otter and Meci. "I will take my wife and these outsiders to my house until their fate has been decided," Shadow Dancer stated loudly, as though daring any of the villagers, including his chief, to dispute him.

Gray Otter nodded his head thoughtfully. "You may take these intruders for now, Shadow Dancer. Soon the high council will gather and their fate will be declared to all!" His words were a dire threat that was not lost to anyone, including those who could not understand the language of the valley people.

"What is going on, Iva?" Delbert asked as soon as she and Shadow Dancer began to lead the small group through the village streets in the direction of their home. Many of the villagers followed, curious about the newcomers who had so unexpectedly come amongst them and anxious to witness any other

310

excitement that might occur because of their being in the village.

Iva swallowed hard, not yet willing to tell Delbert that his life was in jeopardy. She could well imagine the hardships he had been forced to endure while searching for her, and she did not want to be the one to tell him that all he had suffered had led only to his death.

As Prairie Bird Woman rode atop the packhorse that Shadow Dancer led, she kept her silence. It was Willy Handcock who enlightened Delbert. The prospector spat a long stream of tobacco juice into the dust at his feet; then he matter-of-factly said, "They be aiming to kill us, boy, if'n that fat Injun and the priest have their way about it!" With little concern showing in his dark eyes, he swung them from Delbert to the village, taking in the wealth around him and the seeming advanced manner in which these people lived.

"Kill us?" Delbert stopped dead in his tracks, refusing to go a step further until someone told him what was going on.

"The high council will decide your fate at the meeting of the council." Shadow Dancer spoke English, knowing that his wife was feeling too much pain to explain the situation to the young man; and wishing to spare her from having to be the one to tell her friend that he might well be put to death, he tried to soften the action his tribe had decided to take in regard to the intruders.

"What high council? Why would your people want to kill us? I only came to rescue Iva!" Delbert disliked and distrusted the tall, bronze warrior who was speaking English and who appeared far too familiar with Iva Cassidy!

"We will explain everything once we reach the house. There we can be comfortable," Iva stated softly. Not wanting Delbert to be angry with Shadow Dancer, she had intervened in the conversation. Once they reached her husband's house, she believed they would be able to

311

work out some plan to save Delbert's life and the lives of those who had come with him into the hidden valley.

"Whose house are we going to, Iva?" Delbert balked, wondering if they were being led into some kind of trap! He was determined to stand firm until he got the answers he wanted.

"We are going to my husband's house, Delbert." Iva stated this as kindly as she could, for she well remembered the feelings her dear friend had harbored for her and she did not wish to cause him any more grief than he already bore.

"Husband?" The single word came out a gasp, for at that moment Delbert Benell felt as though he had been mortally wounded! *Husband! Iva has a husband!*

As Iva stared into her friend's face, she glimpsed the emotions churning in him. "I will explain everything when we reach the house," she promised, and taking his arm, she forced him along with the others. It would be up to her to explain to Delbert that she had fallen in love with her abductor and had married him. There was hurt in her heart at that moment for the pain she knew he was suffering.

Chapter Twenty-Six

Aquilla opened the front door with the sun sign on its face as the small group arrived, and taking one look at the aged Apache woman who was being helped from her horse, she hurriedly showed her to a chamber.

Prairie Bird Woman had heard what Gray Otter and the priest had said. She knew the high council would be deciding the fate of the intruders and she would not be allowed to speak until the pale ones had been dealt with. As she laid her head down upon the sleeping couch, she reflected on the one known as Gray Otter. He was the chief of this tribe, and with the thought, she knew that he was the son of her father's cousin!

Willy Handcock gazed greedily around the interior of Shadow Dancer's house. Never in his entire life had he seen such splendor. There seemed no end to the wealth displayed in gold, silver, and precious jewels.

Delbert had no interest in any of this. He barely noticed where he was being led as Iva drew him out into the gardens. He could think only about Iva being the wife of the large Indian. *My Iva!* he told himself. The young woman he had always dreamed about claiming as his own had told him she was wed to another!

"Please, Delbert, come and sit down beside me," Iva beseeched. Knowing how he felt, she ached for him. "You must be weary after your long trip. Aquilla is preparing some refreshments and will bring them out shortly." She eased herself down on a garden bench as she tried to get Delbert to say something to her.

Despite his hurt and his raging jealousy, Delbert at last seemed to come to his senses. For the first time, as Iva sat there upon the bench, he noticed that she was no longer trim. The tunic she wore had concealed the fact that she was pregnant, but now the material bunched around her stomach and it was plain that she was carrying a child. His hazel eyes filling with outrage, Delbert could not help staring at her protruding belly as he sputtered, "How could you, Iva?" And since he did not consider the tone of his voice as he questioned her, he drew the attention of the others standing in the garden. "How could you have given yourself to him? He's an Indian, for God's sake!" His last words were almost an agonized cry.

In mere seconds Shadow Dancer was standing next to Iva, glaring darkly at the youth who dared to verbally abuse his wife.

"It's all right," Iva said to him. "Please let me talk to him. I have to explain." She rose and gently placed her hand upon her husband's arm, feeling tensed muscles straining with unleashed power.

Turning his regard from the young man standing before him, Shadow Dancer looked upon Iva, and slowly his anger waned. He could read on her face a deep sadness for this young man's hurt. With a tender hand, he helped her to regain her seat upon the bench. "This one and I will leave you and your friend alone to talk for a time while we see what is delaying the meal." He understood that she needed time with this youth to straighten out some of the hurt that Delbert was feeling, but before leaving the garden, Shadow Dancer directed a glare in the young man's direction to warn him not to mistreat his wife in any fashion.

Iva smiled appreciatively at her husband. She did need to be alone with Delbert in order to explain what had taken place in her life since last she had seen him. She knew that she owed Delbert this much.

"It was never my intention to fall in love with Shadow Dancer." She spoke softly, and once again Delbert's eyes rested upon her. "Nor was it my intention to be taken away from my father's farm. It just happened, Delbert, and no one is to blame!"

"You love this Indian?" He could barely force the words out of his mouth, but he knew he had to.

Without any hesitation, Iva nodded her head. "With all my heart."

"But what of me? What of my feelings, Iva? I love you! I have always loved you!" Delbert could not help himself; his emotions just spewed out. He had traveled so far in the hope of regaining Iva. Every moment since leaving the Cassidy horse farm he had only thought of the time when he would see her again, when he would be able to once more hear her soft, lilting voice, to see her beautiful face. And now that he had found her, she was telling him she loved another!

"Delbert, I do love you." Iva stood and, gaining his side, lightly touched his arm. "I love you now as I always have. As my friend, my playmate from my childhood, as my brother. I could never stop loving you, but what I feel for Shadow Dancer is so much more." Tears filled her eyes as she looked upon him and begged him to listen and to understand.

"But I always thought that one day you and I . . ." He could not finish the sentence, but Iva knew what he meant.

"I am so sorry, Delbert, but even if Shadow Dancer had never come into my life, I am afraid it would not have worked out in that way for you and me. What I feel for you is not the love a woman feels for the man she would wed." Iva saw his disillusionment on his face.

"Perhaps you have these feelings only because he holds you captive. But I have come to rescue you, Iva!"

Delbert grasped at anything that would keep his dreams alive. Perhaps this Indian called Shadow Dancer had somehow forced Iva to believe that she cared for him. Perhaps now she would reconsider, now that she could return to the Cassidy farm.

Slowly Iva shook her head, hating to see the bright lights in his green eyes once again fade but knowing she could not allow him to believe her love for her husband was so shallow. "Because I was Shadow Dancer's captive, I at first fought off the attraction he had for me. I fought it until I could fight my feelings no longer! I love him, Delbert, with all of my heart."

Delbert ached as though his own heart had been pierced, but as he looked upon her, after hearing her feelings for her husband so plainly revealed, his own feelings for her forced him not to begrudge her this great love she had found. Within him was a deep void because he had for so long been in love with Iva, and suddenly he knew she and he would never be. His gaze roamed from her face to her enlarged stomach, and as though unable to stand upon his feet any longer, he eased his frame down upon the garden bench next to her. After a moment of silence, he took her hand within his own. "I have always loved you, Iva. That first day when your father brought me to the farm and I looked upon you with your long, golden hair, I fell in love with you." His sad green eyes looked directly into hers as though he had harbored all these feelings for so long it was a relief to get them out.

"I know, Delbert." She patted his hand as his grip tightened upon hers. She had always known of Delbert's feelings for her, but what the young man did not know now was that they would pass and one day he would meet the woman meant to fill his life. When that day came, he would know what true love really was.

Drawing a deep breath and forcing himself to face the truth, Delbert at last asked, "What of your mother and father, Iva? They have been distraught since you were taken from the farm. Your father searched for weeks after your abduction, but found no lead to you or the Indians that took you from the farm. When he returned, I set out to look for you, and it was only with a great deal of luck, and a lot of searching through Apache villages, that we found Prairie Bird Woman. She was the only one who recognized the headband dropped at the farm during your abduction. She led us to the valley, having claimed that her father had given her directions years ago. But even now Bain and Katherine don't know whether you are alive or dead!"

"Shadow Dancer and I plan to visit mother and father at the farm after the baby is born." Iva was more than a little relieved that the initial storm had passed and Delbert was not so angry he could not converse peaceably with her. With a small smile, she added, "You will be able to take them word of my safety. Shadow Dancer and I both worry about their reception of the news of our wedding, but when you return you can explain some of what has taken place, so that they will have time to deal with their feelings toward my husband before we make the trip."

"You are assuming I will survive to return to the farm with news about you!" Delbert was still deeply hurt, but he was now trying not to allow his anguish to show. Iva had explained her feelings, and he could plainly see that he could not change her mind about this man she claimed as her husband, so if he desired to remain her friend, he knew he would have to put aside his own hurt.

Iva knew how hard all of this was for him. "My husband's closest friend, Dark Water, will stand in your defense before the council. He is very well liked and respected in this village." Iva offered the only hope she could at the moment, for she knew that Gray Otter would press for the death penalty to be meted out to Delbert and to the prospector who had come to the valley with him. She was not unaware that Gray Otter's motive was to inflict pain upon her and Shadow Dancer.

As she acknowledged this her husband returned, Willy Handcock at his side, to find his wife and the young man in conversation. He was pleased for Moon Flower's sake that the one called Delbert was handling himself well. Seeing her husband entering the gardens, Iva went over to him to explain what had taken place between herself and Delbert.

Willy's dark eyes still held the sparkle of greed as he followed Shadow Dancer back out into the gardens, and seeing an opportunity to have a moment alone with Delbert, he wasted no time in speaking his thoughts. "Well, boy, we did it. That's fer sure! We done found the valley of gold, just like I told ya we would. Ya can count on old Willy! Now all we got's ta do is get us some of these fine trinkets lying around fer the taking and then hightail it out of this valley! We can come on back later with more help ta teach these Injuns a lesson and get whatever we want that was left behind!"

Delbert could only stand and stare at the older man. Did Willy really think he would leave Iva so quickly now that he had found her? But staying in this valley might well mean death for both of them. "Don't be stupid!" he said to the old prospector. "If we're going to leave this valley, we had best not bother with anything that belongs to these people! We'll be lucky to get out of here with our skins intact!"

"What?" Willy couldn't believe what he was hearing. "Do ya think I came all this dabblamed way fer nothing? You can bet yer sweet life old Willy Handcock ain't leaving this hidden valley without his pockets bulging. I'm getting what's due me, and that's a fact, boy!"

Delbert did not doubt that Willy Handcock would stand behind these words, but he was hoping the council would decide in favor of their leaving the

318

valley, and hoping Willy would not cause him grief!

A short time later Dark Water arrived at Shadow Dancer's house, his mood solemn as he approached the group in the gardens and stood before his friend, Shadow Dancer. "The council has made their decision, my friend," he announced, and his dark gaze went to Moon Flower and then back to Shadow Dancer as though he were offering the couple an apology.

Shadow Dancer knew without being told that something had gone wrong. Silently he took Iva's hand in his own, wanting to lend her some of his strength. He feared that the council had gone along with Gray Otter and Meci, and had ruled that his wife's lifelong friend and the old man were to be put to death. Such news would be devastating to his wife.

Drawing in a deep breath before beginning, Dark Water looked directly at Shadow Dancer. "I am afraid, my friend, that things did not go well. I tried my best to defend the one that you claim as kin, but the voices of Gray Otter and Meci were more powerful. All that I could gain for the intruders is the chance to leave the valley alive." Dark Water could not allow himself to look at Moon Flower. He could not bear to see the pain in her eyes.

Shadow Dancer was not sure what Dark Water meant by a chance to leave alive. Whatever this might prove to be, he told himself with some relief, it was a chance! "What was the council's decision?" He waited for Dark Water to tell him everything.

Dark Water appeared nervous about going on, but having no other choice, he tried to remain calm as he repeated what the council had determined. "In order for the outsiders to live, the young man must climb the sacred eagle cliff and touch the golden arrow that resides in the bottom portion of the eagle's nest. He must do this before tomorrow's afternoon sun casts its shadow between the two cliffs and touches the sacred eagle's nest."

319

Shadow Dancer frowned darkly at this news, and his hand automatically gripped Iva's tighter. The quest set out for this young man was not totally impossible, but it took skill and a great deal of caution and quickness.

"There is more, I am afraid." Dark Water was even more reluctant to go on, but there was no help for it. The words had to be spoken. "The council voted that if the young man does not perform the quest in the allotted time, then it is Moon Flower who has displeased the gods, and she must be sacrificed to appease our gods' displeasure for the pale-skinned one's presence in the valley. She is to stand alone upon the opposite cliff from the sacred eagle cliff and await her fate as the young man performs the quest. I am sorry, Shadow Dancer. I swear to you that I tried my best to sway the council." Dark Water knew that this news would be taken hard.

For a moment Dark Water's words hung ominously in the air. "No!" Shadow Dancer at last shouted, his anger mounting by the second, and at the same time Iva expelled her pent-up breath.

Unable to understand fully what was taking place, Willy Handcock stood back and observed the two braves and the golden-haired woman as Delbert hurriedly made his way to Iva's side.

"What are they saying, Iva?" Delbert questioned, concern in his green eyes. By the way everyone was acting, he knew the Indian called Dark Water did not bring welcome news.

"My wife shall have no part in this! The gods ordained her coming to this valley!" Shadow Dancer lashed out at his friend, and Delbert was ignored for the time being.

"I did all that I could, Shadow Dancer. The council could not be swayed!" Dark Water defended himself before the fury of his friend.

It was Iva who at last brought some reason to the moment. "It is not your fault, Dark Water. Shadow

Dancer and I both know that you did everything you could. It is Gray Otter. He hates me, and he is jealous of my husband. I am sure no one could have done more than you."

"I will take my wife from this village, and we will not return as long as Gray Otter lives!" Shadow Dancer declared, not willing to risk his bride's life.

"And what of Delbert and his friends?" Iva asked. She had no intention of leaving Delbert and the old man to their own fate. Shadow Dancer knew this; he was just very angry at this minute. "Is this quest that Dark Water speaks of so very hard? Can Delbert not perform the feat in the allotted time?" Her blue eyes traveled first to her husband and then to Dark Water.

"He will have no choice but to try!" Dark Water stated softly. "Gray Otter has ordered both men to be taken from your house and placed under guard until tomorrow. At this moment their guards are awaiting outside."

"Please tell me what is happening, Iva." Delbert got this out during a lull in the conversation.

"Of course, Delbert, I'm sorry." Iva turned to the young man, realizing that he was totally in the dark about the decision the council had made concerning his very life. "The high council has declared that you must perform a quest, if we are all to go free." She tried to soften her words in order to spare him the full impact of what lay ahead.

Before Delbert could question her, Shadow Dancer spoke up, "I myself have performed it. It is not impossible, but you must focus all of your attention and energy upon the ordeal."

Delbert absently nodded his head. "What did you mean, Iva, when you said this quest would determine if we are all allowed to go free? Are you going to leave with us?" Once again a spark of hope warmed his heart.

Iva caught the glimmer in his eyes and had to shatter his dreams once again. "Gray Otter has convinced the

321

council that if you do not reach your goal in the allotted time, it is the will of the gods that I be the one to pay the price for your coming to the valley."

Delbert could say nothing; he could only stare at her in wide-eyed disbelief. No wonder the brave called Shadow Dancer had sounded so angry!

Seeing the distress that instantly came over him, Iva went to Delbert and lightly hugged him. With some assurance, she stated, "I know that you will do what is necessary, Delbert. I trust you now, just as I did when we were children. I know you will be able to perform the quest in time."

"I . . . I will do my best, Iva, but I don't even know what it is I am required to do!" Delbert began to stutter, his nervousness increasing at knowing that Iva's life depended upon him.

"You are to climb the side of the eagle cliff that you passed through when you entered our valley, and you are to touch the golden arrow that lies at the bottom of the eagle's nest. All must be done in the afternoon sun, before the shadow cast by the opposite cliff touches the nest." Shadow Dancer stated this bluntly. He hoped in that moment to take the boy's measure, so he might determine what action he should take before the next morning. If the boy acted as though the feat set out for him was impossible to perform, Shadow Dancer would take his wife from this valley, even if that meant he would be leaving these two men to their fate!

Swallowing, Delbert stared at those around him. He remembered riding through the canyon that led into the valley: Prairie Bird Woman had spoken about the sacred eagle cliff. Was he truly expected to climb all the way up that solid stone wall to reach the arrow that protruded from the nest?

Not willing to put his faith in this young man, Shadow Dancer turned back to Dark Water. "Perhaps I can speak to the council and convince them that I should be the one allowed to perform the quest.

After all it is I who brought Moon Flower among my people."

Earlier Aquilla had heard her husband enter the house, and she, too, had silently listened to his sharing of the council's decision. Now she stood at his side as he responded to Shadow Dancer. "I am afraid that Gray Otter anticipated this. He has proclaimed that only the young man can perform the deed. It is the will of the gods, he has told the high council, and with Meci backing him up, there can be no changing the decision!"

"Delbert will do whatever is necessary!" Iva declared, showing her faith in her friend on noticing her husband's disappointment at Dark Water's words.

With Iva placing her trust in him, just as she had when she had been a little girl who looked up to him as to a big brother, Delbert swore to all that no matter what he had to do, he would not let them down. "I will climb the cliff and touch the arrow in time!"

Only Shadow Dancer was not heartened by the young man's statement. The climbing of the sacred eagle cliff had been a test of strength and endurance over the centuries among his people, and few had been able to succeed. Wind Cryer himself had been the first, when he had placed the golden arrow in the bottom of the eagle's nest, but there had not been many to follow in his steps. Many had reached the nest moments after the sun's shadow had been cast upon the arrow, and many more had not even done that well. If tomorrow's outcome did not go well, it would be Shadow Dancer's wife who would pay, and the price was far too dear. Moon Flower's life!

Chapter Twenty-Seven

The guards waiting outside of Shadow Dancer's house made their presence known, and soon the two prisoners were walking through the village between the pair of braves sent to escort them to the small house that would be their prison for the night.

As the afternoon hours lengthened into early evening Dark Water and Aquilla went to their home, leaving Shadow Dancer and Iva to retire to their chambers.

Shadow Dancer was in no way resigned to his wife's standing on the opposite cliff while the young man Delbert performed the quest, the outcome of which would determine whether she would live or not. For some time he had waged an inner war that left him quietly brooding as the couple prepared for bed. "My heart cries out to me to take you away from this valley and not risk your life and that of our child," Shadow Dancer confessed as he lay upon the sleeping couch and drew Iva down next to him. His large hand reached out and settled over her abdomen, and as though the child within welcomed the touch of its father, it kicked out against his hand, the movement increasing Shadow Dancer's protectiveness of his family.

"I know well your feelings, my husband, but I see no way that you and I can run away from what is happening. We cannot allow Delbert to face the wrath of Gray Otter alone. Your cousin would have him set upon and killed even if he were able to perform the quest set out by the council. All we can do is trust that Delbert will be able to climb the cliff in time and touch the golden arrow." Tears filled Iva's eyes as the thought that Delbert might fail came to her mind. That she might have to leave this life and all the happiness she had found in the arms of her husband filled her with dread. What would eternity be like without Shadow Dancer standing next to her? Would nothingness consume her, leaving her lost until the time when he would find her? Her hand covered his on the mound that was their baby, and with her husband's love surrounding her, she fought these dark feelings.

"I will go to this young man, Delbert, early in the morning and I will tell him all that I know about climbing the sacred eagle cliff, perhaps I will be able to aid him in his effort." At the moment this was all Shadow Dancer could offer. He felt powerless because he knew that his wife would not desert her friend and flee the valley with him to escape the council's judgment. They could only put their trust in the young man.

"I fully trust you, Shadow Dancer." Iva's blue eyes caught the dark regard of her husband, and as a soft moan came from her lips, he drew her into his embrace, his lips settling over hers in a hungry blending of their inner emotions.

How could he chance losing her? Shadow Dancer's heart ached with the fear of what tomorrow would hold. "I love you with all my heart, Moon Flower," he whispered as their lips parted and Iva snuggled tightly against the length of him; and deep within his being, he began to pray to his gods that his wife would be kept safe!

"I have no fear as long as you are near," Iva sighed softly, content for the moment to try to chase away what tomorrow might bring. "Hold me tight, Shadow

Dancer," she murmured, wanting to feel the strength of his arms.

Delbert and Willy Handcock had been led to a small building near the ceremonial lodge. The two braves that brought them to the hut were outside the hide flap that served as its door, but as the hour grew late, their small campfire dimmed and they settled down for the night on the sleeping mats they stretched out near the fire.

Willy had been unusually quiet since he'd learned of the council's decision about the outsiders. Shortly after arriving at the hut, he had told Delbert he wanted to flee the valley as soon as it grew dark. "We can gather us some of these Injuns' riches and hightail it fer help," he had declared after peeking around the door flap to make sure they weren't being overheard. If Shadow Dancer speaks the white man's tongue, there's no telling what other Injuns in this village can, he told himself.

"But we can't run away like that," Delbert had objected. "Iva would be left alone to face the council!" And Delbert did not doubt that her fate would be sealed by their desertion.

"Listen here, boy, we's got ta be thinking about ourselves! The girl seems right happy enough with her Injun brave. As I be seeing it, it's up to this Shadow Dancer to take care of her! Ya done yer part by searching her out, there ain't no more ya can be doing fer her! We should be sticking together and getting out of here as soon as it gets dark!"

"There is something that I can do!" Delbert argued, "I can climb that cliff to the eagle's nest and save Iva!" It was the only way Delbert could see getting out of the situation.

Willy Handcock burst out laughing in the face of Delbert's bravery. "Are ya daft, boy? Yer not going to climb the face of that cliff and save the girl's life or anyone else's! Yer a dumb, greenhorn who couldn't even shoot straight before ya met up with old Willy!" His guffaws once again filled the hut.

"I don't care what you say, Willy, I'm not running out on Iva. I could never live with myself if I did!" Delbert would not be swayed.

"Well, as I see it then, it's each man fer himself." That was Willy's last word on the subject.

With images of all the riches he had seen that day running through his mind, Willy Handcock lay upon his pallet and waited. It was well after midnight when he slowly rose to his feet and, finding Delbert sound asleep, cautiously made his way to the door of the hut.

Drawing a deep breath, he pulled back the door flap and silently looked around. Finding the two braves asleep on pallets near the fire, Willy chuckled to himself. It sure is plain that these Injuns ain't used to having no prisoners, he thought.

Without a glance in Delbert's direction, for as far as Willy was concerned the boy had made up his mind to stay in the valley and face what came, Willy walked away from the hut and headed to the right of the ceremonial lodge, where there was a small group of houses. When the guards had led him and Delbert to their makeshift prison, he had noticed several men sitting outside these houses, each man busy making jewelry out of gold and silver. His plan had been quickly contrived. He would silently get what he wanted and then be shed of this valley until he returned with more help. As he approached the first building, once again his thoughts went to Delbert. It was too bad the boy had to be so dagnab hardheaded! But there's nothing I can do, he told himself. Like he had told the boy earlier, now it was every man fer himself.

Using all the stealth his large bulk would afford, Willy easily slipped into the first house after finding no barred door. In the front room, he quickly found what he was looking for. This house must belong to the silversmith, he told himself as he eyed the intricate pieces of silver jewelry lying upon a long table in the front room, and spying several chests filled with priceless pieces of silver sitting on the floor, he did not hesitate but began to fill a leather bag with handfuls of the stuff.

The second house Willy approached was very similar. The front door also had no lock, and the front room contained the owner's handiwork. In this house Willy found precious jewels in a variety of colors and weights—rubies, emeralds, blue and yellow topaz. He shoved them all into his leather bag, then quickly went on to the next house.

It was in the third house, as he was greedily filling a sack with gold nuggets and gold chains, that he was suddenly grabbed from behind. "What the hell's going on here!" He spun around as the hand settled over his forearm, and was confronted by the hard, angry glare of one of the guards posted outside the hut.

In his excitement at finding so much treasure his for the taking, Willy Handcock had made a terrible mistake. He had forgotten to close the front door of this last house after entering it.

One of the two guards had awakened shortly after Willy had escaped the hut, and checking on the prisoners after relieving his bladder, he had found that one of the pale-skinned men had fled. By chance the guard had seen the front door of the goldsmith's house standing open, and finding that odd at this late hour of the night he had looked inside.

Caught in the act, Willy Handcock knew a tremendous fear as he was spun about, the abundant wealth he had stolen spilling across the floor; and with the evidence of his thievery so plainly visible, the guard's grip tightened. He dragged Willy back to the other guard, and the two braves began to speak excitedly in their native tongue.

"Now looky here, yer both taking this whole thing all

wrong!" Willy spoke the Apache tongue as he tried to bluff his way out of the situation, but the two guards began to drag him away. "I was only trying to see what kind of jewelry yer people make!" Willy wailed as he was hauled down the dusty road, his pleas for release totally ignored.

It was to their chief's house the braves took their prisoner, and Gray Otter was not in a pleasant mood when he was summoned to his front door in the middle of the night and given the news that one of the outsiders had been caught in the act of stealing bags of gold and silver.

A crooked smile came to the fat man's scarred face as he looked upon the prospector who was attempting to shake off the hands holding him. The punishment he would order quickly came to Gray Otter's mind. He was only sorry that it was not the young man who claimed kinship to Shadow Dancer's wife standing before him. Gray Otter would have delighted in ordering the death of that young man, and in so doing he would have known the pain he caused his cousin's family. "Take him from my house! He is vile. Our people do not steal from one another! Give him the fitting punishment for any who steal," Gray Otter commanded. "Death is all that he deserves!" The guards held on to Willy's flailing arms and dragged him away from their chief's house. Gray Otter's leering smile never wavered. Tomorrow afternoon I will see the rest of the intruders taken care of, he thought with some pleasure as he turned back into his home.

At this late hour Willy Handcock's muffled cries for release were the only sounds heard in the village besides the barking of a dog. There was no one about as the two guards obediently carried out their chief's orders. Dragging the prospector to the edge of the village, one brave pulled from the sheath strapped to his side a large hunting knife. The blade gleamed in the moonlight, and that was the last thing Willy beheld. In a swift,

329

silent motion his fate was forever sealed.

The following morning Delbert found that Willy Handcock was gone from the hut. Questioning the two guards still stationed outside the door did him little good, for they could not understand a word he said and he could not understand them. For a few minutes he tried to use sign language in an attempt to find out if they knew Willy's whereabouts, but this also seemed to get him nowhere. In the end Delbert decided that Willy had made good his talk of leaving the valley. He only hoped the old man had not run into any trouble in his attempt at freedom.

A little later Shadow Dancer arrived at the hut, and after he talked to the two guards and gave his word that the young man would not attempt escape, they placed their prisoner into his care.

"I came to show you where you will start your climb and to try to help you with what I learned from my own experience," Shadow Dancer explained.

Delbert only nodded his head, still reluctant to open up to this Indian that had stolen the only woman he had ever loved.

Shadow Dancer could understand the young man's feelings, and as he led Delbert out of the village and they made their way to the cliff, he talked of his everyday life in the hidden valley. He wanted his wife's friend to know how much he cared for her—and how much hinged upon his ability to perform the quest in the allotted time.

By midmorning Delbert was beginning to trust Shadow Dancer more, and as he listened to his advice about the climb, he was glad this man had taken the time to pass on his experience. Perhaps he would have a chance. He grasped this slim thread of hope as he looked up at the towering, sheer wall of rock that he would shortly have to climb!

Chapter Twenty-Eight

As the morning slowly passed Iva attempted to occupy herself while Shadow Dancer was away from the house. She tried not to dwell on the fact that she would soon be led away from her home and forced to stand upon the cliff opposite the one on which Delbert would be performing his quest. All morning she had tried to think positively. Delbert never let me down, she kept telling herself, and he won't now!

Nokie arrived while Iva was sitting in her chamber and sewing on a small gown she was making for her child in order to keep her mind off the ordeal ahead. Looking up as the other woman entered the room, she smiled warmly.

Nokie smiled in return and taking a seat across from Iva, she studied her stitching for a moment before she spoke. "Moon Flower, I wish to take your place on the cliff this afternoon."

Iva's expression revealed her surprise. Setting the tiny gown down in her lap, she wondered if she had heard the other woman correctly. "You want to do what?" she questioned.

"I know you must truly think me mad for asking you, but if you think about it, my request is not all that unreasonable." The large dark eyes held upon Iva, serious intent in them.

Looking at her friend Iva thought her much more pale and thin than she had seemed in the past. Slowly Iva began to shake her head as she realized Nokie was not jesting.

"Listen to me, Moon Flower." Nokie left her seat, and going over to where Iva sat, she took both of her hands in her own. "You have a husband—a child—to think about. You cannot risk the chance that your friend will touch the eagle's nest before the afternoon shadow touches it! I have no one except myself; no husband, no children!"

"And you think that because you have no husband and no child you can chance that Delbert will be able to perform the quest in time? You would place your own life in such jeopardy?" Iva could not comprehend how Nokie would wish to deliberately place herself in such a perilous situation. "I could never allow you to take my place."

Nokie became anxious as she tried to make her friend understand that she had no choice. "Truly, Moon Flower, I do not fear for myself. I spent all of last night praying to Coyolxauhqui, the moon goddess, and while I beseeched her for her help, her voice came to me and told me that it should be I who stands upon the cliff when the quest is performed. It is the will of the gods that I take your place!"

"No!" Iva cried, and she tried to pull her hands away. She did not want to listen to any more of this. All of this talk about gods and goddesses was insanity! What kind of deity would demand of this woman that she take her place upon the cliff and risk her life?

"But you cannot refuse me, Moon Flower. You must allow me to take your place. There is no other way." For a full moment Nokie stared into Iva's gaze, and deep within her eyes there was a pleading light Iva could not break away from. Finally Nokie spoke again, her voice very low as though she were speaking in confidence, "I had not planned to speak of this, but I

332

see now there is no other way." She took a deep, ragged breath before continuing. "The circle of my life path has all but come to an end. I have not long now to live upon this ground that my forefathers claimed as their own."

Iva shook her head slowly, unsure of what the other woman was trying to explain to her.

"I am dying, Moon Flower." Nokie released a soft sigh. "I have known for some time, and I am well prepared to join my ancestors. Sharaza herself has bid me to join her, but it has been the will of the gods that I tarry here for a little while longer. Last night they told me the reason. I am to take your place, and then my journey will begin."

"Dying?" Iva repeated the word as though it were entirely foreign to her. "But this is impossible!" She at last broke free of the other woman's hold upon her hands, and in that moment she felt that her entire world was falling apart. "This cannot be true! You cannot know when you are going to die!"

"Think not of yourself then, Moon Flower, but of the child that you carry in your body. Would you deprive this child of the life I alone can give it? I will take your place upon the cliff, and if your friend is victorious no one need ever know. But if he does not succeed, then at all costs the child must live!"

Iva pressed her hands over her ears, trying to shield herself from her friend's words. "I will not hear any more of this! How can I choose my life, and my child's, over yours?" She dropped the tiny gown at her feet, ran to her sleeping couch, and flung herself upon the soft bed of furs, weeping as though her heart were breaking.

For a full moment Nokie stood and looked down at her cousin's wife, pained by the other woman's agony. Going over to the pitcher of water in the chamber, she silently filled a mug and slowly approached the bed. "I do not mean to cause you such great distress, Moon Flower." The gentle, dark-haired woman spoke very softly as was her custom. "I have grown to love you deeply, my friend, and would offer my life as the only gift I have left in this world to give you." For a moment longer she listened to Iva's sobs. "Come, I have brought you a drink. We will speak no more about this subject of the quest, if that is your will." She waited for her friend to calm herself.

Iva wiped at her tears as she reached out for the drink Nokie held out in offering. It was all just too much for her to take at one time! First Delbert's arrival in the valley and the council's decision about the quest, and now her dear friend was telling her she did not have long to live and it was the will of the gods that she was to take her place upon the cliff.

Nokie watched as Iva drank from the silver goblet. She silently waited, and when the draught was finished, she pulled the furs upon the sleeping couch back in an inviting fashion. "You should rest now for a time, Moon Flower."

Looking at the furs, of a sudden Iva did find that she felt tired. Stifling a yawn, she resisted the invitation of the soft couch for just a moment longer. "I can't sleep now, Nokie. Shadow Dancer will be coming soon. For the quest. I will have to be there." But even as she spoke Iva found her eyelids growing heavier by the second, and she had to fight off her great desire to rest.

"I will take care of everything, I promise you, my friend. Sleep now for a time, and everything will be fine." Nokie lulled her with a soft invitation, which Iva was unable to resist.

"Perhaps for just a few minutes it won't hurt to sleep," she softly mumbled as she tiredly climbed onto the bed of furs.

Nokie sat beside the sleeping couch and lightly brushed away the golden strands of hair lying across Iva's cheeks. "Think only of your baby and your husband, my dear friend. I will take care of everything else," she whispered softly to a now-sleeping Iva.

Nokie had known there was no choice when she had poured the sleeping draught into the mug of water. It was the will of the gods that she take this woman's place upon the cliff, and nothing must stand in the way of destiny.

Later, when Shadow Dancer came to his chamber seeking out his wife, Nokie met him at the door. "Moon Flower is exhausted, Shadow Dancer. Do not wake her now." She spoke softly as though she herself feared that the sound of her voice would wake the other woman.

Shadow Dancer slowly nodded his dark head as he looked across the chamber to the sleeping couch, and his heart ached for his wife who still had much to go through this day.

Nokie easily read her cousin's grave emotions upon his usually indomitable features. "Shadow Dancer, you should return now to the young man who came to this valley seeking your wife. I am sure that he is in need of your wisdom and support."

Shadow Dancer admitted to himself that he had felt somewhat guilty at leaving Delbert alone in the hut, but he had hoped to spend some time with his bride before the quest. "I would spend this time with Moon Flower, Nokie."

"It is better for her and the babe, Shadow Dancer, that she sleep now. Do not worry. I will see that all is taken care of," Nokie promised her cousin, and with a firm hand she led him out of the chamber.

The hour for the quest drew near and at the appointed time the two braves who had watched over Delbert arrived at Shadow Dancer's house. When a young woman was brought to the front door by Aquilla, the two braves led her, draped from head to foot in a dark blanket—her shroud—to the position on the cliff where she was to stand and await the results of the young man's efforts to perform the quest in the allotted time.

The entire village had turned out to witness the event, and as the covered figure was brought to the edge of the ledge that overlooked the long drop from the top of the cliff, every eye beheld her silent stance. Shadow Dancer felt as though his heart were being pulled from his chest as he stood next to Delbert and was forced to witness his beloved standing all alone to await her coming fate.

"I swear to you, Shadow Dancer, I will do everything I can to climb the cliff in time." Delbert could see the warrior's desperation. He had found, over the course of the morning he had spent with Shadow Dancer, that he rather liked this man Iva had chosen for her husband; this Indian did not hide his feelings for Iva. He was a man both strong and wise, and he had a sense of duty toward this village and the people within it.

Shadow Dancer's strong hand gripped the young man's shoulder tightly in a display of camaraderie. He knew of Delbert's deep love for his wife, and he believed the young man would do everything in his power to save her life. "Do exactly as I have instructed you and you will succeed." For a moment dark eyes locked with Delbert's green ones as though both men were communicating their inner thoughts, but the contact was broken as a drum beat sounded throughout the valley. Delbert moved away from Shadow Dancer, toward the starting position for the quest. His eyes sought the opposite cliff, and heart hammering in his chest, he murmured a prayer that God would be with him so Iva would be saved.

Anxiously, Delbert awaited the signal to begin the quest.

Chapter Twenty-Nine

Earlier, as the villagers had gathered at the base of the sacred eagle cliff, Gray Otter had climbed the angular path and had positioned himself upon a jutting rock near the sacred eagle nest. He had insisted yesterday before the council that it was his duty as chief of his tribe to be the one to shoot the arrow, if necessary, that would send Moon Flower to her death. Now standing tall upon the rock in his most colorful headdress and ceremonial mantle, he glared darkly at the pale woman draped with the blanket on the opposite cliff. Eagerly Gray Otter's fingers caressed the arrow he had selected and now held in his hand, savoring the moment that was soon to come. Adding to his eagerness to have the quest begin, Meci's words rang over and over within his mind. *Even if the young man reaches the eagle's nest in the time allotted before the shadow is cast, do not linger, Gray Otter! Let your arrow fly! Once we are rid of the golden woman, we will then be better able to take care of Shadow Dancer! In his grief over the woman, I will arrange for him to be taken unaware and left for dead in the desert!* At the time when Meci had instructed Gray Otter, the chief had remembered that a few months past the priest had had the golden woman taken from the village and had planned to have Shadow Dancer killed. Today,

337

though, there would be no mistakes. Gray Otter felt a trembling of anticipation, for the moment he had awaited so long was now at hand!

As the signal to begin the quest was given, Delbert drew a deep breath and tried to focus all of his energies on finding a sure footing and a grip for his fingers so he could pull himself upward. He recalled Shadow Dancer's cautioning words of reassurance: *there is jutting rock to grab hold of; do not give in to panic.* The key to the climb was to stretch his body to its very limit, and then to pull up the weight of it with the strength of his arms.

Those standing below watched the young man known to them as the outsider slowly pulling himself upward. All knew the danger and the physical hardship of the quest, and as the tension mounted the villagers were keenly aware of the importance of the outcome of this young man's endeavors. Their gazes shifted from the one climbing to their chief standing upon the jutting rock near the eagle cliff and then across the pass to Moon Flower standing silently alone.

Twice Delbert almost lost his grip upon the rocks and the villagers gasped aloud, causing Shadow Dancer to flinch. His dark gaze rested only upon the covered form of his wife, and he silently prayed for the young man to succeed.

The minutes passed by all too quickly, and still Delbert reached one hand up and over the other, each muscle in his body straining as he groaned with his efforts and sweat glistened off of his naked upper body. His only thought was to reach the eagle's nest!

It seemed to take forever, but the eagle's nest at last came into Delbert's upward vision. His hands grasped one small rock and groove after the other as he pulled himself upward, ever upward.

With the eagle's nest in his sight, Delbert saw the golden arrow gleaming dully yellow, in the same position it had held for centuries. His heart pounded,

338

his chest heaving with labored breathing, and tears poured down his cheeks as he raced the climbing shadow of the sun sinking behind the opposite cliff.

Feeling the coolness of the shadow upon his back, Delbert's hand reached upward, the nest not far from his fingertips. A cry tore from his lips, and he heaved his body up, clutching at anything that would aid him, his face pressed against the cool rock surface of the cliff, in his mind's eye the form of the blanketed woman standing on the opposite cliff. He was going to make it! He was going to save Iva!

At that exact moment Gray Otter notched the selected arrow. Slowly he drew back the string. His dark eyes silently watched the shadow creeping toward the eagle's nest.

Just as the young man's hand stretched out to its limit, his fingers slowly being covered by the shadow, Gray Otter, with a cruel smile on his lips, released the arrow!

"Noooooo." The cry, torn from Delbert as he heard the hiss of the bow string, echoed over the valley floor. Turning his head slightly, he saw the dark, blanketed form fall down the side of the opposite cliff. As an eternity passed he remained pressed against the smooth surface of the rock near the eagle's nest, his eyes now shut. But in his mind he saw that silent form plunging to the earth below.

Shadow Dancer stood where he was, stunned. The woman he loved had plunged to her death! A trembling sob racked his body; a portion of his soul silently howled with grief. He looked around at the faces of his people, in a daze. It was Dark Water who came to his side and offered him the comfort only a friend could.

Shadow Dancer exerted an iron will over his shattered control. He shook off the hand that was offered, though at that moment he could have easily fallen to the ground and beaten his fists against it, so helpless was he feeling. His Moon Flower was gone from him! Moon Flower and the baby they had both awaited were no more. "I must see that the boy is safe." He would deal with the heart-shattering ache in his body later, he told himself. He knew this was the only way he could keep from falling apart. Turning his inner misery into action, he could stand before his people a whole man.

"Did you tell him of the trail?" Dark Water questioned, only able at this moment to imagine the pain his closest friend was feeling.

Shadow Dancer nodded his head. "He knows of the trail which will bring him down the cliff, and I have already made sure that his horse is ready so he can leave the valley." Shadow Dancer was determined that the young man would leave this valley without being harmed, and after he was safely away, Shadow Dancer swore that he would deal with Gray Otter! It was the fault of his kin that his wife had been killed. Gray Otter had at last won, but he would shortly find, to his distress, that the price of his victory was dear indeed.

The entire village now stood silently awaiting the presence of the chief and of the outsider who had been only seconds too late in reaching his goal to save the life of Shadow Dancer's wife. Many of the villagers who had been watching the young man with bated breath, believed that Gray Otter had shot the arrow a moment too soon, but none would dare speak this out aloud. Their very silence now told of the tension that gripped each one of them as they wondered what would next take place.

It was Gray Otter who tried to bring everything to a telling head as soon as he reached the bottom of the trail, only a few steps in front of Delbert. "All of the intruders must be killed! It is the will of the gods that they be destroyed, so that others of their kind cannot find their way into our valley! The pale ones hold poison in their hearts, as our forefathers found it in the hearts of the mighty Spanish conquistadors many years ago! They made our people slaves! They stole the riches of our ancestors, just as this one's friend tried to steal from our own people last night, and if he had not been caught by our guards, he would have escaped to bring back more evil, pale ones! We cannot allow such people among us! We must put an end to this now!"

There were murmurs of agreement, but as Shadow Dancer boldly strode to his cousin's side, few dared voice an opinion until they heard what he would say.

His visage was as darkly foreboding as a thunder cloud, and he spoke slowly but loudly so that all could hear. "This one will go free! You have taken your revenge against my family, Gray Otter. You shall go no further!"

As Meci stepped from the crowd to Gray Otter's side, the caution that had settled into Gray Otter at Shadow Dancer's approach slowly began to dissipate. With the priest at his side, he felt victorious over his cousin! "You hold no power here, Shadow Dancer! My word is law, for I am chief of these people!"

"The boy goes free!" Shadow Dancer growled from deep within his chest, and he stepped closer to the fat, gloating man he was forced to acknowledge as his kin and as his chief.

At that moment neither Meci or Gray Otter dared to defy Shadow Dancer. They could read in his features the chill of suppressed rage. They held their silence until Gray Otter's cousin had strode away, the young man at his side.

"Do not let them leave the valley!" Meci cried to several warriors standing closeby. This was the moment he had been waiting for. If Shadow Dancer resisted, the warriors would kill him. He would not have to wait for him to be overtaken and disposed of in the desert; this matter would be finished with now, and then Gray Otter would proclaim him high priest before the high council as he had promised.

Dark Water and several other braves who had been silently outraged by the whole affair, and who had also had lifelong friendships with Shadow Dancer, made their way to his side and offered him their loyalty.

The warriors who had been ordered to stop Shadow Dancer and Delbert did not make a move to hinder them when the number of braves at Shadow Dancer's side grew.

Turning away from the angry eyes of Gray Otter, Shadow Dancer led Delbert to his horse and then mounted his own. He silently led the young man toward the canyon that would lead him out of the valley.

At the end of the pass when Shadow Dancer brought his horse to a halt, Delbert finally spoke. "I guess they killed Willy Handcock too." He dared not say Iva's name aloud, for he knew he would break down in front of this man if he did, and he did not wish to inflict more pain on the Indian he had come to respect.

Shadow Dancer forced his expression to remain impassive as images of his beautiful wife came to mind. Slowly he nodded his dark head in agreement to the other's words. He remembered that the prospector had disappeared and that Delbert had mentioned his belief that old Willy had run away during the night. "There is food and water in your bags." He made no mention of the clay jar filled with gold nuggets that he had put in Delbert's parfleche. "I would ask of you one thing." His dark eyes looked upon the younger man with a sadness that could not be equaled.

"I will do whatever I can for you, Shadow Dancer." Delbert truly admired this large Indian warrior, and he knew his pain was deep over Iva's loss.

Reaching up Shadow Dancer pulled the necklace he wore, with the round disk and its painted scene, from around his neck. "Give this to Moon Flower's parents. When the child was born we were going to go to them, but now . . ." He could not finish.

Tears filled Delbert's eyes, marring his vision as he reached out for the necklace that was being extended toward him. "I am sure that they will treasure it, Shadow Dancer." As he wiped away the tears, he glimpsed the scene upon the disk, a golden-haired woman standing next to a powerful, bronze warrior and a small girl with flowing, dark hair. He clasped the necklace tightly in his fist, and swallowed hard, trying to get a grip on his emotions. "What will you do now, Shadow Dancer? Will you stay in the valley?" Delbert could not imagine this man accepting what had happened to him without retaliating.

"I am not sure, but Gray Otter must pay for what he has done to my family!" Shadow Dancer answered truthfully. His only thoughts were of returning to his village and challenging his cousin to a fight to the finish. He had wanted to insure this young man's safe departure from the valley before he confronted Gray Otter, for he knew how deeply his wife had cared for this young man, and desired to do this one last thing for her. If he survived, after facing his kin, he knew not what he was going to do with the rest of his life. His soul was empty. He was lost without his heart.

"If you are ever near the farm will you stop in? I know that Bain and Katherine will wish to meet you." Delbert dreaded telling Iva's parents of their daughter's death, but he knew it was left to him, and he must also tell them of the happiness Iva had found with this man, even if that had been shortlived.

Shadow Dancer could not answer him; his inner feelings threatened to converge and overwhelm him. Turning his pony around, he started back down the canyon, his goal set. He had but one thought in mind, to confront the one who had so devastated his life. To face Gray Otter and put an end to any more pain that his cousin could cause!

*   *   *

By the time Shadow Dancer returned to the village to confront Gray Otter, the villagers were all gathered within the communal lodge. The high council had convened as an open session for all the village to witness. Gray Otter, with Meci still standing near his side, ordered loudly that the old Apache known as Prairie Bird Woman be brought forth to accept her punishment for entering the valley along with the outsiders.

Not caring who was to witness the vengeance he intended to inflict upon Gray Otter, Shadow Dancer entered the ceremonial lodge boldly, his hand resting on the hilt of his large, hunting knife. As he strode toward the center fire, for a moment thoughts of his wife and of the evening of their joining ceremony settled over him. Had it been only months ago that he had pledged himself throughout this life and all eternity to Moon Flower? He could still envision how beautiful she had been as she had stood all alone before the ceremonial fire, and he recalled that he had watched the fear in her blue eyes turn to warm love when she recognized him in the joining costume of his people. His thoughts were intruded upon by the strong, carrying voice of a woman.

"I am no outsider! My father was known as Golden Eagle. He was the descendant of Wind Cryer and Sharaza, the chief of this very village years ago!" Prairie Bird Woman stood in defiance of Gray Otter and Meci before the ceremonial fire.

"You speak a lie, woman!" Shadow Dancer easily recognized the voice of Gray Otter. "You are the one that brought the intruders to our valley, and now you must stand and bear your guilt alone!"

"My only guilt is that years ago I did not set out on my own to seek out this valley as my father had made me promise to do before his death! It was not until the young man came to my village with the headband bearing the sun sign of my father's household that I

344

made good the oath I had given Golden Eagle so long ago. I swore to him that I would bring word to my father's people, tell them what had happened to him, why he had been forced to leave his tribe."

"Golden Eagle disappeared many years ago. His bones were never found, and it was determined by the people that he was attacked by some wild animal. It was the will of the gods that Golden Eagle travel down the star path." Meci spoke loudly as Gray Otter strutted importantly before the Apache woman, his features ugly as he glared upon her. He believed that she would be unable to get around the priest's words, but the villagers began to murmur among themselves about the possibility of her claim.

"Yes, Golden Eagle did disappear many years ago!" Prairie Bird Woman's eyes were as hard as those of the two men before her at this minute. She had waited many years to tell this story, and all the heated injustice she felt for her father's lot was in her voice. "He disappeared from his village, but it was no wild animal that parted him from his family and friends. It was his cousin, Sky Hawk, and his cousin's younger brother who took him into the desert with the allure of a hunting trip. There they could not bring themselves to kill him, so they put his eyes out and left him to the mercies of the wild animals!" The old Apache woman stood straight and defiant before Gray Otter and Meci. After all these years, she at last knew her father's disappearance was being truthfully explained.

Gasps of astonishment and cries of disbelief that such an outrageous attack would have befallen the legendary Golden Eagle circled the lodge, and angry murmurings could be heard as well because Sky Hawk had been Gray Otter's father.

"You have made all of this up. You have no proof!" Gray Otter appeared paler than he had been a few minutes ago when he had demanded the old woman be brought before the high council. "You are only an outsider!" he shouted, hoping to stir up the people's displeasure against her once again.

"If I am but an outsider, how is it then that I know the language of your people?" But before Gray Otter could reply, Prairie Bird Woman continued. "I will tell you how I know the language of my father's people. When my father had been left in the desert to die, my mother's tribe came upon him. His soul was longing for Spirit Boy to capture him up, but the gods willed that Golden Eagle survive, if only to insure that one day word would be brought back to his village.

"My mother, Desert Flower, was a widow, and on viewing the injured man, she took him to her lodge. She nursed him back to health, for she was a healing woman of her village. But with Golden Eagle's eyes having been destroyed, he was helpless to leave her Apache tribe and return to his own. Desert Flower took Golden Eagle as her husband, and the following winter they had a daughter. I am that one born to Desert Flower and Golden Eagle!

"I am the only person my father ever told about this hidden valley. He told me the way through the mountains, and he taught me the language of his people. I do not lie, Gray Otter. I speak only the truth."

Shadow Dancer, like the rest of the villagers, was taken by surprise at this new development. If what the old Indian woman said was true, she would be his aunt. And if her other claims were true, Gray Otter's father had taken over the chieftainship by foul means! Here was another evil deed to avenge. He would have taken the steps toward his cousin then, to at last free the surging anger that filled him, but he stopped when another disturbance drew his attention.

Two of Gray Otter's most trusted braves, amidst the confusion which was taking place in the lodge, made their way to the center, where their chief stood facing the old Indian woman.

"What is it?" Gray Otter questioned as they drew his

attention, not at all pleased that he was being disturbed at this moment. He knew by the tone of the crowd that he had to stop this Apache woman from saying anything else. Everything he held dear was at stake here, and he sensed that Prairie Bird Woman held the power to destroy everything he had built up over the years!

Both braves appeared nervous as they faced their chief, but at last one stepped forward. "The news we bring to you is not good, my chief." The taller brave swallowed hard, then speaking quickly, all in one breath said, "We retrieved the body of the woman at the bottom of the cliff as you instructed, but it was not the one we all believed to have been sacrificed."

Gray Otter was as stunned as those standing around him. He had ordered these two braves to bring the body of Moon Flower here to the ceremonial lodge with but one purpose in mind, that of tormenting his cousin. "What do you mean, it was not the one we thought to be standing on the cliff? It was Moon Flower that I shot!" His fat cheeks flushed with anger as he inwardly cursed the fates that would allow such a mistake to have taken place.

"It was not the golden woman known as Moon Flower that we found lying at the bottom of the cliff with the arrow in her breast." The braves seemed to have a hard time speaking the name of the one that they had found.

"Then who was it?" Gray Otter shouted, and at that moment his gaze locked with Shadow Dancer's.

"It was your own daughter, Nokie." The answer came with much regret, for even these two braves had been fond of the young woman known to have special powers given to her by the gods.

Cries of disbelief went up in the lodge as the villagers heard this news. All had loved the kind and gentle Nokie, and many would mourn her loss.

"Noooo! This cannot be true!" The words burst from

Gray Otter's lips, and at the same time, his dark eyes broke contact with his cousin's. The chief fell to his knees, the devastation of knowing that he had killed his own child so overpowering, he beat his chest as agony beset him. "I killed her! My own dear child. I killed Nokie!" He thought of the pleasure he had felt when he had notched the arrow he had selected, and of how he had allowed it to fly even as he saw the young man's hand touch the eagle's nest! His tear-filled gaze went to the one standing next to him, Meci. "You told me to kill her! I should never have listened to you! It was you who had Moon Flower stolen from the temple, and you who promised Shadow Dancer's death as well. I should have never plotted against them; the price is too great to pay!" His last words were drawn out on a long, ragged sob.

Meci turned, intending to leave the lodge before Gray Otter's condemnation could set the villagers upon him, but as he tried to walk away from the ceremonial fire, he came face to face with Atlacol, the high priest. "He lies!" Meci pointed a finger at Gray Otter as he stood trembling before the only person in this village that could sit council over him. "His grief has destroyed his reason, and he accuses me falsely!"

Atlacol's features remained impassive as he looked upon one of his own priests and knew the man was guilty of all the charges made against him. "Take him to the temple. He will be dealt with there before a tribunal of his own peers!" Atlacol spoke to the warriors who had come up behind Meci, and as they took hold of the evil priest's arms, the high priest sadly shook his head. Meci had often tried to stir up dissent among the priests, but Atlacol had always thought his thirst for power would ease. He now knew that he had allowed things to go too far. He would make sure Meci did not again have a chance to damage lives. Drawing his dark robe tighter around his frail body, Atlacol turned toward the village chief, knowing that more would be revealed this day than the dark soul of one of his priests.

Standing silently, as though stunned, Shadow Dancer looked on as Meci was taken from the ceremonial lodge, past Gray Otter who was bent over in grief on the tile floor. Turning away from the ruined man, Shadow Dancer staggered out the door. *Nokie had been standing upon the sacrificial cliff.* It had been his cousin who had been killed by Gray Otter's arrow! Disbelief weighed heavily upon him even as his long legs began to hurriedly move down the street toward his house. As his speed increased tears began to roll down his bronze cheeks. He cried because Nokie had died and because his wife had been spared!

Within moments he was sprinting through the door that bore the sun sign upon its panels. He had believed his beloved dead, and his shattered heart would not mend until he saw for himself that Moon Flower had not been standing upon that cliff!

Coming face to face with Aquilla, he wasted little time. "Where is she?" he demanded, even as his feet took him down the hallway to his own chambers.

"There was nothing I could do, Shadow Dancer, Nokie insisted that she be allowed to take Moon Flower's place. She told me that the gods had ordained it, and who am I to rebel against what the gods decreed?" Aquilla hurriedly tried to explain as she followed him down the hallway.

Throwing back the chamber door, Shadow Dancer stood still as his dark gaze quickly went around the room. *Where is she?* he asked himself, ignoring Aquilla. Suddenly he heard a small moan coming from the furs upon the sleeping couch. Still held in the grasp of disbelief, he tentatively drew closer. How could Moon Flower be alive when he had felt her loss so deep within his soul?

At first glance the bed appeared empty, but another moan drew him closer. Slowly golden curls came into view when the mound of furs was pushed away as Iva fought the engulfing darkness that had gripped her.

In that moment Shadow Dancer's entire world was returned to him. His heart hammered wildly in his chest as he gathered this woman of his heart in his arms.

"What is wrong, Shadow Dancer?" Iva questioned groggily as she tried to pull herself out of the drug-induced sleep she had been in.

Shadow Dancer unashamedly allowed his tears to fall as he ravished her with kisses, his arms wrapped around her in a grip he had no intention of ever breaking. "We will talk later, Moon Flower. Now I only wish to hold you."

This is how Dark Water found Shadow Dancer and Iva some time later. Standing next to his wife in the doorway of the chamber, he announced, "Shadow Dancer, the council has taken a vote. Gray Otter confessed to having knowledge of his father's sins against Golden Eagle, your grandfather. It has been agreed by all that the chieftainship of the village should once again be held by the line of those that carry the sign of the sun. You are our new chief!"

Silently Shadow Dancer nodded his head in his friend's direction. Quietly Dark Water edged his wife from the room and shut the door. There would be time later for Shadow Dancer to be thankful that the line of Wind Cryer and Sharaza had been set aright, and also time to grieve for the loss of Nokie. Now he wanted only to hold Moon Flower against his heart. The gods had blessed him! They had brought his soul back to life, they had given him back his wife and child!

As his arms tightened around Iva, he knew that his life was now full. "I love you, my heart," he whispered softly against Iva's brow.

Epilogue

Inside the bedchamber of the hidden valley chief, a single brazier dimly sent its light into the recesses of the room. Upon the fur-covered sleeping couch a man lay naked, his tanned and muscular body stretched out, at ease. His agate eyes watched expectantly for the woman who was his bride to come back to his side.

Her soft, gentle voice came easily to his ears from the far corner of the chamber where she tended their daughter. The soft cooing sounds she made for his child caused his chest to swell. He sighed lightly with his pleasure.

Tomorrow they would leave the village to visit his wife's family. The Cassidys had been sent word that their daughter was well and would visit them when her child was of an age to travel. It is well that I will meet the parents of Moon Flower, Shadow Dancer silently thought to himself.

The statue that he had ordered in the image of his cousin Nokie, to be placed in the gardens of his house, had been completed this day. Shadow Dancer once again reflected on the fact that the gods had always had his life within the boundaries of their keeping. They had led him to the golden woman, now known to all as Moon Flower, and by bringing her to his village, the gods had changed the future of many.

The priests at the temple had taught him at an early age that people were just instruments used for the pleasure of the gods, but not until he had found Iva had he fully believed it.

Light footfalls upon the tile flooring brought his attention back to the room. The light from the brazier silhouetted her outline as she crossed the chamber; the man upon the bed felt his heart begin to race in a rapid tattoo. The sheer tunic she wore as her night garment was translucent and left little to his imagination, as his eyes boldly raked over her form.

She stood for a few lingering seconds as though sensing his mood. Then, reaching up, she brought the gown over her head and allowed it to fall in a soft wisp to the tile floor.

Slowly she glided over the remaining space, all temptress and woman now that she was alone with her man. "Little Nokie is at last asleep." Her words were a seductive invitation. Her blue eyes took in the powerful body eager for her own.

A fire burned like molten liquid in his loins as her eyes went from his toes to his dark hair and then returned to his ebony eyes, staring, seeming to convey an open promise.

"Come to me, Moon Flower." He reached out for her silken skin. His voice, a husky vibration from deep within his powerful chest, sent chills of anticipation through Iva.

Her body had the taste of ambrosia, and he marveled that after all this time, he still felt as though he could not get enough of this woman. Each time he held her in his arms, it was as if it were the very first.

A delicious contented purr came from Iva's lips as she lay down in his waiting arms. "Love me, Shadow Dancer," she whispered as she felt the hard length of him.

"Forever, my heart." His lips descended boldly.